Advance Praise for *Equilibrium*

"Tender, heartbreaking, and beautifully realistic. A family—full of secrets—struggles to keep its balance on a tightrope of grief, guilt, desire, and the need for love. Fans of Anita Shreve will be riveted by this intense and compassionate story."

—Hank Phillippi Ryan, Agatha-, Anthony-,
and Macavity-winning author

"In this impressive debut, Lorrie Thomson skillfully maps the emotional landscape of mother-daughter relationships. *Equilibrium* is an uplifting tale of familial love triumphing over tragedy: emotional, complex, and deeply satisfying. I couldn't put it down!"

—Lisa Verge Higgins, author of
One Good Friend Deserves Another

Equilibrium

LORRIE THOMSON

KENSINGTON BOOKS
www.kensingtonbooks.com

KENSINGTON BOOKS are published by

Kensington Publishing Corp.
119 West 40th Street
New York, NY 10018

Copyright © 2013 by Lorrie Thomson

All Kensington titles, imprints, and distributed lines are available at special quantity discounts for bulk purchases for sales promotion, premiums, fund-raising, and educational or institutional use.

Special book excerpts or customized printings can also be created to fit specific needs. For details, write or phone the office of the Kensington Special Sales Manager: Kensington Publishing Corp., 119 West 40th Street, New York, NY 10018. Attn. Special Sales Department. Phone: 1-800-221-2647.

Kensington and the K logo Reg. U.S. Pat. & TM Off.

ISBN-13: 978-0-7582-8577-5
ISBN-10: 0-7582-8577-9
First Kensington Trade Paperback Printing: September 2013

eISBN-13: 978-0-7582-8578-2
eISBN-10: 0-7582-8578-7
First Kensington Electronic Edition: September 2013

10 9 8 7 6 5 4 3 2 1

Printed in the United States of America

For Sylvie Kurtz and Ellen Gullo

Acknowledgments

To my dear friends and tireless critique buddies Sylvie Kurtz and Ellen Gullo. Thank you for reading every word—several times—your support, and enduring friendship.

To my wonderful agent at BookEnds, Jessica Alvarez. Thank you for believing in my bright future, working with me to ensure the manuscript was ready for prime time, and sharing my excitement every step of the way.

To my editor at Kensington, Peter Senftleben. Your insight brought the manuscript up another notch and ensured the characters were depicted as I'd originally intended. Thank you for that, your patience in explaining the myriad steps for the publishing process, and the smiley faces in your e-mails. You get extra credit for collaborating with the art department and helping them design the perfect cover.

To my Kensington cover designer, Kristine Noble. Wow. I'm amazed by how well the image resembles the Klein house, reflects the inner landscape of the family that resides within its walls, and conveys the entire novel's tone. Thank you for your genius and for *not* using any of my suggestions.

A special thank-you to Dr. Ken Adelman, who educated me on bipolar disorder, answered all of my many questions, and helped me figure out Jack and Troy.

Thank you to friends who read earlier versions of the manuscript, either in whole or in part, and offered helpful suggestions: Colleen McKeon Murphy, Liz Butler, Denise Jacobs, and Martha Chabinsky.

Thank you to my children, Ben, Josh, and Leah, who let

me write and sometimes even paid attention to the sign hanging from my doorknob: *Quiet, please, novel in progress.*

A great big thank-you to my husband, Bill, for his love and encouragement. Without having read a word—preferring to wait until my novel was published—you've always believed in me and assumed I had something important to say. Here it is.

Chapter 1

The first time Laura Klein saved her husband's life, she'd found his side of the bed cold at four a.m. Her throat clenched around the hard-edged understanding he'd gone off his medication again. She stumbled down the stairs in her nightgown, checked the yard, and raced down the street in her station wagon, her bare foot pressed to the accelerator. Half a mile away, she located his Corolla flipped on the side of Forest Road with Jack pinned beneath the dash, his leg broken in three places. After the Jaws of Life cut him from the wreckage, her atheist husband had smiled up at her and, with a wink and a grimace, declared himself born again.

The second time, Laura had followed a serpentine trail of spilled sleeping pills between the house and the toolshed and discovered Jack curled between the lawn mower and snowblower. She'd shaken him till a mild protest bubbled from his lips, and then, fingers twitching with relief, speed-dialed 911.

The third time Jack had tried to end his life, Laura had found his body.

Laura stood in Jack's writing studio, the printer chugging out a copy of his estate tax returns behind her back. The late winter sunrise streamed through the wavy glass window and fell across the recently purchased futon. For months, the empty space had served as a reminder. Now, with the replacement futon back in its proper spot, she'd thought she could keep herself from rehashing the last moments of Jack's life.

She'd thought wrong.

Laura snapped up the original returns and slipped from the studio into the mudroom that doubled as her home office. From the pocket of her robe, she took the skeleton key and locked the door behind her, wishing it were that easy to confine her memories. She set the papers on her desk and slid her checklist off the bookshelf. If she wrote things down, then she wouldn't need to worry. Not as much.

Friday: Clean house, especially bathrooms, and split firewood. Pick up groceries at Market Basket. Bring Jack's tax returns to the post office.

Serving as executor for Jack's estate had kept Laura busy for more than ten months. She preferred her role as Jack's editorial assistant, even though revising one of his literary novels often took longer than Jack spent writing a first draft.

A first draft would mentally exhaust him, depress him when he should've been celebrating.

Several weeks later, Jack would trumpet his accomplishment and turn the house upside down, searching for the credit cards she'd hidden from him. Despite her best efforts, till the day Jack died, the man acted as though he'd no clue how thin a respectable mid-list author's advances and royalties spread over a year.

"Jack." She stroked her husband's name and touched two fingers to her lips, mimicking the pressure of his soft mouth. Last kiss. "I love you so," he'd said, and she'd glanced over her shoulder. Jack's tall frame had filled their bedroom doorway the last time she'd seen her husband alive.

A thread of nausea tickled her throat, and she swallowed against a rapidly forming knot. She wrestled with her breath and recognized the excessively deep inhalations, a sure sign of hyperventilating. At Jack's funeral, a panicked rumble had moved through the crowd, and her friend Maggie had held a crackling brown lunch bag over Laura's nose and mouth, chanting breathing instructions. If she grayed out today, no one would come to her rescue.

She closed her eyes and focused on her breathing the way Maggie had taught her. Breathe in through the nose, out through the mouth. In and out, in and out. From the next room, the kitchen clock ticked the seconds. Her mind settled. Gradually, her breathing slowed.

Laura sighed, blinked her eyes open, and shoved the checklist onto the bookcase, disturbing the crowded shelf. Elastic-bound papers tumbled head over heels, then slapped the floor at her feet. Laura crouched and gathered up three manuscripts of hers she'd never complete, but couldn't bear to toss. A story of family secrets. A journey of self-discovery. And a tale of losing and finding love. Each manuscript had grown from a facet of her life at the time of its writing. Each manuscript represented a missed opportunity she could never get back. Each manuscript stirred a stomach-plummeting falling-apart sensation of loss she resented. She needed to give herself a break. Her life hadn't exactly been normal. She could barely remember normal.

Maybe six weeks from now, after commemorating the one-year anniversary of Jack's death, she could finally work on a brand-spanking-new creation. Unless she'd ignored inspiration so many times, she'd run out of chances. Over the course of their marriage, whenever she'd carved out a slice of time to focus on writing fiction, Jack would dive into a real-life crisis she couldn't ignore. How could she blame him for his perfect timing? She shook her head, told herself her eyes stung from an allergy to dust, and forced the manuscripts back onto the shelf.

Family always came first.

★   ★   ★

Even when Laura climbed the stairs to wake up her kids, she stepped lightly on the brass-anchored Oriental runner, trying to avoid the squeakiest treads. She'd adopted the habit back when Troy and Darcy were toddlers, when her fondest wish was for a few more solitary moments to herself. Now, she would've gladly traded solitude for the squeals and laughter of Jack and the kids roughhousing. Troy would back off after Jack had gently tossed him aside for the third time. But Darcy, dimpled arms and legs wrapped around Jack like a Velcro monkey, would cling to her father long after he'd insisted the game was over.

Music pulsed through Troy's bedroom door, the song too distorted to identify. Between Troy's and Darcy's affinities for loud music, she'd surely go deaf before she reached thirty-six.

Laura pounded on the door, and the music cut out.

Troy flung his door wide, revealing her fully dressed son smirking as if he'd gotten away with something. "Hey!" he said in a voice she wasn't yet accustomed to.

His voice had deepened several octaves over the winter. On an especially cold night, she'd sent a thirteen-year-old boy to bed, and he'd transformed into a thirteen-year-old man by the time he'd bounded down the stairway for breakfast the next morning. As a toddler, he'd shown the same propensity for perfectionism, seamlessly flowing from crawling to running within a twenty-four-hour period. He'd waited to get the details down exactly right before even attempting upright mobility.

She resisted the urge to tousle his hair and rearrange the umber spikes created by his vigorous towel-drying method. He ran his fingers through his hair in response to her stare, lengthening the front peaks. "What's up?"

After Laura mailed the tax forms, there was nothing more she could do for Jack. Beyond the anniversary, no task, however mundane, would connect them. Her hands ached. Her lower lip trembled, and she forced a smile. "Want to come with me to the market after school?"

The half-hour drive would provide Troy with barely enough time for one of his elaborate stories aching for release, folktales with his friends as the heroes and heroines. If she were especially lucky, Troy would distract her with a couple of goofy jokes, too. Today, she would've gladly paid for cable just so she could zone out to Comedy Central, Food Network, HGTV. Anything.

"Basketball," Troy said, and Laura nodded.

Purple-gray half-moons curved beneath Troy's dark lashes, evidence he'd slept in fits and starts last night. Evidence of the sporadic insomnia they all suffered.

If she'd realized Troy was up while she lay awake, she would've comforted him back to sleep with milk, cookies, and a sympathetic ear. "Do you need to talk about Dad?" Directness never worked with Darcy; she required a more subtle approach. But Troy came to her with his problems, actually answered her questions with relevant responses she could trust.

"Nah, I'm good." Troy took a step in her direction, sensitive to her shifting mood. "But I could skip practice."

A son shouldn't have to play the man of the house at such a young age. Not for the first time, Laura marveled *she'd* become the man of the house. She'd never intended for her children to grow up the way she had. At least they'd known their father. "Never mind, sweetie. I'll ask Darcy."

He burst out laughing, squinting at her through the bright blue of Jack's eyes. She didn't resist tousling his hair this time, simultaneously connecting with her son and the color Jack's hair had held until premature gray set in along with accelerated illness. "You never know. She used to love the market."

Laura kept doing that lately—remembering Darcy as a preschooler, skipping along by her side. Was that her daughter's baseline personality or was the annoyed fifteen-year-old the real deal, what Darcy had been maturing toward all along?

She'd been monitoring Darcy's many mood swings. If her easygoing son exhibited any erratic behavior, she'd monitor him, too. She wouldn't want to frighten her children with her worries about their genetic predisposition to their father's bipolar disorder. Any diagnosis at their young age would most likely contain the phrase "wait and see."

Troy tagged along to his sister's room, right in step with his mother. Laura tapped on the door with her knuckles, creaked it open, and then leaned against the doorframe. Hallway light purled over the threshold and caressed the frosty green-and-blue alternating walls. Mounds of clothes and books rested equidistant from each other along the floorboards. At the foot of Darcy's bed, the face of a mammoth sunflower smiled from the open pages of a Burpee seed catalog. Darcy's fraying dictionary sat at her bedside, pen and notebook serving as bookmarks. As long as Laura didn't tell her daughter reading the dictionary remained one of her favorite pastimes, there was a chance Darcy would continue. "Time to get up."

Darcy grumbled from beneath a pile of blankets.

Troy charged past his mother and hurled himself atop the quilted mound. He synchronized his sister abuse with each spoken syllable, four resolute bounces. "I. Love. You. Darce."

Darcy wrestled from her covers, knocking Troy onto the floor. "Asshole!"

"I was just trying to help." Troy looked so innocent sprawled on the floor, Laura almost believed him.

"Watch your mouth, Darcy." Laura tried not to giggle.

What the heck was wrong with her this morning? A peace offering of food often worked. "Want something special for breakfast?"

"Yogurt's fine."

Fine wasn't the point. She didn't have to cook yogurt. She wanted to cook for her children. This morning, she needed to cook. "Troy?"

"Not hungry. Heading out early. Walking to school."

No wonder her son was so even-tempered. More exercise might help her daughter. Chasing boys didn't count. Troy jumped up from the floor, flew past Laura, and trampled down the stairway before she could insist on feeding him.

Darcy peered from beneath a mane of wavy auburn bed head, much like what Laura often sported. "Want to come with me to the market after school?" The cab of her Outback provided the ideal environment for distilling information from Darcy, Laura's only glimpse into what might be playing out in the theater of her daughter's life.

Darcy shook her head. "Plans."

"Okay." Darcy always had plans. What had happened to Laura's constant companion, the little girl in the blue velveteen twirl dress, black Mary Janes, and sequin-covered purse who'd studied Laura's every move, longing to be just like her mother? Troy's perpetual motion veered into athletic pursuits, while her daughter had become the social director of the high school this past year.

After the year they'd all endured preceding Jack's death, who could blame her? At least Darcy could now safely invite kids over to the house without checking on her dad's mental status. Amazing how quickly her daughter's friends' nickname for Jack went from Funny Dad to Scary Dad. Jack's off-putting habit of taking over every conversation put Darcy in the impossible position of defending her father as though she were his wife.

Laura fidgeted with her wedding band, imagined the inscription rising through the gold: *Forever, Jack.*

"Mom, Mom. I need to get dressed." Darcy swung her legs over the side of her bed and glared toward where her mother was standing.

Laura shook her head, trying to clear away the fuzz that sometimes bogged her down, the kind of forgetfulness she'd experienced after the birth of each of her children. "I'd like you home for dinner."

"Dinner's not as much fun as—" Darcy said. When Laura caught her eye, Darcy lowered her gaze, then shook her head. Laura might not always know what Darcy was thinking, but she could tell when an image of Jack stretched across her daughter's mind, exposing the same billboard of loss Laura concealed.

True enough, dinner wasn't the same without Jack's non-stop joking and teasing. His impersonation of Laura chiding him had prevented her from taking herself too seriously and had made her laugh till her jaw ached.

"You miss Daddy," Laura said, and Darcy's eyes misted over for half a second before her expression blanked out. Laura knew better, but she pressed on. Maybe this time Darcy would open up to her. Maybe this time would be different. "Would you like me to take you to the cemetery?"

"Why?"

"What do you mean, why?"

"I mean why bother?" Darcy scraped her forefinger along her thumb, working a hangnail. "It's not like he's there. Not like we're visiting the rest home or something. Going to take dear old Dad out for the day. Take him for a drive around town, bring him to his favorite restaurant. Honest enough for you?"

"Crude's not the same as honest." Laura approached the bed and sat down a good foot away from Darcy, hoping to get closer.

Darcy sprang to standing. "I'm getting dressed now," she said, earning the seven-days-and-counting Laura-diagnosis of moderately oppositional.

Distraction worked wonders.

After Darcy sailed out the door, Laura put on a pot of coffee and took out the ingredients for pancakes, tried focusing on colors and textures. The shiny gold of the yolks, the manila powder of the flour, pools of cool ivory milk reflecting the curve of the toaster.

Elle's Explorer pulled into the driveway, the engine's hum as familiar as her friend's voice.

Laura peeked out the mudroom window. Elle was sitting behind the steering wheel, blowing her nose. She tilted her face toward the vanity mirror and dabbed foundation beneath her eyes.

Memories about Elle's ex-husband, Rick, were the only thoughts that could set off her upbeat friend. She'd replay events, opening her emotional scar tissue along its purple seam, as though she sought pain to keep the relationship going.

Laura returned to her pancake batter, beat the egg yolks, and folded wet ingredients into dry. Years of slogging with Jack through his mood disorder made gentling Elle through garden-variety regret seem like a cakewalk. This problem she could fix.

Elle stumbled into the mudroom and shut the door against a cold blast of late February air. "Howdy!" She stomped week-old snow from her Ugg boots and left them at their reserved spot on the welcome mat. She hung her wool coat next to the ski jackets Darcy and Troy refused to wear unless they were in fact skiing down a slope. "Mind if I stop by?"

Laura approached Elle and hugged her first. Temporary loss of control embarrassed Elle, rendering her uncharacteristically shy.

"Just tell me what you need." Laura smoothed her rumpled morning attire, a jarring contrast to the starched business suits Elle wore daily as proprietress of her in-town antiques and collectibles shop, Yesterday's Dreams. Unlike Elle, no one would notice if Laura stayed in her robe all day, like an unmade bed in a vacant house. "Have you eaten?"

"I don't like eating alone." Elle headed straight for the abandoned pancake batter and stirred with a vengeance.

"Sit." Laura nabbed the spoon from Elle's hand, stopping her mid-stroke.

"Can't you let me take care of you?"

"You have taken care of me plenty." Laura lifted her chin and motioned at the kitchen table.

Elle and Maggie belonged to the book club Laura had been sporadically attending ever since she'd moved to Greensboro, New Hampshire, more than a decade ago. Her friends formed the closest thing to an extended family she'd ever had. Elle was like a cool older sister, Maggie the wise aunt. Days after Jack's funeral, they'd descended on her house, refusing to leave until she snapped out of the blues. The two women had dragged her out of bed, forced her into a too-cold shower, and would've masticated her food for her if she hadn't started chewing on her own.

Asserting that she was nowhere near a clinical depression didn't seem to impress her friends. Six weeks was the definition, so why not leave her alone for another five? She'd collapsed under the weight of her loss, thinking she'd deserved a mind vacation, even though her body had refused to budge.

Apologizing to Darcy and Troy wasn't good enough. Right when they'd needed the strong mom they'd always depended upon, she'd, however briefly, scared them to death by shutting down and staying in bed for a week. Hell, she'd scared herself. Never again.

"Rick's marrying Trixie," Elle said, and her face contorted.

Laura put her arms out to Elle and drew her close. So Elle's meltdown was about a *new* Rick drama. Her ex-husband was marrying his live-in girlfriend. Five minutes must've set some kind of record for Elle. Less than three minutes usually passed before she'd divulge what troubled her, even though she never set out to reveal herself. Nobody ever did.

Public tears worked as a catharsis for Elle of the you-get-what-you-see personality. In contrast, Laura craved privacy. She held Elle at arm's length and made sure she was paying close attention. "Do you want Rick back?"

"Hell, no. I should thank Trixie for ending our marriage."

"That's right. You're a wonderful person. You deserve someone better than Rick."

Elle nodded, exhaled a delicate sigh. "I know, I know."

Laura poured batter onto the ready griddle and set a pitcher of maple syrup in the microwave. The bubbling pancakes and heating syrup melded with the aroma of brewing coffee.

Elle slid out a chair, reclined in the ladder-back. She crossed her legs, and her tweed skirt hem rose, revealing a swatch of forty-three-year-old thigh without a trace of cellulite. If Laura didn't love Elle, she'd hate her.

Laura set their breakfasts on the table, amber syrup dribbling down the fluffy stacks. She fixed two cups of coffee, even though Elle hadn't asked. Black for Laura. Cream, no sugar, for Elle, just the way she liked it.

Ten minutes later, Laura wiped her mouth, then cleared her plate from the table. "Why the suit? Isn't this your day off?"

Elle spoke through her last bite of pancake. "I'm redoing the display windows, getting them ready for spring. Want to help?" Elle's face brightened with the idea. "We had so much fun the last time we dressed windows together!"

Laura attempted to reconfigure her mental to-do list and find a slot to assist her friend. Elle needed moral support, and Laura enjoyed proving her creativity beyond the pages of Jack's manuscripts.

Jack. Laura's shoulders tensed. "Oh, I, uh . . ."

Elle squinted at Laura, then dashed into Laura's office and returned with the hard copy of her list. Any friend of Laura's

knew nothing around here manifested as real unless it journeyed from mind to paper first.

"After months of stressing over the estate, I thought I'd feel
relieved, but I don't. I'm feeling a little unwell today," Laura
said, and recounted the graying out she'd skirted in the mudroom.

Elle looked up from Laura's notepad, revealing tears ready
to drop and ruin her recently repaired makeup. "Why didn't
you say something? I should be helping you clean, not rear-
ranging knickknacks at my shop."

"Don't you dare start, or I won't be able to stop. We'll be
two fools crying in the kitchen all day." Laura tightened her
fabric belt, crossed her arms, and exhaled like a blowfish.

Elle wrestled a tissue from her blazer's breast pocket. "I
can't believe it's been nearly a year," she said through the tissue.
"Did you ever get around to putting an ad in the paper to rent
out Jack's studio?"

"No," Laura said, even though Elle already knew the answer. Laura had discussed the idea with the kids months ago.
Troy had thought it was a logical way to use the now-empty
space. And Darcy had said she couldn't care less, practically a
glowing endorsement. But Laura wasn't ready. Not yet.

Elle meant well. She was just looking for visible change,
evidence of the forward passage of time.

Laura had made a small change to the studio that might
pacify Elle. "Want to see something?"

"Sure?" Elle shrugged and followed Laura through the
mudroom to Jack's studio door. Laura drew the skeleton key
from her robe pocket and twisted it in three convoluted angles. The door gave way and soughed open.

Elle flinched.

"Oh, right. You haven't seen his studio since—it's okay. It's
all fixed," Laura said.

Elle swung her long hair over her shoulder and walked ahead of Laura, trailing false confidence. "It looks exactly like I remember it." She directed her gaze toward the denim futon and lost all natural color beneath her tawny blush.

"It's a new futon," Laura said. "Just picked it up last week."

"You couldn't have chosen a different slipcover?"

"Then it wouldn't look the same."

Elle shook her head, agreeing to nothing. Instead, she focused on the floorboards—the cherry stain and polyurethane finish worn off unevenly, in even worse condition than the neglected pine flooring in the rest of the house. Laura had once talked of actually hiring a service to refinish all the floors, but that was before.

Elle looked her in the eye. "So how's the money situation? You have enough?"

Laura tried a laugh, but it came out like a hiccup instead. "Enough for now. Thanks to Jack's posthumous sales boost, his royalty check will keep us for the next nine months." And thanks to Jack's previous suicide attempts, he'd never been able to obtain life insurance. She shrugged. "We're used to living royalty to royalty."

Elle touched Laura's shoulder with her fingertips. "By the way, a guy from my spinning class is looking for a rental. This studio would work great." Elle clicked her tongue against her teeth, counting out imagined money. "You could probably get eight hundred a month, if you include utilities. Easy passive income."

Elle and her schemes. Her friend's ex-husband-related tears were real, but they weren't the primary reason for Elle's "impromptu" visit. Laura should've known as soon as Elle had uttered "by the way." The fact Elle had crunched numbers for Laura sealed the deal.

"I'll think about it." Laura didn't like seeming unappreciative. She simply wasn't ready to give up Jack's studio, the seat of his soul, even when Elle's solution for her money troubles made perfect sense financially.

"But he's looking now. Just talk to him. His name is Aidan Walsh. He's a nice guy."

"I said, I'll think about it."

"After all Jack put you through." Elle's lower jaw quivered. "How can you enshrine him like this?" Elle looked around the room, swiping her arm through the air, as if she wanted to strike every object, from the denim futon to Jack's handwritten sticky notes framing the computer monitor, the ink smudged where Laura had tried absorbing her husband's last words through her fingertips.

"That's not how I see it. I owe him everything." Marrying Jack and having his children gave her the only family she'd ever have, her reason for getting up every morning. She understood the difference between her husband and his mood disorder. Besides, playing the blame game wouldn't rewrite history and return the only man she'd ever loved.

"No. He owes you everything. You single-handedly kept the man alive for a decade. I mean, how many times did he go off his meds? How many times did you call the police to track him down before he hurt himself, before—" Elle pressed her lips together, restraining the words she'd intended to say. "I am so sorry. I didn't mean that. It's just really hard hearing you defend him."

Laura swallowed through a suddenly sore throat. "Okay."

"Okay, what?"

"Okay, I'll talk to your friend," Laura said, if only to pacify Elle and give herself time to decide.

Elle stared at her, unblinking, as though waiting for Laura to change her mind. Elle raised her hands. "Hallelujah! Let's go clean those bathrooms!" She took Laura by the elbow and guided her from the studio.

"Elle? I really don't want you cleaning my bathrooms. The overflowing trash, Troy's lousy middle of the night aim." Laura gave Elle's crisp outfit a once-over. "And you're not dressed for scrubbing toilets."

Elle held a finger in the air and pulled down an alternate solution. "I'll send my cleaning lady over, my treat."

Laura shook her head. "I need some time alone. Know what I mean?"

"Positive?"

She could blast some of her favorite music—Adele, Ray LaMontagne, Train—and scrub the bathroom grout until either her mind silenced or her knuckles bled, whichever came first. "I'll be fine." Laura flashed her practiced smile. "Get to work and don't worry about me."

A few steps away from Jack's studio, healthy color was already seeping back into Elle's cheeks. "How about tonight? Need me and Maggie tonight?"

"Tonight?" Her last night with Jack, Laura had served his favorite dinner, brisket and red potatoes. His gravelly voice had thrummed through her body, and she'd resonated with his every word. Hands firm along her waist, he'd guided her up the stairs to their bedroom. He'd warmed her through the night.

"I need, I need . . ." Laura said.

Elle nodded. "Uh-huh. Maggie and I will be over at five," she said, and kissed Laura on the cheek.

Laura had meant to say, "I need to be alone with the kids," but one look from Elle and, *poof*, the sentence had vanished.

Soul sisters like Elle got you into the habit of telling the truth, whether you wanted to or not.

Chapter 2

Impersonating a dumb blonde got them every time. Darcy waited until the Monte Carlo stopped directly in front of the high school entrance, timed the cleavage reveal perfectly. Hanging out with a cute boy after school was way better than Market Basket with Mom. She unzipped the hoodie her homeroom teacher insisted she wear for the entire day, despite the school's overactive heating system. "No midriff showing," Mr. Burke had said, while staring right at her bare belly button. She glanced at Heather and handed her backpack to Cam, bounced to the driver's side of the idling stack of metal, and rested her elbows on the window frame until Nick got a good eyeful.

"Got room for three more?"

"Three more what?" Nick grinned like crazy, deepening his ever-present dimples. She could see why all the girls were going gaga over the newest boy in town, but she didn't impress easily.

Darcy signaled to her waiting friends without acknowledging Nick's lame joke. The plans she and Nick had made during lunch on Monday didn't include her best friends as chaperones, but she liked first-date protection. "Nick—this is Cam and Heather."

Nick nodded at her chest, as if she'd introduced him to her

boobs instead of her best friends. Cam opened the side door and held the bucket seat forward for Heather. Heather did her best to avoid contact with Cam after he climbed into the backseat, angling her legs to the side.

"*You* sit next to me." Nick looked up from her cleavage for the first time and gave her a tiny jolt when his violet eyes made contact with hers. Maybe he had promise after all.

"Whatever." Darcy came around to the passenger seat and grappled the shoulder strap across her body while Nick peeled out of the parking lot. Serious testosterone overload, even for a junior.

The boys' middle school basketball team ran down the snow-cleared sidewalk between the middle school and high school for their daily warm-up. Darcy picked Troy out from the line. Apparently brain-dead, she waved, giving her brother permission to jog backward, flailing his arms as if he were signaling a plane.

"Where to?" Nick said.

"The lake would be good." She angled a glance at Nick, checked out his blond highlights, his overuse of hair products.

"Is the park open?" At the stop sign, Nick dialed up the heat and turned on the stereo, blasting heavy metal through the vehicle.

Darcy lowered the volume and changed the station to the rock she preferred. "Of course not. But we're not going to the park. We're going across from the park. Take a left."

"Oh, yes, ma'am. Show me the way."

What kind of girls was Nick used to? Darcy had heard all the rumors, of course. How he'd hooked up with a zillion girls. How he'd been kicked out of school in Nashua for dealing drugs. How he'd hit a teacher. But rumors weren't always true. She of all people should know how stories got out of control and took on a life of their own.

Darcy reclined in the seat, letting the lyrics for "Breathe" wash over her body. Sing it, Missy. She could relate. Life sucked, and then you died. "Got anything to drink?"

"Cooler's in the back. Pass my girl a beer." *His girl?* Give her an eighth of a break. She wasn't anyone's girl, not since Daddy had died.

Cam fished through the cooler's ice cubes and handed Darcy a Bud.

"Thanks." Her two best friends in the back, a cute boy, cold beer. One more thing would rocket the afternoon into nirvana. "Got anything else in the cooler?"

"Nope, in my pocket." Nick grabbed her hand and held it against the herb-filled bulge on his thigh. "Enough for everyone."

"Good." Darcy withdrew her hand and pretended to need two hands to open her beer. Mom would pitch a fit if she found out she sometimes partied. Since elementary school, Mom had warned her and Troy about the dangers of doing drugs and alcohol, leaving out the part Darcy had figured out on her own: their odds of getting Daddy's bipolar disorder and how nonprescription meds would make it worse. But Daddy had listened to his shrink's warnings, and look how well that had turned out. "Take a right at the lights, then it's the third driveway. Says *private drive.*"

"Your folks' place?"

Darcy popped the tab and took a sip. Beer misted from the can's mouth, tickling her nose. "Don't know whose house it is."

"Gotcha." Nick smiled, seeming to understand their tradition of trespassing.

"She doesn't have folks, just a mother," Heather said, chiming in only to save Darcy from explaining her life. Yet again.

"Leave the car facing out, in case we have to bolt." No movement in or around the abandoned cottage. No sign warning

against unauthorized entry. No reason to obey the law. Darcy un-
latched her seat belt. "Still looks empty. It's our place now."

Nick cut the engine and let out a whoop, startling spar-
rows from a low bush into the pines.

Heather untangled herself from the backseat and ran
ahead.

"Wait a minute!" Darcy chased Heather to the cottage, her
sneakers sinking into the snowy yard. "You okay?"

"Sure, why?"

"You're kind of quiet today. I mean, more than usual."

"Hey, that wasn't here last fall." A weathered hammock
hung between two spindly pines. The trees listed inward. The
ropes strained. Heather gave the hammock a halfhearted prod,
and the crapped-out netting swayed.

Darcy felt herself shaking her head, her whole body saying
no. "Don't touch it."

Cam came up behind Heather and swung the cooler into
her butt. "Quit it," Heather said. Cam set the cooler down and
pretended to sulk.

Nick ran past Darcy and hurled himself sideways onto the
hammock, pitching it back and forth.

"There's room for two. Come to Daddy." Nick held out his
arms to Darcy, as if she were a toddler needing direction.

"Shut up, Nick." Heather crossed her arms against the
image Darcy couldn't block out, no matter how hard she tried.

The backyard hammock at home had been their special
place for years. Even when Daddy was too down to manage
anything else, they'd swing for hours. Sometimes he'd ask her
to memorize poems and recite verse back to him. Darcy found
out the hard way that some poems served as a foreshadowing
of events to come. She should've understood the cautionary
tale when he'd asked her not to tell her mother about their secret Shakespeare sonnet.

No longer mourn for me when I am dead
Than you shall hear the surly sullen bell
Give warning to the world that I am fled

Darcy snatched up the cooler and ran down the trail to the beach. She squeezed through the overgrown bushes and climbed up the slippery rock path to her favorite perfectly flat boulder. Snow covered the lake, and she blinked against the reflected light till her sight adjusted. She sat, drew up her legs, hugged her knees. Her throat burned, dry as a bone, and she gulped at the beer.

"What the fuck, Darcy? You're pissing Nick off, you know." Cam came up the path alone, sent as a messenger. He plunked down on the rock and stretched out his legs.

She knew what to do with a messenger. "I was just wondering. Could you possibly use less creative language?" Even she sometimes cursed, but only for shock value. "Sure *fuck* could be construed as colorful language. But swearing is generally used as a defense mechanism, a lazy man's way to communicate," she said, repeating her father's warning word for word.

"You used to be nice, Darcy." He spoke through a swallow of beer, wiped dribble off his chin with the back of his hand.

Evidently, she'd disappointed him by changing into someone he had trouble recognizing. She didn't even recognize herself lately, so she kept experimenting.

Cam frowned. He swung the heel of his sneaker into a patch of ice, breaking off chunks. His outrageously long eyelashes curled up to meet the mane of thick curls drooping over his forehead. When they were both eight, he'd begged her to trim his feminine lashes for him, and she'd slipped. Instead of telling, Cam had covered for her. Told his mother he'd fallen against a fence picket during a game of tag. A flesh-toned scar still cut across his brow bone.

"Sorry." Darcy rubbed Cam's shoulder, trying to erase the verbal jabs she'd given him.

"Heather thinks Nick's going to ask you to the prom."

It was Darcy's turn to sputter on her beer. Last week, she'd mentioned wanting to go to the junior prom to Nick as a joke he'd apparently taken seriously. Something ridiculous like a bunch of teenage girls dressing up like fairy princesses might prove a worthy distraction. For the boys, the evening suggested a promise not evident in any fairy tale she'd ever read. No happy ever after, just happy for about fifteen minutes. Or so she'd heard. Despite rumors to the contrary, she was still holding on to her virginity, wearing it like a hoodie she could unzip for optimal impact when she was ready.

"Am I supposed to tell you my answer before he even asks me? Take away all the suspense? What would be the fun in that?"

Cam shoved her with the heel of his hand. "Quit it, Darcy. You're such a pain in the ass."

"Umm." She totally agreed with him. Even she had trouble swallowing how nasty she could get, how far she'd go to produce interesting reactions. Sometimes, she'd get really quiet inside, and her mind would slow down to listen to words she could hardly believe she was saying. Like the way she spoke to her mother this morning about going to Daddy's grave.

From this vile world, with vilest worms to dwell.

Cam flipped his sweatshirt's hood over his head. For warmth, he tucked his right hand into the sweatshirt's left sleeve, his left hand into the right, a ritual he'd practiced since preschool. What would she do without her quirky Cam?

Cam glanced over at her, responding to her unbending stare, the close scrutiny of his every move. He shook his head, stood up, and guzzled down the rest of his beer.

She should really be nicer to Cam, instead of treating him like her brother. Cam refused to discuss her father, even though Cam's father had been the first person her mother had called after finding Daddy's body. She wondered what exactly her mom had said to Mr. Mathers. Something like, *Uh, Tom, I think I found one of your guns.* Then Mr. Mathers must've told Cam's mom, energizing the story of her father's last drama through the small town, leaving no one untouched. Each person took the story way too personally, like Cam, or not nearly personally enough.

Heather and Nick crunched up the path, walking in perfect unison—right leg, left leg, arms swinging in agreement. Heather had told him. Everything. Why else would he be looking at her like that? Meeting her gaze, then staring at his feet, as if his shoes would tell him what to do next. Stay or flee.

Darcy pulled her legs up under her, took a sip of beer, and stared out at the lake. Nature never shied away from you. Last week, she'd stood in the yard, catching snowflakes on her tongue. Another six weeks, and spring would come. Then white dandelions would pop up across yards all over town. Then little girls would close their eyes, blow on the fluff, and pray they'd remain their daddies' sweethearts forever. Then her daddy would be gone for a whole year.

Nick sat down right beside her, shoulder to shoulder, and took a beer. He held the can between his knees, depressed the tab, and hooked an arm around her shoulder. She didn't mean to shudder from his touch.

"I'm sorry about your dad," he said. "I didn't know."

She tried to gauge his level of pity, how repulsed he might be by the story of her life. His eyes didn't give him away. Nick had moved to Greenboro a few weeks ago, and nobody had clued him in to one of the town's most notorious former citizens—writer in residence and crazy person in residence Jack Klein. Well, good. The story must've finally died down and been replaced by more recent gossip. Come to think of it, Nick was the most recent gossip.

The notion of their going out together suddenly made perfect sense.

"I like your earring." She slid her finger over the thin gold hoop straddling his left lobe, then dropped her hand when Nick didn't look away.

"Want it?" He fussed at his lobe and offered the earring to her. "I have others." He pushed back her hair to reveal the diamond studs she always wore, a gift from her dad.

On reflex, Darcy covered her earrings.

"Okay." Nick heaved a sigh and snapped the hoop back on his earlobe. "I don't have a dad, either, you know."

"Is he dead?" It was a disgusting thought, but the very possibility of someone finally understanding actually excited her.

"No, not dead. Just divorced. I only wish he were dead."

"Why?" She'd given up wishing years ago in favor of bargaining with God, telling Him she'd be good, do more chores, if only Daddy would get better. But she'd never wished him dead. He'd done enough of that himself.

"It'd be easier. I like things easy. That's what my mom says."

Didn't sound exactly like a compliment to Darcy, but Nick seemed to think so, judging by the way he was smiling at her. Heather and Cam sat at the boulder's edge, dangling their legs. A few feet away, they were in their own world. Good for Cam. He'd had a crush on Heather forever. Heather never seemed to notice how Cam trotted by her side, like a lovesick puppy. Darcy even thought they looked good together—Heather's stick-straight blond hair working to balance out Cam's thicket of dark curls. Whenever Darcy tried bringing up the subject of any boy lately, not just Cam, Heather would change the topic. As if fussing over trouble with hair and acne were more amusing than boys. Nothing was more amusing than boys. Darcy placed her hand on Nick's pocket and gave him a moment to consider what she might be after.

"Oh, princess wants some weed."

"I'm not a princess." In all the Disney movies, the heroines were either orphans or came from single-parent households. Hey, maybe she was a princess. And he was Prince Charming, sliding a baggie of marijuana from his low-slung jeans and sprinkling the dried leaves into a tidy row on a rolling paper.

He licked the end of the paper with practiced precision, then handed her a nice thick joint along with his lighter.

She concentrated on the glow of flame, slurping it up through the crisp paper until the end lit scarlet on its own. She held the smoke and imagined it billowing across her brain. Her fingers ached for it while Nick took his turn.

"You like it? Grew it myself in Nashua." Nick inhaled deeply. "Just popped a heater in my grandmother's green-house, started up a new crop here," he said in a strained voice, without releasing any telling smoke. "She hasn't used it since my mom and I moved in. I thought, why not get a head start on the growing season? Make a few bucks while I'm at it." So that part of the Nick rumor was actually true.

The sweet weed lured Cam and Heather. Heather plunked down beside her, cross-legged, not allowing for any space be-tween them. What was wrong with Heather lately? Couldn't she see how much Cam liked her? He'd seen her red-nosed from colds, freaking out over grades, and beyond comforting when her dog had died. Yet, amazingly, he still liked her.

Darcy could never show a boyfriend how sad her father made her, way worse than a red nose and freaking out. Way beyond comforting. She couldn't think of Daddy anymore without remembering how he'd died.

Nay, if you read this line, remember not
The hand that writ it; for I love you so.

Darcy passed the joint to Heather and found a new expres-sion clouding her friend's features, equal parts concern and eagerness. Nick set up a second jay, twisted the end, and passed it to Cam. "Don't drool on it, buddy. Okay?"

Nick didn't have to worry about Cam slobbering all over the joint. Mess didn't coexist with Cam's neatness addiction or his neurotic organizing. He tore through more pads of paper than her mother with his perpetual list making. Probably, he'd made sure he got through all of his homework in study hall so he could scratch it off and arrive at number two on the list: getting stoned.

Nick stood and stretched, crossing his arms behind his head. His open jacket and T-shirt rose, revealing the kind of six-pack you only saw in movies. The kind she and Heather watched late at night after Mom was asleep. Darcy would stare straight at the screen with what must've been a goofy grin on her face and shift in her seat, like she was doing now.

"Want to go for a walk?" Nick took her hand, and she sprang to her feet.

Cam waved them on, like when her father had sent her off on her first date. *Have her back by eight, young man.* She could still hear Daddy camping it up.

Holding hands didn't mean anything, but by the time they'd walked to the end of the beach, Nick's pulse was heating her palm, and her hand was sweating. The snow on the lake glimmered, perfect and white, unlike the graying slush in town. She thought she'd noticed the thermometer outside chemistry edging above freezing, maybe even hitting forty. But that had been midday, when the sun hit dead-on. That had been when Nick wasn't watching her.

She dropped Nick's hand and stepped past the shore's edge, crunching through the untouched snow. The bottoms of her sneakers slid against the ice, and her heart pulsed in her ears. She ignored the cramps in her feet, how her toes ached with cold.

Nick followed her lead and stepped onto the lake. He paused for a beat as if considering his next move, and then picked her up and spun her through a panoramic view of the lake, the pine trees, the shore. She steadied herself against his chest, realizing the effect his homegrown pot was having on her for the first time. The way it gentled her down so she could see things more clearly. The curved line her sneakers sketched into the snow.

"Darcy," Nick said. His eyelids lowered; his gaze trained on her mouth, and she licked her lips.

Nick edged his whole body closer, adjusting his legs into a wide-legged stance so he wouldn't be too tall for her. She tilted her chin. His lips curled into a grin before they touched hers, tentative at first. He pressed harder, and she closed her eyes. Sunlight darted across her eyelids, and standing still, she was sailing across the lake.

Flavors slid off Nick's tongue like layers of a parfait. She expected the slightly bitter beer, the savory pot, but the last layer came as a surprise: a sweet cinnamon candy. She swallowed. A low growl rose in Nick's throat and vibrated into her mouth like a warning signal of going too far. With the heels of her hands, she pushed him away.

"Wow. You're a great kisser. Except for the part where you stopped." Nick's face had that soft sleepy look, as if he wasn't sure they'd really stopped kissing.

Darcy slipped from his arms and trudged farther across the lake. Petal-soft snow slid beneath her sneakers. She couldn't feel her toes, but the rest of her burned with Nick's kiss.

"Hey, what're you doing?" Nick asked.

"Snow angel." She lowered herself to the ice, lay on her back against the snow. She ignored how the sudden shift in temperature weakened her entire body and fanned her arms and legs. Clouds painted milky swirls across the too-blue sky.

Nick's face smiled down at her. "What the hell." He lay

beside her, fanned his arms and legs, and then scrambled to his feet. When she started to get up, Nick swept her legs out from under her and cradled her knees over one strong arm. She wrapped her arms around his neck, and he ran, carrying her across the ice against his shivering chest.

At the shore, he lowered her onto the ground with more care than she'd expected from him. Her whole face throbbed from laughing. His blue lips leaning in for a frosty kiss didn't slow the giggles. Not even when he found himself making out with her teeth. Now Nick was laughing, too.

"I was gonna ask you something, but I can't remember what it was. I need another kiss."

She cupped his pink cheeks and pressed her lips to his cold mouth.

"Okay," he said. "I remember. Would you—you're going to think it's stupid."

She couldn't quite believe his sudden shyness, how innocent he looked soaking wet and shivering. His wet hair made him even more striking. Drops of water glistened at the ends of his dark-blond lashes. She touched his jawline, and a fake tear slid down his cheek. "I'm listening."

"Would you go to the prom with me?"

She took her time gathering her hair over one shoulder into a controllable bundle, and then squeezed until a torrent of melted snow flooded down her arm. Her scalp tingled. "I don't know, Nick. When is it?"

"It's the end of May, I think—I could find out—the paper—" He brushed at the snow caking his arms. "Jeez, I lose everything."

She put him out of his misery. "I'll go with you."

"What?"

"I said, I'll—"

"You were messing with me."

"What makes you say that? I wouldn't mess with you."

"You're doing it again." He liked it, judging by the grin running rampant. He got right in her face, flattening his features. "You talking to me? I said, *Are you talking to me?*"

"Robert De Niro, *Taxi Driver*," Darcy said. "My dad used to do that."

"Yeah? Mine too. Scared the shit out of my mother. Let her know what was coming next." Nick clawed at the snow, as if searching for something he'd lost.

Darcy's dad didn't look any more frightening when he tried the classic movie lines out on her than the boy shifting snow through his fingers. Daddy's impersonation of a deviant taxi driver intimidating a baffled stranger always cracked her up. Her father only scared her when he wasn't consciously trying to.

Daddy.

There he was again, throwing a shadow over her shoulder. No, it was just Cam come to interrupt her moment of improv identification.

"Got any food at your house? Heather and I are starving." Cam crouched down behind her, glanced over his shoulder at Heather waiting on the rock. "We've got wicked munchies."

"Are you kidding? We always have food at my house. It's like part of my mother's religion." *Thou shalt not go hungry.* Come to think of it, she was hungry, too. Famished. "Want to come over my house?" she asked Nick.

"Like this?" Nick pointed to his sagging, wet jeans.

"My mom won't be home yet, and I can put your pants in the dryer. No biggie." A shiver hunched her shoulders.

Nick nodded and took her hand to help her up. "You look cold," he said. He wrapped an arm around her, but Darcy slipped from his reach and caught up with Heather. "Hey!" Nick called after Darcy, and a laugh cracked his voice.

Heather swiped at the brush, knocking clumps of snow to the path. "So what happened?"

"We made snow angels." Darcy smiled, not thinking about the snow, but about Nick's lips and the sound he made when she kissed him back. The path spilled into the property's yard, and she twirled, actually twirled, into the open.

"Well, duh. I know that—I have eyes. I mean, did he ask you to the prom?"

"Yes."

"Oh." Heather glared at the cottage, the foliage, the hammock beside her. Not exactly the response Darcy had imagined.

"I know it's silly, but I don't know—it could be fun. I love to dance and, hey, we can go dress shopping. You can help me with my hair. And—"

Heather was crying.

Heat flooded Darcy's face and pulsed at her temples. "What's wrong? What is it? Is it the thing with Vanessa? I only hang out with her so I can tell you all the stupid things Loudmouth says." Heather used to hang out with Vanessa, too, until she and Vanessa had a disagreement. Heather had found Vanessa annoying and Vanessa hadn't agreed.

Heather almost smiled, but she wouldn't give up an answer.

At Nick's car, Darcy tried again, although she really wanted to shake Heather till whatever was wrong rattled from her mouth. "Do you want to go, too? I don't think Stevie has a date yet. Wait, I'm an idiot. It's Cam, isn't it? Did something happen? Did he ask you out? Did he not ask you out?" Too bad Cam couldn't ask Heather to the prom till they were juniors next year.

Heather leaned against the car and retied her sneakers, as if Darcy were totally clueless. "Just forget it, okay?"

No, not okay. "Whatever."

"Hey, girls." Nick sauntered into view, Cam trailing behind. "Darcy tell you the good news yet?" He slipped an arm around Darcy's waist and drew her to his side. "Darcy's gonna let me take her to the prom."

Heather crawled into the backseat, refusing to respond to Nick's big announcement.

"What's with her? Did I do something wrong?" Darcy and Nick slid onto the front seats. Nick twisted toward the back. "What did I do?" he asked Heather.

Heather pressed her cheek against the window, and Cam just shrugged.

"Braaar!" Nick shook his wet head, splattering the windshield. He cranked the heater and checked his hair in the rearview mirror.

"Looks the same as always," Darcy assured him. How was she ever going to tolerate a boy more high maintenance than she was?

He smirked. "You're messing with me again. Come here."

He leaned in and clutched her face, forcing a long kiss right in front of her friends that left more than the taste of sweet cinnamon. A shiver thundered through her chest. The pins-and-needles sensation of thawing nerves pierced Darcy's toes, and Nick's kiss burned her tongue, like a fireball candy she'd once held in her mouth on a dare.

Chapter 3

Years before Jack Klein's once-lucrative teaching requests had dried up due to his reputation for cutting his own classes, he'd taught his student Laura how to analyze a character's behavior.

Mid-afternoon, and Jack's tax returns still sat on her desk, and the fridge still awaited restocking. Laura couldn't help herself. If she wanted to find the motivation behind her real-life husband's suicide, she'd need to study the hours leading up to his death one more time. The thought weakened her foundation, as though she were sinking into a hole.

Laura wasn't really trying to torture herself, merely gain closure. She went into the living room and obtained a small measure of stress relief from stirring the woodstove's coals and squeezing three thick logs through the side door. She opened the flue and watched the pyramid catch fire.

Jack had wanted ice cream, and she'd run out to Yogi's to buy a pint. Resurrecting the memory stirred up the sight of her Jack lounging in bed all tousled and sexy, and the coarse texture of his hair beneath her fingertips. Laura inhaled, and then huffed an exhalation. She required a lot more than refreshing the fire to release her angst. Arms clasped behind her back, she bent at the waist and raised her arms until her shoulder blades opened.

He'd asked for Chunky Monkey, their favorite flavor since their first date. He'd wanted to start over, to go back to a time when he wasn't sick. And, the thing was, he'd seemed so happy, in a balanced sort of way . . .

She tossed on her fleece, laced up her duck boots, and stepped out to the yard. At the shed, she slid the maul ax from its shelf and headed for the woodpile. From beneath the green tarp, she drew a sixteen-inch log and placed her victim dead center on the splitting block. Every single time Jack had messed around with his medication, taking too little lithium or going off it completely, he'd lost control. She raised the maul, set her focus on the log, and released all her energy into the wood, splitting off a satisfying chunk.

He was sick. He couldn't take it anymore. The rapid cycling—

Jack would've told her, the most obvious reasons for a character's action were usually wrong, excuses masquerading as explanation.

He'd stayed on his prescription that last week, choosing to follow through with a plan he'd hatched when the sun was setting on his mood.

Jack had asked her to get him Chunky Monkey ice cream, and the tightness in his voice had straightened her spine. Purse on her shoulder, hand clutching her keys, Laura had paused at the edge of their bed. And he'd kissed her. Dear God, he'd kissed her. He'd studied her face, scrambled to her side of the bed, and he'd kissed her.

He wasn't sick when he'd killed himself. He'd made a rational decision, and then did whatever was necessary to carry it out. He knew she was looking for a sure sign of his mental health, so he gave it to her.

Jack had used her.

She squinted through the glaring sun and rolled her shoulders. *Damn you, Jack!* She gave herself a split second to aim, then swung the maul and nailed the sucker. *Whack!*

"Man!"

She whirled around, ax guarding her chest, and found a stranger standing a few feet away from her, grinning as if he'd witnessed the ninth wonder of the world. She sized him up. Young, somewhere in the middle of his twenties, and fit, too, judging by the shape he took beneath a gray-and-white wool sweater. But she had the home turf advantage. The stranger was on her property, and she had a sharp-edged maul she wasn't afraid to use. She could take him.

The stranger raised his hand and produced not a weapon, but a stack of papers he offered to her. "Elle said you'd be home."

"Elle?" Laura laid the ax down beside her, hands shaking from the adrenaline rush of her body preparing for battle. She took the papers from his hands and flipped through the thick pile—completed rental application, verification of employment, credit check. The stack even included a personal note from Beth at Hometown Real Estate stating that she found no record of court proceedings against the applicant. So Elle had found herself an accomplice. Or, more likely, Elle had left Beth in the dark, too, claiming she was doing Laura a favor by helping to rent out Jack's studio.

"Aidan Walsh." The man offered his hand and left it between them while she juggled the paperwork.

Oh, okay. Elle's friend from her spinning class. Not at all how Laura had pictured him. She'd imagined someone who'd recently experienced a reversal of fortune, a middle-aged man with a face like an English bloodhound. This young guy was almost too good-looking. "Laura Klein."

He kept hold of her hand longer than necessary, maintaining that irritating grin, as if he knew something deliciously gossipy about her. Well, join the club.

"What a surprise." She'd told Elle she'd talk to her friend. She didn't expect a prescreened tenant, hadn't even allowed the idea of renting out Jack's studio to fully form. Now she'd better think fast. She glanced down at the first page of the application and noted that someone—either Elle or Beth—had highlighted eight hundred dollars, so Laura couldn't miss it.

"Sorry about that, surprising you," he said. "I don't usually sneak up on women splitting wood."

"Good to know." The nearest Laundromat was forty-five minutes away in Milford. A tenant would have to use the laundry room off the kitchen, right in the middle of her family's personal space. She must be nuts even considering this. Still, eight hundred dollars.

"Let me ask you something." Heat from splitting wood thrummed down her arms, but a subtle chill laced her spine. "What exactly did Elle tell you about the apartment?"

His grin faded, and he shifted in place. "I'm very sorry about your husband's death."

At least Elle had the common sense to offer up the truth. "And you're all right with that?" Plain logic hit hard. This guy might be the only person in all of the Monadnock Region willing to rent out the studio where her husband had killed himself.

He shrugged. "Doesn't bother me."

The idea of death in general and a self-inflicted death in particular not bothering this man cast him into a tiny minority. Most people did their best to shield themselves from gruesome reality, covering their eyes like kids at a horror flick. *Tell me when the scary part's over.* This guy didn't even flinch. Perhaps, like her, he didn't believe in ghosts. Memories were enough of a challenge. "Right this way then."

The stranger, Aidan Walsh, followed her across the snowy yard, keeping a respectable distance until they came to the mudroom. Laura unlaced her boots and peeled off her fleece.

She was about to ask him to take his shoes off, but he beat her to it. He set a pair of broken-in work boots on the rubber mat. What the heck was his story? She'd noticed Memorial Hospital listed on his application but had missed his occupation. Maybe he was a young intern, needing a place to crash in between graveyard shifts. That would make sense.

She turned the skeleton key and assisted the studio door with her hip, then glanced over her shoulder and found herself staring into Aidan's dark brown eyes.

For her, Jack's studio was like a memorial. But to what? Jack giving up? Maybe if she disassembled Jack's studio, her family could move past the dark side of Jack's history. Renting out the studio could provide both financial support and an emotionally cathartic spring cleaning.

A sense of synergy flowed into her body as natural as the day's first wide-awake breath. While Maggie would explain this everyday miracle as descending from the universe itself, Laura simply attributed her luck to the intensity of Elle's love for her coupled with especially good timing. "I could empty it out pretty fast, if you need to move in right away."

A few minutes ago, renting out the studio as a one-bedroom apartment wasn't even a wisp of a thought in her mind. Now she was inviting a strange man into her home. Elle and Beth had screened him for her, but so what? If he were an especially clever serial killer, he wouldn't even have a police record, just a trail of unexplained murders dotting every town he'd ever graced.

Laura waited by the desk, giving Aidan the opportunity to discover the quirky apartment on his own, beginning at the far reaches of the studio and working his way backward. She could hear him open and shut the rarely used outside door leading to the side yard. He tried the water in the small but ornately tiled bathroom, checked the cabinets in the galley kitchen, and then climbed up into the loft overlooking Jack's office space.

The gate at the front of the loft creaked open, and he climbed down the recycled library ladder, whistling during descent, as if each wrung inspired a unique note. "Really nice. I even like the paint color. Reminds me of pumpkin pie."

"I think so, too." Sometimes, just gazing at the walls inspired her to whip up the dessert, even in mid-July.

Aidan made his way over to Jack's computer desk and studied the collage of black-and-white family photos. "These are your kids? Elle told me you had a son and a daughter, but I imagined them as toddlers. You must've been a child bride."

Was he trying to butter up his potential landlady? She'd given up associating herself with the word *young* a long time ago. Whenever she looked into a mirror, she half expected to see an elderly woman staring back through timeworn skin. Fortunately, the effects of stress weren't quite so harsh.

"Yes, I was a youngster." She left it out there, couldn't resist waiting until he squirmed a little, no doubt visualizing her barefoot and married to her first cousin at age thirteen. She even placed a hand on his arm. Laura didn't usually tease strangers, but the look on his face was too priceless to give up.

"I was eighteen, fully legal." Laura slid her hand from his arm. She didn't usually *touch* strangers, either.

"Uh, okay. You got me." He rubbed at the back of his neck, tried finding a place to rest his gaze. "So anyway."

What was wrong with her? Surely, she was scaring the poor guy away along with his rent money. The prospect of eight hundred much-needed dollars a month must've sent her over the edge of propriety, setting her in the camp of overeager. "Are you interested?"

He smiled, raising a curve to the left of his mouth.

"In the apartment." She couldn't let him think she was flirting, even for a second. She did not flirt. "I mean it's a large space, but no laundry room. We'd have to share mine off the kitchen. I'd need to chart a schedule, do an every other day thing."

Relax, Laura. It's only laundry. She hardly recognized the sound of her voice, the singsong cadence. She was stumbling about verbally, vacillating, working out her decision in public. The last time she'd babbled in front of a strange man, she was a college freshman sitting in the front row of Jack's Creative Writing 101 class, biding her time until she could get him alone. All her logic had gone out the window, every ounce of common sense discarded as quickly as she could shed her clothes in Jack's campus office. She'd just had to have him.

Aidan cocked his head, stared at her as if she were a 3-D puzzle. "I'm used to a separate laundry room. You'd only have to tolerate me, say, once a week. I'm not a clothes kind of guy."

What was he then? A nudist?

Great, so now *she'd* need to decide *and* erase the pulse-quickening thought of him naked. "Would you like something to drink? Coffee or tea?" Sipping a cup of joe would give her time to go through the application more thoroughly and bring up any questions that came to mind.

"Coffee'd be great."

She led him into the kitchen and motioned to a ladder-back chair pushed away from the table, as though waiting in readiness. She flipped on the filtered water, left the carafe in the sink, and leaned against the counter.

"I'm having a little trouble switching back and forth between day and night shifts," he said. "Not exactly looking forward to rotations and an additional thirty hours a week, but I'll live."

"Intern?"

He shook his head. "Nope."

"Not an intern?"

"Guess again."

She poured the filtered water into the coffeemaker, scooped grounds into the filter basket, and flipped the switch. "I don't have to guess." She went for the application package she'd left on the kitchen table, sat down across from him, and skimmed her finger down his verification of employment. *Emergency medical resident, second year.* That set Aidan at about twenty-eight, a bit older than she'd guessed. Something about this guy beggared her mind. Rugged male labor EM resident seeks apartment in home of local widow. There was a piece missing here, probably several. "What brought you to emergency medicine?" Laura asked.

"Ever since I was thirteen years old, I've wanted to work in the ER, almost as much as I wanted to become a professional baseball player," he said. "Figured I had a better chance as a doctor."

The blips from the coffeemaker gurgled to a stop. "Just a sec." She jumped up, poured two mugs of coffee, plunked them on the table along with cream and sugar, and then returned to the exact sitting position she'd vacated.

The more this guy talked, the more questions he brought up. At thirteen, most boys were learning about the basics of adolescent body changes, not pondering a career as specific as an emergency room doctor. "I don't usually speak for my thirteen-year-old son, but I'm positive he has no interest in emergency medicine. So what happened?"

"What happened?" he said. Surely, the guy was playacting, noticing her eagerness and delaying story gratification.

She rested her chin in her hands and inched forward. "What happened to make you interested in emergency medicine?"

"Oh, that." He held up his index finger, dug in his back pocket, and produced a worn leather wallet. He unfolded a newspaper clipping and smoothed it flat before sliding it across the table.

The boy's baseball cap in the old photo caught her eye first, then the smile with the curved dimple set to the left. The boy was sitting next to a girl propped in a hospital bed with a bandage covering her lower arm. Laura read the caption: *Resourceful thirteen-year-old Boy Scout, Aidan Walsh, saves ten-year-old sister Anna's life by applying a tourniquet after girl puts arm through a glass door.*

Well, that said it all. At the age of thirteen, the younger version of the man sitting across from her must have gotten permanently hooked on life and chose to spend his days, and nights, saving lives. The precipitating event. She took a second glance at the photo, and then passed the clipping back to Aidan.

He regarded the photo with fresh interest before putting it back away.

"So you keep the old photo to explain to curiosity seekers why you chose emergency medicine?"

"Well, sure, it works okay for that, but mostly I keep it to remind me." He sipped his coffee, and she waited for clarification.

"Say on a day when I'm getting burned out, the magic is lost from it. It's like, oh heck, not another blunt force trauma. I haven't had my lunch break yet." He tapped his pocket. "Take out the photo to remind me the woman on the gurney is more than an injury or disease. She's someone's mom, a daughter, maybe even a goofy little sister. Then I'm right back there in a world of wonder, and nothing else matters."

A world of wonder. Not the kind of eloquent speech she'd expected from a young guy, even a doctor. "So how's little Anna doing?"

He grinned. "Arm works great. Got a free ride to UMass on a softball scholarship. Swings a bat like a pro."

He stood, pantomimed a killer swing, and then held his hand like a visor, gazing past the sun's glare at the fast-moving softball. "Yup, over the wall again! Go, Anna!" Aidan Walsh was a proud older brother and a physical storyteller.

His unbridled enthusiasm spilled over, and she couldn't stop smiling as she riffled through the application, looking for his current and past housing situations. He was staying with a couple in Greenboro he'd listed as friends, and until a few months ago, he'd been living with a woman in the North End of Boston. Probably his love interest, although he'd left the relationship line blank. Unless this Kitty—God, she hated that name—was a platonic housemate. She went by a different last name, but these days, that didn't prove a thing. Laura tapped the blank line next to Kitty's name. "Kitty is, was, your wife?"

He shook his head, and the exuberance drained from his face, as if Laura had siphoned it out herself. "Girlfriend." He drank down the rest of his coffee. "So, yeah, I figured I'd rent in Greenboro for a while, see if this is the kind of town I'd like to settle in before I look for a house to buy, put down roots. I visited my old college buddy Finn here a couple of years ago, really liked it, but it wasn't the right time. Things changed, and then I got an offer from Memorial, so I just had to jump, take my chances." *Bing, bang, boom.* He spilled the rest of the story, no longer inspired to drag out the details. This Kitty must've been quite a girl. Where had the spirited storyteller gone? She wanted to lure him back onto the stage of her kitchen. *Encore, encore. Tell me more.*

He pushed away from the table and stood. "My cell phone number's on the app. I like the apartment. Think it'll do fine. Why don't you call me when you decide? Just leave a message." He took his empty mug to the sink, rinsed it, and set it in her dishwasher.

He rubbed the back of his neck and turned to meet Laura's gaze. "Were you really looking to rent out the apartment? I mean, before I showed up and interrupted your chopping?"

"I told Elle I'd talk to you, but no. Not quite yet."

"Yeah, got that impression. Guess we can both thank Elle. She's kind of—how can I say this? Pushy."

"Pushy?" That sounded about right. He backpedaled. "In a real good-natured way."

"Oh, sure. It's a compliment."

"Maybe *friendly* would be a better word."

"No, no. Stay with *pushy*."

He stifled a chuckle and rubbed at his chin again in what she now recognized as a nervous little gesture, a sudden shyness. "So, um, call me when you decide. Okay? Either way."

They went into the mudroom, and he leaned against the wall, worked his feet into his mud-caked boots. He hunched over, tightening the dirt-striped laces into snug bows as endearingly off-center as his dimple.

"When would you want to move in?" Saying the words hollowed Laura's center, as if she were free falling.

"Right away. Finn and his wife have been great, but I'm sure they'd like the slob to get off the couch and give them back their living room."

Slob, huh? She tried picturing Aidan's scattered belongings. Lug-soled work boots with graying laces peeking out from beneath the sofa skirt. Medical journals. Photos of his family sprinkled across his unmade bed. She preferred everything neat and tidy, yet for some inexplicable reason the idea of this man's strewn belongings in her home soothed her.

She inhaled down to her toes, but her lips still quivered. "I've decided."

He nodded. "I understand. Thanks for showing me the apartment."

"You can move in. Today." Her heart was pounding through her chest wall, unused to spur of the moment decisions. Sometimes you just had to go for it. Wasn't that what her daughter always said? *Oh, come on, Mom. Just go for it!* Besides, who could say no to an emergency room doctor with such sweet eyes? She doubted she'd discover anything off-color about this guy through further digging. She considered herself a good judge of character, and first impressions usually proved themselves accurate. Besides, she could really use the money.

He stopped at the side door and turned around, a big grin leading the way. "Really? Are you sure? I mean I wouldn't want to be pushy."

She nodded, getting the joke. "In a good-natured kind of way."

"Well, thank you for the compliment." He checked his watch. "What time works for you?"

Oh, heck. She still had to drop Jack's tax returns at the post office and pick up a few groceries at the market. Then there was the matter of hauling Jack's furniture into the shed. "I have a few errands," she said. "And I'll need to clean out the studio."

"I'd be happy to move your furniture for you. Finn and I could empty the place, oh, I'd say, in about thirty minutes, if you can wait till five o'clock. I need to go spring my stuff from storage."

"Five's perfect."

"Great. It's a date then." He offered his hand to seal the deal. This time, he let go first. She followed him out the door in her socks, and the cement step iced the soles of her feet. She crossed her arms against the cold.

Aidan jogged across the driveway to a midnight-blue Toyota pickup, then turned back around. "Bye, Laura! See you at five!"

She nodded, hoping he wasn't looking at her. A wave of prickly heat struck, as if she were still a shy fifteen-year-old. Whenever a cute boy spoke her name, she'd blush painfully, embarrassed by thoughts of connection.

Now she stood on the cement steps watching Aidan

Walsh climb into his truck, shuffle in his seat, and slam the door shut. He keyed the engine, rolled down his driver's side window, and hung his head out the window. "Nice meeting you!" He smiled, showing the full depth of his lopsided dimple, before ducking back into the truck's cab. The pickup bumped to the edge of the driveway, and Aidan waved out the window, palm exposed in her direction, signifying both an ending and a beginning.

Chapter 4

An unfamiliar old sports car sat in Laura's driveway, and she pulled up alongside it. A few scraps of robin's egg blue, reminiscent of more colorful days, remained against the canvas of matte gray. Two tremendous fuzzy dice hung from the rearview mirror. A joke, she hoped, not some boy's earnest attempt at decorating.

Many times, Laura had cautioned her daughter about the dangers of fast-talking boys with fast cars and even faster hands. Many times, she'd come home and found Darcy with a new boyfriend in her kitchen. And many times, she'd reminded Darcy about the no-friends-without-a-parent-home rule.

One more time wouldn't kill Laura. But Darcy better watch out.

Laura slammed the car door, then hurried to the side of the house. She held her breath as she turned the key and exhaled when the door swung open and the sound of Heather and Cam wafted out to greet her, along with the static of a radio station that never came in right. At least her daughter wasn't alone with the owner of the pile of rust parked in her driveway.

Laura jiggled her keys to sound the adult-in-the-house alarm. "I'm home!"

Laura kicked off her boots harder than necessary and carried the grocery bags into the kitchen. She tossed her handbag onto the table and headed for the faint sound of wheezing. On the far side of the kitchen island, Cam was tickling Heather into oblivion. Heather curled up into herself and left nothing showing but her light blond hair blazing across the floorboards.

"Enough, Cam!" Laura said. She came around the island.

Cam removed his hands from Heather's armpits. She leaned against the cabinets, catching her breath and swiping at the tears washing down her cheeks.

"Hey, Mrs. Klein." A blushing Cam kneeled and tried to help Heather up.

Heather swatted at his outstretched hand, sprung up unaided, and turned on the for-adults-only charm. "Sorry about the mess."

Bits of crackers and chip debris lined the countertops, evidence of a hastily consumed festival of carbohydrates. Two glasses of homemade soda—Laura saved the real stuff for birthdays—stood guard to the crumbs. Seltzer and juice rose up through the bendy straws, dribbling orange onto the countertops. Water gurgled in the teakettle, quickened to a rolling boil. Two waiting mugs held drifts of untouched cocoa, the brown powder coming to rest at identical angles. Darcy only drank cocoa when she was near freezing to death.

"Hot chocolate?" And two mugs. Soon, Laura would meet the owner of the barely blue wreck parked in her driveway.

"They're cold," Heather offered, getting a thinly veiled look of warning from Cam. Between Darcy's two best friends, Laura always pieced together the truth.

"Who's cold, honey? Darcy and a friend?"

Heather's pale lashes leaped up to meet her brows. "Uh-huh."

The last time Laura had found her daughter cold enough for cocoa, they'd earned a visit from Officer Keith Holmes, come to explain how trespassing and skinny-dipping on private property were prosecutable offenses. She doubted that would be the charge today. What mischief had Darcy gotten into this time? And where was the boy?

"Cam? Where's Darcy?"

Cam's gaze darted to the door of the guest bathroom.

Laura listened for her daughter's voice, uncovering the thump of clothes in the dryer from behind the closed door. Darcy was not in the habit of doing the wash when she had friends over. At least Darcy wasn't upstairs with a boy. Laura's pulse pounded in her ears. As if the bathroom were a more suitable place for her daughter and a strange boy.

The kettle shrieked, mimicking Laura's internal pressure gauge. She flipped the switch to off and poured water into the mugs. Stirring the cocoa did nothing to slow the boil. Laura marched to the bathroom door, then rapped on the frame. "Darcy, are you in there?" Laura jiggled the door handle. Locked.

"Just a minute, Mom." Darcy's muffled giggle filtered through the door. The rich tone of a boy's whisper reminded Laura of Jack's seductive voice seventeen years ago. Three weeks after Laura had buried her mother, Jack had invited her for their first secret as sin student-teacher conference. Behind the closed door of Jack's university office, rug burning her back, she'd thought he was exactly what she'd needed.

Were Darcy and the boy naked on the other side of the door? She released the doorknob and put her mouth up to the interface of door and frame. "Open the damn door!"

Laura nabbed the turkey lacer from the kitchen island.

After she disengaged the lock, she'd use the utensil to lace the boy's zipper shut.

Please, Darcy, don't do this. Don't give a part of yourself away you can never get back. Especially not like this! Did Darcy think so little of herself?

Had Laura?

Eyes moistening, Laura aimed the turkey lacer, ready to jab the lock, and the door swung open, revealing her fully clothed daughter and—

Her late husband.

Heat slapped her cheeks. Her hand flew to her mouth. She blinked.

Not her late husband, but the owner of the heap on wheels, was tightening the belt of the light blue terry cloth bathrobe Jack had left hanging on the door hook over a year ago. Laura's hand drifted from her mouth, and she fisted her hand to cover the shaking.

The boy grinned. Unlike Jack, his smile showed off the deepest dimples Laura had ever seen. Clad in nothing but her late husband's bathrobe, the boy didn't have the common decency to appear the least bit embarrassed by his inappropriate behavior. Exactly. Like. Jack.

Time for the turkey lacer.

Was it too late for Darcy to plead make-out amnesia?

She was expecting her mother to get home soon, but she'd lost track of time. Mom clutched the turkey lacer, the tool she'd use when Darcy and Troy were little and had accidentally locked themselves in the bathroom.

Today, Darcy had locked the door accidentally on purpose.

Mom tilted her head toward Darcy. Her lips trembled into a smile, then relaxed, trembled, then relaxed. Now Nick was staring at Darcy, too. His entire face seemed ever so slightly distorted. He double-knotted the belt on the terry cloth robe.

Daddy's robe.

What the hell was she thinking? She should've shrouded Daddy's robe in shrink-wrap, kept it in cold storage. How could she explain some strange boy wearing her father's bathrobe?

Nick placed a hand on her shoulder. She was supposed to say something, she just couldn't remember what.

Nick took a step toward her mother and offered his hand. "Hi, I'm Nick."

Mom raised the turkey lacer to waist height, paused, and then switched it to her left hand. She shook Nick's hand, accepting nothing. "Mrs. Klein, Darcy's mother," she said, heavy on the *mother*.

"Thanks for the loaner robe. Darcy and I got carried away. It was really all my fault." Nick splayed his right hand over his heart. "Couldn't resist starting a snowball fight. My jeans weighed a ton wet, so Darcy said I could use the dryer. She was helping me figure out the settings. My mom, she kind of spoils me, still does my wash and all."

Nick played Mom just right, nodding until she joined in. Thank goodness he hadn't told her mother the truth. That they'd walked out onto the lake while the temperature hovered above freezing.

Mom tucked a strand of hair behind her ear. "Well, that's what moms do."

Nick flashed Mom one of his best grins, the kind reserved for getting out of detention. "Yeah, she's pretty incredible."

Nick's praise for his mother must've completed his trick. Mom replaced her rocky-road grin with a for-real smile until Nick started for the kitchen. Mom shook her head. "Oh, Nick. Go check the dryer, please. I'm sure your clothes are dry by now, from the snowball fight."

"Yes, ma'am," he said, and ducked back into the bathroom. The way she emphasized *from the snowball fight* . . . Why didn't her mother trust her? Mom took her self-satisfied smile into the living room. The clank of metal against metal meant she was stirring the woodstove.

Cam and Heather were waiting in the kitchen with her cocoa, just what Darcy needed to clear her head. She snatched up a steaming mug and raised it to her face, breathed deeply until she fooled her tongue into tasting chocolate before sipping for real. Heather and Cam munched through a second sleeve of Stoned Wheat Thins.

Nick came out of the bathroom. The pockets of his faded jeans showed off two not quite dry splotches.

Heat pulsed Darcy's face even as she shivered. She swiped at the perspiration beneath her damp hair and glanced over at Nick. He hid behind his steaming mug and winked so quickly she wasn't sure if she'd imagined it.

Was she blushing? She'd need to have a talk with her body about giving herself away. Nick didn't need to know her every reaction, how she wanted to take him by the hand, bring him straight to her room, and let him do what she'd put off for the last three boyfriends. That hadn't stopped the boys from bragging about what they'd done, after they'd dumped her. Like Daddy had always said, never let the truth get in the way of a good story.

Darcy sputtered on her cocoa, dribbling onto the kitchen island. So not cool! She wiped her face with her hand and touched her fingertips to her swollen lips. Nick had kissed her hard, pressing her between the warm thumping dryer and his warm thumping body. He wasn't afraid to let her know his every reaction. *Don't go there!*

Nick's shoulders hunched in a shiver, and he set his mug on the counter. He came over to Darcy, pressed her face between his cocoa-warmed hands. "I think I'd better go home and figure out my grandma's dryer."

Heather put her glass in the sink. "I should go, too."

"Don't leave." Mom had scared off Nick, but Cam and Heather were used to her mother. Besides, Mom was actually nice to them. She probably liked them better than Darcy.

Cam jumped to standing. "I'll walk you home," he told Heather, but gave Darcy a wide-eyed warning. Okay, she got it. He wanted to walk Heather home, even though she and Cam lived on opposite sides of town, and Heather didn't need an escort.

"I could give you both a ride," Nick said before Darcy could stop him.

"Sure!" Heather raced for the door.

Darcy rubbed Cam's shoulder, mouthed *sorry*, before he chased Heather out the door to Nick's car.

"I can't believe you're leaving me alone with the drill sergeant," Darcy told Nick. She put on an exaggerated pout, but the fake expression made her stomach sink.

At the door, Nick glanced over his shoulder to make sure her drill sergeant mother wasn't around. "See you in school, pretty girl." He gave her a quick peck on the lips, and then leaned his forehead to hers. He crossed his eyes till she gave in and laughed.

When Nick's car rumbled from the driveway, she went back to the kitchen and sipped the last of Nick's cocoa. The grainy liquid slid lukewarm down her throat.

Mom came into the kitchen and frowned at the crumbs on the counter. "Where did Cam and Heather go? I thought they'd stay for dinner."

"You scared them off, along with Nick," Darcy said, and chewed the cocoa's chalky dregs.

"Really, Darcy?" Mom stared at her, then sighed. "Since you insist, I will reiterate the rules you've broken. No friends over when I'm not home. No riding with a boy, or anyone, without prior permission. And no locking yourself in a room with a boy."

"We weren't doing anything," Darcy said, which could've been true. They weren't doing more than she'd done with other boys. Except for the part where Nick's hands had wandered under her shirt, and she'd let him—her cheeks tightened with heat.

Mom peered into her face, and Darcy turned her head.

Two sharp knocks sounded from the side door. Mom headed to the mudroom, shaking her head. Mom's voice greeted visitors, and then the overwhelming scent of artificial pine tweaked Darcy's nose. A hint of ginger softened the horrid cologne. A man's voice thrummed the air. Her mother's giggle reached around the corner, a wind-chime's laugh Darcy hadn't heard for at least a year. Her too-serious mother rarely joked. Mom acted more like an old lady than a woman in her mid-thirties, as if thirty-five wasn't ancient enough.

Mom peeked into the kitchen and hooked a finger in her direction, and Darcy swallowed down the last of the chocolate dust.

Two guys stood in front of the door to Daddy's studio. Guy number one Darcy nicknamed Hollywood—a tall paparazzi-worthy piece of eye candy. Guy number two was definitely the wearer of the pine stench. With a blaze of hair and a matching copper beard, Red stood a few inches shorter than Hollywood.

Of course, her clueless mother probably hadn't even noticed the hot Hollywood guy.

Mom used her private-with-other-people-around voice. "Do you remember us talking about renting out the studio?"

"Yeah-ha." Hollywood caught her staring. He raised a hand in greeting and shot her a half smile.

Mom touched Darcy's cheek till she redirected her attention to her mom's eyes. "I found a tenant. Dr. Walsh, the taller man. He's moving in tonight," Mom said, and Darcy followed Mom's gaze back to Hollywood.

Mom nodded. "His friend is here to help him move in. You okay with that?"

"What?" Darcy said, right when she finally understood. Mom had rented out Daddy's studio. Which was weird since Mom had acted as though Daddy still needed the space. She'd even bought him a new futon last week. Darcy understood what her mother was saying, but it still didn't make any sense. "That's great, Mom."

"Really?" Mom said, and she broke into a grin.

"Whatever, I—"

"Let me introduce you," Mom said, using her formal voice to summon the guys. "Darcy, this is our new tenant, Dr. Walsh." Mom turned to Hollywood. "This is my daughter, Darcy."

"Aidan, Aidan's fine." *You're telling me.* Aidan shook her hand, pumping three times and revving up his smile.

"And this is Mr. Smi—"

"Finn," Red said. His pink hand nearly crushed hers.

"Oh!" Mom squealed. "Almost forgot." From her pocket, she took two keys—the silver hardware-store-issue key that unlocked the studio from the outside of their house and the antique gold skeleton key that unlocked the inside door. "For you," Mom said, and she placed the keys side by side in Aidan's upturned palm.

Warm cocoa rose in Darcy's throat and soured her mouth, and she swallowed.

Aidan turned the key. He and Finn slipped into the studio and shut the door behind them.

Daddy's door. She'd practically memorized that door, with its worn finish, the permanent scratches. The lengthwise crack in the frame she used to peer through when she was little and Daddy wouldn't let her in, no matter how hard she'd cried. Now what would she see if she looked through the crack? A red-faced doofus and Aidan, grinning like an idiot.

"Yoo-hoo!" Her mother's dizzy friend, Elle, pushed into the mudroom with Maggie, middle-aged hippie woman, in tow of her tailwind. Oh, great, the goon squad had arrived. Soon Maggie would entice them into joining hands in a misguided attempt to conjure her father's ghost. *Count me out!*

Mom hugged Maggie against her chest, squeezing the patchouli out of her. Maggie plucked a chunky knit cap from her head and shook out her gray curls.

Elle unwound her red scarf. "Saw Aidan's truck," she said, as though she were teasing.

Mom wagged a finger at Elle. "I don't know whether I should kiss you or kill you."

Elle hugged Mom and planted a kiss on her cheek. "It was Maggie's idea."

"I bet it wasn't," Mom said.

Troy flung open the storm door and said exactly what Darcy was thinking, "What's going on?"

Mom rushed to Troy; she always rushed to Troy.

"Two guys just carried Dad's desk out into the yard," Troy said, sounding winded. "Are you giving his stuff to the Salvation Army or something?"

"Sweetheart, no, I rented out the studio."

Troy's voice reverted to his adolescent high-pitched croak. "No way." He glanced over his shoulder out to the driveway. Aidan leaned into the bed of his truck and passed a guitar case to Finn. "Both of them?"

"No, just—" Mom leaned out the door. "Excuse me, Aidan!" She ushered Troy outside, and Darcy followed behind them. Not much cracked little brother's voice. Darcy wasn't going to miss this.

"I'd like you to meet my son, Troy," Mom said. "Troy, Aidan Walsh, our new tenant."

Aidan nodded. "Nice to meet you, Troy." Aidan put down a box and shook Troy's hand.

"Finn, friend of Aidan," Finn said, but Troy's gaze lingered on Aidan.

"So where're you putting the desk?" Troy asked, and Aidan exchanged a glance with her mother.

"I asked Aidan to put it out in the shed," Mom said. "But we could find a place for it in the house, if you'd prefer."

Troy cleared his throat. "The house would work," he said, but his voice didn't return to normal. Troy stared after Aidan as the two men carried Aidan's guitar and moving boxes into the studio.

"I just—I don't get it," Troy said. "You never do stuff without telling me and Darcy first. You don't like to surprise us." Surprises were Daddy's specialty. Mom, they could predict.

Mom pressed her lips together and lowered her voice. She held her arms against the cold. "Troy, I asked you months ago, and you were okay with it."

Troy looked right at Mom. "Well, I'm not okay with it now," he said, and Darcy found herself nodding in agreement with her little brother.

Shivering, she trudged back into the house and sat at Mom's desk. Cold banded her chest. Elle's and Maggie's annoying voices carried from the living room. Footsteps, Drew's and Aidan's, sounded from behind the closed door of Daddy's studio.

She couldn't pretend anymore Daddy was home, safe and sound, writing away. She couldn't trick herself into thinking any second now he'd open the door and wrap his arms around her, so she could bury her nose in his citrus-musk scent. She couldn't—

Darcy dug her nails into her thigh. The flesh gave, and she inhaled sharply.

She vaguely remembered Mom asking her and Troy for permission to rent out Daddy's studio. Something about unused space, and money that Mom insisted wasn't crucial. *Yeah, right.* Darcy might've even said she couldn't care less.

It wasn't fair.

That was before Darcy had realized she cared a lot, before she understood Daddy's studio without Daddy's things killed her father double dead.

Chapter 5

Other than Aidan, what kind of guy would whistle off to work, psyched to head to the emergency room, her mother's least favorite destination?

For the past few weeks, Darcy had tried convincing Mom something was very wrong with a man who couldn't wait to mess around elbow deep in blood and guts, when most men would faint. Last time Darcy ran into Aidan, he'd told her about popping some guy's dislocated shoulder back into place, complete with sound effects, and she'd nearly gagged. Yet Mom wondered why she'd refused to step inside Daddy's studio since Aidan had taken it over.

Come to think of it, she might gag today.

On the other side of the kitchen table, Troy was busy eating a bowl of Honey Nut Cheerios in the most disgusting way humanly possible. Little brother had it down to a science. Scoop milk and cereal, slurp milk from spoon, and then munch the Os. Darcy's bowl of cereal sat untouched. She pushed the bowl away from her and kicked at the overflowing laundry basket by her feet.

Sunday was laundry day, her laundry day. But when she'd come downstairs this morning, the washing machine was already humming with Aidan-the-weirdo's wash. The dryer churned with Aidan's clothes, too, making Darcy think of how she'd made out with Nick against the dryer. Of what she'd let him do in there. Of what she hadn't let him do since.

Not that he hadn't tried. But whenever Nick came over to her house, Mom lurked. Whenever they parked at the lake, Cam and Heather came along. Darcy made sure of it. And she always had a ready excuse why she couldn't hang out at his grandmother's house, where nobody was home. Better to lie than admit she was scared to be alone with him. She'd learned from experience—juniors wouldn't go out with a virgin for long. The washing machine beeped, but no weirdo emerged from Daddy's studio. Troy chewed his cereal, humming through his nose. She glared at Troy, and he waved. Had he stayed up all night figuring out ways to irritate her? En route to the bathroom, Darcy bumped into Troy's chair with her laundry basket. Twice. Troy chewed with his mouth open.

Aidan's dryer load rotated on warm, the done button lit. Darcy pressed clear, opened the door, and scooped the warm wash into Aidan's waiting basket. Jeans, T-shirts, boxers, and light green scrubs with a small questionable stain. Okay, she really was going to hurl.

She needed to get her wash started and shower before Nick came to take her to a movie. The last time they'd gone to a movie, they sat in the back row of Cinemagic. As soon as the room went black, Nick rubbed her neck and pressed his mouth to hers. He drew an ache up from her toes that left her wiping her eyes when the credits rolled, although she hadn't watched a single frame. The best part? Nick had held her hand all the way to the car.

No wash, no shower, no Nick.

Darcy blew past the still-chewing-humming Troy and knocked on Aidan's—Daddy's—studio. No answer. She put her ear to the door, and shower sounds washed through the crack. First Aidan had swiped her laundry time, and now he was hogging all the water!

She stomped to the bathroom, opened the washing machine, and shoveled Aidan's wet clothes on top of his dry duds. Let him figure it out. She lifted the basket and—

"What're you doing?" Mom, dressed and wearing lipstick. On a Sunday morning. In the house.

"You going somewhere?" Darcy asked.

Mom took Aidan's laundry basket from her arms and walked into the kitchen. She squeezed Aidan's jeans on the top of the pile and furrowed her brow. "They're wet."

"It's not my fault. He left them there. What am I supposed to do? Besides, the clothes underneath are dry, so the heat can rise up and—"

Mom's eyes bugged out. "That's worse."

Aidan strolled into the kitchen, shower-fresh and barefoot, as if he lived here. As if he belonged.

Troy had been giving Aidan the hairy eyeball since he'd moved in. Little brother would stop whatever he was doing and stare after Aidan, his face concentrating like when he was puzzling out a school assignment. Maybe Troy's Einstein ways would spook Aidan. Nice one, odd little bro.

Troy chewed faster, then swallowed. He set down his spoon.

Aidan glanced sideways and eyed his laundry. "That looks strangely familiar," he told her mother.

Mom laughed. "And familiarly strange," she said, some dumb as dirt back and forth they'd devised. No surprise Aidan knew Elle. He acted like one of her mother's girlfriends. Well, maybe not *girl*friend. Last week, Darcy had caught him checking out her mother's ass when she wasn't looking. Must be desperate. Yet another reason Mom shouldn't trust him.

"Unfortunately, at least half your wash is still wet." Mom

looked at Darcy and lost her sense of humor. "Darcy, take Aidan's wash and put it back in the dryer, including anything you caused to dampen."

She wasn't about to do Aidan's wash.

"Darcy?"

"Tell Aidan if he wants to do wash on Sunday morning, he shouldn't leave it for hours."

"Darcy Ann, speak directly to—"

Aidan stepped between her and her mother, and Troy took his bowl to the counter to get a better view.

"Watched the clock," Aidan said. "Dryer stopped ten minutes ago. Wash finished five minutes ago."

She wanted him to get all red in the face. She wanted him to stammer. She wanted him to raise his voice till a vein popped out on his forehead. She didn't want him to tell the plain truth. Darcy sucked at her bottom lip. Mom folded her arms, angled her a what-do-you-say-to-that glare.

"Something else bothering you?" Aidan asked.

Darcy wanted to knock the perfectly reasonable look off his face. "I do wash on Sunday," she said, which sounded lame, even to her.

Aidan nodded, offering Darcy an I-know-how-you-feel frown, like she'd shared something deep. " 'Kay. So you'd like me to stay clear of the laundry room on Sunday?"

"Uh-huh."

Aidan flashed her a toothy smile. "Why didn't you say so?"

Mom shifted Aidan's laundry basket off her hip.

How was she going to get out of—?

"Darcy?" Mom said.

"Fine." Darcy ripped the basket from Mom's hands. She hoped her voice dripped with attitude.

Troy tilted his bowl in front of his face, slurped down the

last of his milk, and came up grinning. "What's so funny?" Darcy asked.

"You are."

"Listen, dork, I don't s—"

"Hey, Troy, know a decent bike shop around here?" Aidan said. "Looking to replace my tires."

"Road or mountain?"

"Road."

"You planning on riding on ice?"

"Nah, I'm counting on an early thaw."

Troy set his bowl by the sink. "Souhegan Cycleworks on the Milford Oval."

"You wanna come along to navigate, if your mom doesn't mind?"

"Take him," Mom said, her voice practically chirping.

Why should Mom care whether Troy got along with her newest buddy Aidan? He wasn't related to them. Mom used to play at tearing her hair out of her head whenever Troy and Daddy argued. Darcy had kind of liked it. No matter the issue, she was always on Daddy's side. Right now, she liked being on Troy's side about Aidan.

"What d'you say, Troy?" Aidan asked. "Want to come along?"

Troy gave Aidan one of his long looks. Aidan spoke one of Troy's two languages: geek and jock. Come spring, her brother sprouted wheels for legs and biked to school and back without breaking a sweat. He'd started riding a two-wheeler at age four, Darcy's, not his. After watching her struggle without training wheels, he dragged the kitchen stool outside, hopped on her pink banana seat, and pedaled down the street. Still, Troy wouldn't—

Troy nodded. "Need a few things, if you don't have any plans."

"That is the plan," Aidan said.

"Cool. I'll go get dressed then." Troy breezed out of the room and jogged up the stairs, leaving Darcy dazed, holding Aidan's laundry, and staring at Troy's empty cereal bowl. The geek. The jock.

The traitor.

Chapter 6

Sometime after eleven that night, Laura noted her mind drifting off into sleep, and she spiraled down into a nightmare.

Her bedroom door sprang open. A shot rang out. Blood
splattered the walls. Jack's blood webbed between her fingers.

Laura was awake, upright, in bed, a gasp caught between
her teeth.

She flicked on the overhead light, and the brightness scared
away the nightmare along with the shadows. Her circulatory
system pulsed madly. She held a hand to her chest, waiting for
the drumbeat's retreat.

A nightmare had hijacked her memory, forcing her to re-
live the worst day of her life.

She gathered her hair away from her perspiring neck, fashioned a loose braid, and cool air whispered over her nape,
sending a shiver down her bare arms. She slipped into the
cream-colored satin robe at the foot of her bed and headed for
the relief of the hallway, a place where spectral blood did not
splatter.

In the bathroom, she considered taking either the Valerian
drops Maggie had given her as a sleep aid or the prescription
sleeping pills. She'd tried each of them exactly once, and she'd

hated herself exactly twice for having needed mind-altering medications.

Thanks, but no thanks.

No sound from Darcy's room. Laura pushed the door open with one finger, stepped inside, and listened for the cadence of her daughter's breathing. Well, it sounded as if her daughter were fast asleep, but Darcy had fooled her before.

The *Union Leader* sat on Darcy's bedside table, the newspaper still folded open to the apartments for rent Darcy had shown Laura she'd circled for Aidan. She'd even "borrowed" Aidan's rental agreement and knew they could ask him to leave within thirty days. But Aidan wasn't the culprit, just a convenient scapegoat for her daughter's grief. Darcy scoffed at the idea of visiting her father's grave. Instead, Jack's former studio served as her in-house memorial. The problem was, Jack didn't live there, either. Laura had only recently figured that out herself.

Laura pulled the covers over Darcy's exposed shoulder, wishing she could protect her more thoroughly and rewrite her daughter's childhood to include a father who could do no harm. Heaven forbid either one of her children got sick like Jack. The secondhand effects of mental illness posed enough of a burden. Laura sighed and kneeled down next to the bed, an old habit gone by the wayside. If Darcy were really asleep, then she wouldn't wake from her mother's nearness. Laura gazed at her daughter's relaxed face. "I'd do anything to keep you safe, angel."

At Troy's door, she blew her son a kiss across his darkened room, not wanting to wake her light sleeper, her easy child. She'd do anything to keep her son safe, too. When Troy had climbed into Aidan's truck for their drive to the bike shop, she'd slumped into her desk chair, limp with relief. Troy had worked through his eleventh-hour resistance to renting out the studio quietly, in his own internal way.

Darcy's methods were a lot more external.

Laura padded down the stairs, switched on the kitchen light, and preset the oven to 325 degrees. She didn't know what she was about to bake, rarely knew until she began these middle of the night cooking frenzies. Showing up and answering the call to the kitchen usually set her creative process in motion. She refastened her satin belt and sat with her chin in her hands.

She took out two well-used cookie sheets and lined up all the ingredients for gingersnaps, the spicy cookie recipe she'd long ago committed to memory. If she moved really quickly, reciting the list of ingredients and paying special attention to the task at hand, then she could drive away the nightmare's afterimage. She didn't need the yoga Maggie swore by, the supposed meditation in motion exercises she taught in group to relaxing Indian music. Laura had her own methods for producing equilibrium.

She placed the butter in the microwave and gave it a minute on defrost to bring the hardened sticks to room temperature. Thinking of the blood she'd touched in the nightmare, she washed her hands and dried them on rough paper towels until the pockets between her fingers grew raw. Damn him. How dare Jack haunt her so? Was this the thanks she got for loving one man so completely?

The word *raw* boomed inside her head, conjuring an image of Laura at eighteen. After her mother's death, she'd been open to influence, and Jack Klein had been a taker. He should've waited, should've helped her process her grief. Instead, he'd helped her bury it, along with her childhood. Was it any wonder Laura worried about Darcy's vulnerability to a charmer like Nick?

The microwave ding bristled her all over, a disproportionate startled response. She shook her head, trying to regain composure, although she was her only witness to the overreaction.

She poked the butter to test its give, then added a bit of the dark brown sugar. Drizzling the dark molasses over the golden hills blasted the image of the cramped kitchen from her childhood and the tiny fatherless apartment she and her mother had shared.

Her tiny fatherless life.

She readied the dry ingredients and added more ginger than the original recipe called for.

Sift, sift, sift, sift. She squeezed the metal handle, tried enjoying the snowfall of flour and spice, and the way the beige mounds rested at soft angles, sloping against the rim of the glass bowl.

She hadn't had a family, really. None except for her quiet mother, a woman who kept to herself. Kept herself from her daughter, too. So many times, Laura had asked her about her father, always with the same result. Mama smiled her rueful smile, leaving her to wonder whether the look of regret had as much to do with Laura as her conception. Now she'd never know for sure.

She dumped the dry ingredients into the wet and blended with her favorite wooden spoon, folding dark grainy stripes into the dry sands. Her arm muscles tensed and picked up speed.

Each and everything she'd made for her family had blossomed from that emptiness she'd felt as a child, the feeling as if she were the only one without any family to speak of. She'd always craved open fields and mountain views, even though she'd spent her childhood on city streets, conjuring small-town life from all the books she'd read. For a while there she'd even grown to believe in the power of her imagination to influence her life, although she'd never spoken of magic out loud.

Now she believed only in what she could see. The readers who never knew Jack the person didn't suffer the consequences of his real-life actions, those that diminished rather than elevated their children. Those that—

The *crunch-snap* of wood brought her attention to her spoon broken into two tidy sections, not a splinter in sight, and a very well mixed dough. She rubbed at her spent muscles, tossed the doomed utensil, and spread a plastic-wrap bonnet over the bowl.

Now what? Letting the dough sit for half an hour provided way too much time to think, when that was the last thing she wanted. She cleaned the dough dribbles off the counters, wiped the completely clean kitchen table, and then made her way to the broom closet. No matter how many times a day she swept the kitchen, she'd always discover more dirt.

Swish, swish, swish.

Sometimes, in the middle of the night, the notion that she was an adult woman responsible for two teenage children seemed preposterous. Deep inside of her lay the young girl who had willingly stayed up all night, reading under the covers with a flashlight borrowed from her mother's emergency car kit. Later, she'd set her intentions to paper, deciding exactly what her life would look like ten years down the road, and the precise steps needed to birth the dreams of marriage, children, and a published novel by age thirty. She certainly hadn't signed up for widowhood at age thirty-four or a fatherless life for Darcy and Troy.

Laura stopped sweeping, visualizing another girl hiding beneath a white bedsheet with a silver flashlight in hand. She headed straight for her desk to jot down the sketchy character before the story seed dissolved.

When the ideas thinned, she read what she'd written and chuckled her way down the page. Okay, either she was entirely too smart for herself or just a BS artist. Maybe both. Really, whom was she kidding? Even if she found a story train, what right did she have to follow it? Time was running out on her free lunch. Come fall, she'd need a job. A paying job. Best-case scenario for writing and selling a first novel would get her a check for a few thousand dollars in about four years.

Jack was one of the few writers who'd actually earned a decent living out of his passion. Thank goodness for the long tail of royalties. The ideal of the struggling writer never included a thirtysomething widow with two teenagers in need of financial support they could depend upon.

She rubbed at her eyes and stood to her anklebones crackling a protest at finding themselves up and about so late at night. Then another sound drew her attention outside her weary body. The music of a strumming guitar flowed seamlessly from Aidan's closed apartment door, through her office nook, and penetrated her chest.

One note, then several successive notes rippled the air. She couldn't make out the tune, but she adored it right away. The flowing melody thrummed bittersweet, the strings plucking chords of deep regret and unspeakable sorrow, making her think he was playing her song, like in the old Roberta Flack tune "Killing Me Softly." A joy just below the surface kept popping in, refusing to bow to the song's initial mood.

Laura padded to the apartment's door, and the upbeat secondary melody gained momentum, running away with the song. She'd noticed Aidan's guitar when he'd first moved in but had yet to hear him play. Could she have slept through other concerts? Mistaken his playing for Darcy's or Troy's music?

She pressed her hand against the door, and the vibrations sang through her palm. The music stopped, but her hand still buzzed. She raised a fist to the door, then paused, getting a full-frontal memory flash of the classic movie, *The Good-bye Girl.* The single mom, Marsha Mason, upon hearing sub-leaser

Richard Dreyfuss playing the guitar in the middle of the night, walked into his room and found him naked as a jaybird, obscuring his nudity with a well-placed guitar.

Apparently, her late-night mind was dipping into music and movies from as far back as preschool and elementary, and broadcasting from her '70s archives. Smiling, Laura tapped on the door with the knuckles of her middle finger.

Nothing. Oh, great. The poor guy probably thought squirrels were scampering through the walls. She knocked harder. "It's Laura."

Panic now, as she realized her foible. Aidan, her tenant, her new friend, deserved privacy, not a midnight visit.

"Laura! Door's unlocked. Come on in." His response sounded as if he were expecting her.

She pushed open the door, trying to look less like a grinning idiot.

There he sat.

The light from the mudroom followed her through the doorway and laid a carpet of illumination across the weathered pine boards, then climbed up a dark leather recliner and onto Aidan himself. In the minimal light, she made out his bare feet, the folds of his jeans, and the curve of the guitar he clutched in front of his shirtless chest. Not naked as a jaybird, thank God, but close enough to give her pause.

You like him.

The words played in her head and sounded a lot like Elle. Laura was no good at this, years out of practice, so she couldn't say for sure whether his response to her visit indicated interest.

For Laura, his nearness awakened every secret place.

"Was I too loud? Did the music wake you?" Aidan said, and the gentle rhythm of his rich voice tweaked the pulse at the base of her throat. He got up and turned on the overhead light, making Laura wish for the anonymity of darkness. She straightened beneath the thin satin layers of a nightgown and robe, not exactly appropriate garb for their professional living arrangement.

Her bed-sock feet relaxed against the smooth wood floor, responding to a palpable softness in the air. Yet, the distance between her and Aidan contained an energy that shifted her balance forward. A corresponding internal tug spun her thoughts. "Goodness, no. I was cooking. In the kitchen."

He raised his eyebrows into identical arcs.

"I was getting some dough ready. For gingersnaps. I haven't really baked anything."

He nodded, as if her nonsensical speech made all the sense in the world.

"You have to let the dough kind of meld together. So I was writing." She didn't wait for his reaction; she just barreled forward. "Not really writing. Sketching out the framework for a character that came to mind while I was baking, but not really baking. You have to let character sketches meld, too."

"Sure." He took a step in her direction.

"Loved the music. I don't think I've heard it before though. I was wondering if you could tell me what it's called."

"Nope."

"Not even a clue?" She tried looking him in the eye, even though his bare chest was vying for her attention. Just a sprinkle of dark hair at the center. And that waist—she gazed over his shoulder.

"I've never heard it before, either. Never played it before tonight."

"You write music?"

"Occasionally. When I can't sleep."

Her new friend, Doctor Aidan Walsh, wrote music and strummed the guitar like a virtuoso.

Well, she couldn't look *past* him when he was standing so close. "The music was beautiful." He was beautiful. "You should write it down." She should stop offering unbidden advice. "I could let you know when the cookies are done, if you like." She turned to leave.

"Um, Laura." He waited for her to turn toward him. This time she held his gaze, and he grinned. "Do you . . . would you like some company?"

"Sure." She exhaled her response, and it came out all breathy, as if she were trying to sound sexy. Either sexy or asthmatic.

"I'll just be a minute." He scrabbled up the loft ladder, and she stared at the ascent of his fantastic firm-looking bottom. He peered over the railing and nodded toward his bicycle on the indoor training stand, the source of the early morning whirring sounds. "Great shop Troy brought me to. Way better than driving into Manchester."

Who? Laura touched her face, reconnecting with the anchor of reality and translating the boy's name: Troy, her son, the other bike enthusiast. "Glad it worked out," she said. Now they'd have to work on Darcy.

Aidan nodded and climbed down the loft ladder, shrugged into a white T-shirt. The apartment's radiator clanged into gear, even though the temperature was kept a steady ten degrees warmer than the rest of the drafty house. Laura chanced a last peek at his chiseled abs, imagined touching his heated skin.

Just make the cookies, Laura.

In the kitchen, she threw on the overhead light, not wanting the room to reflect any of the inappropriate notions flowing not so much through her mind but through her body.

A buzzing sound, and Aidan slipped his cell from his back pocket. On call at Memorial? He checked who was phoning, shook his head, and pocketed the cell.

Aidan opened and closed his hands at his sides. "How can I help?"

She uncovered the hill of melded dough she'd pulled from the fridge and tilted her chin toward the right-hand cabinet. "You can take out the parchment paper for me."

"Will do." Without her asking, he tore off two strips of the brown paper and laid them on the waiting cookie sheets.

His mother must've taught him well.

"When I was a kid, my mother and four sisters used to bake every Sunday. Parchment was the extent of my job. That and eating. I excelled at the eating," he said, as if reading her mind.

Laura paused with her hands in the silverware drawer, rewinding to the last words she'd said out loud. *Take out the parchment paper* didn't segue naturally to Aidan's comment about his mother. "And your dad? Does your dad cook?" Jack had left anything remotely kitchen-related to her. He'd scurry through to pinch a taste of whatever she was cooking, and then throw his hands up and back out of the room.

"Yes." He gave the parchment an extra press into the baking sheet. "My dad *cooked*. He passed away . . . let's see, I was fifteen. So, wow, thirteen years ago." He smiled. "Doesn't seem like that long ago."

"I'm sorry about your dad." Even an old loss deserved condolence. Laura added this new information to the Aidan file. Becoming the man of the house at fifteen explained even more than his unexpected foray into emergency medicine at thirteen. No wonder her son was warming to Aidan.

Laura left the teaspoons on the counter and reached past Aidan into the cabinet. Then, hands clasped around pastry bags, she tensed with the full-body-tingle feeling of being watched, of Aidan's warm gaze sliding from her braid to her waist and lingering on her backside before gliding back up her spine. She turned back around and couldn't mistake his half grin, the facial expression equivalent of a shrug.

Or she could be losing her mind.

Aidan held up a spoon and a pastry bag. "What do I do with these?"

"Spoon dough into the opening?" she said.

"Like this?" Aidan scooped dough and played at trying to force the dough through the smaller opening.

She shook her head, laughed, and shoveled dough into her bag's wide mouth opening. "No, like this."

Aidan winked and followed her lead. "After my dad died, my sisters and I didn't sleep much. We'd stay up talking, get hungry, and they'd end up baking all night. Big brother," Aidan said, pointing to himself, "got to oversee the operation. We never had all the right ingredients, so they'd improvise. The worst results were the most fun, at least for me. I'd make my sisters play 'I dare you to eat it.' "

"Oh, you're bad." She smiled at how thinking about teasing his sisters splashed a mischievous grin across his face. "Your family sounds great. I mean, really close."

"Yeah, too close sometimes." He stood beside her, pastry bag at the ready, and watched her squeeze dough along the tray into satisfyingly well-ordered rosebuds.

She kept her gaze on the cookies, her piping, but her awareness focused on his inches-away nearness and the way his movements paced hers. Her awareness deepened her breath. Her robe gaped open and, for a second, Laura let herself imagine the warmth of Aidan's steady hands on her chest before covering herself. "I didn't have any siblings, never knew my dad, and my mother died when I was eighteen."

Aidan stopped piping and angled toward her. "Laura . . ." he said, his voice soft with concern.

She waved her pastry bag at him. "Not a big deal! I'm just giving you my bio to be fair. You know, since you had to fill out an application."

He nodded, but she couldn't figure out his underlying reaction. So what if her childhood wasn't ideal? Whose was? You worked with whatever family you were given. Sometimes family taught you a lesson in reverse: how *not* to behave. She sighed, thinking of how her friendless mother had died alone, felled by a massive heart attack two weeks short of her fortieth birthday.

Aidan headed to the oven with his cookie sheet.

"Where do you think you're going?"

"Heard ovens work swell for baking."

"Just a minute." She filled a small peach bowl with warm water, tested the temperature with her finger, and then crooked a finger at Aidan.

He jogged back across the room in response to her correction and set his tray back at the starting position, then stood at attention, awaiting further instruction.

"Wet your finger in the water."

He stared helplessly at his dangling hands. "Which one?"

"For goodness sake." She snatched up his right hand, dunked it into the bowl of water, then brought his index finger to a mound of cookie dough and pressed the first circle flat. "Now continue."

She looked up from the tray and made contact with Aidan's dark eyes. She couldn't mistake the way he was looking at her, piercing the surface of her being and trying to go deeper. Waiting to gauge her response.

How long since a man had made love to her? How long since she'd even been touched? Is that what had happened to her mother? Heart failed from lack of use?

Heat didn't contain itself in Laura's cheeks. Sleep deprivation, nightmares, and overwhelming worry couldn't account for the sheer magnitude of what she was feeling, despite its wrongness. After all, she was the elder, the responsible party. Her heart pounded an alarm in her ears, and she made herself look away.

He dipped his fingers into the bowl of warm water. "So, yeah, what were you saying?" He didn't wait for a response before fingerprinting the rows of gingersnap dough.

Pressing her fingers along her identical rows of dough made her wish instead for the tactile experience of touching his skin. She sighed, threw open the oven door, and forgot to wait a beat before stepping into the fire breath. She slid their baking sheets onto the metal rack, shut the oven door, and set the timer.

Aidan leaned against the counter, scraping the curved glass bowl with a spoon, and then popped a sizable glob into his mouth.

Horror should've struck. He was eating raw eggs and risking salmonella poisoning. Instead, an irrational thought slammed her: she wanted some, too.

"Any left for me?" Her logic center was shutting down, the way a teenage girl's mind responded to a cute boy. Likely, the way Darcy reacted to Nick. Laura could only hope she'd sufficiently brainwashed her daughter about the dangers of premarital sex. At the moment, Laura couldn't recall any of her own warnings. The image of Aidan pressing his mouth to hers, her fingers in his hair, his beautiful body—

She nabbed a tablespoon from the drawer, scraped up a glob of her own, and leaned against the counter, mimicking Aidan's stance. She gazed into the center of the kitchen and sucked batter from the spoon till nothing remained but the cold taste of metal.

"Your mom," Laura said. "Did she ever remarry?"

"Nope."

"Thirteen years is a long time."

"She says no one can compare to Dad. They were childhood sweethearts, married at eighteen. Mom still wears her wedding band." Aidan set his spoon and the bowl in the sink, then ran the hot water.

Laura had always thought of Jack as the love of her life. And after nearly a year without him, the loneliness hadn't subsided. If anything, it had gotten worse. On the day Jack had died, her body had turned as cold as Jack's side of the bed. But tonight she was craving another man's touch. What kind of person did that make her? "Your parents sound very romantic."

Aidan shut off the water and turned toward her. "My father was a great guy. But I tell my mother all the time he'd want her to find someone else." His direct gaze slid a heartbeat of warmth between her legs, and her mouth fell open.

The oven timer beeped, like a parent flickering a porch light. "Cookies," she said ridiculously as she tried shaking the cobwebs from her pheromone-saturated brain cells.

She took out two trays of perfectly browned gingersnaps, his and hers, and inhaled their sweet heated spice. The notion of reality split down the center. Earlier this same night a nightmare had spilled from dreamland to a wide-awake horror show. Now she stood in her midnight kitchen, sure she was wide-awake, but playing at the kind of fantasy she'd refer back to all the next day.

The phone squealed a jarring trill behind their heads, and they both jostled. She frowned at the phone, knowing only Elle would call her at this late hour, and only she would answer her friend's call. Oh, what the heck. She nabbed the receiver off the wall, if only to prevent a second irritating ring. "Hi, Elle." Silence at the other end of the phone met her greeting. "Hello?"

Laura was about to put down the receiver, but the sound of a throat clearing followed by a rather congested exhalation stopped her. "May I speak with Aidan, please?" A woman, and she wanted to talk to Aidan, the man with the disorienting gaze. Aidan had given Laura's phone number to Memorial, for emergency purposes only. She doubted the call was work-related.

"Whom should I say is calling?" Maybe Laura was acting nosey, but hey, it was still her house.

The woman hesitated. "Kitty."

A middle of the night call from a snuffling ex.

"I'm so sorry to disturb you, but I'd really appreciate—"

"He's right here." She thrust the receiver at Aidan. "It's Kitty."

He stared at the phone, and his entire body tightened, starting with his eyes and washing down until his toes must've curled. He nodded and took the receiver, covering the mouthpiece with his palm. "I'm sorry," he whispered, but she'd already turned off the oven and was hightailing it out of her suddenly crowded kitchen.

Two was company, and three irked her beyond reason.

Upstairs presented a quandary. Even though Aidan had looked anything but pleased with his midnight caller, he'd taken the call anyway. Kitty still held a couple of his reins, however flimsy.

When Laura turned off all the lights, sensory deprivation washed blood down the walls. She jumped out of bed, yanked the pretty little hydrangea nightlight from the hallway, and jammed it into the bedside outlet.

Then she plumped an extra pillow behind her back and reclined halfway under the covers, waiting for a few precious hours of sleep to claim her from the predawn clash between darkness and light.

Chapter 7

Going out with the same boy for six weeks in high school practically set a record. Mom should've been cooking an anniversary dinner for Darcy and Nick. Instead, Mom had invited all their best friends over for the anniversary-eve commemoration of Daddy's Death Day. Nick, Cam, and Heather for Darcy. Maggie and Elle for Mom. And Michael, Troy's best friend since nursery school. Right this minute, Mom was fussing over shish kebabs, making sure she cooked the meat the way her father had liked it, bright pink at the center. She thought it was a little sick since he wasn't the one eating them.

Troy and Michael weren't home yet from the middle school track practice, and Cam had dragged Heather outside on the pretense of a predinner walk. Despite the fact Heather was so not interested, Darcy had to admire Cam's perseverance. But Mom's girlfriends' annoying voices resounded from the kitchen, so Darcy couldn't even pretend she was alone with Nick in the living room.

Nick sat alongside Darcy in the one marginally comfortable dent of the rickety old couch, playing with her hair. They fit perfectly, snuggling under the cranberry throw, for privacy, not warmth. This week, the weather had flipped from winter to spring. The red line on the living room window thermometer hovered above seventy, a veritable heat wave.

"Hey, kids!" Elle peered around the corner, a surprise attack. And the reason Darcy had made sure to make herself and Nick scarce whenever Mom's friends came around. Her mother was enough of a fright. "Darce, your mom would like you to come set the table. 'Kay?"

"I'll help, too." Nick dropped his hand from the nape of her neck, and the throw fell from her shoulders. He walked ahead of them, showing off the back of his jeans.

Elle waited until Nick left the room, then turned to Darcy, all girly and conspiratorial. "So cute!" she whispered loudly, as only she could. Yeah, he was adorable, but not deaf.

Elle put an arm around her, guiding her into the kitchen. "Your mom tells me you guys are an item."

"One of the distinct parts of a whole?" Darcy shot off the dictionary meaning, getting the designated reaction. Elle removed the unwanted arm and gave Darcy the appropriate five feet of personal space. Who cared if Elle widened her eyes at her mother? But Mom didn't need to smile and sigh in agreement. Mom pointed at the silverware drawer. "Do you have any idea where Troy is? I'm starting to worry."

"No clue."

Nick took the utensils from her hands, playing the helpful boyfriend.

"Dining room tonight." Mom gestured toward the narrow galley that somehow fit a farmer's table with seating for ten. "Did Troy mention anything to you about a track meet? I mean, I think he'd call, but you never know."

"I said, I don't know." Oh, this was novel, her mother worrying about the good child for a change. "Wait."

Her mother paused, clutching a fistful of napkins.

"I know for sure he doesn't have a meet today, just practice. And he already told the coach he'd skip the meet this weekend, due to Dad's De—the anniversary." Mom might think she preferred honesty, but Darcy knew better than to share the term Dad's Death Day with her.

"Okay, thanks, baby." Mom caressed her cheek, and Darcy cringed. Mom didn't seem to know where her body left off and Darcy's began. *My body, your body. See the difference?*

Nick required similar tutoring. Darcy leaned against the dining room table, sensing Nick's heat before he came up behind her. He reached around her body to arrange the place setting just so. Not bad at all. He even knew to put the smallest fork on the outside of the arrangement, awaiting the salad.

She inhaled, intending to get a hit of Nick, but coughed on the unmistakable scent of patchouli-redolent Maggie instead. Didn't she need to save a rain forest or something? Maggie stood in the doorway, stock-still, reviewing Nick around his edges. Her flowered skirt shifted slightly, swaying from the melody of Woodstock coming through the speakers in her 1960s brain. *Get back to the garden, sister.*

Maggie nodded her whole body, completing her visual assessment of his energy field. "A bit heavy on the root chakra, mostly red and orange."

Maggie sashayed her flowered bottom past them and into the kitchen.

Nick stared toward the spot Maggie had vacated. "What was that?"

She couldn't blame Nick for cracking up. Not everyone had heard the Buddhist lessons of her mother's New Age friend. Darcy liked the idea of energy vortexes circulating the life force of the universe through her body, although she'd never admit it to her logic-loving mother. "Chakra one, seat of sexuality, survival. Chakra two, how you express your feelings."

"Meaning?"

She leaned over and cupped a hand around his ear. "You're horny."

"That's because you don't stroke me," he whispered.

Heat flashed through her body, a surge of wanting to cry. How long before Nick figured out she was too much of a baby to give him what he wanted? How long before he tired of snuggling and kissing? How long before he broke up with her?

Nick twittered his fingers at the hem of her T-shirt. She grabbed his hand and gave him a kiss on the cheek.

Mom, Elle, and Maggie fell silent when she entered the kitchen, as if she'd tripped their off buttons.

Darcy glanced over her shoulder, and Nick bit at his fisted knuckles. "I have eyes at the back of my head," Mom said without parting her lips, even though Darcy hadn't done anything wrong.

Darcy dragged out the beat-up cow-stenciled stool and stepped onto the lowest wrung, feeling three sets of eyes burning her back. Her mother, Elle, and Maggie never failed to bug her when they worked in unison. Three against one wasn't playing fair.

Darcy took down a stack of mismatched sherbet-colored plates, her mother's idea of pastel mood therapy.

Mom untied her patchwork apron and hung it on its hook. "We're going to have to start soon. I don't want the meat overcooked." She opened the door to the back deck. The aroma of grilling meat wafted inside, and Darcy's stomach rumbled.

The mudroom door flung open, and Troy burst through, as if the smell had called him to dinner. He raced past them through the kitchen, stomped up the stairway, and continued the stampede across the second floor.

Michael slipped into the mudroom. Since the fall, Darcy had to remind herself Troy's turned-cute-over-the-summer friend was a few months younger than Troy, and not a few years older. Michael shook his dark hair from his eyes. "Hey, Darcy. Can I talk to you for a minute?"

Nick leaned against the doorframe.

Michael glanced at Nick. "Alone?"

"I don't think so, buddy." Nick folded his arms, his muscles primed, reminding her of Daddy's reaction when another dad had flirted with Mom at last year's high school open house. Daddy had smiled at the man, if only to show his teeth, and his eyes had said, *Back off or I'll kill you.*

Nick's eyes spoke the same language. Darcy imagined the raw smell of blood, a disaster only she could prevent. Her fingers jittered.

"It's about Troy," Michael said.

"Nick can stay. I don't mind," she told Michael, but she was really reassuring Nick. Darcy placed her hand between Nick's shoulders and rubbed his back. Nick stretched an arm around her shoulder. He tugged her to his side, and his fingers pressed against the muscle of her arm.

On the way home from that open house, Mom had teased Daddy that he'd acted like an overgrown boy. Nothing extreme. But she'd kept her hand on Daddy's leg till they'd pulled into their driveway. Then they'd gone straight up to bed.

Michael slid his gaze to the shaking ceiling. "Troy's kind of hyper or something."

"He's always had tons of energy." *Hyper* was not a word anyone in her house used lightly, too close to *manic*. Michael knew better.

"After practice, he kept running, like he didn't want to stop. No, like he couldn't stop. Then he sped off ahead of me on his bike. Didn't even stop at a red light."

Troy usually stopped on yellow.

"He didn't want to be late for dinner?" she said, and instantly regretted the way her statement curled at the end.

"Yeah, right," Michael said, and his deadpan expression reminded Darcy he was just a stupid kid.

Why was Michael getting all worked up? Why was he trying to get *her* all crazed? Nobody told her what to think, but the thought of her little brother—

"Screw you, Michael! I'll go see for myself." Darcy untangled herself from Nick, bolted through the kitchen, and raced up the stairs. So what if Troy ran a few extra times around the track? Extra energy didn't necessarily mean anything bad. Not always.

She paused at Troy's closed bedroom door, remembering one of the many times her father had rapid cycled between depression and mania. Daddy had been sitting in the kitchen, forehead resting on his arms, still as a stone. Darcy had tried to tiptoe around him. And then, *boom*! Next thing she knew he'd jumped up, sprinted for the door, and started running in circles, while she, her mother, and Troy had sat out on the deck. They'd tired from hours of watching him before he'd even slowed. "Troy? Dinner's up. Let's go."

Darcy creaked the door open, expecting to see her brother jogging around the room.

Troy hunched over his desk beneath the watchful eye of his favorite poster, Albert Einstein sticking out his tongue. He scribbled in a wire-bound notebook. The pen scratched in agreement with his twitching legs, his rocking body.

She'd never seen her brother look so much like Daddy before. "Hey, what's going on?" she said, trying for a light tone. Instead, her voice came out in a whisper.

He mumbled to the notebook, waving her away with his free hand.

Earth-smelling air flowed through six wide-open windows. The slight breeze circulating throughout the room should've cooled her down and stopped her from itching with perspiration. Troy continued his nonstop writing. She'd learned about hypergraphia years ago after Daddy started wearing wrist guards to save him from worsening tendonitis. His writing compulsion would evolve from pounding the computer keys to filling notebooks with a frenzy of swirls and loops.

"Just gotta finish this." Troy jumped up with the notebook, and Darcy startled. He read to himself in front of Darcy's favorite Einstein poster, the one declaring that imagination was more important than knowledge. The sentiment was lost on her brother.

"Oh, this is so great!" Troy snapped the notebook shut, unleashing a flood of words. "D'you remember when we were like six and eight, and we went camping at Hermit Island in the boys' and girls' tents, and Dad was, like, so clueless, and you and Mom slept through that storm, and me and Dad ended up in a freakin' puddle, and me and Dad slept in our old van, and he gave me all the blankets, and he didn't even sleep?"

"Kinda." He'd lost her at *tents*.

"The scarlet moon howls, and the sun flames, a color burst descent brightening the skies. Children's book illustrations are so emotionally evocative, so in sync with the—"

"Troy." She spoke his name clearly, like Mom often did when Dad grew unreachable.

He ran his fingers through his hair. "Dad was the only other person in the whole world who liked tapioca pudding, and now it's too late to thank him for that and for that vase I broke and all those cool rubber bands and—"

That's it; she'd better get her mother. Mom would know what to do with Troy. Tents, a moon, a flaming sun. She never could handle her dad when he talked at her instead of to her.

"Darcy, Troy! Dinner's ready!" Mom yelled up the stairs in her singsong sticky-sweet voice.

"Do me a favor. This might sound weird. Could you bring me up a dinner?"

"Troy."

"Maybe I should go to the library. What time does it close

on Friday?" He shook his head. "Doesn't matter, I can get Dad's info online."

"We have to go down to dinner." If she told her mother Troy was acting all hyped out, the entire crowd downstairs would get involved, convinced Daddy's genes had finally kicked in. Maybe her brother was just a little jazzed due to the anniversary, showing off the far reaches of normal? Mental illness wasn't an exact science. What if she were wrong?

Worse. What if she were right? She had to tell Mom.

"I can't go downstairs, not now. Say I'm sick."

Nobody got out of one of her mother's family dinners unless they were at death's door. "Mom would be out of her mind. I mean, you know, upset. You have to come downstairs for dinner."

As if on cue, her mother called up the stairs a second time. If they didn't go down, she'd come and get them. The woman took stairs two at a time if she sensed noncompliance.

Was her little brother scared, too, worried about their shared family history?

"We'll do it together." She took his hand and gave it a squeeze, hoping he didn't notice the tremors running through her hand. The image of her mother calming her father superimposed over their entwined fingers. So her brother experienced a little mania, so what? Once didn't necessarily mean anything, right?

Chapter 8

Darcy and Troy took an abnormally long time navigating the journey from the second floor. Laura could've sworn her often-battling children walked into the jam-packed dining room holding hands.

Magical thinking had played tricks on her before. After one of Jack's manic episodes, she'd gone out into the backyard fields. She'd taken a heart-shaped worry stone from her pocket and set it next to a freshly picked white dandelion. Illogical behavior, but she couldn't help herself. She'd prayed to her artifacts, icons to suggest her love for her husband should release to the wind and heal his mood disorder.

Most likely, her children hadn't been holding hands at all, merely digging their fingernails into the soft flesh of each other's hands and attempting to draw blood.

Darcy and Troy hovered behind the dining room table, and Heather's voice cut through the din of conversation. "Switch places!" she said, setting off the kids' fun-loving tradition. Chairs scraped against wood. Laura leaned one knee on her seat at the head of the table and counted nine guests. She wouldn't need to move Jack's chair from its place at the sideboard.

Cam and Heather had popped up in the dining room minutes ago, part of the furniture. Maggie and Elle lit a row of tea lights on the sideboard, physically depicting their perpetual emotional support. Michael settled for the seat between Cam and Heather, and Darcy angled in between Troy and Nick, but she didn't sit down.

"Mom, I need to talk to you," Darcy said.

Later, Laura mouthed.

Darcy stamped her foot. "Now."

Laura looked to the ceiling and decided to ignore the mini-tantrum. She didn't need another Darcy melodrama, not when Jack memories, the good memories, had been simultaneously buoying her and priming her for tears all day. Jack building intricate sand castles for the kids on summer vacations. Writing poems for her birthdays. Wrapping an elastic band around the kitchen sprayer each and every April Fools'.

Last week, wrapping the kitchen sprayer herself hadn't worked. No matter how hard she'd tried, she couldn't manage to fool herself.

Laura tapped her fork prongs against her beveled water glass. She waited till the room quieted. She waited till Darcy sat, elbows on the table, glare aimed at Laura. "No kissing. I just want to say a few words, if I might." The whispered remains of conversations lulled to a finish.

She took a deep breath, and her mind quieted. Even Nick appeared reverent, keeping his randy hands off her daughter and awaiting further instruction. "I'd like to thank all of you for coming to dinner tonight."

She reined in her memories from the past year like a movie reel set on accelerated rewind, and then unrolled them on fast forward. The easiest days ended with reading herself to sleep and collapsing into forgetfulness, way better than making mental lists until sunrise roused her from a companionless bed. "I couldn't have made it through this year without the support of my dear friends, and I know that my kids couldn't have done it without their friends, either."

Elle blew kisses her way, mouthed, *We love you*, and then dabbed the corners of her eyes with a napkin. Maggie held her palms together, thumbs against her chest, and bowed her head slightly in Laura's direction.

"I know Jack would be so proud of all of us, so—"

Steps approached the dining room. Aidan stood outside looking in, lips slightly upturned, gaze open. "Sorry to interrupt. Plumbing's all set," he said. "Didn't want you to worry." Aidan's gaze narrowed on Laura like a spotlight, and the heat of connection dusted her cheeks.

A few hours ago, he'd returned home from work to find the feed line under his vanity had blown. The sight of water flooding his bathroom had nearly done her in, until he'd revealed plumbing as one of his many and myriad skills. She'd told Aidan about Jack's anniversary but hadn't wanted to embarrass him with an invite to commemorate a man he hadn't known. Which now seemed silly. Aidan was her friend, a thoughtful friend.

"Join us for dinner," she said, a bit too loudly.

"I wouldn't want to impose," Aidan said, and the formal sound to his voice betrayed the discomfort she'd feared.

Laura nodded at the sideboard. "Pull up a chair."

"I really—"

Elle jumped from her seat and carried the chair to the table's head herself.

She wagged a finger at Aidan. "House rule number one, you don't say no to a dinner invitation from Laura."

Aidan nodded. "Don't say no to Laura. Got it, chief." He saluted Elle, and she poked him in the ribs, a bit too flirty for Laura's liking. Elle was well over forty, way too old for a man in his twenties.

"Darcy, please get Aidan a place setting," Laura said.

"Talk with you in the kitchen?" Darcy said, and the pleading tone in her voice snagged Laura's attention.

Laura shouldn't bow to her daughter's impatience. "I'd be glad to speak with you after dinner."

"But Mom—"

"Thank you, Darcy."

Darcy scowled, pushed away from the table, and plowed past Aidan.

Seconds later, Darcy edged through the door. She dropped a place setting in front of Aidan and slid back into her chair. "Mom—"

The table shook, Troy's knee twitching against a support leg.

"Ow!" Troy yelped, and the table settled.

"Is there something you'd like to say, Troy?" Darcy must've nabbed him with a kick or a pinch, her special modes of brother torture. Why would he even risk sitting next to her?

Troy's gaze skittered back and forth across the guests. "Good food, good meat, good God, let's eat!"

"Guess we're eating, folks." Laura slid half of a skewer onto her plate—cubes of aromatic meat, bright red cherry tomatoes, crisp green peppers, and her favorite, cream-colored mushrooms caps. Mushrooms always appeared so optimistic, springing out of the musty gray earth when all else failed to thrive. Maybe Jack should've behaved more like a mushroom. That made no sense at all. She cracked up, leaning over her side salad.

Elle came up behind her and poured merlot to the brim of her wine goblet. "Drink. Red wine's good for your blood cells."

Laura was being conned, but so what? She slouched and edged her mouth over the lip of the glass, sipped until she could safely raise the glass by the stem without fear of spilling onto her ironed white tablecloth.

Troy and Darcy looked to her for direction, a road map for the one-year anniversary of their father's death. She could not, would not, follow the trail of grief and lose her composure now. Dwelling on the negative would hurt the whole family. At the other end of the table, Aidan slid a bite of meat between his lips. He smiled as he chewed, deepening his dimple. Aidan the healer. Aidan the proud big brother. Aidan the exuberant. Maybe Jack should've behaved more like Aidan. Okay, that notion was even more preposterous than Jack as a mushroom. If Jack hadn't died, she never would've met Aidan Walsh.

Of course, she'd give anything to have her husband back, alive and well and trying her patience. But why could something so good—her friendship with Aidan—only come from her greatest loss?

Aidan looked up from his food and raised his wineglass. *Delicious*, he mouthed.

Laura lifted her glass. She held his gaze, and the energy of his smile rooted her to her seat. The morning after their cookie baking, she'd decided her midnight crush had been one-sided, a punch-tired delusion. Now she wasn't so sure. Warmth hugged her torso moments before the alcohol's secondary heat flowed through her.

Maggie came around the table and massaged Laura's perpetually tight shoulders. "The wine's fine, but try and eat more. You need your strength."

Laura reached back and took hold of Maggie's warm hand. "Thanks, sis." Soul sister, blood sister. It was all the same to her.

Nick showed off his version of multitasking, navigating food into his mouth using his right hand and rubbing her daughter's leg under the table with his left. Darcy's face twitched with the effort not to show any expression.

Jack had liked to paw Laura under the table when they went out to dinner, making a sport of seeing how long it took until Laura's cheeks fired. But that was different—married people playing married games. *Hands above board, buster!* One sideways look from Laura, and Nick's left hand magically materialized in plain sight.

Troy hung over his plate. He prodded his meal, separating each food and leaving white space between mounds of meat, rice, tomatoes, and peppers. Laura thought he'd matured beyond that stage, but then, even her overachiever son could regress now and again. Troy yanked a pen from his back pocket, smoothed his napkin, and scribbled on the makeshift paper.

"I really need to talk with you about *Einstein's* latest project." Darcy spoke more loudly than usual, emphasizing her facetious nickname for her brother.

Laura shook her head. She'd have to speak with Darcy about her jealousy problem but not during dinner.

Troy glowed, as if on fire with a new idea. He swiped Darcy's napkin from her lap, glanced up, and then hunched to write.

"Troy, honey, why don't you eat while it's hot?" Laura said.

Darcy bowed her head down to Troy, looking as if she might bop him again. The threat must've been a good one, causing him to drop his pen and stab at his food. Stab, chew, stab, chew. He gobbled relentlessly, stuffing his cheeks full, then shoveling more food into his mouth before swallowing down the previous glob.

"Troy," Laura said. "Slow down."

Troy washed his food down with water. *Glug, glug, glug.* He wiped his mouth with his hand, then rubbed at his upper lip, as if he'd never before noticed the skim of dark fuzz. His hand floated down from his face. "Who's gonna teach me how to shave?"

Troy kneeled on his seat and engaged the project-to-the-last-row voice Jack used at signings. "I can't even remember how Dad made all those cool shaving cream piles around the sink," he said, and the room fell silent.

"Those ridges that looked like cloud castles. And the bathroom would get all steamed up after his shower, and we'd close the door to keep it all hot and soap smelling, and when he left, all the cold air came rushing in. Why'd it get so cold like that? Huh? Why'd it have to get so cold?"

Troy hadn't watched Jack shave for at least five years, the time when he'd begun to pull away from his father. Laura shivered and dropped her fork. Her son was not himself. "You can watch Mr. Mathers," she said, and her voice warbled.

"That's the dumbest thing I've ever heard!" Troy stood up, knocking over his water and toppling Elle's wine. Merlot splashed across the tablecloth.

Laura approached Troy, and he backed into the sideboard. Tea lights flickered. Shadows tarnished the wall.

"What? Am I supposed to sleep over Cam's so I can watch his father shave?" Troy's gaze jounced to the right, and then settled on Cam. "I know! I'll borrow his dad and go hunting with him, too. Mr. Mathers can teach me how to shave and shoot!"

Cam pushed back in his seat.

"Troy Edward Klein, apologize to Cam right this very minute!" Laura said.

"Jacob Abraham Klein!" Troy said.

Her late husband's full name stole Laura's voice, as if Troy had resurrected Jack's ghost. Laura pressed a fist to her mouth.

Troy's mouth crumpled. His shoulders quaked. A shriek of laughter squawked from his lips. He folded into himself, and his laughter turned soundless.

Laura counted to ten before his silence turned into wheezing. If she were dealing with what she termed Jacked-up behavior, Troy would wear himself out.

Was she?

Laura shook her head, then swallowed. Swallowed again. Not her baby. "Troy—"

"I think Troy needs to work on his project," Darcy said. "Can he please be excused?"

"What? Darcy, no . . ."

Troy's spasms of laughter slowed. Carrying on in front of friends wasn't at all like her mature son. Adrenaline surged through her chest, thrummed her spine. The primal call to fight or flee, no doubt, activated from years of tuning in to her husband's illness, and certainly not due to the current situation.

"That's enough, Troy." Using the same firm tone as when he was a toddler set off a conditioned response. Even teenagers craved consistency.

Troy sucked at the air, quelling residual chuckles. He coughed and forced a straight face.

Laura caught his gaze, and a fresh batch of tremors bunched his shoulder. He stared at the floor and fisted his hands. Tears washed down his cheeks.

Laura closed the space between them. She wrapped Troy in her embrace, tucking his head under her chin.

"No!" Troy yelled in Laura's ear. He shoved her away from him.

Laura gripped the edge of the sideboard. Crying and laughing were intimately connected, two extreme faces of the same emotional coin. Troy had done so well this year, dealing with his father's death without any noticeable side effects. The anniversary was hitting him hard tonight, catapulting him into out of character behavior. The poor baby needed a good night's sleep. They *all* needed a good night's sleep.

Darcy chewed at her lip. Her eyes glistened in sympathy. "I tried to tell you," Darcy said, splitting Laura's heart down the center.

Aidan pushed Troy's chair out of his way. "Hey, Troy, help me with this tablecloth?" he said.

Troy raised his head. "What?"

Aidan mopped up the wine spill with a fistful of napkins, but his gaze rested on Troy. "Better get this in the wash right away. Learned from experience."

"I don't—I can't—"

"Let's all clear the table," Laura said. She gathered up the serving dishes, moved them to the sideboard to free the stained tablecloth, and gestured to the guests to follow suit.

Good call, Aidan. This wasn't the place for Troy to vent his emotions, yet she'd allowed him to suck her into his black hole of regret. How Jack-like of Laura to escalate Troy's public fit. How un–Jack-like of Aidan to distract him.

Silverware clattered against plates. Diagonally across from Aidan, Laura took up a corner of the tablecloth.

The dinner guests clamored past Troy, and his hands relaxed.

Darcy followed behind Nick. "You never listen to me," she told Laura, and slipped out the door.

"Not helpful," Laura wanted to say in her defense. Instead, her shoulder muscles bunched, and she inhaled through her nose. She had to admit, sometimes she didn't listen to her daughter.

"Grab the other side," Aidan told Troy.

Troy stared at the tablecloth through tear-dazed eyes and blinked. He wiped his nose with the back of his hand, and then helped Laura and Aidan fold the mess into the center. Aidan scooped up the tablecloth.

Troy took a watery breath. "Um, I'll help you."

"Really appreciate that." Aidan aimed a smile straight at Laura, and she allowed herself a full breath.

Laura followed Aidan and Troy into the kitchen. A year after Jack's death, Troy was responding to a man with a temperament the polar opposite of Jack's. Jack would've loved the irony.

Troy was responding to a father figure.

Tears clogged Laura's sinuses, and she blinked them back. At the sink, Maggie was scrubbing a serving dish and Elle was drying a wineglass. "Did you see that?" Laura asked her friends. She hugged Maggie around the shoulders, steadying herself so she wouldn't cry.

Elle leaned in and whispered loudly in Laura's ear, so Maggie could hear, too. "Yeah, I know. Nice ass."

Laura shoved her away. "Shhh! You're impossible," Laura said, glancing toward the guest bathroom's open door. "I was talking about—"

"Told you he was a nice guy," Elle said.

Maggie shook water from the serving dish, then placed it in the draining rack. "Very peaceful aura, lots of blue."

The click of the washing machine shutting echoed into the kitchen. Laura put her finger to her lips and cocked her head toward the bathroom. Aidan's voice, then Troy's, but she couldn't make out the words. The washing machine hummed to life, and Troy walked into the kitchen. He stood up straight, arms relaxed, features smooth. Still, Laura suspected his fit had evidenced the tip of an iceberg.

"How you doing?" Laura said.

"Sorry about the tablecloth."

"And Cam?"

"I owe him an apology."

"Yes." Troy's paler than usual skin sharpened the blue of his eyes. For the millionth time, Laura marveled at the beauty of her son.

"Heading upstairs."

"Okay. Do you—"

Troy race-walked from the room.

"Need me?" Laura shook her head. "Excuse me," she told

Maggie and Elle, and headed in the opposite direction of her son.

"Hey, there," Aidan said when Laura stepped through the guest bathroom door. He dragged a rag over detergent splatters atop the rumbling washer. "Just finishing up."

"You've done more than your share already. Really. You're officially exempt from any more cleaning. And thank you, thank you so much for distracting Troy."

"I could do more." Aidan scrubbed a hand across his five o'clock shadow and widened his eyes at Laura. "I'd be glad to share my shaving expertise with him."

Troy could easily get a friend to show him how to shave. She'd seen Michael sport pieces of facial tissue stuck to his face, newbie shaver wounds. Troy's problem went deeper.

Her son worried who would teach him how to be a man.

"Troy's little display. It wasn't really about grooming." Laura met Aidan's gaze, and she hoped she wouldn't have to explain further.

Aidan nodded, and he firmed his jaw. "He's just a boy missing his dad."

"Yes," Laura said, and her voice hitched.

Only that wasn't the truth, either, not exactly. If Jack had been alive, Troy's uncharacteristic behavior would've snagged his attention. Jack would've questioned Troy. He would've encouraged his son to delve into his emotions, for all the wrong reasons. Jack would've interviewed Troy the way a reporter interviewed a subject. Coldly. Objectively. Relentlessly. Jack would've used Troy's pain as research material for his next great work of fiction, because Jack Klein's real-life family wasn't half as important to him as the characters that inhabited his prize-winning imagination.

Jack hadn't always acted selfishly. He'd played the attentive boyfriend and husband until Darcy was born. The precipitating event that changed Laura from a girl into a woman had set off Jack's first manic-depressive cycle, leaving Laura the only adult in charge from that day forward. Leaving Laura with the understanding that in a flash good fortune could turn on you. No need to overanalyze the situation. Celebrated writer Jack Klein was simply good at writing and bad at life.

"Hey, hey there. You okay?"

To Laura's horror, her face was heating, but not from grief. Like Troy, she wasn't missing the husband she'd known and loved, the brilliant man with all of his weaknesses. Laura was missing the man Jack had shown her during the honeymoon phase of their relationship. For fifteen years, that husband had lurked, popping up on holidays.

A strange new sensation swirled through her chest. Jack would've asked her what she was feeling, and she would've told him, "Not a thing." He'd felt more than enough for the two of them.

Aidan tossed the rag in its bucket. "I get it. You told me to stop cleaning. House rule number two. Listen to Laura."

She laughed. "It's true. I do like when people listen to me."

Aidan mirrored her smile. The overhead light reflected off his dark eyes, that peculiar sensation in her chest deepened, and its meaning came to her.

For fifteen years she'd loved and cared for a sick man, enduring his changeable moods, the quirks of his self-indulgent personality. Now she was standing inches away from Aidan Walsh, a man who was simply good at life. How did that make her feel? In a word?

Cheated.

Chapter 9

The desk lamp Laura had taken from Jack's studio directed oblong gray patches against her bedroom walls, casting the collage of relocated black-and-white photographs into darkness and dimming their entire family history. Laura paused at the threshold, clutching a stack of books against her nightgown to balance the research material's heavy weight. She squinted through the dimly lit room until she reached her bed, and then let the books tumble from her hands.

She slid out a notepad from beneath the rubble of books. Using all capital letters, she filled the top margin with one word: TROY.

After Troy's dinner performance and the Aidan save, and after she'd kicked Elle and Maggie out of the kitchen, she cleaned up the rest of the mess herself. By the time she'd made her way upstairs, Troy was standing in the bathroom doorway, wearing plaid sleep pants, and working winter mint toothpaste into blue foam. Her son was desperate for sleep and was smart enough to listen to his body. How could she tell, how could anyone tell, whether one fit on the anniversary eve of Jack's death meant her son was sick?

She'd read every single manual on bipolar disorder, known

as manic depression when Jack was diagnosed, and had memorized most of the symptoms psychiatrists used for diagnosis. Depressed mood, feelings of guilt and worthlessness, and recurring thoughts of death pointed to depression. On the flip side, pressured speech, flights of fancy, and Jack's favorite, hypersexuality, highlighted mania.

She couldn't imagine her son succumbing to a lifelong illness with no chance of a cure, just an endless array of hills and valleys regulated by doctors and tiny beige tablets. Even the supposed miracle drug lithium required constant monitoring of kidney functions as the therapeutic dose easily crossed the line into toxicity. Jack didn't mind the weight gain and hand tremors. It was the foggy thinking that he couldn't brook, the memory loss, and the overall mental sluggishness. *Please, Laura, let me finish this novel on deadline, and I promise I'll be good.*

She saw not her late husband, but Troy, down on bent knee before her, begging for her help. Her belly trembled, signaling the feeling of helplessness she abhorred. From the foot of her bed, she took the red knit throw, another transplant from Jack's studio, and wrapped it around her shoulders.

She didn't need Jack, not now. She'd taken care of their children pretty much on her own for their entire lives. Her husband had chosen to kill himself and take the easy way out of a tough situation. This wasn't the first time she'd nicknamed him Slip-Out-the-Back Jack.

Where had that come from?

Unsympathetic, for sure, possibly even downright mean-spirited. She fisted her hands, squeezing hard in a vain effort to squelch the negative energy. A restless sensation weakened her left arm, shoulder to wrist. "Four, two, three, seven. Eight, seven, six, three." Laura spoke the last four digits of Elle's phone number, and then Maggie's, like a whispered prayer. Earlier this evening, before Maggie and Elle would agree to leave, they'd made Laura promise to call if she needed them, and she loved them for it. But she wouldn't want to alarm them with a midnight call.

Besides, it wasn't so much soul emptiness she was experiencing as a mild hunger centering in her belly. She hadn't managed more than a few bites of dinner when Troy had initiated his sideshow, cutting the meal short. She touched her son's name at the top of her jam-packed worry list, then added Jack's psychiatrist's name off to the side. She wouldn't wait until things grew worse. She wouldn't repeat the mistakes she'd made with Jack. One appointment didn't mean a thing; Dr. Harvey could set her mind at ease.

She plucked her satin robe from the closet and slipped it over her nightgown. The garment delivered an all-over twinge of cold instead of the warmth she'd expected. A floorboard creaked under her weight. She clicked the closet door shut. The latch popped, the door creaked open on rusty hinges, and she startled.

It's just a room, Laura. Relax.

After all, she didn't believe in *that* sort of thing. Ghost stories were the living's overintellectualization of what happened when a person died, myths to keep the fear of death at bay. You were alive, and then you were dead, so why worry about it? The dead didn't walk around mourning themselves. They left misery to the living.

How many times had she wished misery would release its grip on her husband? She'd sail into the kitchen on an updraft of joy, only to find Jack sulking over his coffee, unaffected by the sunshine blazing through the windows.

Laura padded down to the kitchen. No sounds came from the studio, but the knowledge another stable adult was living in her house eased the edge off her worry.

Laura thought of the leftover gingersnaps and discovered their freezer container, empty save for a few crumbs. Instead, she slid three frozen chocolate chip cookies into the microwave for a quick defrost and gazed through the behind-the-sink window, searching through the night for the tranquil distant hills. Instead, the eight-by-eight panes reflected blue-black darkness. Troy was not sick.

She yanked the microwave door open before the third annoying bleep and released her cookies, her only visible moral support. She stood over the sink and bit into the biggest cookie's chewy moistness, crunching salty roasted pecans. Rich chocolate melted on her tongue. Troy was not sick.

She never did find out where Jack had disappeared to after Troy's birth. Jack had dropped her at their off-campus apartment with their toddler and newborn son. She spent the week in a blur of diapers and feedings, convinced that he'd never return, that at twenty-two, she'd become the sole parental support for her two children. Even after Jack had returned at week's end, she held fast to her assertion, never letting down her guard. Tensed and at the ready. Troy was not sick.

A full glass of ice milk, transparent bubbles peeking over the rim of green-tinted hobnail, never failed to please her. She sipped through the tickly froth, and then sucked down the frosty liquid without pausing until she reached the transparent emerald bottom. An immediate brain freeze scraped across her forehead. She held her hands against her temples, trying to contain the pain. She had to smile. Worse than the kids.

The ceiling moaned above her head. Troy's room. She counted five steps, not enough to take him to the hallway bathroom. A rumbling told her he was rolling his desk chair across the floorboards. If Troy couldn't sleep, they should at least endure wakefulness together.

She nuked three cookies for her son and poured a brimming glass of milk. No ice this time; she'd learned her lesson. She carried the offering atop a hand-painted floral bed tray, careful to keep the surface steady as she climbed the stairs toward Troy's bedroom. No sound through the barrier of Darcy's closed door, although Laura couldn't shake the conviction Darcy was wide-awake, staring at the ceiling.

Troy's door stood open a crack, and a skinny line of light trickled across the hallway. Laura paused where the beam faded to nothingness, as though waiting to ford a stream into unknown territory. Ridiculous, for sure. Almost as irrational as the shudder splashing down her neck and washing over her shoulders.

She nudged the door with her hip and stepped into the dim room. "Troy, sweetie."

Hard to tell if her son heard her or, really, how loudly she spoke his name, if she spoke it out loud at all. Troy sat at his desk, the twitching of his bare shoulder blade evidencing his swift jotting. He ran a hand vertically through his pillow-molded hair, and then continued on his writing rampage.

"Troy." Laura was reasonably sure she'd said his name out loud this time. "I brought you some cookies and milk. Thought it might help you get back to sleep." Okay, that was dumb. Her son was in no way interested in sleep tonight.

Laura slid the bed tray atop Troy's waist-high bookshelf. "Do you want to talk? It helps when you say your worries out loud. I mean, in my opinion."

He glanced over his shoulder. "That's very funny." Troy returned his attention to his desk, leaning over his work and shifting his back toward where his mother stood.

Troy chuckled to himself, as if he'd already forgotten Laura was standing behind him. He slouched over his work and blew gently across and down, setting the fresh ink before turning the page with exaggerated slowness. He ran his hand over the stark blank page, as if memorizing the territory he planned on desecrating. Another chuckle, and he fell upon the page like a lion on its prey.

In Jack's most agitated manias, he'd plunged into the bottomless waters of hypergraphia, thinking he was writing a best seller. But Jack's so-called inspiration, when under the magnifying glass of his mood disorder, produced pressured writing, copious pages of nonsense.

Troy was not—

The undigested cookies churned within their milk bath in her belly, threatening to revisit her throat.

Laura tiptoed to the desk and peered over Troy's shoulder. Her son had inherited her notoriously impossible to read cursive. No matter how hard she tried, she couldn't make out a single word.

"Do you think you could tell me what you're writing? I'm just so curious."

Troy swiveled his chair around and regarded her with the deliberate eyes of a pundit. The tips of his ears glowed scarlet; a telltale sign of her son's extreme exhaustion. Charcoal pools rested beneath his black velvet lashes, making him appear like an older version of himself, one she hadn't expected to see for another decade.

A smile flickered over his face. He nodded, coaxing the words, and his speech flowed at a normal rate. "I'm writing about Dad for the anniversary thing tomorrow. I keep waking up in the middle of the night remembering stuff I'd forgotten, like about watching him shave, and tapioca pudding, and camping, and even how we connected all those rubber bands end to end and stretched them across the house. All the good stuff I'd forgotten because I was always so pissed off at him." He shook his head, and his voice thickened. "I'm still pissed off, Mom."

"Oh, honey, it's okay to feel angry." Thank God! Troy was finally talking to her. Aidan was right. Nothing was the matter here, just a boy missing his dad. She breathed into her belly, then sighed.

She could smell him then, the unmistakable body odor of an adolescent who exercised without showering, and then added a second layer of sweat. Troy usually showered *twice* a day.

Laura rubbed his bare back, getting a moist palm for her efforts. Now she was perspiring, too, judging by the prickly heat needling the back of her head. "Can you read it to me?"

"Sure." He hung his head and stared at the page, his back muscles tightening beneath her hand. "I can't. I can't read this. Stupid lousy handwriting." He shook his head, and his gaze flitted around the room. "Fuck," he whispered.

Her breath caught. "It doesn't matter. Everything, all your memories are inside of you. Your dad's inside of you."

Troy looked at her as if he'd never seen her before. "What's the matter with you? Don't you get it? I don't want Dad inside of me! That's the point. That's the fucking point!"

Her chest jounced, and she pushed down the useless panic. She reached for Troy, and he stood to avoid her touch. "I'm so stupid! What an idiot!" he said.

"Troy. Stop that. Give yourself a break."

"Imbecile, moron." Troy zigzagged across the room.

Laura raced to block the doorway. "Troy!"

He spat out a slew of profanities, daring Laura to make him stop. Maintaining eye contact with Troy proved more challenging than listening to his self-abatement. Her son didn't really hate her.

Behind Laura, Darcy's voice rang out like a shot. "Quit it!"

Troy's jaw worked, but no sound came from his lips. His face contorted, evidence of internal turmoil boiling not so far below the surface.

Laura's gaze focused on her son, maintaining a measure of restraint, and she reached for Darcy's hand.

Laura waited until his breath settled into a steady cadence. Agitated mania begged for assistance, the barest suggestion of support, although it rarely looked as if it desired company. "It's okay. I'm right here with you. Your whole family's here," she said and squeezed Darcy's hand.

Troy stared at Laura through downturned eyes.

"Your family," Laura repeated, and Troy fell into her arms. His sobs broke against her chest. Hot tears pooled in her neck, and Darcy hugged her from behind.

Laura stroked Troy's perspiration-damp hair. "It's okay, sweetheart. Let it go." She'd make that call to Dr. Harvey first thing Monday morning.

"Why don't you lie down? Hmm, Troy? Put your head on your pillow? You'll be more comfortable." Laura couldn't tell if Troy heard her through his sobs, but he let her guide him to his bed. She helped him slide beneath the snug covers, a letter in an envelope, just the way he liked it, and he took a breath. "Do you remember the time Dad started that pillow fight?" Troy said.

"Sure I do," Laura told Troy, and his sobs began anew.

Darcy leaned against the doorframe, her hair curling around her face. Her hazel-brown eyes glowed like amber under water.

"Bring me some tissues and a glass of water, please?" Laura asked Darcy, just like Laura had done countless times before when Jack had been in the midst of a crying jag, and she couldn't leave his side. Petite powerhouse Darcy nodded and slipped from Laura's sight.

Laura kissed Troy on the forehead, and her lips registered a low-grade crying-induced fever. Déjà vu all over again. She may not believe in ghosts, but she couldn't deny Jacob Abraham Klein was haunting their son.

Chapter 10

Troy was missing.

Beside her son's empty bed, Laura bolted to sitting. Daylight seeped around Troy's shades. She threw off the blanket she'd used as a makeshift bedroll and scanned the room. Her gaze touched every dark corner.

No Troy.

Her throat clutched. She belted her robe and went into the hallway, poked her head into the empty bathroom. She even peeked into Darcy's room. She wasn't expecting to find Troy tucked in with his sister beneath her green-and-blue patchwork quilt, but on this day of days, she couldn't rule that out, either.

No Troy.

She rushed down the stairway. No Troy in the living room, but her son's chipper voice echoed into the kitchen. She followed the sound of Troy's chatter through the studio's open door. Menthol steam opened her airways, loosening the knot in her throat. A tingle cooled the back of her neck.

Yes, Troy.

With his back to Laura, Troy stood inside the apartment's tiny bathroom. Laura hugged him around the waist, intending to make him laugh. Instead, she caught sight of Aidan standing over the sink and burst into hysterics herself.

"Easy there, you're going to damage my delicate ego." Face covered with shaving foam, Aidan's bright smile crept all the way to his eyes. His right hand held his razor, while his left hand kept the towel around his trim waist from dropping to the floor. The well-defined contours of his chest told Laura he must do more than cycling. Cycling alone didn't carve an upper body like that.

"Are you done laughing?" Aidan asked. "Got to give the kid a shaving lesson before my face hardens."

"Yeah, you're going to make his face harden," Troy said.

Laura wiped at the corners of her eyes. "Up all night, punch-drunk," she said by way of an explanation.

"Likely story," Aidan told Laura.

Aidan turned to Troy, and her son leaned toward his voice. "Now *as I was saying*," he said, glancing at Laura. "After a shower is best, when your face is nice and soft . . ."

A facial-hair shaving lesson was a male-only rite of passage, but Laura couldn't bring herself to miss the event. Truth be told, she wouldn't have missed it for the world.

"You angle the razor like so," Aidan said.

Troy tilted his head to follow Aidan's razor as it cleared the foam from his upper lip. Aidan raised his chin to reach his beneath-the-chin stubble, and Troy mirrored his movements.

Laura's sleep deficit had really and truly left her punchy, a ball of laughter caught in her throat. In contrast, Troy's exhaustion had served to reset his mood back to its familiar from-the-day-he-was-born mellow.

"Any questions?" Aidan asked Troy.

"I don't think so."

"You've got your basic Barbasol cream," Aidan said, shaking the barbershop pole-striped can. "Some guys prefer gel. Got a razor?"

"Nope."

"Hang on a sec." Aidan reached down into the vanity cabinet and handed Troy a can of Barbasol with an attached disposable shaver.

"How did you—?"

"Bought two, got one free." Aidan rinsed his razor under steaming-hot water, tapped it against the counter, and laid it on the side of the sink.

Troy gave the can of shaving cream a couple of shakes. "Thanks for the stuff. I'm off to shower," he said. "I mean, soften my face." Troy blew past Laura, and she smiled after him, committing his boy-mustache to memory.

"You may need some Band-Aids," Aidan said.

Laura stepped into the bathroom. Steam cushioned her like a whole-body hug. "My first-aid kit is full. The rest. The shaving supplies—the advice—words seem insufficient. Once again, how will I ever thank you?"

Aidan's dimple grinned at her a beat before his eyes brightened. "You'll think of something." The intimate tone of his voice teased like a feather down her body, crossed the line of friendship, and, sure enough, had her thinking about a very specific something she could no longer deny.

He liked her.

The urge to connect with Aidan prickled Laura's cheeks. He took a hand towel from the rack and patted his face. With his features covered, he could've been Jack standing in his studio bathroom, freshening up after a deadline-induced all-nighter.

Only Jack and Troy wouldn't have been discussing shaving. A conversation required two parties, and somewhere along the line, Troy had decided his father wasn't worth the effort.

A dab of shaving cream shone along the sharp edge of Aidan's jawline. "You missed a spot," she said.

Aidan swiped a hand above his lip, then swiped more when Laura shook her head. For some reason, men could feel neither food nor shaving cream on their faces.

"No—it's—let me." Laura touched her fingers to his newly smooth skin, noted the strong shape of his face. His gaze flicked from her eyes to her lips and back up to her eyes. Heat ached between her legs. Her mouth fell open, and Aidan's lips parted, a whole conversation.

Laura's pulse raced forward, but she took a step back, reminding herself who she was: Jack Klein's widow on the morning of his graveside visit. And Aidan was exactly what she needed now, a trustworthy friend and a role model for her son. She didn't need to add another layer of complication to her complication-riddled life.

"You were great with Troy," she said, and to her horror, her voice betrayed a slight breathlessness.

Aidan pressed his lips together and nodded. "Troy's a good kid."

She took a covert cleansing breath. "He's a bright one." Troy's IQ hovered in the genius range, but Laura was referring to her son's emotional intelligence, evidenced by all of his Jack love-hate remembrances.

By the time Troy had turned ten, he'd realized Jack wasn't like other fathers. Other fathers didn't swing from days of pitch-black brooding on the couch to too hyper to tolerate. Other fathers didn't use your parent-teacher meeting to pitch their novel in progress. And other fathers didn't make your mother call off a Lego playdate with your best friend, Michael, the one you'd been looking forward to all week, because your dad wasn't "feeling well," and a visit would've taken your mother's attention off him.

To this day, Laura wasn't sure Troy had ever gotten over that disappointment.

Laura leaned forward and gave Aidan a pristine kiss on his

menthol-scented cheek, for showing Troy how to shave, for taking care of her son in a way his father had not.

"What was that for?"

"My way of thanking you without words." As Jack was fond of saying, it was better to beg for forgiveness than to ask for permission. Which pretty much summed up Jack's entire philosophy.

"No need to thank me," Aidan said. "Troy heard me up and knocked on the door, so I asked if he'd like to hang out while I shaved. I got a kick out of his enthusiasm. Figured a shaving lesson was the least he deserved."

"That's my low-maintenance boy for you."

Troy had always required so little, and Jack had given him even less.

Chapter 11

The smell of fresh coffee seeped into Darcy's dream, spiriting her to a roadside diner. Waitresses, wearing striped uniforms, swarmed through the dimly lit restaurant—hot pink bands against retro black-and-white checkered linoleum and shimmering candy-apple booths. Darcy waited for a gray plume of cigarette smoke to rise toward the vaulted ceiling. He was sitting sideways, so she only managed a glimpse of her father's face, the suggestion of a smirk. Ceramic stoneware dishes clattered, and a waitress stepped in front of her. A pair of pushed-up-to-her-neck boobs blocked Darcy's coveted view.

"What'll it be, sugar?" The waitress slid her pencil out from behind her ear, and a few strands of bleached hair came along for the ride. Her pencil hovered above the order pad. "Just coffee again?"

"Coffee, Darcy." *Wait a minute.* Her mother's singsong voice sucked Darcy out of the dream diner and into her too-real bedroom.

She opened one eye and caught sight of her mother carrying the infamous floral bed tray with a cup of decaf coffee. Her overprotective mother would never let her drink *real* coffee, as if caffeine were a gateway drug, leading directly to heroin addiction. A sunny-side up egg shone atop Mom's favorite multi-grain toast—light on flavor and heavy on revolting texture. Her mother's smiling face held steady above her offering, like a cheerful highway billboard.

"Morning, angel." Angel. Mom never called her that pet name anymore.

Mom sat down on her bed and placed the tidy breakfast tray atop Darcy's outstretched legs. "Thought you might need a special wake-up call after last night."

Ah, that explained the decaf, something Mom allowed her on only a few select occasions. Today, she supposed, gave her mother a double reason: the anniversary of her father's rather messy suicide and the morning after little bro's freak-out.

"Thank you for last night. You were a big help." The admission caught in Mom's throat. Her mother didn't always accept help, but she had no trouble delegating half of the grunt work to Darcy last night. Mom had barked out orders like a drill sergeant, sending Darcy to fetch tissues and ice water for Troy, and then a plate of heated leftovers when he finally grew hungry from his nonstop crying and blabbering about Daddy. He'd kept switching back and forth between good and bad stories. Troy loved him; Troy loved him not.

"Troy?" Darcy said, and his name tightened her throat. Not even her twit of a brother deserved her father's illness.

Mom turned her head and, as if in response, the radiator rattled, and water flooded through the pipes. "He's showering. I've never seen anyone recover so quickly." By *anyone*, her mom meant that her father had never come out of a manic episode and landed on his feet right away.

"He seems, like, normal?"

"Actually, he seems better than normal."

Darcy sliced through her egg yolk and waited for the bright-yellow liquid to soak the toast before cutting the first bite. She couldn't imagine what depression would look like on her brother. Even in his sleep, he held a steady smile. Well, except for last night. "Are you sure he's not faking?"

Her mother shrugged. "I'm going to bring Troy to talk to Dad's Dr. Harvey." Light filtering through the curtains highlighted the shadows beneath her eyes. After Troy had fallen asleep, Mom had made up a bed for herself on Troy's floor so she could sleep with a hand against the edge of his mattress. "I'm sure Troy's exhausted. I'd say that's as normal as it's going to get for today." A sigh quaked through her mother's petite body.

The sound of water cascading behind the wall came to an abrupt halt as Darcy munched through the last bites of sticky toast. A few minutes later, Troy trotted to the doorway holding a towel around his waist and a blood-speckled tissue to his upper lip. What do you know? Little bro had learned to shave without Daddy.

"Thanks for everything," he said, and then lowered his eyes and dashed to his room.

Mom stared after Troy with a weird grin on her face. "Found Troy in Aidan's studio earlier, getting a shaving lesson," she said. "You know, you really should take a peek . . ."

Again? Darcy must still be asleep because she was having a recurring nightmare. She gulped at the coffee, but the caffeine-free imposter didn't jolt her awake. Only near-scalding water could wake her brain after four hours of sleep.

"Maybe another day."

"I need to shower, Mom."

Mom took a while to realize she should get up off Darcy's bed and leave her room, as if Mom were working on a five-second delay. She rested at the threshold.

"You know one episode doesn't necessarily mean anything. I mean, if it even was an episode." Mom nodded, as though she were trying to convince herself, too. "In about ten percent of the cases, the illness never reaches beyond one distinct episode. Okay, Darce?"

Darcy squeezed her face into what she hoped passed as a grin. "Sure, Mom." And in ninety percent of the cases, mania evolved into lifelong bipolar disorder. With odds like that, who needed enemies?

Darcy adjusted the shower to the hottest setting, tugged her T-shirt up over her head, and then let her drawstring pants and underwear drop to the tile. Steam billowed out from the shower curtain, but she shivered anyway. She climbed into the claw-foot tub and pulled the curtain tight to keep in all of the warmth. Hot water pinged off her back. She eased into the rhythm and turned slowly to cover each section of her body with the numbing heat. Breathing in the humidity relaxed her, and the spectral image of her father sitting in a diner booth, just out of her reach, returned.

She lathered her body with the slippery bar soap, and then worked shampoo into her scalp, attempting to scrub out the dream Daddy. Inhaling the almond suds didn't prevent her from remembering the last time she saw him alive.

"Hey, wild thing. Did you pack a sweater in your duffel? It's supposed to get cool tonight," Daddy had said, calling out from the wing chair in her parents' bedroom.

Darcy had scrambled to gather up what she'd need for the weekend at Heather's, and Heather had been waiting for her out on the porch rocker. The sound of creaking boards had come loud and clear through open windows. *Hurry up.*

"All set, Funny Dad," Darcy had said, effortlessly falling into their routine banter. She hadn't even bothered stepping into the bedroom. She'd just stood at the doorway, looking past her father, thinking of her plans for the evening and what cute boy she might kiss.

"Darcy? I love you so. You know that, right?"

"Sure, Super Writer Guy."

"Darcy—"

Too late. Darcy was already hightailing it away from her dad and pounding down the stairway faster than his words could travel. She'd never know the last words he'd meant for her ears alone.

"I love you so," Darcy spoke out loud, trying to chase down a lost connection. She held her hand below the showerhead. Near-scalding water pierced her palm.

For I love you so. Inhaling the steam drove the connection home, like a nail to her heart. *Nay, if you read this line, remember not the hand that writ it; for* I love you so.

Their secret Shakespeare sonnet.

Her legs went soft beneath her, and she slid down into the tub.

That I in your sweet thoughts would be forgot. She spoke the words inside her head, using her father's voice. She'd kept her pace safely ahead of Daddy's borrowed verse, while the unsympathetic hallway had absorbed his very last plea for help. Daddy had never, ever recited the poem inside the house where her mother might overhear, so Darcy knew for sure.

Her apathy had killed her daddy.

Her high-pitched screams echoed off the walls. She clamped her hands over her ears, but she could still hear the pathetic wailing.

The sound of feet stampeding toward the bathroom confused her. Women's voices called out to her. Mom burst through the door. "Darcy! Are you all right?"

Darcy was shaking, but she sucked it up fast. One family member completely losing it within any twenty-four-hour period filled the quota. She understood her mother's unspoken rule, and she couldn't even blame her for this one.

Darcy shut off the water and poked her head out from the

shower curtain, holding it around her face like a hood. "Sorry to scare you, Mom. I slipped and twisted my ankle, but it's fine. Guess I overreacted." Darcy batted her lashes, pretending not to notice Elle and Maggie outlining the doorframe. *Leave me alone! You don't even know what I did!*

Mom stared, trying to siphon the truth through sheer determination. Maggie and Elle fell back, responding to a glance from her mother.

"I'm just *so* tired," Darcy said.

"Oh, Darcy." Mom started forward, heading straight for where Darcy sat in the tub bare-naked. Mom crouched to pass her a towel, and Darcy wrapped it around her quaking body snug enough to mask the subtle movement.

Darcy would've kicked her mother out of the bathroom, but she knew a chance when she saw it. "Please don't make me go to the cemetery. I need to remember Daddy *my way.*" Mom was big on individual self-expression, as long as she oversaw the details.

"Angel, I don't think you should be alone today." Mom shook her head, but Darcy could tell by the way Mom's pupils lost focus that she was already thinking up a compromise.

Maybe if she pleaded. "Please. I want to stay home, where I last saw him. . . ." Darcy didn't mean to start crying again, but the snag in her voice seemed to trip up her mother the required amount.

"Would you mind if Maggie stayed here with you? She'd sit downstairs, in case you needed anything."

Would she mind? No, she'd love to hang with the scary weirdo. They could string love beads and burn incense. Maggie could even teach her how to read tea leaves, decipher her undeniably rosy future from the graying dregs. And there were always the tarot cards. "That'd be great, Mom."

Mom nodded, even though she hadn't even asked her friend yet. She unfurled herself from her tub-side seat.

"One thing," Darcy said, pausing her mother at a kneel. "Please tell Maggie I need privacy. Okay? To explore my *feelings*." That should do it. Mom was so easy to play. All she had to do was push her dazzling array of buttons.

Darcy tried molding what she'd told her mother into something resembling the truth. After all, if she wanted to connect with the memory of her dad, what better place than their home? Their house remained exactly the same as a year ago, like those preserved in amber insects she'd learned about in earth science class.

Mom used to move furniture around with the seasons and repaint the walls to reflect the weather. Darcy would come home from school and discover the suede-mocha walls in the dining room had transformed into what Mom called a spring-savoring buttercream wash. An ottoman would morph into a coffee table, furnished with an antique cocoa carafe Mom found at a yard sale. Across the living room wall, silvery stenciling would offer words of encouragement. *Dream. Believe. Do.*

Darcy tiptoed into her parents' bedroom, careful not to disturb Maggie sitting watch at the foot of the stairs. She creaked open the walk-in closet and discovered Mom had hung Daddy's robe on the hook beneath hers. On the rod, evidence of Daddy's last hurrah before Mom took his credit cards greeted her. All twenty-seven of Daddy's cashmere sweaters remained exactly as he'd left them lined up in obsessive-compulsive color wheel order: cobalt, blue violet, violet.

She went for his favorite sweater and slipped the cobalt V-neck over her head. She didn't expect to smell her father; his citrus-musk scent had worn off several months ago, but she tried anyway.

She couldn't even resurrect his scent through memory, couldn't even remember what he looked like, not exactly. She flung the sweater back on its stupid cedar-lined hanger and clicked the closet door shut. The black-and-white picture of him in the gilded frame didn't really look like him, either. She'd never understand why Mom would want his most recent dust jacket photo on her bed table. He wasn't even smiling beneath the wreath of fingerprints.

Darcy touched the straight lips on Daddy's photo and imagined them curling up at the corners, showing off his straight white teeth.

No longer mourn for me when I am dead.

What did that mean? That she'd mourned for him while he was still living and that she should've stopped when he offed himself? Her mother always said it was his choice, and the phrase tumbled effortlessly from her lips, as if it didn't even hurt.

Was Mom really that stoic? What was the point in Darcy even attempting to please her mother? The refined widow/domestic goddess/editor did everything so well. Darcy could never approach her mother's level of nauseating perfection.

How could Daddy have left her with a mother who just didn't get her? Even though she and Daddy looked nothing alike, he'd often remark how similar they were inside. Extreme Man and Extreme Girl understood each other. And she'd let him down, missing his coded cries for help.

She hugged Daddy's photo to her chest and thought of how Daddy had taken her to get her library card the day she'd turned five. She'd worn a blue velvet dress and tights, and Daddy wore his best suit with a blue tie to match, like they were going on a date. He'd lifted her onto a stool so she could reach the counter. He'd let her use his for-signings-only pen.

Each and every year since middle school, he'd come into her homeroom to talk about the writer's life and answer students' questions. He'd tell the class she was his inspiration.

Now he was just gone.

With shaking hands, she put Daddy's photo back on the bureau. She was so sick of missing him, so sick of living under the suffocating cloud of what her father had done. So sick of jamming the pillow into her mouth every night so Mom wouldn't hear her sobbing. So sick of this house and everything in it.

Darcy went into her bedroom, slid open her top dresser drawer, and took out the emergency joint hidden beneath her underwear. She sniffed the sweet weed through the paper's length. The scent made her feel better, as if help were on the way, even though she was breaking her self-inflicted rule about partying twice in one week. When she'd told Nick on Wednesday about Mom's plans for Daddy's Death Day Eve dinner, he'd suggested they celebrate their six-week anniversary a few days early with a reenactment of their first date.

She made sure she wasn't a total pothead. She didn't get high every day or even every week, making the treat into a special event. Today definitely qualified as a holiday. This joint wouldn't get her very far though. The cheapo stuff she'd purchased months ago from the loser in the high school girls' room wasn't half as good as Nick's homegrown. His powerful weed sailed her within three hits to her favorite vacation spot: anywhere but here.

She couldn't call Nick. She'd told him she was busy today. She'd resigned herself to family time at the cemetery. Besides, she would not play the role of the clinging girlfriend. Mom had been right about the don't-call-boys rule. Boys liked you better. She'd call Heather if her best girlfriend weren't such a drag lately. She needed entertainment, not more doom and gloom. For a good time call . . . Nick. Thinking about making out with Nick set her heart beating madly, which only made her want more.

What if she broke her self-inflicted dating rule, too, and made the anniversary of her father's suicide into a day of living dangerously?

From beneath her bras at the back of the drawer, she dug out the box she'd been saving, tore it open, and ripped off a shiny red packet. Loudmouth Vanessa had given her the Trojans, and then enacted a demonstration for Darcy, complete with a mold-slick cucumber. The poor vegetable had looked ridiculous, like something no one in her right mind would go near. Still, remembering her embarrassment heated her cheeks, heated places in her body she'd never shared before.

Sure, she'd kissed plenty of boys. She and Heather had kept lists since their first spin the bottle game five years ago, and they regularly reviewed them to compare stats. About a year ago, they were running neck and neck. Now she bested Heather by at least ten boys. How could Heather stand it?

Darcy dialed Nick's number before she could chicken out. He probably wouldn't be at home today, anyway. *It's ringing.* Probably, he'd gone for a drive to visit old friends, or he could've gone to the library. He'd told her last night he might go to do homework, which had really shocked her. *Another ring.* Not that she thought he was stupid or anything. She just didn't see him as the library type.

"Yeah?" Nick answered, sounding as if he'd just come through the door and had yanked the phone off its receiver.

"Wait a second." Nick's voice came from a distance, along with clattering and thuds. "Sorry, just cleaned the house." He chuckled. "Who is it?" Well, there he went. Her boy pulled it together.

"It's Darcy. What's going on?"

"Swear to God, I was just thinking about calling you. Thought you were doing family stuff today, so I was gonna wait until later and call or swing by or—"

"Could you swing by now?" She slid the useless joint inside the box of condoms, tossed the box back in the drawer, and slipped the foil packet into the back pocket of her jeans.

"I can do anything you want." Nick lowered his voice, and the special spot where he kissed her neck tingled.

"There's just one not so small matter," she said. Her mind sped, jazzed with the challenge of working up an escape plan to circumvent Maggie on guard duty in the living room. "You have to park on Lake Street and wait for me there. Think you can do that?"

"Know I can."

"Thata boy." Darcy hung up and docked her iPod. She set the volume loud enough to mask the sounds of her climbing out the window and clambering down the iron fire escape, a lucky leftover from the house's previous owner. The random song selections would play infinitely, leading Maggie to believe her charge was enjoying a bit of alone time, grooving to the beat.

She threw open the sash and screen, and inhaled the rain-scented air. Far-off storm clouds mingled above the mountain-tops, threatening a future deluge. She should probably grab a jacket, but she couldn't risk going downstairs. Besides, who was afraid of a little rain? Her mother's eventual punishment carried a much more imminent threat. Darcy didn't have a clue how she'd explain her mother's discovery of her friend guarding an empty bedroom. The porch-side wind chimes tinkled, and she laughed. Who cared? What mattered was now, sneaking out, and getting with Nick. *Dream. Believe. Do.*

She tiptoed down the slatted steps, and then dropped to the squishy spring ground. Delicious dangerous energy danced through her body. She touched the condom in her pocket, checking in with Daddy's Extreme Girl. She ran up the hill, away from her house, took a shortcut through a neighbor's property, and then sat waiting at the corner, writing Nick's name in the curbside sand with a stick.

The ratty Monte Carlo pulled up alongside her, and she checked her watch. Ten minutes—he must've flown. Nick got out, came around to the passenger side, and even opened the door for her. "Where to, gorgeous?"

Her last trace of doubt fell away. "Anywhere but here."

Chapter 12

Jacob Abraham Klein.

No matter how many times Laura visited Ever True Cemetery, she'd never get used to seeing her husband's name inscribed on a gravestone. Reading Jack's name narrowed her windpipe, numbed her legs, and sucked the joy out of her life.

She lowered herself to her knees between Elle and Troy, and stifled an urge to rock. Purple-and-gray clouds hung low, swollen tight like overripe fruit. The musty-compost smell of impending rain filled her nose and burned the back of her throat. To stave off the chill, she tugged the lapels of her bright-coral trench coat around her neck. She set a bouquet of daffodils in the cemetery vase, proof that Jack had been gone for a full year and the world had not come to an end.

A year ago, she'd stood in this spot, buoyed by a sea of friends and neighbors, with the knowledge that Jack's body lay in the grave below, dwelling, as he would say, with the vilest of worms. Then she'd gone home, and the discovery that Jack wasn't waiting there for her had knocked her on her ass.

Logic, be damned.

She no longer expected to feel the warmth of his body when she skimmed her hand across her bedsheets. She no longer expected to hear his voice wending its way to her from the kitchen as she headed up the stairs. And she certainly didn't expect to see Jack emerge from his study, gray hair poking around his head in odd angles, blue gaze unfocused with thoughts of the fictional characters in his head.

Over the past year, the surface understanding that Jack was gone for good had seeped through her skin, traveled through her bloodstream, and embedded itself in her heart. The anniversary served as an exclamation point. Jack didn't need her anymore.

But did she need him?

"We've really missed you," Laura said, feeling slightly ridiculous talking to her atheist husband at his burial site. What the hell? If Jack could actually hear her, then the joke, for once, was on him.

Irony, be damned.

"The kids are doing . . . as well as can be expected," she said, thinking of Darcy closing herself off from Laura, all her Daddy's-girl hurt misdirected. Troy pitching a fit, his thirteen-year-old heart and mind overwhelmed with the sadness Jack had caused. Herself. Well, that hardly mattered. "Do you want to say something to Dad?" she asked Troy.

Her son had decided to leave his Jack-memories notebook filled with his Laura-like impossible to read handwriting back in his room. Sharing memories with Laura till the wee hours of the morning had been enough of a tribute.

Big plans, be damned.

Elle rubbed Laura's arm. Elle's breathing betrayed a readiness to cry. Laura loved Elle, but she probably should've asked Maggie to come to the cemetery in her stead. Troy's emotional state was enough of a worry.

Color rose in Troy's cheeks. His nostrils flared, and he stared at the gravestone, reminding Laura of the expression on

Troy's face when he'd tried to talk to Jack about his interests, and Jack had only half listened. Listening, she supposed, had been her job.

Jack had always told Laura he was proud of their son. Laura would've preferred it if Jack had shown that to Troy.

"Maybe tell Dad about making the A-team for basketball? Placing for the mile run in track?"

Troy shook his head, and he sucked his lips between his teeth, as though trying to hold back his words.

Elle made a sound at the back of her throat, a cross between a growl and a suppressed sob. Her hand dropped from Laura's arm.

Troy took a loud breath, and his exhalation vibrated the air before them. He slid a daffodil from the cemetery vase, worried a yellow petal between his fingers.

"Your science project?" Laura said.

Troy plucked the petal, and it dropped to the grass.

"Shaving?" her high-pitched word hit the air. Power of suggestion, she inhaled the lime smell of her son's freshly shaven face. An image of Aidan's clean-shaven face flashed over Jack's.

Troy plucked two more petals and crumpled them in his fist. Troy's chin dimpled, and he flung the ruined petals to the ground.

"Never mind, baby."

"How about telling your dad how you really feel?" Elle said, and Laura's jaw clenched. She cut her gaze to Elle and gave her the universal arched-brow signal to back off.

Troy stopped in midpluck, his fingers buried in the remainder of the yellow blossom. Tears pooled in the sleep-deprived wells beneath Troy's eyes. He looked to Laura for approval.

She nodded. Her whole body shifted toward Troy. After last night's headfirst dive into Jack memory lane, what could Troy have left to express?

"I liked how you made Mom laugh during dinner," Troy

said, and Laura let out a breath. "I liked that time we tried to beat the Guinness World Record for stringing rubber bands. Especially the part where we caught Darcy in our giant spiderweb. And camping. I miss climbing the giant anchor with you at Hermit Island. I miss that a lot."

"Me too, sweetheart. Those were good times." And took place years ago. Laura rubbed Troy's back, and he stared straight ahead. His fingers plucked, crumpled, and then tossed the daffodil's petals until nothing remained but the stalk, stamen, and pistil, trembling in his hand.

"This year's been okay. Mom's sad," Troy said.

Laura held a hand to her throat and reminded herself to breathe. She'd never wanted to burden her children with her grief. She thought she'd hidden it well.

"But now Darcy and I can have friends over without worrying you're gonna embarrass us. And Mom's not all preoccupied with you."

She'd mostly hidden that, too, with the possible exception of the few times she'd forgotten to pick up Troy after school in the second grade. And once when he was in fourth. "Dad was sick," Laura whispered.

Troy turned to her. "He was also a jerk!" Troy said, debunking Laura's conviction that she knew the difference between her husband's personality and his mood disorder.

How could she? How could anyone?

Elle took a tissue from her jacket pocket and blew her nose. She looked from Troy to Laura. "I'll go wait in the car," Elle said, and she got to her feet.

Oh, sure. Start trouble, and then run for cover, leaving her to deal with the mess.

Just like Jack.

Except Laura could criticize Elle. She hadn't let herself get mad at Jack until recently. For years, she'd buried her anger and resentment, so it wouldn't bury her.

"I'm so sorry, Troy."

"What if I don't miss him?" Troy said. "What if, sometimes, I don't miss him at all?"

Sometimes Laura was too pissed to grieve. Sometimes, in between spikes of loneliness, she couldn't miss the man who'd torn their family apart. She'd hoped she'd hidden that from Troy, too.

I'm so sorry, Jack.

"I think that means we're making progress."

Laura's ponytail holder strained, pulling the hairs at the nape of her neck. The sky rumbled and brightened between the maple trees, illuminating fuzzy rhubarb-colored buds. Last year, she'd missed all the signs of spring. This year, she was determined to pay better attention.

"One, Mississippi. Two, Mississippi," Troy said, and Laura grinned, remembering the trick Jack had taught the kids to estimate the distance from the storm.

"Three, Mississippi. Four, Mississippi. Five," they said together. On six, thunder smacked the sky, the storm nearly upon them. Raindrops splattered against Laura's trench coat, darkened Troy's unzipped navy fleece, and wet the red silk of Jack's tie he'd insisted upon wearing.

"Think Dad's the rain king?" Troy asked, and he started to cry, a perfectly normal reaction.

Sadness, anger, resentment. All these emotions fell under the umbrella of grieving. So why was she planning on bringing her son to a shrink?

"King of the heavens?" Laura said. "Sure, honey. Why not? Anything's possible." She imagined Jack in one of his grandiose moods, loving the title.

Another flash and a boom, and the sky cracked wide open, releasing a downpour. Laura imagined Jack gazing down on them, happy at last, and something inside her released, too.

Then she imagined Jack, the day after one of those moods, seeming perfectly normal. He'd play mind games with her and rationalize his previous day's behavior, trying to convince her he didn't need to see Dr. Harvey.

She hugged Troy to her side, tilted her face to the skies, and let the rain numb her face. Good thing for Troy, Dr. Harvey had a supersensitive BS detector, honed from years of listening to patients like Jack.

Chapter 13

Nick pulled away from the curb, and Darcy took a good hard look at his light blond hair, curling up at the ends, and full lower lip. His double layer of shirts, short-sleeved brown over a long-sleeved beige jersey, got her craving coffee ice cream and chocolate sauce. Got her craving him.

Nick turned a corner and caught her staring. "What? Do I have food on my face or something?" He checked the rearview mirror, scrubbed a hand across his chin, picked at imagined remnants of meals gone by, and flicked them onto the floor.

Darcy smiled. No, he was perfect. She could climb on top of him and lick his face, bite his yummy lips and eat him up like a hot fudge sundae.

"So what's with the secret meeting place?" Nick asked.

"I kind of sneaked out of the house, left one of my mom's friends guarding an empty bedroom."

"How'd you manage that?"

"Fire escape." Darcy made climbing motions, getting a secondary rush from the memory.

Nick issued a low whistle through his teeth. "You are in deep."

Well worth the risk, considering the alternative of hanging around for more doom and gloom. She'd had more than her fill. Nick careened through the hokey small-town square, past the statues of children reading on the green, nearly clipping the curb by the drugstore that still served ice-cream sodas to customers twirling on vinyl-covered stools. Elle wasn't working today, but the usual cast of characters would be wandering the brick-lined sidewalks.

Darcy slid down in the bucket seat below window level, far enough to evade detection. Nick tossed her a questioning look. "My mother knows half the town," she said by way of explanation. Her mother not only knew everyone in town, but also kept them in her employ, hiring them as unpaid freelance kid watchers. Darcy couldn't make a move in Hicksville without her mother receiving a full report, complete with eight-by-ten color glossies, like the photos featured in "Alice's Restaurant." Every Thanksgiving, Mom made her suffer through the song. Family tradition.

God, she was tired. She closed her eyes, a trick she'd learned long ago for heightening the other senses. Cool air brushed her cheek, and her mouth fell slack. The car engine shook, vibrating through her body, starting at her bottom and working outward in a series of unbroken waves. She smelled rain and lightning, and a sour taste puckered her tongue. Nick's heat opened her eyes.

No more acting like a baby.

She reached past the stick shift until her hand hovered above his lap in temporary indecision, then she dared herself and went for it big-time. She let her hand fall to the lap of Nick's jeans and spread her fingers across the folds.

"Darcy." Nick not so much spoke her name, as breathed it. He adjusted her hand and wriggled beneath her massaging fingers, his gaze on the road. If he looked down, he would've seen her whole arm shaking, a current running from her shoulder to her fingertips. She couldn't believe she was really and truly touching a boy. "I was going to suggest a movie, but this is way better. Hang on," he said.

She nabbed the door-side handle in time for an impromptu hairpin turn Nick navigated, jostling her hand from between his legs. She walked her trembling fingers back to his lap, and he kept her hand at bay, lacing his fingers between hers. "Not yet."

Back roads whizzed by, and Nick drove with one hand on the wheel. What did it matter where they were going? She had exactly what she needed sitting right beside her.

The car bumped along unpaved streets. Nick turned down a dirt driveway, avoided a major pothole, and jammed the stick shift into park. The sky hung heavy with swollen clouds. Strands of electricity rippled neon white. She could see them now, and her electrified hair stood on end. Beyond the tree-tops, clouds clashed. The first shock of lightning startled the air. The sky brightened. Her lips puckered.

"One, Mississippi. Two, Mississippi," Darcy counted, and Nick joined in, estimating their distance from the storm's center, the way Daddy had taught her. They barely reached six, and the sky exploded, the storm within a mile's reach. Darcy shrieked, even though she'd expected the noise.

Rain splattered against her T-shirt, and she rolled up her window. A tiny blue beat-up house, not much larger than a double-wide trailer, stood at the end of the pockmarked drive-way. Sickly evergreens dotted the front yard, and pine scent gave rise to the associated taste of peppermint candy canes, staple ornaments for the Klein family Christmas tree. Daddy, a devout atheist, never begrudged Mom's winter holiday with all the trimmings.

"Grandma's house," Nick said. "You okay with this?"

Nick asked her over to his house at least three times a week, where his two-job mom rarely lurked and his one-job grandma left him to his own devices. Where they'd be left to their own devices. No turning back.

Darcy licked her tingling lips. She leaned across the seat and kissed his mouth into a smile. "Thought you were gonna make me wait forever," he said.

Nick came around to open her door, and she kept one hand over the red foil packet in her pocket. Probably, Nick thought she was Little Miss Sexually Experienced, that she'd slept with half the boys in the school, or at least gotten them off. She was going to have to tell him the truth. Until Nick, she'd always stop boys when they tried to touch her.

She'd never let a boy get her all worked up. She'd never let a boy see her like that.

Nick followed her gaze to the ramshackle house. "You sure about this? We can find another place. . . ."

"This is fine." Did he think she was some kind of snob? She of the psycho family had visited her father in a variety of locked wards, so a shoddy bungalow didn't even register on her snubbing scale. She hurried out of the car and touched Nick's arm, morphing his scowl back into the dimpled smile she adored. Her vision fuzzed before her open eyes into a cascading zigzag pattern.

"You okay?" Nick took her arm, steadying her, as if she were a little old lady needing assistance to cross a street. Only he wasn't exactly the Boy Scout type.

"Sure." Her brother's mental health was cracking, her dad was rotting in the ground—his choice—and her mother was a control freak. Even the Mad Hatter wouldn't stick around for her father's warped anniversary. "Let's go inside."

The tentative raindrops had already doubled in size and number, splattering the grassless front yard, and tilling the soil into a seed-ready medium. The earth aroma she loved mingled with the rain smells, blending until she could no longer single out each distinct scent. This year, she might actually create the garden she'd tried last spring when nothing would grow.

"Wait." Nick pecked her cheek, a ploy for getting a good hold around her waist and sweeping her into his arms. Her stomach somersaulted with the sudden change of position, and the rain's patter heightened into a downpour. She nuzzled into his neck, the only dry spot, and dared a tentative nibble at the tender underside of his chin.

"You're not making this any easier." Nick stumbled across the rock-strewn yard, mud sucking at his sneakers, and then placed her lightly on her feet when they reached the front porch overhang. "Geez, you're light."

Stacks of boxes were piled high along each side of the tiny porch, and she squeezed through the cardboard-scented passage, eyes on her prize.

Nick fumbled through the keys on his keychain till he found the one for his house. "Ta-da. Beats the hell out of me why Grandma insists on locking the door. It's not like we're in the city. Not like anyone would want her stuff." He released the dead bolt, and the flimsy-looking door flung wide and knocked into the wall. He laughed, shaking his head at yet another pile of junk. More boxes snaked through the living room. Darcy spied a pea soup–green and pumpkin-orange flowered sofa that she could've sworn she'd seen on the side of Underhill Road.

Last week, she and Heather had watched a TV show about a woman who couldn't throw anything away. The pack rat even kept used Band-Aids, in case she wanted to revisit an old scab for its sentimental value. Darcy and Heather had screeched with laughter, trying to gross each other out over made-up collections: bloody tampons, dingle berries, earwax. Now evidence of a hoarding addiction didn't seem the least bit funny.

Nick knelt by the doorway leading to the rest of the house.

A skinny black-and-white cat padded down two steps, and then lay down at his feet. One look from Nick, and the cat started purring. Nick picked up the cat, held it to his cheek, and stroked it beneath the chin. The purring grew louder. In Darcy's limited experience with cats, they ran the gamut between complete owner loyalty and utter disinterest. She'd never seen one purr so readily though.

Nick let the cat down. "There you go, Sissy."

A girl. That explained the cat's over the top enthusiasm for Nick.

Nick leaned at the doorframe, picking long cat hairs off his T-shirt. "Want something to eat?"

She shrugged. She didn't want to seem rude, but Nick's grandmother's house didn't exactly pique her appetite. The smell of cigarette smoke made her a little queasy. The surroundings dampened her more personal hunger, too. "Some water would be great."

Nick led her up two steps to the kitchen and tickled her palm with his fingertips, rushing her blood flow to lower ground. If only she could block out the pack rat–infested house.

She looked past a sink full of soaking dishes, wilted nachos floating atop cheesy water. She chose not to notice maroon sauce splattering the stove top or the strands of burned spaghetti hanging from an open pot, like dried twigs ripe for snapping. But she couldn't ignore when something squished underfoot. She bent to pull noodles from her sneaker treads and crumbs dug beneath her fingernails. *Gross!*

Nick clattered through the sticky-looking cabinets, searching for two clean cups. "Ick, yuck. How embarrassing." Well, at least he was with her on that one. He produced two cloudy glasses, scrubbed them at the sink, and then held his hand under the tap, waiting for the water to run cold.

He handed her a slippery glass, and she dipped her tongue

into the tepid water and pretended to sip. Nick chugalugged his water, gulping until he'd drained the disgusting liquid, and came up gasping for air. "Sorry, I get thirsty when I'm nervous." He tried looking her in the eye, then broke off his gaze. "To tell you the truth, I don't know if I can do this. You're, like, too pretty."

"Thanks." Okay, he thought she was pretty and they were going to have sex, the real deal, going all the way. So what was the problem? Didn't he like her?

He set his glass on the countertop behind her. "I can barely even look at you at school. I get so worked up, I think maybe I'm gonna lose it right there in front of my locker."

The image in her mind's eye of Nick standing in the middle of the high school hallway, scrambling to conceal a wet mess oozing down the leg of his jeans seemed as real as the solid boy in front of her. She couldn't say a word. She just stood there blushing like the virgin that she was while Nick played with her hair. He kissed her, and an unmistakable bulge pressed through his pants. Nick might've thought he was shy, but his body had other ideas. "I have something to show you."

Her mouth itched, like when she'd jam her pillow into her mouth to keep from crying. He'd better not pull it out right here, right in the middle of the filthy kitchen. She wanted to do it, sort of, but not like this, not like some kind of skuzzy whore.

"Oh, my God, I scared you. You're shaking."

"No, you didn't." Maybe she should leave, break up with him right now, and forget about the stupid prom. Who cared about limo rides and floor-length gowns with delicate spaghetti straps? Who cared about dance contests and prom queens? Happy endings belonged to other girls, those whose fathers didn't shove gun barrels into their mouths and blast their heads into a million little pieces.

A million little pieces. The bullet that killed her father must've scrambled her brains, too. Whatever she felt, whatever she thought she felt, kept changing like the weather.

"Darce, I just wanted to show you *my room.*"

Yeah, she bet he did.

What the heck was wrong with her? Did she want to give it up or not? She'd better decide fast. Sometimes, she was certain equal and opposing forces lived in her, battling until she couldn't feel anything at all, couldn't be certain of her own name.

Nick examined her face, as if trying to figure out what she was thinking. Good luck with that. "I would never do anything you didn't want me to," Nick said. "I'm not like that. I'm not my—I'd never hurt a girl."

She nodded, and Nick's flash of annoyance vanished. "Follow me."

Imagination offered up way too many guesses as to what Nick had in mind, if not sex. Maybe he'd show her his latest marijuana seedlings angling toward a makeshift sunlamp. Maybe his claim that he wouldn't hurt her was a joke, the standard lie of a serial rapist. Maybe he'd butchered the mail carrier, buried the bloody pieces beneath the floorboards, and slept to the rhythm of his victim's telltale heartbeat, an Edgar Allan Poe copycat murderer.

Her telltale heart pounded in her chest. Maybe Nick wanted to share some really strong weed he'd hidden under his pillowcase. That'd work.

Nick opened the closed bedroom door and stepped back to let her enter first.

"Wow." She hadn't meant to say it out loud, but really, wow. Walking into Nick's bedroom reminded her not of Edgar Allan Poe's gothic *The Tell-Tale Heart,* but of C. S. Lewis's mythic Narnia tales. She'd made her way through the jam-packed wardrobe of his grandmother's house, and now found herself entering another world.

Unlike her messy bedroom, no clutter obstructed Nick's tiny room. She could see clear from the doorway to the windows outlining the opposing wall. A bed with a gleaming pine headboard and a clean—she couldn't get over that one—shearling comforter nestled beneath two windows. A cable ran between and across the two windows' frames, and faded denim curtains gave the illusion of a single jumbo window. Air billowed the curtain and helped dry the freshly painted robin's-egg-blue walls. The wind's direction was on their side, and not even a mist trickled through the screens.

Nick shut the door, keeping the new-paint smell in and keeping out the less pleasant odors that stank up the rest of the house. Two bright-orange lockers functioned as Nick's bureau, fitting neatly against the right-hand wall. He kicked off his high-tops and walked across the pasta-free vinyl flooring.

Darcy unlaced her sneakers, following his lead. She had to sit down and touch the comforter's nub and process this new information about Nick. She got it. Nick didn't only want to show her his bedroom. He wanted to show her who he was, separate and distinct from his less than stellar family unit. Nick made a selection from the iPod docked on his makeshift bureau, and the music played.

"Oh, I have that album. I like it." She adored the scary-cool Nickelback cover art, too. An aquamarine eye was crying, shedding molten metal tears. She knew the drill: boys cried bullets. She appreciated the music better after adding the lyrics to her MP3 library and studying every word. Songs about family dysfunction and desperation, losing hope and smoking dope.

Nick crawled over the bed to open one of the windows the rest of the way. The rain upstaged the rock music—pelting the tin roof, rushing across the gutter, and surging into the rain barrel she'd noticed by the front porch.

Nick nestled in beside her. "First song's my favorite. Re-

minds me what I need to do if my dad ever breaks the restraining order Mom took out against him. Reminds me of
when I saw my parents fighting for the first time."

The song "Never Again" was about a guy who beat his
wife. Until the day the wife decided she'd had enough. Then
she shot him.

Darcy's throat went dry, like when she'd climbed a tree,
looked down, and the earth tilted on its axis. "What do you
need to do, Nick?"

When she caught his gaze, he flashed his trademark dimpled grin, but his eyes darkened. "Kick his ass, of course.
Thought you knew the song." He laughed—a sharp burst that
sounded forced—and then jumped up and turned up the volume.

The kid in the song, the son of the wife beater, did want to
kick his father's ass. True.

Daddy used to joke about killing himself, or at least
claimed he was joking. Also true.

Nick snuggled back next to her and curled an arm around
her shoulder, so gentle. He swallowed, and sadness edged his
eyes. Sad enough to kick some serious ass, but her Nick wasn't
a killer. "So what was I saying?"

"About your parents fighting?" she said. "About your
dad?"

Her parents had never really argued. Not unless you counted
the hushed discussions that trickled through closed doors. Always about the meds, always about why Daddy needed to go
back on lithium. Mom could've played a recording of the same
lecture every few months. Daddy never listened to her medically
sound reasoning. Her father should've taken a restraining order
out against himself.

Thinking about her dad brought up a clear image, as if
Daddy were in the room with her.

Nick shook his head, stared at her lips. "Uh-uh. Before

that." He tickled her waist, coming at her with both hands until she'd scrambled backward against the pine headboard.

Darcy swiped at her eyes, pretended the tears were from laughing instead of crying. "When I was little, I liked to play Doctor Darcy and bring my dad Band-Aids for his forehead. Sometimes, when he was having one of his moods, he'd bang his head against the wall until it bled. I was, like, four." Nick stroked her hand, and the Daddy image faded, blissfully faded, then disappeared entirely. To her surprise, Nick looked her in the eye, his expression neutral. "How old were you when you first saw your parents fighting?" she asked.

"It doesn't matter, Darce. I don't exactly feel like talking right now. Know what I mean?" He hugged her, kissing her neck. Nick's ear peeked through strands of glossy blond hair— so cute—and she kissed the bare lobe, then whispered, "It matters."

He untangled himself from her, stood up, sat back down. When she rubbed his back, he gifted her with a Nick smile she'd never seen before, the corners of both his eyes and mouth turned down this time. He cocked his head and shrugged like a little boy, and she imagined him as a towhead in fire engine– red footed pajamas. She couldn't see inside of him, but she sensed he was about to give her a box seat.

"I was maybe five or six, when I first saw my parents going at it." He paused and shook his head. "You don't want to hear this."

"Yes. I do." She stroked his hand, taking the lead, and he followed her to the headboard, as far back as they could go.

Nick closed his eyes most of the way, either to make re-membering easier or avoid embarrassment. "It was the middle of the night, and I was thirsty. I remember thinking I can hear my parents talking, so I'll go ask for a glass of water. What's the harm in that? I tiptoed up to my bedroom door, and by the time I got there, they were already going at it. Not really yelling but talking really loud. Well, at least he was. I couldn't even hear her voice. She was doing her thing. You know, talking real soft, practically whispering, so she didn't make him any angrier. Don't want to make the big guy angry." He stopped talking and took a labored breath.

"It's okay, Nick. Go on."

Another breath, and he squeezed her hand. "He was right in her face, and she couldn't just walk away. She couldn't get away 'cause that would've made him angry, too. *Everything* pissed him off. Mom always left my door open a bit so she could hear me if I needed her, you know, and I was peeking through the crack." Nick sat up straighter, opening his eyes all the way. "I swear I don't know what she said to him, probably didn't even matter what it was. He was just aching for a fight. He . . . he got even closer, yelled point-blank, and this part I heard. She said two words: 'Nicky's sleeping.' And just like that he threw her onto the floor, started whaling on her like she was a punching bag. Just whaling the shit out of her." Nick stared straight ahead, no doubt revisiting the scene that often tormented him.

Darcy could relate. "And he's not even around to answer your questions," she said. "That's the worst part. Like, how could he do what he did? Why couldn't he stop himself? He was supposed to be the grown-up, so why didn't he *act* like one and get it together?" Their Daddy stories weren't exactly alike but close enough for her to sympathize. Fathers were supposed to protect you, not kill themselves, not beat on your mother. Why did everything have to hurt when she just wanted to feel good?

They turned toward each other, and Nick leaned in only partway for a kiss, making her come the rest of the way to him. She slid down onto the bed pillows, and he edged down beside her. The rain was pounding so hard, drowning out her thoughts.

She just wanted to feel good.

Under the covers, warmth and darkness. The delicious closeness of Nick's body pressing against her and producing the kind of sparks she'd never before let a boy ignite. Periwinkle splotches beneath her closed lids mingled with orangey-red orbs of light.

Nick unbuttoned her jeans and slipped his hand into her underwear. No way she could deny how close she was to going over the top. She took her mouth off his, and he started in on her neck. "Nick, stop."

He glanced up at her. "It's okay, babe. I've got protection." He removed his expert hand, kicked his pants and briefs off from around his ankles, and then lunged to extract a half-empty box of condoms from under-bed storage.

Nick calling her *babe* should've cooled her down. The half-empty box of condoms should've sent up warning flares: call off the misguided mission. But amazingly, energy still sped through her body, seeking an exit route.

She just wanted to feel good.

He crawled back toward her, squashed red box in hand, massive smile on his face. She almost hated to tell him. "Nick, I'm a virgin."

Two-second delay before the big horny grin faded, then returned. "Never kid a kidder, Darce." He knelt with one knee on the mattress and pulled his T-shirts up over his head, making sure she reviewed a whole lot more than just his unbelievable cut abs.

"I'm completely serious. I've never even let a boy touch me until you." She'd never seen a boy without his clothes on, either. Accidentally walking in on her brother didn't count. She was still wearing her underwear and T-shirt, but she shivered. She pulled the covers over her legs and waited for Nick's reaction.

"The hottest girl in school is a virgin." Nick wouldn't stop smiling, as if he wasn't going to dump her and tell all the boys at school what they'd done.

This time would be the worst. This time the story would be true. This time she'd hoped Nick was different and really liked her.

She got up on shaky legs, looked away from him, and started pulling up her jeans bunched around one ankle like a little girl's skip-along toy. She could walk part of the way home, and then hitch. Hitching wasn't so bad; she and Heather had thumbed rides all over southern New Hampshire last summer.

"Don't go!" Nick grabbed her hand. "I'll take care of you."

Her near-sleepless night must've turned her goofy. For a second there, she thought Nick was proposing marriage, of all ridiculous things, instead of sex. Despite her best efforts, she couldn't prevent the giggles from trickling from her belly and bursting through her mouth. "I'm sorry! I'm sorry!" She let go of Nick's hand and left the poor guy waiting for her fit of laughter to come to a close. The poor *naked* guy. She fell back onto the bed with her jeans still dangling.

No use. Every time she looked at Nick, she cracked up again. "It's not you, I swear!" Darcy turned toward the window. She tried listening to the swish of rain and the background rock music, tried focusing on the subtle shades of blue in the window's denim curtains. She shoved her face into Nick's pillow, but the sound of muffled laughter only made her hysterics grow.

The mattress shifted, and Nick rubbed between her shoulder blades, trying to calm her down. "Heard somewhere that people laugh when they're nervous. Guess it's true 'cause the day my old principal found a dime bag of pot on me, I cracked up in the guy's face. Told him, 'No, really. I've got no clue where the crap came from, never seen it before.' Even asked him what the stuff was in the bag. Was it, like, fertilizer or something?" Nick lay down behind her and whispered in her ear. "You don't have to be scared, but it's okay if you are. It's okay."

Nick really got her. Darcy rolled back around, smiling. "You are so smart, maybe even a genius." No, seriously, she wasn't trying to be . . . what was that word? *Facetious.* Only her real friends had the guts to tell her the truth about herself. First Heather, then Cam, and now Nick.

Darcy propped on one elbow, working hard not to laugh despite her fluttering belly. She swiped a hand in front of her face and pantomimed pulling her expression rigid. "I want you to know that I'm not being facetious."

"Okay." Nick removed her dangling jeans and tossed them across the room. He reclined next to her and caressed her from ankle to waist, until his fingers teased her belly. "You're not whatever it was you just said." He rubbed across the outside of her underwear, paused his hand right where she liked it. "So do you want to do it?" His hand started moving again, and he brushed his lips against hers, like the flick of a feather, leaving her in need of more intense pressure.

"Wait a minute." Darcy sat up, wrestled her tight-fitting T-shirt over her head. Her mother's many warnings about sex floated through her mind.

She could get pregnant. Even the health teacher at school had to admit that when used properly, condoms prevented pregnancy ninety-nine percent of the time. Wicked good odds, as far as she was concerned.

Disease. Condoms once again galloped to the rescue, brave little knights in red capes.

A broken heart. This last warning almost launched a fresh barrage of giggles. Maybe sleep deprivation made her fearless; her legs weren't even shaking anymore, at least not in a bad way. Maybe the last year had toughened her up, maybe her entire crazy life had led her to this place where she couldn't imagine any boy breaking her heart. What hurt could possibly compare to Daddy's suicide?

Just the same, something was missing.

She'd imagined doing it for the first time so often, maybe she'd ruined it. Nothing could compare to the fantasy movies in her mind.

But she still wanted to feel good. "Do you think we could—" She paused, stalling to gain courage. "Do you think we could maybe just touch a little?"

Now it was Nick's turn to laugh. "I think we could touch one hell of a lot."

She unhooked her bra and slipped it off before she could change her mind, her heart pounding louder than rainfall on the tin roof. Nick's stare revved up the thudding, making her wonder whether fifteen-year-olds could suffer heart attacks. He held back the bedding, and she eased into their cozy bed cave. Only the swatch of her cotton underpants remained between them, a just for show boundary. Nick yanked her underwear down over her hips, and she pushed them off the rest of the way, making her decision final.

What did Nick think he was doing to her boobs, squishing them like glitter-filled gel toys? He stopped kissing her. "Darcy, I'm sorry, but I can't hold on. You're gonna have to finish me fast." Finish? Back up. She'd just gotten started.

He took her hand, demonstrating exactly what he'd meant by *fast*. The way he drove should've clued her in; the kid had a need for speed. Okay, this was both boring and gross. She counted out two sets of twenty, and her arm tired.

"Don't stop." Nick scrunched up his face and gave a series of embarrassing wounded sounds, losing it all over her hands, losing way more than the well-directed spoonful she'd imagined.

Yuck! Talk about disgusting! Darcy wiped her hands on his sheets, depositing the slime all over his nice clean bedding.

The rain was still pelting the roof and Nickelback was still trickling through the speakers, although she didn't much care about the lyrics. Nick sprawled across the bed, eyes shut and mouth slightly open, as if he'd exhausted himself when she'd done all the work. She touched his arm and smiled when he twitched in his sleep.

A phone rang somewhere in the house, and soft chatter she'd wrongly identified as rainfall clarified into women's voices. She could hear two women talking on the front porch, fussing at the stuck lock, and sending the lightweight door flying into the living room wall. She shook Nick by the shoulder and whispered as loudly as she dared, "Someone's here. Wake up!" He only stirred slightly.

Oh, shit. Shit, shit, shit. Normally she'd care, even worry, that she couldn't uncover a more suitable word to express herself and she was taking the lazy way out. But right now, who the fuck cared? Her jeans lay in a crumpled heap halfway across the room, which meant they were halfway to the door that might open any second. She jumped into her underpants, nabbed her T-shirt and bra from the foot of the bed, made a mad dash across the bedroom, and slid into her jeans. She didn't bother waiting until she'd fought her way into her bra and T-shirt before renewing Nick wake-up duty. "Wake up now! We're not alone!"

That did it. Nick scrambled into his clothes and yanked the comforter over the entire bed mess. Good, the phone had finally stopped ringing. One of the women must've answered the call. That should give them a few more much-needed minutes to figure out a plan. Even with their clothes on and the bed covered, the whole scene looked suspiciously rumpled. If her mother ever found her alone with a boy in her bedroom and the door closed, she'd send down a life sentence and ground her for life. Just for starters.

A tentative tap at the door sent Darcy into a panic. Already, her cheeks were burning. She could lie to her mother, but a stranger might not be so easy to fool.

"No biggie," Nick whispered to her, and then headed across the room. "Just a minute! I accidentally locked the door."

"Nicky, I've got a woman on the phone looking for her daughter?" Probably the woman speaking through the door wasn't shouting, but it sure sounded that way, louder than the clash of thunder.

Nick opened the door, revealing a woman of indeterminable age—not really old, but worn out like a birthday balloon two days post party. The woman offered her the cordless receiver. "Darcy? Your mother's on the phone."

Quick, call 911. She was having a major heart attack.

Chapter 14

Daughter Darcy was definitely off her game.

Home from Ever True Cemetery with Troy and Elle, rain-spattered and muddy, Laura had found Maggie meditating in the living room, and Laura had basked in the light of her peace. Until Laura had followed Troy upstairs and discovered her daughter missing, the evidence trail as troubling as her absence. In her haste, Darcy had left her underwear drawer open, revealing a twelve-count box of Trojans with only eleven remaining. To top it off, a lone joint had taken the place of the missing prophylactic. At least Darcy had taken protection.

Nick's phone number had been even easier to find, dangling from Darcy's fabric memo board, thumbing its nose at Laura. *Neener, neener.* When Laura had called, Nick's mother, Hope, said she'd just gotten home. She hadn't known Darcy was in her son's bedroom, but she hadn't seemed all that surprised, either.

Laura peered at the driveway through the distortion of antique glass, waiting for Nick to return her daughter. She would've driven across town to retrieve her daughter herself, but she wanted the two of them here, on her home turf. One look at them together would likely speak volumes.

"I am so sorry," Maggie said, for the third or fourth time. "This is the last thing you need."

"Not your fault," Laura said. "She played me." *Please don't make me go to the cemetery. I need to remember Daddy* my way. Cue the tiny violins and Darcy's pleading look. Cue the tears. Darcy didn't want to explore her feelings about her father; she wanted to explore her boyfriend.

Laura couldn't even wrap her mind around the idea of her fifteen-year-old daughter having sex. She prayed she'd get to the truth and Darcy's little afternoon adventure wouldn't produce any lasting consequences. Like a grandchild, for instance.

Tires ground into the wet driveway, and Elle handed Laura a cup of tension-tamer tea. Wiper blades whirred and cut out. An engine coughed to a halt. Laura took a sip of tea and burned the tip of her tongue.

"Sure you don't want us to stay?" Elle asked, even though she likely knew the answer. Laura relied on her friends for moral support, but the kids she handled herself.

"I'm sure," Laura said.

Maggie looked at her sideways.

"I promise not to harm the dear children, just make them squirm."

"Wish I could stay for the show," Elle said, and gave her a pat on the arm. Maggie and Elle ducked out the door, and then Elle popped back in. She held her forefinger and thumb up to her ear, the call-me sign, and Laura nodded.

Darcy slunk in the house first, Nick two steps behind. When Laura had spoken to Darcy on the phone, she'd told her to make sure Nick came in the house with her. She'd told Darcy she'd like to have a word with him. She'd told Darcy she was not pleased. She'd wanted to give Darcy and Nick something to chew on during the car ride home.

What she'd given them, she now realized, was time to coordinate their alibi.

"What happened?" Laura asked Darcy, and her daughter's big eyes got even rounder.

"What do you mean?" Darcy pulled her head back, and twin pink splotches bloomed on her cheeks.

Dear Lord, give her strength. Laura wasn't about to question Nick about what he and Darcy had done while they were alone at his house. That interrogation she'd save for Darcy. But her daughter's instant embarrassment reminded Laura of how she'd sat in the front row of Professor Jack Klein's class trying to hide the shame firing her cheeks.

Laura took a breath and reminded herself to exhale so she wouldn't turn blue. "Let's start from the beginning. Why did you sneak out of the house, today of all days?"

Darcy opened her mouth, then snapped it shut. Her gaze dropped to her untied sneakers. "I don't know."

Laura tried Nick. "Didn't you know Darcy wasn't supposed to leave the house? Didn't you know she sneaked out of the house to be with you?"

His gaze darted to the ceiling, evading. He edged closer to Darcy till they stood arm to arm. Darcy straightened her spine. She peered from beneath her paintbrush lashes and tugged at a hairstyle that bore a striking resemblance to morning bed head.

Laura sighed and decided to play good cop. "I'm sorry, Nick, but if you encourage Darcy to go break house rules, I can't allow her to see you." She was bluffing, sort of. Nothing united a couple faster than having to sneak around behind people's backs. That explained why she and Jack had invited Laura's dorm mates and Jack's colleagues to their wedding.

Nick shook his head, met Laura's gaze, and the words gushed out of him. "She told me she had family stuff, but she didn't have to go. I'm sorry, Mrs. Klein, really sorry. Honestly, I didn't know."

Laura squinted at Nick, decided he was lying his ass off to try and save Darcy's. He had to have known her family was busy visiting her father's grave while she was busy, well, getting her hair rumpled.

"This cannot happen ever again. No sneaking out. And for goodness sake, the two of you," she said, shifting her gaze between Darcy and Nick. "No lying."

"He's telling the truth," Darcy muttered.

"Darcy Ann!"

Darcy jostled, as if she hadn't realized what she was doing. Her lying had become that automatic.

"Do we understand each other?" Laura asked Nick.

"Yes, ma'am. No sneaking out and no lying," he parroted. At least the boy could memorize rules. Only time would tell whether he'd any intention of following them.

"You can leave."

Nick turned to Darcy, and his gaze went hazy, as though he thought he could kiss her good-bye.

Laura opened the door for Nick. "Right now."

A look passed between Nick and Darcy in place of a good-bye kiss, and Nick stepped out the door into the afternoon drizzle. His on-its-last-legs-looking car started on the first try and screeched from the driveway, no doubt leaving a nice deep rut.

"Upstairs, please." Laura took Darcy by the shoulders and turned her around.

Darcy brushed off her hands. "Don't touch me," Darcy said, and Laura spoke without thinking, entirely from her bruised heart: "You're grounded."

"What else is new?"

That wasn't fair. Laura only grounded Darcy when she'd

broken one of her many reasonable rules, each and every one set up to keep her daughter safe. She didn't like grounding her daughter. It had been nearly nine months since Darcy's punishment for the skinny-dipping incident.

Laura paused on the stairway to regain her composure. Breathe in, breathe out. She caught up with Darcy in her bedroom, shutting her underwear drawer. "I've already found your stash," Laura said. "The joint, I got rid of, but I left all of the condoms. Minus the one that's missing."

Darcy bit at her lower lip and reached past Laura to swipe a lip gloss from her dresser top. She wrenched off the cap and smeared wild cherry–flavored gloss across her lips.

"Angel . . ." Laura began, even though the angel-Darcy from last night was nowhere to be found. Long ago, Maggie, mother to three grown daughters, had warned Laura about the Dr. Jekyll and Mr. Hyde stage teenage girls went through. Laura never really believed it would happen to her daughter until Mr. Hyde had smacked her upside the head.

Laura sat on the edge of Darcy's unmade bed. "Talk to me. What's going on?"

Darcy capped the lip gloss, mashed her lips together, and set it back on the dresser.

"Look, I realize you like Nick, and he certainly seems like he's fond of you. I just don't want you doing something you'll regret. And no matter how smart you are—" She caught Darcy's attention. "No matter how smart, you simply cannot make an informed decision if you're stoned."

Darcy couldn't hide the sneer in her voice. "We weren't stoned."

"I'm very glad to hear that," Laura said. "So something happened? Darcy, do you need to see a doctor?"

Darcy's gaze flashed on Laura. She gathered the scatter of books from her floor and stomped over to her bookcase, arranged the books into a tidy stack of five.

Either Laura's question had lighted on the truth or she'd pissed Darcy off with the intrusion. Laura shuddered a sigh. She was about to bargain with God and toss up a prayer to keep Darcy safe from Jack's risk-taking gene, when her mind picture turned on a dime into an image of her teenage self. She'd offered herself to Jack, as though her virginity were a jacket she'd outgrown. One heedless act had changed the course of her entire life. She didn't regret it. How could she? But she'd be damned if she let Darcy follow her example on this one.

Using a boy's attention as a substitute for her father's love could only lead to further heartache. Laura should know. "Were you *intimate* with Nick?"

Expressionless, Darcy just stared at her mother. It must've killed her not to respond to Laura's word choice.

Okay then. "I don't want you to have sex before you're ready. At least not until you've graduated from high school. Although I'd prefer college graduation as a precursor, I'm a re-alist."

This claim earned a snort from her daughter.

"You're too young, Darcy, and having sex doesn't make you mature. If anything, it messes up the process."

Darcy knelt, picked up a pair of jeans from the floor, and found a neighboring hanger.

Laura went to Darcy, got down to her level, and stroked her cheek with the back of her hand. She gazed at a girl hell-bent on rushing headlong into womanhood and saw herself in her daughter's eyes. For a moment, Laura thought Darcy might speak. Instead, she brushed at the spot where her mother had touched her face.

Just like her father. Jack wouldn't listen to Laura's sage ad-vice, either. No, he'd nod and smile, and then do whatever the heck he pleased as soon as he got the chance.

Laura stood. She rubbed at the grass stains spoiling the

knees of her slacks—evidence of where she'd knelt by Jack's grave, seeking closure. It made sense that at Ever True Cemetery, she'd felt an almost imperceptible lightening. Jack's body rested in peace. But what remained of the stubborn as hell facet of her husband's spirit was sitting on the floor, pretending to sort her wash and stonewalling like a pro.

Chapter 15

Ten past two on Friday usually meant the beginning of the Darcy party: free time and friends. Instead, today's end of D block bell would usher in her first full weekend of grounding. Two entire days stuck with her family, no friends allowed, practically constituted abuse.

Vanessa bounced by Darcy's seat, depositing a scrunched-up note into her hand. What was wrong with her? Darcy had told her she was grounded for sneaking out with Nick and getting caught in his room, so she couldn't hang out after school. Loud-mouth turned Queen of Nosey had stared at her and Nick throughout lunch period. Her entire table of look-alike Vanessa Wannabes took turns ogling them, giving Darcy the big-time creeps. Nick, on the other hand, seemed to enjoy the attention, making a show of feeding her black olives until the memory of his naked body made her chest ache.

Darcy slipped the note beneath her desk, unfolded the crumpled paper, and read Vanessa's oversized scribble: *Give it up, Darcy! Did you and Nick do it or what?*

Darcy's smile started at her lips and flooded the rest of her body. That was for her to know and Vanessa to never find out. Let the pervert imagine whatever she liked. This morning, Vanessa had asked Darcy if she and Nick had enjoyed the box of condoms she'd given Darcy along with the ridiculous cucumber demonstration. Amazing how a few well-chosen words uttered during first period could crack Vanessa's teeny-tiny brain.

Vanessa turned around in her seat, looked over her shoulder, and made sure Darcy watched her doing Vanessa's favorite pantomime. Eyes partway closed like a blind mole, she scrunched her face and pushed a shiny drop of spittle through pursed lips. For the first time ever, Vanessa's imitation of a penis erupting made Darcy's cheeks burn. Vanessa was getting way too personal, guessing at what had happened between her and Nick and simultaneously making fun of it. Nearly as mortifying as her mother's useless sex lecture.

Darcy clutched the strap of her backpack and angled a foot into the aisle. She zoned out the office announcements squeezing through the tinny intercom and stared up at the clock's fat black numbers until the trill of the bell put her out of her Vanessa misery. Darcy jumped from her seat and flew past the desks, then race-walked through the traffic-clogged hallway and burst out of the front of the school doors. She leaned against a concrete pillar, gazing up into the cloudless sky until the familiar scent of tropical fruit came up behind her.

"What's with you? I called your name, and you kept going." Heather unfastened a crooked purple hair clip, pulling her perfectly straight blond hair into the kind of smooth curve Darcy could never manage with her wild hair. Welcome to the land of excess. Boobs too big, hips too wide, legs too long for pants that otherwise fit her just right. Darcy and her best friend stood at the exact same height, but Heather was the only one who looked like a Barbie doll.

"So when are you off grounding?" Heather clicked her barrette into place, and a second wave of tropical conditioner scent rolled over Darcy. Mangos, pineapples, and an endnote of coconut.

"Sunday night."

Heather groaned. "But that's, like, *after* the weekend. I really, really need to talk to you now." Heather's eyes darted to the side.

"Uh, what are we doing now, if not talking?"

Heather sighed. "You sit with Nick at lunch. Whenever we meet at your locker, he pops up, like he's a stalker or something." She peered over her shoulder. "Okay, I wasn't going to say anything, but I get a really bad feeling from him. He's kind of scary."

"Uh-huh." Darcy thought Nick was kind of sweet, and Heather was totally jealous.

A hand from nowhere tickled Darcy's waist. She squealed, and Nick jumped out from behind the pillar.

"See what I mean?" Heather said.

Nick ignored Heather's glare. He hugged Darcy as if he hadn't seen her in weeks, even nibbled at her neck. "Ready to roll?"

"I gotta go. I'm in serious trouble if I don't get back on time." Darcy mouthed, *Sorry.* Heather didn't know Nick the way she did. She hadn't seen his sensitive side.

"I'm parked down the road." Nick wrapped his arm around her shoulder and turned her away from Heather.

Mom never allowed phone privileges during grounding, but Darcy usually managed to sneak in a call or two when her mother went to bed, her after-hours calling plan.

Darcy leaned around Nick and yelled to Heather. "I'll call you after hours! Okay, LU?" *LU*, their secret code for *Love you.*

Heather instantly brightened. "Right back at you, sister!"

"Could you call me after hours, too?" Nick asked.

He was so clever, picking up on her little get-around-grounding trick. "Sure thing," she said.

Nick snatched up her hand and swung it between them as

they squeezed down the narrow sidewalk lining the busy road. "She's got it in for me, you know."

"Heather? I don't think so." Heather was feeling left out, but what could Darcy do? Heather knew the drill. Whenever one of them was seeing a boy, their friendship took a backseat. They'd agreed on it years ago.

Next week, she'd figure out a girls-only day, plan on some shopping therapy—try on spring clothes they couldn't afford, test body butters, and gobble up ice-cream sundaes. Oh, and she couldn't forget looking for the right prom dress. A color and cut that would show off her body, but keep within the school dress code would definitely prove a challenge. Maybe she could even convince Heather to go to the prom, too. Note to self: find out if Stevie was still looking for a prom date. Getting ready for a big dance with her best friend, helping each other with hair and makeup, was almost as much fun as the event. Almost as much fun as going with her best friend to the ladies' room and talking about their dates.

The middle school track team ran down the street, Troy waving at her in his usual village idiot way. He looked normal on the outside, but next week Daddy's shrink would look inside of him to decide whether last Friday night's fit meant Troy was more like Daddy than she was. According to Mom, getting Troy an appointment with Super Shrink within ten days of her phone call evidenced a major miracle. Darcy waved like a fool, right back at her lucky little brother.

Nick opened his car's passenger door. Two spaces down the row a metallic orange Element backed out, jam-packed with boys Darcy recognized but didn't really know. In sync, windows rolled down and masculine voices called out, as if rehearsed. "Darcy!"

She giggled and held her hand up to wave.

Nick stepped in front of her and waved using only one finger.

The Element stopped right next to them, and the driver, Jared, a boy she'd talked to a few times at parties, hung his head out the window, dark blond hair covering his eyes. "Hey, chill out, dude!"

Nick marched to the driver's window. "You talking to me?"

"Yeah, I'm talking to you! I said chill—"

Nick whacked the windshield with both hands. "Get out of the car!"

Darcy froze, and her stomach plunged into her socks. She thought of Daddy eating lasagna once. Three uneventful bites, and he'd Frisbee-tossed his plate across the room, beheading a bouquet of pink peonies before gouging the wall.

She thought of Troy's out of nowhere dinner fit.

This was not happening.

Jared's car edged backward. "What's your problem?"

"Get out of the fucking car!"

"Nick, stop," Darcy said, but her high-pitched voice barely rose above a whisper.

Nick grabbed the top of the driver's window, and it started rolling up. He jogged backward alongside the car, jerked his fingers out of the way at the last possible moment. Wheels squealed, and the Element hightailed it down the road, deep voices yelling at Nick.

Darcy ducked into the Monte Carlo, trying to catch her breath, as though she'd run alongside Jared's car, dangling from the window, too. Her T-shirt stuck under her arms, and she pulled at the fabric. She was shell-shocked and paranoid. Everyone wasn't bipolar, like her father. Everyone got angry, right? Anger was normal.

Nick went around to his side and slipped behind the wheel. He slammed his door. He kneaded the leather steering wheel cover. Glared through the windshield. A faint mist of sweat beaded on his upper lip.

"What was that about?" she asked, and her lips tingled.

"I don't like them looking at you." Nick turned his glare on Darcy, and her chest flushed. "And I don't like you flirting with them."

"I wasn't." She couldn't think of what she'd done, other than wave. Nick had once said he wasn't good at sharing, but this seemed over the top jealous. Still, she couldn't help feeling a thrill at his possessiveness, as if she were a girl worth fighting for.

"Damn!" Nick whacked the steering wheel, and she startled. "You don't get it," he said. "Do you think they're your friends?"

Darcy stared at Nick, his wide-eyed intensity, and her hand edged toward the door handle. Sure, anger was normal, but was Nick?

Nick's mouth edged into a sneer, and he shook his head. "Do you think they just wanna hang out with you? You think they just wanna talk?"

A few months ago, she'd heard rumors Jared had said she had a good personality. He thought she was pretty, too. But he'd never asked her out, never—

"They want to *do* you, Darcy. You know what I'm saying?" Nick clenched his jaw. His gaze slid away from her, and that scared her more than his outburst.

If she'd heard the nice rumors about Jared, then he must've heard the not-nice rumors about her. That explained why he'd never asked her out and why a whole carload of boys she barely knew had called her name.

Nick, on the other hand, knew for sure the rumors about her weren't true, and he still wanted to go out with her.

Darcy touched his cheek, then turned his face so she could see his eyes, and his expression softened. That's right, her sweet Nick.

"That stuff, that stuff I told you about my folks, about my

dad. That's just between us, okay? I don't go around telling people my life story." Nick's pupils reflected two identical Darcy pictures, like black-and-white arcade photos.

Darcy knew about keeping secrets. Secrets meant love. She nodded and swallowed twice. "Your secret's safe with me." She found his lips, that familiar hard bite of cinnamon sweetness, and sighed into his mouth, but Nick wouldn't smile.

Darcy remembered something Nick had tried to give her months ago. She remembered the look on his face when she'd turned him down. He was wearing that look right now.

Darcy took off one of the diamond earrings that never left her ears and pushed it to the bottom of her pocket. She un-hooked Nick's gold hoop and snapped it onto her naked ear-lobe. Nick nodded, and a smile flooded his face, the look that meant he thought she was special.

Slowly, he backed the car from the spot. Darcy fastened her seat belt across her chest. Her hand wandered to her earlobe, and she traced the hoop's curve, the not-Daddy shape. Back in third grade, another girl's dad had died in a head-on collision with an elderly driver going the wrong way on 101. Darcy had barely known the classmate, but she'd cried for a week, along with the rest of the town.

Darcy stared straight ahead, slid her sunglasses from her backpack and onto her face. She couldn't let Nick see tears stinging the corners of her eyes. She couldn't explain what she didn't understand. She could understand missing someone who'd died by accident.

But how could you miss someone who'd left you on pur-pose?

Chapter 16

In the early days of A.S.—after suicide—Daddy's natural citrus-musk scent had hung heavy in his writing studio and clung to all the surfaces. Back then, Darcy couldn't tolerate hanging out there for more than a few minutes at a time. Entering with a full stomach pretty much ensured serious muscles cramps, not to mention nausea extending to her fingernails.

Months ago, Darcy had searched Daddy's desk for his smell and came up with nothing but a nose full of lemon polish.

Today, she knew what she wanted. But first, she needed a snack.

Darcy let the screen door slam, announcing her return. Mom must be losing it. She didn't pounce on her, asking about her day. Didn't happen upon her, checking out whether the outfit she was wearing this morning had miraculously transformed into scandalously revealing non school-approved clothing. Okay, so where was she? She'd better be home.

Darcy kicked off her sneakers. Her mother's giggle reached around the corner. Then another laugh, deep and throaty, a full manly guffaw. Mom's buddy Aidan was having trouble keeping to his part of the house again. For once, Darcy would take this as a good sign.

Might as well go for it, after that snack.

Darcy peered into the kitchen. Mom was sitting sideways, her legs crossed in faded jeans, her pink-painted toenails shimmering. Darcy squinted. Her mother rarely painted anything except walls.

Aidan was staring at Mom as if she were the most fascinating woman on earth. He was grinning like that goofy kid who'd followed Darcy around freshman year, drooling on his shoes. Hands resting on his thighs, Aidan leaned back in his seat, legs falling apart at the knees in the way only a guy could sit, the designated Y-chromosome position. Give those manly 'nads breathing space.

He couldn't have seen her, but he stopped laughing and sat straight up as soon as she came around the corner. "Hey!"

Mom uncrossed her legs and offered Darcy an explanation she hadn't asked for. "Aidan has today off and, lucky me, he happened to pull into the driveway right when I needed help with the groceries."

Darcy glanced around the kitchen. Mom's usual Friday lineup of grocery-filled blue canvas bags blocked the cabinets. Okay, and who cared?

Darcy's stomach churned so loudly that Aidan narrowed his eyes.

"You need a snack, honey?" Domestic goddess Mom flew in to save the day. "I bought a ton of strawberries. I could whip some cream, too, if you like."

Mom turned to Aidan, and Darcy could've sworn she brushed her hair out of her eyes in a soap opera–type gesture. "Low blood sugar."

Okay, now she felt not only like a gross noisemaker, but a sickly wimp loser. Not that she cared what Aidan thought. She was only putting up with him for Troy's sake. The guy had totally calmed Troy down when he'd gone off on his Daddy rant during dinner, something her mother hadn't even been able to do. That had scared the wits out of Darcy.

But she didn't have to like him.

She'd eat something, and then ask Aidan for what she wanted. Nothing yummy sat out, but Aidan and Mom both had a kind of full look about them—leaning back in their seats, eyes slightly glazed, movements slow. And Aidan kept touching his mouth, as if checking for cookie crumbs.

"Where are the cookies?" Her fingers twitched from more than low blood sugar.

Her mother laughed, then shook her head. "I didn't bake today, but last I looked, there were still a few chocolate chip cookies in the freezer. Do me a favor and finish them. I can't trust myself around desserts," Mom said as much to Aidan as to Darcy. Actually, more to Aidan than to her. He needed to know her mother's weakness for sweets because why?

Darcy grabbed the freezer container and tossed four cookies onto the bare microwave carousel, glanced over her shoulder to see whether her mother would notice and insist on a paper towel. She pressed the keypad, then whacked the on button with the heel of her hand.

"Take some milk with that," Mom said without turning around to witness the cookies on a potentially germ-infested surface.

Well, she had been going to take milk, but she hated following her mother's dumb instructions. The woman acted as though she'd invented cookies and milk.

Darcy leaned against the sink, shoved a cookie into her mouth, and bit down hard. Ah, she felt better already. She got to the third freezer-burned cookie before she gave in to the crumbs clogging her throat and poured a glass of milk. The third gulp dislodged the scratchy lump down her throat and into her stomach. Okay, now she was way too full, but at least her fingers had stopped twitching.

Might as well go for it. "I want to see the apartment," Darcy blurted out, and then stifled a burp.

Mom blinked at her and pressed a hand to her heart. "Are you sure?" she said, even though she'd been asking Darcy for weeks.

When Mom met her gaze, she felt like crying, and her stupid chin quivered.

Mom got up and hurried across the kitchen, coming to her rescue when she didn't want rescuing. "Sometimes, seeing what you're worried about diffuses the worry," Mom said. "Most times, nothing's half as bad as what you're imagining."

What did her mother know about what she was imagining? Sure, Mom would often ask her about her concerns, hopes, and dreams. But then, right when Darcy was considering a truthful response, her mother would grow restless with the silence between them, and insert *her* concerns, hopes, and dreams. What was the point of getting real with her mother when she was so good at one-sided conversations?

Darcy made certain she caught Mom's eye, even threw in a smile for good measure. "It might be weird, but I want to."

"Cool," Aidan said, and led the way. He opened his apartment's unlocked door and stood back to let them enter. "Ladies first," Aidan said, and Darcy forced herself not to roll her eyes.

She stepped inside, took an exaggerated inhalation, and tried extracting a hit of Daddy's citrus-musk scent. Walking over to the spot where his desk had sat didn't help. A leather recliner fit into the corner, cradling Aidan's guitar. She'd heard Aidan playing at night, even fell asleep to the rock riffs. The guy was seriously good. Not that she'd tell him.

Her mother held a tentative smile. "So what do you think?"

She shrugged. So far, no muscle cramps and no nausea.

Aidan nudged the recliner with his toe. "My living room furniture. Couldn't wait to spring it from storage."

Couldn't wait to get a babe in here. Miraculous, really.

Aidan had transformed her father's writing studio into a bachelor pad. The nearly empty apartment screamed "low maintenance, travels light." The guitar left accidentally out in the open provided just the right touch. *Shag me, baby.*

Wait a second. She would've thought the front room would work as a bedroom and the back room adjacent to the kitchen galley would work as the living room. She looked around and couldn't locate anything resembling a daybed or sleep sofa. Maybe Aidan had fashioned a retractable bed, the kind that exploded out of the wall at just the right moment when he plucked the appropriate note on his guitar.

She left Aidan's living room and checked out the kitchen. A chunky coffee table, a pile of cushions, and Aidan's muddy bike took up the entire back room. Maybe the guy slept standing up. It could happen.

"Looking for something?" Mom asked.

Well, all right. She turned to Aidan. "I thought you'd make the front room into a bedroom."

"I did." Aidan's smug smile made him even more irritating. "Look again."

She pushed past the joker and scanned the front room—floorboards, recliner with babe-magnet guitar. She scanned the walls, then looked up. The loft.

Darcy burst out laughing and scrambled up the ladder. Peeking over the gate revealed not a cliché water bed, but a mattress on the floor and a puffy chocolate-brown comforter.

Daddy had only used the loft for storage. When they were little, she and Troy would sneak up, hide between the cardboard boxes and accordion files, and watch their father gaze into middle space. Daddy would pound his keyboard in a writing frenzy, all the while pretending he didn't know they were watching.

She and Troy would hide their toys beneath the floorboards

as a time capsule treasure chest—origami paper fortune-tellers, handmade spool dolls, painted-bead jewelry. She pressed through the garden fence–style gate beyond the ladder. "I left something up here."

Mom craned her neck from the base of the ladder. "Darcy, no. I moved all the boxes to the attic. There's nothing."

On her knees, Darcy peeked over the gate, like when she was little and needed to stand tiptoe to see over the counter at the ice-cream shop. "Under the floorboards." She laughed at the bafflement on her mother's face. "Just some toys Troy and I hid." Then she added for Aidan's benefit: "A long time ago."

Mom started up the ladder.

"Toolbox is in my truck, if you need something to pry up the boards," Aidan called from below.

She'd never needed tools in the past, but you never knew. Maybe her fingertips had grown too wide to fit between the planks. "Knock yourself out."

Darcy was already in the corner, bent beneath the sloping ceiling and the skylight's heat. For old-time's sake, she closed her eyes and said the special incantation she and Troy had made up. "Shadows and angels." She dug her not-too-big fingertips through the inch-wide crack, yanked, and then waited while the cobweb dust settled. She spotted the crafted toys right away alongside a completed Lego creation and the tin of Pick-Up Sticks she'd once spent months looking for.

Darcy popped open the cardboard end and looked inside the cylinder. Not a single painted stick, just a folded piece of paper. That didn't make any sense at all. Odder still, when she slid the paper from its housing, a soft puff of musk and citrus escaped. She smoothed the paper, and the Daddy-scent blossomed. Nausea squirted from her body's center and trickled down her limbs.

Darcy stared at the creased verse, her chest tightening with every stanza. She couldn't stop herself from reading through the entire poem, even though she knew every single line of the poem Daddy had made her memorize.

"You shouldn't read that." Mom's voice, so soft now, speaking as if each word caused her pain, the way she'd spoken on the day Daddy had died.

Darcy felt her mother kneel down beside her, and she glanced over her shoulder. Mom was clasping her hands prayerlike before her.

"You know the poem?" Darcy asked, although she already knew the answer. Only thoughts of Daddy at his worst could bend her mother that way.

Mom lowered her eyelids.

Darcy kept her gaze on the Daddy-scented paper, willing the verse to vanish. For the first time, she realized how much she hated that Shakespeare poem, had always hated its scary-sick warning Daddy made her keep from Mom. *No longer mourn for me when I am dead.* The sharing of the poem and the ritual recital had weighted her with first dread, and then guilt. The shame of keeping a dangerous secret that wasn't really a secret, just a twisted lie. For so long, she'd thought keeping Daddy's secret about the morbid Shakespeare sonnet had maybe not caused, but contributed to his death. Turned out, Daddy's game was all about testing her loyalty.

She never could have saved his life.

"You can tell me how you know about the poem," Darcy said. "I already know all the bad stuff. I saw all the bad stuff."

Mom sighed.

"Please." Darcy took a cue from their earlier conversation and flipped it around to the reverse side. "You're right. Sometimes imagining is worse. I just want the truth." That should do it. Use Mom's recently spouted wisdom and toss in The Truth, her life's mission.

Mom laughed weakly, as if she detected Darcy's less than

covert debate methods, but she gave in anyway. "It was an unhealthy obsession. He read it over and over, memorized it, decided it was all about him. He even wanted me to say it with him. No way I would go along with that one and become an enabler to his self-perpetuating darkness."

So Darcy was an enabler. And a second-choice enabler at that. They'd never shared a just between them poem. Daddy had saddled her with an obsession Mom knew all about, words so tortuous he'd hidden them beneath the floorboards. Daddy should've known telltale hearts never remained silent.

Darcy handed the poem to her mother. " 'No longer mourn for me when I am dead than you shall hear the surly sullen bell give warning to the world that I am fled—' "

"Did you just memorize that?"

" 'From this vile world, with vilest worms to dwell.' "

"Angel, I am so sorry."

She couldn't stop; she had to get it out. Her throat burned, as if she'd swallowed poison. " 'Nay if you read this line, remember not the hand that writ it, for I love you so.' "

"Damn him."

" 'For I *love* you so.' " Darcy stopped, suddenly wishing for a dictionary. She questioned the meaning of everything she'd believed before this moment. The father who'd claimed to love her had sucked her into his sick, paranoid obsession and called it love.

And she'd believed him.

Chapter 17

A wood knot on the outside of the bathroom door stared at Laura, taking on human characteristics in the low light of the upstairs hallway. "Are you all right?" Laura asked Darcy through the closed door, although unmistakable retching sounds had precipitated her knee-jerk question.

"Great. Just tossed my cookies." Darcy laughed, the kind of giggle more appropriate for late nights turned punchy than the middle of the afternoon. "So that's where that saying comes from."

"Guess so." Laura splayed her fingers wide against the door, a poor substitute for stroking her daughter's hair. "Daddy loved you. What he did doesn't change that. But he never should've asked you to keep a secret from me. That put you in an unfair position."

"I'm not feeling so good."

"You shouldn't—" The shushing sound of running water silenced Laura voice. *Feel guilty.*

"Brushing my teeth," Darcy said.

She sighed and leaned against the wall. *Back off, Laura.* She could open the unlocked door and barge in on her daughter, insist that Darcy confide in her and accept her help through the latest Jack-related trauma. But getting to the other side of the door wouldn't break down the real barrier between them. She could lead her daughter to conversation, but she couldn't make her talk.

Laura had always tried to strike a balance between telling her children the truth about their father's illness and shielding them from the effects of such knowledge. How could she have known he'd enlisted their daughter to keep part of the truth from *her*? Even now, diplomacy was crucial. Shame the parent; shame the child. Laura couldn't exactly tell Darcy every unfiltered thought she was having about her father. The information Darcy had revealed enlarged his diagnosis to include sociopath. If Laura had known Jack was making Darcy feel responsible for his emotional and physical well-being, Laura would've put a stop to his inappropriate behavior. She would've stepped between Jack and Darcy, and offered herself as a sounding board for the dark poem he'd wielded against their daughter. Words as weapons.

She'd thought incorrectly that the relationship with her husband would end with his death, his self-inflicted one-way road trip. The ultimate book tour. How could a dead man stir up such trouble? Hadn't he caused enough problems when he was alive?

Laura could never really relax unless Jack was sound asleep. Even then, she'd move cautiously, tiptoe downstairs to read or fix a snack for herself. If he awoke in the middle of the night, who knew what reassurances he'd require, how much he'd expect from her? Talk therapy, physical therapy, sex therapy. Jack knew no boundaries. Hang on. Reverse that notion. She knew no boundaries. You showed others how to treat you.

A creak from behind her, and Laura turned toward the stairway.

"Laura?" Aidan walked through the upstairs hallway, the sight of him incompatible with the second floor of her house. He was carrying steaming tea in one of her pink mugs.

Laura had left Darcy for two minutes and had raced downstairs to set peppermint tea in a mug, water in the kettle, and—

She held her hand over her mouth. "I forgot—I don't know how—I didn't even hear the whistle."

"Done it myself a few times." He dunked the tea bag, then handed her the mug. "Thanks for giving me an excuse to see how she's doing."

Ten minutes ago, Laura and Darcy had flown from Aidan's bedroom loft to their upstairs bathroom. Laura didn't think Aidan deserved a mess in his bathroom. Or a cookie tossing.

The toilet flushed.

"She's been better," Laura said.

"She vomited?" Aidan asked, and Laura nodded.

Aidan's gaze went to the door. "She's still upset I'm living in her dad's studio."

"Not exactly." Darcy had been worried seeing her dad's studio might be weird, and it turned out she was right, but in a way neither of them could've predicted.

"This then?" From Aidan's back pocket, he slid out the folded poem. "Dark stuff. Jack wrote this?"

"William Shakespeare."

"A tragedy." Aidan started to unfold the poem, and Laura held up a hand. "Do me a favor and burn it," she said.

Aidan slid the paper back in his pocket, his mouth firmed with what Laura imagined were unasked questions about the mysterious sonnet hidden beneath his floorboards. "The poem—Jack used it as a weapon," she began.

Laura gnawed her lip, and Aidan waited for her to gather her thoughts.

She stepped away from the bathroom and waved Aidan nearer to her, lowered her voice so Darcy wouldn't hear through the door. The best she could, Laura tried to explain to Aidan what made so little sense to her. About the poem and what it meant to Jack. About how he'd tried to use it against Laura. About how, when that hadn't worked, Jack had whittled away at their daughter, a roundabout way to get to Laura.

The whole time Laura told the tale, Aidan stood perfectly still. His head angled to the side, and he looked at her as if she were the most important person in the world.

"And that's my sad little story," Laura said. "One of many." Laura tried a smile. Clutching the mug, her fingers trembled, a dead giveaway to her mood. Tea splashed onto her shoe.

Aidan wrapped his hands around hers. He steadied the mug, steadied her. "Why don't we give this to Darcy while there's still some left?" he said, and Laura grinned.

"Darcy, can I come in?" she called through the door.

"It's your funeral," Darcy said, her voice a muffled croak.

Laura opened the door and found her daughter kneeling over the toilet, white-faced and staring into the bowl. She crouched down next to her, set down the tea, and gentled a hand onto her back. "Oh, Darcy."

"Can I help?" Aidan asked from the doorway. Laura nodded, and he entered the room.

"I want a washcloth, Mom," Darcy said, and the effort sent her over the edge. Dry heaves growled from her gaping mouth.

"I'm on it." Aidan found a washcloth on the rack and waited for the water to run ice cold.

Darcy fell back, then groaned. Her eyes watered. She rested her head against the wall, and her eyes drifted shut.

Aidan wrung out the washcloth, folded it in thirds. He bent down and smoothed the cooling cloth across her daughter's forehead. His eyes softened toward Darcy.

Aidan had a gift, the gift of caring.

Darcy blinked her eyes open. When she shifted to rise,

Aidan took her hand and helped her to standing. Laura imagined Aidan at the hospital, tending women with sick and broken bodies. She imagined those same women, pain-stricken and scared, falling a little in love with Aidan.

"I'm going to lie down," Darcy told Laura. "Can you wake me for dinner? I'll do my homework later."

Laura nodded. "Sure, angel. Whatever you want." How could she make up for how Jack had tormented their daughter, how he was likely still tormenting her?

Laura didn't mind nursing the kids back to health when they got sick. Preparing endless cups of Jell-O, bowls of soup, and cooling compresses made her feel useful while their bodies healed themselves. But she'd always wished for another set of helping hands. She'd always wished for a man who'd listen to her sad little stories, instead of creating them.

Chapter 18

The sound of her gasp jolted Laura awake. The same three times a week godforsaken night terror she'd been having for a month.

Fully clothed, she sprawled on top of the covers, her head crooked at an unnatural angle. The nightlight's glow didn't squelch the image of blood on her hands, the thick taste in her mouth, or the pressure behind her eyes. She went into the bathroom and threw on the cold water, then gargled the rancid taste from her mouth till her tongue throbbed with mint. When the water turned to ice, she washed the image of spectral blood from her vision. The pressure behind her eyes required a different sort of release valve.

A peek into Troy's room confirmed he was asleep. She could hardly believe he was the same boy whose crying jag, exactly one week ago, had kept the house awake through the night. Earlier today, she'd even considered canceling his appointment with Dr. Harvey. But then, she'd thought of the many well-meaning acquaintances that asked her how the kids were doing. She could live without the pity in their eyes, but it reminded her of what she knew too well. The fact bipolar disorder could crop up anywhere between early adolescence and young adulthood necessitated another decade of her vigilance.

In Darcy's room, Laura gave thanks that young ones recovered from physical illness so quickly. By six o'clock, Darcy's color had returned to normal. She'd sprinted down to dinner, taken seconds of the spaghetti pie, and gulped three glasses of water before embarking on a steam-the-paint-off-the-bathroom-walls shower.

Laura leaned over her daughter's sleeping form. "I'd do anything to keep you safe," she said, reiterating her oft-whispered promise. She thought first of how Jack had coerced Darcy into keeping his dangerous secret, and then she thought about Nick. The way he'd straight-faced lied to her after Darcy sneaked out of the house to be with him sent up warning flares. That boy was not good for her daughter.

Downstairs, Laura nestled into her office enclave, settled into her desk chair. The desk lamp spotlighted her free-writing journal; a near-iridescent light reflected off the blank pages and warmed her face. Too edgy to plot fiction, Laura unleashed her real-life worries onto the page. Her purple pen sailed across the pages.

The journal was like a truth detector. She didn't need to mince words when she admitted how she felt about Jack: *angry*, or about her children: *protective*. But when she wrote the word *Aidan*, she stopped, her hand hanging in midair.

A few months ago, Laura had promised Maggie and Elle that after Jack's one-year anniversary, she'd *consider* dating again. She'd thought, maybe she'd go on a few dates to placate her friends and let them fix her up with Sean, the Greenboro police officer with the bluer than blue eyes, or Carl, Maggie's widower friend from New Boston. A date meant nothing. She wouldn't even have to tell the kids, unless one date led to another, unless dating turned into a lasting relationship. And what were the chances of that?

Elle had burned through so many relationships that whenever she told Laura about a new guy, she'd refer to him as her future ex-boyfriend. Most romantic relationships failed.

Earlier tonight, Troy had knocked on Aidan's door to share his book on New Hampshire rail trails. Darcy was harder to win over. But the way Aidan had helped Darcy, the way he did not judge . . .

Laura could never date a man who was developing a relationship with her children, much less date a man who was living in her house. She snapped the journal shut.

With her gaze unfocused, she let her mind wander to the character sketch she'd written weeks ago about a girl dreaming of an authentic life. A girl hiding—

The studio door creaked open, and Laura startled, held her hand to her heart. Aidan's laundry basket peeked into the mudroom and shouldn't have come as a surprise. She'd told him the laundry room was open for business any time of day or night. The hum of the washing machine and dryer, and the tumble of clothes worked like a white-noise lullaby for her and the kids.

"Hey, there, my insomnia friend," Aidan said.

Aidan's presence filled the room, and Laura sat up a little taller, breathed a little deeper. "Hey, yourself." Aidan's lingering gaze stripped away artifice, and she flushed, as if he'd read his name in her journal. As if he were pushing her to complete the entry and name her feelings for him.

"How's Darcy doing?"

"One hundred percent recovered," she said.

"Glad to hear it." He stepped closer and glanced at the journal on her desk and the pen she was clutching between her fingers. "Don't let me interrupt your midnight musings," he said, and dashed into the guest bathroom with his wash, leaving an empty space beside her.

Behind the closed bathroom door, the washing machine's

rusty door squealed open. Seconds later, the ancient machine rumbled to life, and Aidan emerged sans laundry basket. He headed for his apartment's open door.

"No guitar playing tonight?" she blurted out before he could walk through the door.

Aidan turned back around. "Nah, not tonight. Music's the thing after a long day at work. Didn't need it tonight."

"Too mellow to create?" she asked, thinking of Jack's creative process, thinking of her own. Too mellow posed the same challenge as too edgy.

"I've never thought of it that way." He grinned. "Whether I've had a good or bad day, the guitar unravels me."

"You use it to process life."

He considered her, then shook his head. "Don't need to process life. More like, life inspires the music. Work's part of life."

"You love your job."

"It's goofy, but I do." He angled his feet toward her and leaned against the bookcase. His gaze turned thoughtful, and he drew his forefinger across his bottom lip, a gesture she'd noticed this afternoon. Once again, the gesture drew her to his mouth and made her want to press her lips against his inspired half smile. "Whether it's been a good or a bad day, I love it."

"Tell me about a good day." Laura dropped her purple pen into the mason jar at the back of her desk. She rested her elbow on the desktop, her chin in her hand.

Aidan's bright gaze cut through the mudroom's low light. "Guy brought in his nineteen-year-old daughter, complaining of an intense headache, stiff neck, and spiking a fever. Told the dad I suspected bacterial meningitis, and I'd need to do a spinal tap. Poor guy nearly fainted."

"And?"

Aidan's mouth turned down at the corners, but his eyes smiled. He nodded. "Tap turned up what I'd thought. Told the dad what I'd found. Told him he'd done the right thing. Thanks to him, we caught it early. After a course of antibiotics, his daughter will recover just fine. When the dad realized he wasn't going to lose his daughter, it was like . . ." Aidan's gaze drifted, searching for a word.

"Pure joy," she said.

"Yeah, that's the word I was looking for. Joy," he said and looked right at her. "You're good with words."

"Words are my life," she said, and then amended her statement. "I mean my work." She shook her head. "Used to be, anyway."

"You write, like Jack did?"

"Mostly I edited his work," she said. "Helped him with gathering research, revised, revised, revised."

"But you didn't write your own stuff?"

"Well . . . some." She shrugged. "But I never got very far with it."

"Anybody read this writing of yours?"

"Just Maggie and Elle. Oh, and of course, Jack."

"What did Jack have to say?" Aidan asked.

Laura envisioned Jack sitting next to her, breathing down her neck, and hogging all the air. "Not his cup of tea. Too sweet, too trivial, too optimistic. Didn't make the reader want to reconsider life, if you know what I mean." Didn't make the reader want to shove the barrel of a gun in his mouth.

"But you love writing," he said.

"Oh." Heat pulsed her cheeks. "Well."

A grin split Aidan's face. "I bet you're good."

She shrugged again, thought of the hard to believe compliments she'd received from Elle and Maggie: talented, original, as good as the novels on their favorites shelves. Aidan caught her gaze and held it, as though he could see the praise she held close to her heart.

"I bet your—I bet Jack Klein's wrong," Aidan said, and

Laura wondered whether he was avoiding the words *your hus-band*. "Any chance I could read Laura Klein?"

Laura's exhalation whooshed out of her. "Wow, I wasn't expecting that question." No one new had asked to read her writing in years, at least not anyone whose opinion of her she cared about. Her head grew light with heat, which only made her blush harder.

Aidan took half a step in her direction, and the glint in his eyes gave him away. He thoroughly enjoyed flirting with her and making her squirm. Forget logic. She thoroughly enjoyed flirting right back.

"C'mon, you've heard me play guitar," he said. "Fair's fair."

"It's not the same thing."

"Close enough. They're both creative expression. Me, strumming away the blues." He leaned over and performed a wink-quick air guitar riff. "And you, tapping away whatever it is you tap away," he said, and pantomimed her fingers typing.

She wrinkled her nose and tried to keep a straight face. "I don't think so."

"Come on. Come on." Aidan's drawn-out words warmed like sweet talk. His forced pout tweaked her pulse like a dare.

Laura giggled. "No." What if he read her writing and he agreed with Jack's opinion? She imagined Aidan didn't favor relationship novels. He looked more like the action-adventure type. He'd never straight-out insult her. But one look at his unable to lie face, and she'd know. Heaven forbid, he said something purposely vague like he'd found her writing inter-esting. Translated into English, *interesting* meant *torture*.

Aidan folded his arms, sighed. "What are you, chicken?"

"Excuse me?" Laura said. Right now, Aidan assumed he'd like her writing, but what if her writing disappointed him?

What if she disappointed him?

Aidan tapped his foot. From his mouth came strange noises, strange clucking noises. How old was he?

Laura glanced at the ceiling, imagined Aidan's squawking rising through the floorboards and angling into the kids' rooms. "You're going to wake up the house."

He grinned, and the flash from his eyes could've served as a lighthouse for ships.

She was an idiot.

"Cock-a-doodle—"

"On the shelf behind you!" she said, and he held a finger to his lips.

"Now you're talking." He glanced at the jam-packed bookcase. "Where?"

She hesitated, wondering how she could take back her words.

Aidan smiled and chicken-flapped his arms.

"All right already," Laura said, and inhaled so she wouldn't pass out. She took half a second to decide which manuscript to give him, and then got it herself. The tale about losing and finding love wasn't a romance, but contained enough romantic elements to make Jack squirm. *It's fluff, Laura. You can do better than this.* But what if she didn't want to?

Aidan held out his hands, as if he understood her manuscript was like a baby to her.

"Here you go." She placed her baby in his hands. "Whenever you get to it, no rush."

"Uh, I was going to read it right now. Between switching loads."

What had she done? Her mouth fell open. The backs of her knees went soft, like when she'd await one of Jack's critiques. Jack would insist she sat by his side while he read, and she'd try to predict his thoughts from his rapidly darting gaze, the subtle nuances of his changing expressions.

Aidan smirked. "See you in a few," he said, and slipped into the studio.

Thank goodness. Laura opened and closed her journal. She

tried catching the story train of thought Aidan had interrupted, but failed. Her stomach growled.

In the kitchen, she put enough water in the kettle for two
cups of tea, reminded herself not to burn down the house. She
wondered what Aidan's face looked like as he read her work.
Whether his lopsided dimple deepened. Whether his mouth
turned down in sympathy when he read a bittersweet passage.
She wondered whether he was thinking of her.

By the time Aidan returned, she'd finished the tea, the kettle had grown cold, she'd wiped down and reorganized two
spice shelves, and her hands were sweating. She dried them on
the dish towel overhanging the stove handle.

"Back so soon?" she said, and avoided his gaze.

Aidan stood next to her. He leaned against the counter. His
attempt to torture her with silence couldn't have lasted more
than two minutes. He cracked up, turned to her. "I thought for
sure you'd want to know what I thought."

She forced a deadpan expression. "What did you think?"

Aidan rubbed his hands together. "Thought you'd never
ask," he said. "I've come to two conclusions, derived from several thoughts. I thought your—what would you call it, writing
voice—sounded a lot like Jack. Not the type of story, heck no,
but some of your word choices. A bit of the, umm, music."

Laura's stomach tightened around the warm tea. "You've
read Jack's work?"

"Oh, sure, sure. Who hasn't?"

"Lots of people."

"You're changing the subject," he said, and his smile warmed
her toes. "The writing's unique, the observations fresh."

"You went to medical school?"

"And I took Professor Pearlstein's creative writing class as
an undergrad."

She tilted her head. "You write?"

"Got a B, which I didn't even deserve. Should've been a C.

Hey, I write music, not novels." He paused. "As I was saying, the writing's sensual."

"You didn't say that."

"You helped Jack with his writing? You were the assistant behind the genius?"

"His right-hand girl."

Aidan shook his head. "Uh-uh. You know what I concluded from all these really deep thoughts?" He turned toward her, pressed his palm to the edge of the counter, and his bicep stretched the sleeve of his T-shirt. He lowered his voice. "The second thing I concluded is that you were the unsung genius behind the writer."

"Oh, no, no. I untangled Jack's rambling overwriting, made sure the story structure was sound, did some light line editing. Nothing more." At least that's how her job had started. In recent years, Jack had come to rely on her for heavy revisions, a close cousin to cowriting. Another of their little secrets.

Aidan looked to the ceiling. "Unbelievable. I just called you a genius, and that's all you've got to say for yourself?"

"If that was the second thing you concluded, what was the first?"

"Oh, that," he said, and a little-boy-devil grin washed over his face. "The first thing I concluded when I read your writing was that I wanted to do this." Aidan cupped her face in his warm hands, and those dark-chocolate eyes melted her. He leaned in. Touched his lips to hers. Took a tentative taste. His mouth parted from hers, and he licked his bottom lip.

They stood, forehead to forehead, grinning in the stove hood's golden light. "Can't lie," he said. "I've wanted to do that since the day I moved in."

Laura's heart battered against her chest. She closed her eyes, and the space between them vibrated with . . . joy.

Aidan's breathing deepened. His breath fell across her lips, and her hand found the back of his neck. Silk overlaid strength. She kissed him, hard, swallowed the candied ginger taste of his mouth. Her hips rose in the vibrant space between them.

His tongue explored her mouth with unnerving slowness and, dear God, she groaned, surprising herself with the sound of her own need. Aidan took his lips from hers, traced her jawline with his mouth. The edge of the countertop cut into her back, and she didn't even worry that they were making out in the kitchen like horny teenagers.

She didn't even worry.

She could reach for him, unzip his jeans, and open herself to him. She could let him inside of her. She could—

Answer the ringing phone before it woke up the kids!

She dashed across the room. "Hello."

"May I please speak with—?" Laura took the receiver from her ear. Aidan's ex-girlfriend, still snuffling after all these weeks. Laura stripped the affect from her voice. "It's for you."

She wanted to bash the receiver against the wall, smash it into smithereens, and crush the sharp-edged remains under her bare feet. Instead, she handed the receiver to Aidan, her dignity bruised, but intact.

She turned to leave, and Aidan grabbed her by the hand. He waited till she met his gaze. And then, without covering the receiver, he spoke loud enough for the caller to hear, "Don't go."

Chapter 19

Exactly at midnight, right when Darcy was about to call Nick, the phone rang once.

Darcy sat on her bed, listening for the sound of her mother's telephone voice, eyeing her clock's moonbeam face, and rubbing her belly. She'd shaken off the queasiness hours ago, but a bloated hollowness remained.

Silence from Mom's room convinced her the single phone ring she'd heard had been either a wrong number or an electrical burp. For cover, Darcy selected her ocean sounds album and upped the iPod's volume. She could explain needing the lullaby of waves and whales.

An overheard phone call? Not so much.

She switched off the light in case Mom happened by her bedroom again. Faking deep sleep during Mom's earlier drop-in had required Darcy's practiced acting skills. Even now she wondered whether her mother had known she was really awake. Why else would Mom lean close and whisper her enduring loyalty, after everything Darcy had done? Troy might've inherited Daddy's bipolar, but she shared a deeper connection with their father. Sometimes what you didn't tell caused the most damage.

After the great cookie tossing, she'd hastened to bed with

her Webster's dictionary and flipped to the word *love*. But the definitions made no sense at all, lying flat on the page and failing to explain Daddy. Her fingers flipped past the glossy black-and-gold indented letters and found the word that explained her father: *insidious*. Every single definition related back to Daddy. Treacherous. Having a gradual and cumulative effect. Drugs that destroyed the young.

Turned out, a slow-acting drug was growing inside of her, masquerading as loyalty. Reject all that Daddy had taught her, all that she'd promised him, and she rejected him, too. Reject her father, and where did that leave her? Her fingers tightened against her thighs, her nails digging into the flesh before she could stop herself. She rubbed at what she knew would turn black and blue, then nabbed twin tension balls from her desk drawer and squeezed until her hands ached.

With a slow, skilled hand, she lifted the phone from the cradle. If her penny-pincher mom would spring for a cell phone, Darcy wouldn't have to deal with this game. She held the receiver to her face. A woman's wavering voice tickled her ear, and Darcy's eyes widened in the dark. At first she mistook the incoherent whining for Elle, and then Aidan interrupted the whimpering.

"I don't want to hurt you. I really don't. No matter how many times we talk, no matter how you frame it, I'm not going to change my mind about us. Okay, Kit?" A big exhalation from Aidan inspired more female crying. "We're wrong for each other, so it's over. There is no *us*. There just isn't."

A high-pitched wail made Darcy reposition the receiver a couple of inches away from her ear. "You hate me!"

"I don't hate you. Why are you making this so difficult?" He paused. "Finn shouldn't have given you this number. And you can't keep calling my cell every night. Don't call again."

The crying stopped, as if Aidan had sprayed cold water through the phone line. Two clicks ended the conversation for good. Darcy couldn't tell who'd hung up first, but she suspected it didn't really matter.

Darcy pressed the receiver button and waited for the dial tone before tapping out Nick's cell number. The phone didn't even ring on her end, letting Darcy know Nick was waiting by the phone. "Hey, Darce," Nick said in a whispered shout. "What's up?"

"How'd you know I'd call?"

"You said you'd call, and you haven't lied to me yet. Wait a second. Have you?"

Smiling, Darcy sped through her Nick memory bank, seeking fibs and omissions. Nope, no lies to date. Nick wasn't like other boys; she didn't have to lie to impress him. Just being herself was good enough. "No lies."

"All rightie then. So, um, what are you doing?"

She clicked through the still frames in her mind from when Nick had dropped her off through discovering Mom knew all about the sicko Daddy poem, and the sharpness of wanting to cry kept her quiet. She would not turn into one of those girls, like the spineless loser bawling over Aidan.

"I'll go first then," Nick said when she was silent. "My dad called today. He wants to see me."

"I thought there was a restraining order out against your dad. Like, he can't see you, even if he wants to."

"Yeah, well, he can see me all he wants. The restraining order's between my mom and him. He can't get within spitting distance of her, but me, he can spit at plenty." Nick laughed at his own joke. "Pretty messed up, huh? He can beat up my mother, then I'm supposed to go out with the guy for a burger and fries. Act like we're buddies, you know? Like I don't wanna kill him." Nick's voice muffled, as if he were cupping his hand around the cell phone. She imagined him turning away from his bedroom door. "I do want to kill him."

Darcy's heart tumbled at the base of her throat.

On the day Daddy had died, she'd tried to run into the house, and Officer Holmes had caught her in his arms. She'd pounded her fists against his solid chest, trying to explain how she needed to get inside and talk Daddy out of what she knew he'd already done.

But wanting and doing weren't the same. Plenty of boys joked about wanting to kill their parents, a stupid thoughtless expression they didn't mean. If Nick were serious, he wouldn't have told her. He sure hated his father though.

Darcy reached for the tension ball next to her thigh, and her hand wavered, like when she'd slide a bagel from the glowing-red toaster oven. She clenched the ball. "Making you see your dad if you don't want to can't be legal. We'll find a lawyer. There are lawyers who represent kids, I think, stand up for them in court. You have rights. I know you have rights. We'll figure it out together."

In the silence, whales called to each other over the sound of crashing waves.

"You are so damn cute. You know that, Darce? You're like no girl I've ever met before."

"Nick—"

"No, let me finish. I've been thinking on this a lot lately, and I'm really glad we didn't do it. I like that you're a virgin. It makes me crazy, you know. I can't stop thinking about getting inside you."

Nick had it all wrong. He was already inside her.

"Nick—" The line beeped. "Hang on, okay?" She checked caller ID. Heather's cell phone. Darcy put the receiver back to her cheek. "I don't believe her. Heather's calling in. I'd better pick up."

"She's trying to get you in trouble."

Another beep. "No. I don't know. I really should—"

"Okay. I'll hang on."

"Thanks." Darcy pressed the flash button. "Hello?"

"I'm sorry. Is your mother asleep?" Darcy wouldn't have recognized Heather's whispered voice without caller ID.

"I sure hope so." Darcy grimaced, wishing Heather could see her expression through the phone. If Heather were trying to get her into deeper trouble, this would be the way to go. Mom's creative punishments during groundings were the absolute worst. Last time, Mom had made her do Troy's chores, taking out the bottles, cans, *and* the gross compost.

Heather's silence brought on the guilty gremlins. Nick was wrong. Her best friend would never try to get her in trouble. "Actually, you're totally in luck. I'm on the other line with Nick, so the phone didn't even ring. No harm done."

"I just wanted to let you know I'm coming over."

Either Heather was joking or Darcy was even more tired than she'd realized. "Do you mean Sunday night? That's fine. You can probably even sleep over, if you want. Mom's extra easy after a punishment, like she feels bad she's such a sergeant and—"

"Right now. I mean, I'm already *over*. Look out your window."

Darcy tiptoed across the room and pulled aside the heavy insulated drapes left over from the winter. Heather's blond hair shone, reflecting the half-moon. She waved, and her arm gleamed, too.

Darcy threw open her window—glass plate and screen—and gave Heather the one-minute signal, not knowing whether she could see her from the unlit bedroom. Darcy jabbed the flash button. "Nick? Heather's here. Now."

"So tell her you'll call her back later or see her in school Monday."

"No, I mean she's standing outside my window, at the bottom of the fire escape." If Mom weren't so predictably neurotic, she would've dismantled the escape hatch as part of Darcy's punishment, instead of giving her another chance.

"Are you shitting me? That's just all wrong. First, you're gonna get in worse trouble. And second, I should be climbing in through your bedroom window, if anyone. Tell her to get lost. Tell her I said so. Tell her—"

The fantasy that Nick and Heather could become friends died a quick death, reminding Darcy of how Daddy would suddenly need her mother whenever Elle or Maggie called.

Heather needs me, too. "I promise I'll call you back later," Darcy told Nick. "This won't take long."

Nick wasn't even listening. "Tell her to fuck off. Okay, Darce? Can you do that for me?"

She could almost understand Nick getting jealous of boys calling to her from a car. But Heather was her best friend. She wouldn't give up Heather, not even for Nick.

She couldn't imagine her life without Nick, either.

"I'll call you back." She hung up the phone, then stared at the receiver.

Darcy locked her bedroom door and switched on her desk lamp. Heather climbed through the window and sat on Darcy's bed while Darcy shut the screen.

"So what's up?" Darcy said, borrowing one of Nick's favorite expressions. She didn't need a mirror to know her face looked like her mother's, pale with nerves and worry. Pale with trying to please the world.

Darcy sat down beside Heather on the bed, feeling as if a third person were in the room—the problem Heather had been hinting at for months. Darcy had thought she was acting as a friend by not pushing Heather too hard. Now she wasn't so sure. Maybe she didn't really want to know.

Heather drew a breath from her toes, and then turned to look Darcy in the eye. "Don't bother talking to Stevie. I'm not going to the prom with him."

That was what Heather had walked half a mile in the dark to tell her? Darcy blew out a breath. She'd forgotten how sensitive Heather could be, how relatively small issues could blow up blimp-sized unless Darcy diffused them. "No problem. I haven't talked to him yet, and I won't." Then Darcy's whole body smiled, and she laughed. "It's Cam, isn't it?" She should've known Heather would finally take a page from the Darcy rule book and play hard to get.

"It's Amy."

"Who?" Heather must've said *Andy*, but they didn't know any Andys, except for the band kid with the acne problem.

"Amy. A girl."

Was some girl named Amy going after Cam? Heather wasn't looking directly at her anymore, but Darcy noticed the way Heather was staring sideways, and her eyes lost focus. A smile tugged at the corners of Heather's mouth.

Darcy went across the room and flicked on the overhead light. The brightness woke up her sleepy brain, flashing the face of a girl she and Heather had met last summer.

"Amy from the party?" Darcy asked, even though she must've already known the answer. Why else would her voice quaver? Last summer, she'd left Heather talking to Amy and had gotten in line for the bathroom, even though she hadn't really needed to go. Darcy couldn't shake the feeling Amy was peering through a very feminine mask with the eyes of a teenage boy and checking out the girls.

Heather nodded. "Yup. We've been talking since last summer, and she's really helped me understand some stuff."

"What *stuff*?" Since the summer, and Heather hadn't told her? What could she talk to a stranger, this Amy, about that she couldn't discuss with her best friend? Besides, Darcy was reasonably sure Amy was gay, so—"Oh, my God!" Darcy said, automatically lowering her voice to a whispered shout. "You think you're gay?"

"I don't think it. I know it. And Amy made me feel better about it." Nick was right. She should've locked her window and told Heather to come back on another day. A day when she wouldn't claim something that simply was not true. Heather had always been susceptible to suggestion, a follower rather than a leader. But if Amy had gotten into her head, this was going too far.

"You are so not gay. What about all the boys you've gone out with, all the boys you've kissed?" Heather's kissing list that had suddenly and inexplicably halted almost a year ago.

Heather shook her head, frowning. "It just never felt right. It's, like, remember that caviar we had at the freshman dance? The teachers kept swearing it was a delicacy and that we should like it. So I tried it, kept trying it. And each and every time, I kept thinking, *Yuck, fish eggs.* Even if I'd tried it twelve times, it still would've tasted disgusting."

Twelve boys on Heather's kiss list, and each one of them she'd found as unappetizing as fish eggs. Fish eggs!

"Are you sure?" Darcy asked.

"Pretty sure." The hazy, dazed daydream smile. Heather had a crush on Amy.

God, this was so weird. Darcy looked at her best friend as though she'd just met her. Maybe she'd never asked Heather the right questions. "Does Amy know? I mean, that you like her?"

"Oh, I think she has a good idea." Heather wasn't wearing any barrettes, and her usually smooth hair was standing up at the back, the way hair complained if you mussed it before it dried completely. The way hair complained if you'd lain down on a wet head.

"You've been, like, dating her?" Darcy asked.

"Tonight. First date, first kiss."

She'd trusted Heather not to keep secrets from her, and Heather had taken her for a fool. What if Heather had already joined the gay-student alliance? What if she'd come out to other kids at the high school?

What if Darcy was the last person on earth to find out?

Darcy had thought she was so cool, open to anything, but the unkind edge to her voice spoke of something else. "Did you add Amy to your list?"

"No, I started a new list." Heather sounded just as mean, maybe meaner. "What do you care? You have Nick. You don't need to fix me up with boys anymore so we can go to dances together."

"Fix you up? Boys always wanted to go out with you. And we always had so much fun," Darcy said, and the past tense stung.

"Yeah, I know. That's why I was crying when Nick asked you to the prom. I knew I couldn't fake it anymore and go out with another boy. I actually saw a big neon sign in my head: Game over."

Heather couldn't fake it anymore. Back in fifth grade, the three of them had vowed honesty—she, Heather, and Cam. Darcy had swiped alcohol and sewing needles from her house, and they'd taken turns pricking each other's forefingers. They'd stood in the shaded woods and pressed their fingers together until the blood ran together. *Blood brother and sisters. Forever.*

Giving her left-hand ring finger a good hard stare, Darcy could still make out the tiny point of raised skin, the evidence of their shared tattoo. "I just don't think you're gay. Maybe you're just experimenting? Maybe this is, like, that phase where you'd only kiss redheads?"

Heather smirked. "Ever notice there aren't many boys with red hair?"

"What if next week you change your mind and decide you're straight again?"

Heather stood up. "So now you're saying I'm too stupid to figure out if I'm gay or straight?"

"I never said you were stupid, Heath, it's just—"

"Why is everything *you* do okay? Like, you can go out with a delinquent, but I can't have something real? You can't even stand the possibility this has nothing to do with you. It's not about you, okay? It's about me."

"Did you just call Nick a delinquent?"

Heather's jaw dropped, releasing a huff. "I don't believe you! To think I defend you when people talk about you behind your back, tell them how nice you really are, even though you treat me like dirt whenever you have a boyfriend." Heather narrowed her gaze, and her arms trembled even after she'd crossed them. "Now you're blowing me off for a drug dealer, a kid you don't even know."

"I do know him!" All at once, Darcy was trembling, too, her body working hard while her mind tried to figure how to best express Nick to Heather, without betraying Nick's family history. She spoke extra softly, so her voice wouldn't crack. "Nick gets what I've gone through, what I went through with my dad."

"Like I don't! Who did you call whenever your dad was sick? Huh? Who stayed over all week after he—after he died, even slept in the same bed with you, so you wouldn't get scared?"

"You're not going to tell anyone about that, are you?"

"This is not about you! It's about me, what I'm going through, right here, right now." Heather unfolded her arms and dropped her hands to her sides, so Darcy could see the full extent of their tremors. "I'm scared, and you won't even look at me."

True enough; Darcy was staring at Heather's hands. Darcy pulled focus and worked her gaze back to her friend's paler than usual complexion, her quivering lower lip, and her moist eyes. The back of Darcy's head tingled as she saw herself from Heather's point of view: selfish.

What did Heather want from She of the Crazy House?

Darcy had always thought Heather was her soul sister, that she loved her as if they were truly related, even before they'd performed the blood sister ritual. But that was when Darcy had thought she understood the meaning of love, when she'd thought, incorrectly, that love healed, instead of harmed. That, just like in countless corny songs, love lifted you up, instead of grinding you into dust. Maybe her doubts about Heather being gay would work as a backhanded blessing, since everything Darcy touched went to seed.

She went to Heather and gave her the best hug she could muster, all she possessed. Heather's heart fluttered beneath her like the hummingbirds that had fed at last summer's red plastic feeder. Her narrow shoulders leaned into Darcy. You thought you knew someone, thought you understood everything about the why of what they did, and it turned out, you didn't know anything at all.

If she didn't know a thing about Heather, then she knew even less about Troy. She stepped back and handed Heather a tissue, and the need to tell Heather absolutely everything itched her skin until she just had to scratch. "My mom made Troy an appointment with Dr. Harvey."

Heather grimaced, making her wide-set eyes cuddle up to the bridge of her nose. Maybe she didn't remember the name.

"My dad's shrink. You know, the famous guy who's such a great doctor that patients are dying to see him." Right away, she wished she hadn't thought of that joke. She *really* wished she hadn't said it.

"God! I'm so sick of hearing about your family."

Heather's words slapped Darcy across the face, and her cheeks burned. "Troy could die," Darcy said. The three little words she hadn't dared to even think before this moment now hung in the air between them, like a flipped car. Like a bottle of sleeping pills. Like the taste and shape of a gun's barrel in your mouth.

Heather wrapped her arms around herself, her face reenacting the time she'd accidentally bitten into a habanero pepper.

Darcy went in for a second hug, and Heather jabbed out her palm inches from Darcy's face. *Talk to the hand.* "My whole life has just changed," Heather said. "Can you think about *that* for even a minute?"

Heather withdrew the obnoxious hand signal but kept an arm's-length away.

"So what, you kissed a girl. Big deal. Big *fucking* deal." Darcy counted on Heather to remember how funny she used to think it sounded when Darcy pronounced *fuck* so properly. She crossed the invisible line Heather had drawn. "C'mon, Heather. It doesn't necessarily mean anything. Remember how we used to practice kissing and then practically pee our pants, we'd laugh so hard."

"You haven't listened to anything I've said!"

Darcy glanced at her locked door, sure her mother would awaken from the tone if not the volume of Heather's voice. Sure, Darcy had listened plenty. She'd just confided her fear Troy might kill himself, and Heather had equated Darcy's worry with her out-of-whack angst over kissing a girl, as though being gay were fatal.

"I am so outa here," Heather said.

"Wait!" Darcy said, trying to wrangle her scrambled thoughts into something approaching coherence. Trying to decide what to do about their friendship.

"Oh, by the way," Heather said, already halfway out the window. "I want the clothes you borrowed back."

Too late now. Heather had decided for both of them.

Chapter 20

Darcy had just lost her best friend, and now she was supposed to call Nick back for more talk about his wife-beater father. What if Nick really did have to see his father? What if Nick's father beat up Nick?

Daddy used to say, "What would Laura do?" also known as WWLD, whenever Darcy came to him with a problem he couldn't solve. Way funnier than, "Go ask your mother."

Darcy couldn't remember the last time she'd gone to Mom for advice or what the problem had been. But she remembered Mom pulling back her blanket. She remembered climbing into her parents' bed. She'd let her mother stroke her hair, and with each caress, with each whisper and kiss, the trouble had lifted.

She sat on the edge of her bed, twisted open the lid of her special occasion body butter, and released the cupcake aroma. She breathed deeply, dipped into the swirls, and massaged her feet. Darcy didn't doubt Mom's nighttime pledge that she'd do anything to keep her safe, which meant she'd keep Darcy safe from Nick, not that she'd help Darcy keep Nick safe from his father. Mom's pledge guaranteed if she knew about Nick's family history, she'd forbid Darcy from seeing Nick.

Besides, Mom had sworn to keep Daddy safe, proving she wasn't good at everything.

Darcy dug her thumbs into her sole to the point of pain, and her foot relaxed. She rubbed her palms together, releasing more fragrance, and then massaged the remaining moisturizer into her hands.

She hoped it wasn't too late to call Nick and that his household slept as soundly as her mother. What difference would another minute make? Counting out the seconds, she slipped out of her cami and sleep pants and flash-buttered the rest of her body. No time for more massage though. Instead of wrestling her sticky body back into sleep clothes, she left them at the foot of her bed, and slipped her unwrapped cupcake-self between the sheets.

Nick listened to her. She could take care of Nick.

She dialed Nick's number from under the blankets. The phone rang twice, and silence seeped in while she waited for Nick to answer.

"Whazzup?" he said, sounding as if he were dragging himself from the depths of sleep.

"Just me. Go back to bed."

He coughed, then cleared his throat. "No, it's okay. I'm awake."

"Now that I woke you."

"What did Heather want?"

Darcy wasn't even completely sure. Heather had wanted to come out of the closet, she supposed, to reveal her newly acquired gayness. More than that, Heather had been asking for Darcy's acceptance, which she'd given with a hug. Then, out of nowhere, Heather had rejected Darcy's family, rejected her. Same difference.

Heather was so sick of hearing about Darcy's family. "She didn't want anything at all."

"Yeah? Like I said. She was trying to get you in trouble."

"Maybe." Her slight friend, or ex-friend, had made so

much noise clambering down the fire escape that Darcy had been sure her mother or Troy would wake up, convinced of a break-in, and autodial the police. If her mother had woken up and seen Heather, Mom would've quadrupled the grounding, extending it for a month, maybe even stopped Darcy from going to the prom with Nick before Darcy had even asked permission.

"I don't think Heather and I are friends anymore." Probably, Heather would come out to Cam next and form a newly strengthened alliance, a bond that excluded Darcy. "In fact, I don't think I have many real friends left." First Daddy and now Heather. Darcy couldn't ignore the common denominator.

"Are you okay?" Nick asked.

"I'm fine." She actually sounded as if she didn't care about a thing. If she acted as though nothing mattered, then nothing could hurt. "Listen, I'll call you tomorrow night."

"No, wait. I've got an idea. I can't come over, right? But nobody's gonna use the phone between now and sunrise. So let's stay on the line."

"I'm already half asleep."

"Good. I want to sleep with you. Get where I'm going with this?"

"Uh, phone sex?"

"I mean the dreaming kind of sleep. Stay on the phone, pretend you're right next to me." He chuckled. "Yeah, I guess that might turn into phone sex."

"Okay." Now she got it. "I'll do it. The sleeping part, I mean." She didn't dare tell him what she wasn't wearing.

"Hey, I'll take whatever I can get."

She cuddled up to the phone, keeping it near enough so they could talk if they wanted. She couldn't hold down the giggles. "Are you awake?"

"No."

"I feel funny."

"You look funny, too, I bet. Hey, Darce? I just wanna tell you I'm your friend. I'm right here. I'm not going anywhere."

"Okay."

"I'm serious. No matter what. Close your eyes."

She rested her forehead against the receiver and imagined Nick beside her, warming the bed.

"I'm the only friend you need, Darcy."

Words she meant to say danced around her mouth, and then slipped back down her throat. Her eyes fluttered shut. And she was falling into the dreaming kind of sleep.

"All the other guys just want to use you. All the girls are jealous of you. It's just us. You and me. All you need."

All I need.

Oversized barbells shackled her ankles. The weight of water pressed against her lungs, and she knew she was at the bottom of Greenboro Lake. Clad in scuba gear, Nick swam toward her through the murky darkness. Her heart lifted. When he was close enough to touch, when she reached for him, he flashed one of his killer smiles, the smile that meant he really got her.

A riot of bubbles, and Nick stepped on her chest, forcing out her last breath.

Chapter 21

For the third day in a row, Darcy had woken up gradually, not to her mother's nagging, but to the hum of Nick's breath through the open phone line. No more nighttime talk about having to see his father, making her wonder whether she'd dreamed Nick's rant along with that whacked-out nightmare. Her Nick would never hurt her.

She'd spent the whole morning at school searching between classes for Nick, scheming to run into him in the hallways before lunch. Now and again a less pleasant image had nudged Nick from her thoughts, so she stopped at her locker, scooped up Heather's clothes-filled backpack, and went on a mission. *Just go for it!*

Darcy had counted on the scuffle of students on the way to the cafeteria to work in her favor, making the return of Heather's clothing a quick and painless exchange of goods. Now, rounding the corner and finding Heather by her locker in a tight-knit conversation with Cam, Darcy was sure she'd screwed up massively. Seeing Heather totally messed with Darcy's ability to hate her. She should've waited until later, should've gone over to Heather's house, should've made it right between them.

"What do *you* want?" Heather asked, turning in a way that blocked Cam, making Darcy miss him, too.

"I—uh." Heather's old backpack shifted on Darcy's shoulder, and then bopped down the length of her arm, as if the bag had a mind of its own. They all glanced at the bouncing bag.

"Thanks." Heather grabbed her clothes without looking at Darcy.

Darcy felt her head nodding, her legs walking away. So that was that.

"Darcy, wait," Heather said.

Darcy turned around, certain the torture was nearing its end. Certain the worst fight she'd ever had with her best friend was coming to a close. In the space of a breath, Darcy saw them watching a movie Friday night and munching homemade kettle corn. Maybe Cam could sleep over, too. She could sleep in the middle.

"Here." Heather shoved another lumpy backpack at Darcy, similar in vintage and contents to the one she'd given Heather.

Darcy just stood there waiting, for what she couldn't say. For her life to change, she supposed. For something, anything, to improve, instead of growing increasingly worse.

"Everything's in there," Heather said. "I checked twice."

"Check it again," Darcy said as a stalling tactic until she could come up with the right thing to say.

"What?" Heather said, although she'd heard every syllable.

Darcy couldn't think of a single piece of clothing she actually cared about, when all she really wanted back was her best friend. "The pink paisley scarf," Darcy said, remembering the silk she liked to wear as a belt. "My mother gave it to me. She might want it back and—"

"Fine!" Heather shot Cam a look of *what a bitch*, and Cam returned her eye rolling with a shrug.

Heather fished in the backpack and took all of three seconds—Darcy was counting her breaths—to find the scarf.

Heather dangled the scarf in Darcy's face, close enough to blind her. Now who was the bitch? She snatched it out of Heather's hands. Well, she'd tried, hadn't she?

"Cam." Darcy waited until he'd peeled his attention off Heather. "Wanna watch a movie Friday night?"

There she went. Now she had Heather's attention, too. Good.

"Yeah, I dunno, Darce." He looked to Heather, as if he needed her permission and didn't owe Darcy a thing.

Darcy couldn't read Cam's thoughts, but she could always tell when his wheels were churning, grinding down the treads. She shifted from foot to foot. The buzz and rattle of student traffic framed Cam's refusal to speak.

"Whatever!" she said, clean out of patience after counting five breaths. She so didn't have time for this.

Typical of her life, Darcy's worst fear was coming true. Heather and Cam were growing closer, two best friends working together to focus their hatred on the outcast third. The thing that riled Darcy wasn't so much that it was happening, but that she'd imagined, even briefly, that it would not.

From her seat at the front of advanced placement English, resting her chin in her hands and leaning slightly forward, Darcy could hear other students reading aloud their short stories, but could discern no meaning, as though listening to a foreign language she'd never studied.

Darcy straightened up when the bell rang and snatched the wide strap of her backpack.

"I'd like to speak with you about your story." Mr. Sullivan was heading her way.

Wasn't that what they were doing in class? She glanced at his eyes, then focused on the flecks of silver in his close-cropped beard, the way they twinkled like tinsel. "Study hall," she said.

"I've already let Mrs. Levesque know you'll be late."

"Okay." She dropped the backpack in the vacant seat beside her. What had she done wrong? She folded her hands in her lap and squeezed them together, pretending her tension ball lay between the palms.

They waited until the last student left the room and the volume in the hallway trailed to nothing.

"So," he said, moving her backpack over one seat so he could sit right beside her. He scrubbed his hand across his beard, chuckled as though nervous, and then fixed his gaze on hers. "Your story was really, really good. I mean, wow. It just blew me away!"

She released a pent-up breath, smiled. Now she could go!

"The reason I asked you to stay—"

They weren't done?

"Darcy." More fixed gaze coming from Sullivan. "Some of the themes you illuminated very much concerned me. And I thought you might like to discuss them."

No, she did not like.

"Sure." For the first time, Sullivan's unflappable calm rubbed her the wrong way and she sensed a dangerous undercurrent.

While she wondered how to get out of this one, Sullivan got her assignment from his accordion folder on his desk, set the papers between them, and removed the clip from her untitled story about a court of fairies and their ephemeral—God, she loved that word—life on the planet Earth. The happy fairies spent their days sipping nectar from long-necked daylilies and flitting between flowers, zigzagging the fairy garden with their butterfly cousins. But unlike their decor winged relatives, a higher being had bestowed upon the fairies a two-sided gift: the knowledge of their mortality.

"I thought, maybe, we could discuss the king of the fairies?"

Darcy shrugged. "What do you mean? Like his robe that reflects twenty-seven different colors or his territory-marking citrus-musk scent?" She'd found the territory-marking idea by googling an article on predators.

Sullivan grinned, but his eyes said something else. "Your details are unbelievably creative. I especially enjoyed how every spoken word makes a unique color and smell. Your writing really rocks."

Eww! She hated when teachers tried to sound like kids. She slid her story away from Sullivan and flipped through the pages just for something to do with her hands.

"Darcy."

She looked up.

"I'm going to read from your story. All right?" he asked, as if she had a choice.

She lifted her hands off the papers, and Sullivan scanned the pages with his finger until he found what he was looking for. He cleared his throat. " 'Thoughts of his impending death niggle at the king, for he can never hope to know the details of his last breath. Taking control of the deplorable situation, he usurps the role of the higher being and plans his end in great secrecy.' " Sullivan scanned farther down the page without glancing up. " 'After setting the scene with all that had comforted him through his days, silks and jewels, colors that no human could see, he drinks deeply from the forbidden black rose, and sinks into the welcoming arms of the great sleep.' "

Sullivan sighed like an old lady, the type with bad teeth. "Shall I continue?"

"It's your class."

He shuffled the pages, then took a breath. " 'When the fairy princess returns from her travels, nothing remains of the king, except the lightest sprinkling of fairy dust and his citrus musk cloying each and every blade of grass in the silent garden. Her father, the king, only forgot one precious detail when gathering his comforts for the eternal journey. He left the princess behind.

" 'From that day forward, the abandoned princess wears the forbidden black rose over her heart, pinned directly to her skin, securing the secret gateway to her father.' "

Sullivan paused. "Would you like to talk about what I just read?"

The color of the sky kept changing; she could tell even through the grimy school window. Amazing, really, just when she'd get a handle on a particular shade, the baby-boy blue shifted to indigo, the color of Daddy's eyes.

She knew more than one gateway to her father and none of them required sipping from a black rose. Why, right in her house, hiding innocently behind a year-old bottle of Valerian drops—the herbal sleep aid Maggie had given Mom—sat a nearly full bottle of prescription sleeping pills her mother hadn't touched in a year. Darcy had sneaked both when she couldn't take another minute of lying awake staring at the ceiling, and the prescription meds had given her a wicked headache.

Sullivan touched his fingertips to her arm. "Darcy? I said, would you—?"

She looked him in the eye. That's what he wanted, wasn't it? "It's a fairy tale."

"Yes." Sullivan's voice actually cracked. "But even fairy tales tell the truth."

Which apparently was against the law in Greenboro, New Hampshire. Would a great dramatic confession please Sullivan, a teacher she'd liked up until a few minutes ago? Perhaps he was looking for a play by play of the precise moment when she'd returned home from school to find the town's entire police department swarming her house, and the sure understanding her father was gone forever.

Perhaps she could map out how her heart had exploded in her chest.

"I need to know," Sullivan said, "if you're thinking about hurting yourself."

The heel of her sandal jangled against the chair's metal rung. The blue sky had already washed white, barely hinting at indigo.

Sure, she'd thought about it. How could she not, when she had such a legacy to follow, such a fine and shiny example? Car accident, popping pills, blasting your brains out. Daddy had made it look so easy. And she hated him for it.

Sullivan's chair scraped the floor, and before she realized he'd left, he returned with a box of tissues.

Dry-eyed, she pushed the tissues away using both hands. Once again, he'd read her all wrong. The black rose in her story was a metaphor, a snapshot of feelings past. Not the motion picture of her emotions. *Her* private emotions, not Sullivan's. Damn him for dissecting her story. Damn him for believing he understood her.

Damn him for even trying.

"No," she said. Then, just so there could be no mistaking the meaning behind her words, she said, "I'm *not* thinking about hurting myself. Can I leave now?" Despite what Sullivan or anyone else might have thought, she was not her father.

Sullivan scribbled on a scrap of paper. "Here's my cell phone number. Feel free to call at any hour. My door's always open. And Mrs. Gould is here for you, too, Darcy."

Oh, sure, Mrs. Gould, the school shrink, who'd insisted on an appointment last spring and forced Darcy to sit through an hour-long lecture on why her father's death wasn't her fault. That had gone so well.

She slid the phone number in her back pocket, nodded in Sullivan's general direction, and made sure to take her story with her before the idiot submitted it as police evidence.

She slipped into the ladies' room, carried the wire trash basket into a stall, and took out her emergency pack of matches. Copies of her story were safe in her computer at home and the thumb drive in her backpack, as well as her memory. But the paper copy begged destruction. Sullivan had ruined it for her. Not only had he totally misunderstood what she'd written, he'd managed to hold it against her, as if what she'd really meant were secondary to his screwed-up interpretation.

She dropped Sullivan's phone number on top of her story, struck a match, and lit the word-decorated kindling on fire. Then she watched the sharp red and orange tongues lick her A plus, curling and blackening the papers' edges. Remembering the smoke alarms, she dragged the flaming basket back to the sink and squeezed her hands around the faucet, aiming the stream of tepid water like a garden hose.

She stared at what was left of her story, as pleased with the destruction as with the creation. For the life of her, she could not believe Sullivan had read the last paragraph.

The realization starts out slowly, gaining momentum in not merely the princess's mind, but also in her heart. The king, whom she admired, who spent his brief days casting great magical spells over the kingdom of fairies, wielded his talents as a smoke screen for the larger truth.

The king, her father, was a coward.

The temperature must've dropped twenty degrees since this morning, and Darcy shivered when Nick pulled his heap into the private drive leading to the lakeside cottage.

Good, still vacant.

They got out of the car, flipped down their seats, and hunched into the backseat. They didn't have much time. Mom had only given Darcy permission to stay out till nine thirty, half an hour later than her usual school-night curfew. Yahoo's Pizza Shop stayed open till nine, so why not let her and Nick hang out in the safe public place till closing? Still, Darcy could stretch it further, explain her way out of getting home fifteen or twenty minutes later than expected. Traffic jam, stopping for gas, or Nick dropping off other kids. Her mother didn't trust her, so why tell the truth?

Nick started toward her, and she closed her eyes. His body pressured her chest.

"What's wrong?" Nick took his weight off her and sat up suddenly. "Why the tears?"

Finding the wetness on her cheeks made her even shakier, like when she was little and noticed blood after skinning her knee. She thought back through the events of the afternoon, trying to figure out what precisely had stuck in her gut and was now churning out tears. Incredibly, the tears had nothing to do with her.

"Troy's seeing a doctor Thursday," she said. "The shrink I told you about."

"Uh-huh. So that's a good thing, right?"

"Yeah, awesome."

"Sounds like this shrink guy knows his stuff. If your brother has your dad's problem, then he can help. And if Troy doesn't, even better."

"I suppose." If Super Shrink diagnosed Troy with bipolar, little brother could look forward to a lifetime of pills and doctors, with a messy suicide as his final Daddy-like act. Some patients even offed themselves while in the disorder's early stages as a preventative measure.

Nick refused to look away, even though she knew she looked ugly when she cried. A box of tissues came her way for the second time today, and this time she accepted the offering. She blew her nose and pocketed the wet wad.

"Better?" Nick asked.

She nodded. "A little."

"Your family's like mine. Really small. It's just me and my

mom and grandmother, so we stick together. Hang tough through all the crap. There's nothing I wouldn't do for them."

Nick returned to his original position above her and lowered his weight as she slid beneath him. His unfaltering gaze blurred her vision. He felt so good. Smelled so good. Tasted so good. She couldn't tell whose heartbeat was pounding through her chest wall—his or hers.

There was nothing she wouldn't do for Nick.

He unbuttoned her jeans, and she helped him push her pants and underwear down together. He moved his hand over her stomach, past her stomach. A small hitched gasp rumbled through her mouth and into Nick's, so they could both feel the gravelly texture. "Shh, it's okay. I just wanna make you feel good. I won't do anything else. Trust me," he said, and she held her hand to his.

Chapter 22

Monday night found Laura kicking herself, annoyed to distraction by her willingness to please her daughter. Darcy was already half an hour late for her half-an-hour-later-than-usual curfew, making Laura sorry she'd agreed to the exception. She'd called Nick's house ten minutes ago and spoken to his mother. Hope had no more idea what was delaying the kids than Laura did. Well, that wasn't true. Laura had plenty of ideas, and none of them softened her edges.

Laura threw in a load of wash and booted up the computer. For the first time in years, this morning, the writing muse had whispered in Laura's ear.

She'd been resisting the muse's voice all day.

For years, Laura had pictured the muse as a young woman with long, flowing hair, pastel-pink fairy wings, a to the floor lavender gown, and a voice like cool whipped cream frosting. Now the muse spoke to Laura in a voice decidedly male, entirely warm, and completely Aidan's. He'd called her the genius behind Jack's writing. He'd deemed her writing fresh. He'd found her work sensual.

He'd found her sensual.

When Laura thought back to Aidan's encouragement, and the ensuing kiss, she didn't know whether she should apply for a grant to the MacDowell Colony for artists in Peterborough or show up at Aidan's doorstep wearing nothing but a white calla lily behind her ear and a big grin across her face. So far, she'd neither committed to writing nor decided what to do about her spring-fever crush on Aidan. The fact the man was seven years her junior and renting the apartment in her home made him doubly inappropriate for her.

Wasn't that what she'd decided before he'd gone and kissed her? Before she'd, quite aggressively, kissed him right back? After Aidan had taken the call from his ex-girlfriend and told Kitty not to call again, he'd hung up the phone. Laura and Aidan had hugged good night. He'd kissed her on the chin, and it had gotten . . . awkward.

What if Friday night hadn't really happened? What if she'd dreamed it, and the events were no more solid than the unreal night terror she couldn't shake off, even after she'd opened her eyes? What if everything had happened and Aidan regretted it?

Worse yet, what if he regretted nothing?

A knock came at the side door, and Laura flinched. She checked her watch. Darcy, forty-five minutes late, and she'd forgotten her key again. Smiling when she should've been scowling, Laura yanked open the door.

Aidan stood on her doorstep, wearing a big grin. Hands jammed into his pockets, he was fully clothed, and no calla lily poked from behind either ear. "Can I come in?"

Laura stepped back. "Did you lock yourself out?"

He shook his head and stepped into the mudroom, the way he'd entered her home the first day he'd rented the studio. Aidan rubbed at the back of his neck, his adorable sign of embarrassment, and a feathery scratch irritated Laura's throat. He was her renter, and she his landlady. By definition, their relationship was unequal, just like when she and Jack were student and teacher.

Except this time, *Laura* had totally crossed the line of propriety. "I apologize."

Aidan squinted at her. "For what?"

"For kissing you Friday night," she said. "That will never happen again. I don't want you to come in through the outside door. You live here, too. I want you to feel at home. I mean it is your home. You shouldn't have to get all weird and formal around the landlady."

"Who?"

"I'm your landlady, and you're my tenant, and I am so sorry."

Aidan's gaze slid to the side, and a smile tugged at his lips. "You think you took advantage of me?"

"I promise, it will never happen again."

A laugh burst out of him, and he stepped closer. "That's a shame because I came over to ask you out on a date."

"Aidan, no, you don't have to—"

He pressed a hand to his chest. "First a date, then you get to kiss the girl. I haven't really dated for years, so I apologize for my misstep."

"You haven't dated? What about Kitty?"

"What about her? We met in college at freshman orientation, and we were together for ten years. I wouldn't exactly call that dating. See, I skip steps. My bad."

"Ten years is a long time," she said. Judging by Kitty's Friday night phone call and her cry of anguish, she still loved Aidan. Yet, he'd broken up with her and moved on with his life. Jack had left a family who'd loved him. Was love that easy for Aidan to give up, too? "What went wrong?"

"I didn't come here to talk about Kitty. We weren't right for each other. That's all," he said, referring back to the vague reason he'd given Kitty over the phone. He widened his stance and crossed his arms, letting Laura know she'd once again overstepped the rules of propriety.

But she just had to know. "Why not? Why weren't you right for each other?"

"What's with the twenty questions?" Aidan inhaled through his nose. His through the mouth exhalation told of a ten-years-too-long exhaustion. "I grew up. She didn't. End of my story. What's your story, Laura Klein?"

"What do you mean?" she asked, and her words sounded pinched. "You already know my sad little story. I don't want to—"

"But it wasn't always sad, right? How did you meet Jack?" he asked, and her cheeks burned with the memory of her and Jack's secret inappropriate relationship.

Aidan's white-toothed grin flashed victory, but he didn't know. He couldn't know.

"I was a freshman in college when I met Jack," she said.

On her desk, Aidan tapped four times: index finger, middle, ring, pinkie. "Keep going," he said. "I've still got sixteen more questions."

"I didn't—you can't—"

"What did you find interesting about him?" he said, and he held a closed-fist microphone in front of her face.

Laura leaned toward his hand, eager to show Aidan she was a good sport, eager to end this game she'd started. "To me, he was this worldly man. He'd traveled. He was accomplished, making a name for himself as a writer. Which, by the way, hardly ever happens." There. Enough said.

"Oh, oh. I've got a better question," he said, and tapped her desk. "Why did you want to date him?"

"I was young," she said, a lame excuse.

"He impressed you."

"I thought if I can win this man, then some of that great maturity would rub off on me."

Tap. "Did it?"

"Oh, yeah." From the inside of her lips, her pulse ticked a Morse code warning. "Quickie wedding, one kid after another, graduated from college, and before I knew it I was all grown up at twenty-two, and married to a very irresponsible man." She hadn't meant to reveal so much, but something about the close quarters, the nighttime. Something about Aidan . . .

Aidan removed his faux microphone. His fingers did not tap. His expression did not judge. "He never grew up," he said, and his intonation blended empathy and understanding.

"No, he didn't." For the life of him, Jack couldn't manage to get his cereal bowl from the sink to the dishwasher. And the last time she'd asked him to throw in a wash, he'd verified the laws of color mixing. When red and white bedding were laundered together, they did in fact produce pink offspring.

Laura was partially at fault. For years, she'd defended Jack when Elle had insisted she did too much for him. *You're his wife, girl, not his freaking maid.*

Jack was gone. What was the point of defending him to Aidan?

What was the point of Aidan defending Kitty, a girl who'd never matured?

Aidan lifted his fingers to tap. "When did you and Kitty start growing apart?" Laura asked.

"I'm not done tapping."

"How many questions have you asked so far?"

"I wasn't really counting," he said, and he slipped her a bright-eyed smirk. The unique combination of smugness and innocence tweaked her heart.

"How long ago?" she asked.

He pressed three fingers to his lips, as though challenging himself. "Too long."

"But you stayed because you were in love with her."

He offered the barest shake of his head. "Not exactly."

"What exactly, then?"

Aidan scrunched his mouth, and his eyes turned down at the corners, a secondary sadness that Laura had caused. "I stayed because I'd once been in love with her."

Laura had loved Jack till the end. She still loved him. But *in* love was a whole different country.

How could you be in love with a man who demanded you help him with his life's work, and then invalidated your efforts? How could you be in love with a man who, time and again, refused to take responsibility for his illness, in spite of the toll it took on his family? How could you be in love with a man who took you entirely for granted?

Yet, Laura had never thought to leave him. Maybe if Jack hadn't died, and maybe years from now, after the kids were grown and gone, their marriage would've come to that conclusion. Now she'd never know.

"Moving along," Aidan said. "Enough about Kitty. I came here to ask you on a hike or to the movies or to dinner, whatever you want. What do you like?"

"I like you, Aidan."

"That's a start."

"But I can't go on a date with you."

"You're still grieving. You're not ready. I get it."

"I might be ready, but this situation . . . I wouldn't want my kids to find out we went out on a date. They've been through so much, and I wouldn't want them to get, you know, emotionally invested with the thought of us."

Aidan gave her a long look. The corners of his mouth turned up, but he pressed his lips together.

"For goodness sake, say something."

"You think too much."

"Thank you?"

"Just an observation," he said, and he glanced at her desk, the screen opened to NewsBank. "Research keeping you up nights?"

"That and Darcy," Laura said, glancing at the mudroom door. "Darcy's nearly an hour late for her curfew, and I'm waiting for her to walk through the door any minute now." Laura's mouth twisted. "She'd better walk through that door."

"Let me guess. She's out with her boyfriend?"

"Charming Nick."

Aidan nodded. "I know the type. My sister Caroline dated one of those. Couldn't trust He Who Must Not Be Named to tell me the day of the week. Best to assume every word out of his mouth was a lie."

"He lied to your sister?"

"Lied to me, every chance he got. Every damn time they came home late, whenever I asked where they'd been. He was very creative with his excuses. I'll give the kid that much."

"Did he lie to your mother?" Laura asked.

"Didn't give him the chance. Kid had to get through me first." Aidan fisted his hands, puffed out his chest. When he widened his eyes and camped a papa-bear growl, Laura couldn't help but laugh.

"Caroline was how old?" Laura asked.

"Sixteen," Aidan said. "And I was seventeen. Caroline and me, we're Catholic twins."

Laura tried to picture a teenage good-natured Aidan putting the fear of God into a boy nearly his age. "At seventeen, you were disciplining your sister's boyfriend?"

Aidan punched a fist into his palm, softening up a catcher's mitt. "I prefer the term *intimidating*," he said, and his face glowed. "Yup, that boyfriend didn't last long."

The washing machine buzzed, signaling the end of the wash cycle. Perhaps Aidan had some tips she could use, although she strongly suspected if she tried a He-Man pose on Nick and Darcy, all three of them would succumb to hysterical laughter. "Wait right there," she said, and pointed to her desk chair. "And hold that thought. I want to hear more."

In the guest bathroom, Laura switched a dark-towel wash for light towels. Washer and dryer rumbled to life. She checked her reflection in the mirror and wondered what Aidan saw when he looked at her. When he'd kissed her, she'd floated out of time and place. She'd forgotten her name, her age, and her position in life. The silly college girl inside Laura had grinned from ear to ear, giddy with irrational optimism. Even now, the thought of Aidan had her craving his touch the way she craved her favorite decadent dessert, a molten chocolate cake she could eat in three bites.

What would be the harm in going on one little date with him? She didn't have to tell the kids or her girlfriends. The kids' emotional investment would pale compared to Elle's and Maggie's, the precise reason she'd told neither of them about that amazing kiss.

She tried running her hands through her hair, and her fingers stuck in the snarls. From the medicine cabinet, she took an elastic band and corralled her hair. With a click, she opened the bathroom door. A male voice sounded from the mudroom. Aidan's? Darcy's voice, dripping with attitude, Laura recognized, although she usually saved the ennui for Laura. Nick's response, contempt masquerading as politeness, hastened Laura's pace.

Laura no longer had to try and imagine good-natured Aidan intimidating a kid.

"Not cool, Nick," Aidan said, his voice controlled yet booming. "You date a girl, you need to get her home on time, follow house rules, buddy."

Nick and Aidan were about the same height, yet Aidan towered over the boy. An arm's length from Aidan and up against the door, Nick clenched his fists. His nostrils flared. "Don't tell me what to do."

The air thickened. The walls of Laura's cozy mudroom office narrowed to a tunnel. That too-familiar cotton-ball sensation clogged Laura's throat. She glanced at her desk phone, 911 set on speed-dial, like every phone in the house. She hoped to God she'd never have to use it again.

Darcy stood to Laura's right, one hand clasping a bookshelf, the other digging nails into her thigh. "Who do you think you are?" Darcy asked Aidan, her voice shrill as ice. "Don't listen to him, Nick."

"Just looking out for you, Darcy," Aidan said.

Laura appreciated the relief of, for once, not having to do it all herself. But how could she effectively discipline Darcy and gain Nick's respect if Aidan diminished her authority by taking control?

Nick took advantage of Aidan's divided attention and got in his face. Spittle creased at the sides of Nick's mouth. "What're you, some kind of whacko pervert guy who likes teenage girls? Talk to me, loser."

Aidan's jawline ticked, but he didn't budge. "I'm just a friend, and you know it." Close enough to breathe Nick's exhaled air, Aidan set his jaw, crossed his arms, and waited for the boy to stand down.

The situation called for Laura's measured reason, not a testosterone competition. "Guys, why don't we all take a moment and settle down?" Laura said, but neither man nor boy took her bait.

Instead, Aidan treated them to the serious version of his papa-bear scowl. "You want to see Darcy, you need to show respect for women," Aidan said, and Nick's gaze jostled. "Show respect for her mother by getting her home on time."

Laura seconded the sentiment and nodded in agreement. She only wished she'd said it herself.

"I wicked respect women!" Nick glanced at Darcy. "What the hell?"

"You don't have to answer him," Darcy said. "He's not my father. He's just some guy who rents an apartment from us."

Aidan's macho act was misguided, but he was sweet and wonderful and he wasn't *just some guy*. "Darcy Ann," Laura said. "That was uncalled for."

"I haven't done anything!"

"Get the fuck away from me," Nick told Aidan. "I fucking mean it, asshole."

"Disrespectful language, buddy. I don't like—"

"Screw you! So what if we were a little late? We were driving around and—"

"Stop right there. No excuses. The reason doesn't matter," Aidan told Nick, and man and boy glowered at each other.

"This can't happen again. Show some pride, Nick. Know what I'm talking about?"

Nick shifted in Aidan's glare. "I got pride."

"Then show respect for women, and follow the rules."

Nick gritted his teeth. "I told you, I respect women. So get out of my face."

"And next time you take Darcy out?" Aidan asked. "What are you going to do?"

"Jesus!"

"What has to happen?"

"I'll bring her home on time. Okay? Is that what you want me to say?" Nick said, a white flag and a final attack.

Aidan flashed an honest to goodness grin and moved aside to give the boy breathing room.

Nick's gaze flicked to Darcy and back to Aidan. "So we cool, now?" Nick asked through a sneer.

"Yeah, we're cool," Aidan said. "Why wouldn't we be cool?" he said, as if they hadn't been half a shade away from beating each other to a pulp.

"Excuse me. What just happened here?" Laura directed her question to all of the room's occupants, but she hoped Aidan understood she'd designed her tone for him.

"I've got it," Aidan said, and Laura recognized the take-charge expression he'd used when he'd prepared a cold compress for Darcy. This had gone too far. Laura wasn't anyone's charity case. She knew how to discipline her children and their friends. She'd been taking care of Darcy and Troy without any help long before Aidan had moved into her house, long before the man had grown facial hair.

"You've got it," Laura said, forcing a light tone. "But I didn't ask for you to get it."

Aidan met Laura's gaze. A deep inhalation stretched his T-shirt across his chest.

"Mrs. Klein, can I use your phone to call my mom?" Nick asked. "I don't want her to worry 'bout me being late. 'Cause I respect her," he said, and aimed his snarl at Aidan.

Ah, *respect* was Nick's magic word. And *respect for women* was the miracle phrase. Who knew what would've happened if Aidan hadn't stumbled upon Nick's Achilles' heel? "You're welcome to use the kitchen phone," Laura told Nick. "Thank you for asking. I appreciate you not *assuming*."

Aidan blew out a breath. "For Pete's sake."

Laura watched Darcy follow Nick into the kitchen. "Don't ever do that again," she told Aidan. "Taking over like that—just because I mentioned a problem, doesn't mean I was asking you to fix it. Not at all. I'm perfectly capable—"

"Never said you weren't."

"Then have a little respect for my authority," she said, and softened when Aidan caught her gaze and held it. "Please."

The kids came back into the mudroom. "G'night, Mrs. Klein, Mr. . . . . Aidan." Nick glanced at Darcy and lowered his gaze. "And uh, s-sorry about my language." Laura nodded. Nick sent Darcy a final full of longing teenage look before he slipped out the door. Oh, the melodrama.

"Mom, I—"

"Give us a minute," Laura said.

Darcy stamped her foot. "No, I want to talk to you now. Alone. Without *him*."

"His name is Aidan," Laura said, wishing Aidan had asked her kids to call him Dr. Walsh.

"It's all right, Laura."

Darcy glanced from Laura to Aidan to Laura. "What's going on? Is something going on because I don't think I can take another—"

"I said, I will meet you upstairs. Do you understand?"

"No, I don't!" Darcy said. "Where does he get off talking to Nick like that? He acts like he's—"

"Upstairs!" Laura said, and pointed to the doorway.

"Fine!" Darcy shot them her best look of righteous indignation, turned on her heel, and stormed from the room. Her footsteps echoed through the kitchen, the living room, the foyer. On the stairs, each tread received its own Darcy stomp.

Laura sighed.

"I was going to tell you about how much Darcy and Nick reminded me of Caroline and He Who Must Not Be Named," Aidan said. "But that's making an excuse, isn't it?"

"Yes, it is."

Aidan nodded and came over to where she was standing. "I'm sorry," he said, and damn if his voice didn't remind Laura of molten chocolate. He hugged her, and her cheek pressed up against his chest. Caught in his warmth, Laura's body relaxed until her breathing slowed; until it occurred to her the reason the two of them had butt heads. Way before she was a single parent, years of single-parent thinking had honed Laura's personality to the sharp point of independence. Her children had already lost their father. If she fell into a pattern of letting Aidan take care of her problems, her children would lose their mother, too.

Laura and Jack had squabbled due to their differences. But wasn't it worse if a man and a woman were too much alike?

Her heart clenched, and she stifled a sigh. His hands caressed the small of her back, and a tingle rolled up to her chest.

"So are we cool?" Aidan said.

"We're cool."

"Then let me make up for my latest misstep by taking you out on a date. A movie? Dinner? A walk in the woods?"

She smiled at his perseverance. At the small of her back, the warmth of his handprint branded her. Nothing compared to the flame scorching all her secret places. Nothing compared to all her hellfire girlish wants.

She squelched them both and deferred to good old dependable logic. Logic, unlike people, had never let her down. "Aidan," she began, and his hands stilled on her back. His expression soured. And his gaze disengaged from hers, reflecting her response. "I'd very much like it," she said, "if we could be friends."

If anger had a scent, her daughter's smelled like white cake with vanilla frosting.

Darcy sat on her bed, back to headboard, working body butter into her hands with a vengeance. She screwed the lid on the jar and slammed it down on her nightstand. "Aidan's not my father."

Laura's stepped into Darcy's room and shut the door behind her. "No, he most certainly is not."

If Jack had been alive and Darcy had been late for curfew, Jack would have trudged up to bed and left Laura to play the role of the parent. And Jack would have retained the role of Darcy's friend.

Laura wouldn't share that tidbit of information.

"What's going on, then?" Darcy asked.

A flush tingled Laura's cheeks, and she sat on the edge of Darcy's bed. Could Darcy have sensed an attraction between Laura and Aidan? An afterglow from their kiss? Flirtation in their wordplay?

"I mean, where does he get off yelling at Nick? He has no right. It's just weird. He's freaking me out!" Darcy said, and her voice thickened.

Darcy might be getting used to Aidan living in Jack's studio, but taking her father's place was a whole different story.

"Aidan's my friend. He knew I was worried about you missing curfew. Because I wasn't in the room when you and Nick got home, he thought he should act on my behalf." Not much different than how Laura imagined she'd want a man she was dating to behave, except for the part where she'd returned and Aidan hadn't backed off.

That wasn't his fault. He couldn't have known her preference. Now he knew.

"I don't like him. I don't think you should be friends." Darcy's bottom lip jutted out, giving away her pique of jealousy. Darcy was so busy trying to convince Laura she was all grown up, Laura sometimes forgot she was just a girl. A girl missing her father and needing her mother.

Darcy's nostrils fluttered, as if she might cry, setting of a corresponding twitch in Laura's stomach.

"Aidan's a nice man. I enjoy his company. And he's been good for Troy. Why don't you like him?"

Darcy's bottom lip quivered. She went back to the body butter, lifted it from the dresser, and unscrewed the lid. "As I was saying," Darcy said, as if she were trying to rewind the conversation. Instead, she inadvertently gave Laura a truthful response: "Aidan's not my father."

Chapter 23

Late April wasn't supposed to hover in the eighties. Laura wasn't supposed to sleep through her children leaving for school. And she wasn't supposed to shut off her alarm clock so she could continue dreaming about Aidan.

Laura stared at the bedside clock in utter disbelief, peeked into Troy's and Darcy's empty bedrooms, and then ran down the stairs in her short satin nightgown, not bothering with the longer robe. Searching for Aidan's truck, she stepped out the side door and onto the cement steps. Faint tire tracks crisscrossed the sand by his apartment door, marking his early morning departure. She wasn't sure whether she was disappointed or glad she'd missed him.

The way Aidan had rushed to action Monday night, lecturing Nick on getting Darcy home on time and matters of respect had annoyed Laura to no end, true enough. She would never admit it to Aidan, but his toe-crushing misstep had also made her like him even more, right when she was supposed to discourage his crush.

Laura tiptoed across the gravel drive to retrieve her daily *Union Leader*. Underfoot, the sun-charged pebbles burned the balls of her feet, sparking a snippet of Monday night's conversation with Aidan. They'd squabbled and made up, like any new couple learning to navigate a romantic relationship that included kids. The image shouted soul mates. The thought made her question her sanity.

Laura shook her head and, newspaper in hand, stepped back into the house. She couldn't handle Aidan's sense of humor, his gentle nature, his unflinching confidence, or the way his voice lifted when he spoke her name.

Laura.

Her name was written in Aidan's tidy block letters on an envelope sitting on her desk.

She dropped the newspaper, tore into the envelope, and slid out a folded sheet of yellow-lined paper. Based on the ghosts of erased words, the note likely resulted from a second or third attempt.

Are you and the kids available for dinner tonight? I'd like to cook for the three of you. If tonight doesn't work, leave a message on my cell. Otherwise, I'll be expecting the Klein family at eight. I look forward to it.

Aidan

He'd asked her and the kids over for dinner. Not a date. This was a good thing, right? After all, she carried the kind of baggage no fancy-free bachelor need entertain: teenager troubles, financial worries, a son who might be sick.

Troy's appointment with Dr. Harvey was this afternoon, and each of the hours between now and four carried the weight of uncertainty. No matter the diagnosis, she and Troy would enjoy Aidan's lighthearted company. And Darcy? Darcy and Aidan could start over. Who didn't deserve a second chance?

She folded the note over and over until the paper formed a touchstone, a little piece of her dear friend Aidan she'd keep with her all day till she could come home to the real thing.

★　★　★

At a quarter to four, Laura pulled past the gate announcing their entrance into the campus of what Jack had termed U-Nuts. They drove past the cozy cottage of the Women's Treatment Program, the tri-dormered Transitional Living Center, and the plush and all-too familiar Pavilion, where Jack had memorized the meal plan. The private pay hospital ran the gamut of mental health services, ranging from child psychiatry to Alzheimer's disease. Considering the amount the Klein family had spent on Jack's mood disorder, she wouldn't have been at all surprised by a Klein bipolar wing, if not an entirely new structure, sprung up along the collegiate landscape.

The Admissions Building looked exactly as she remembered it—an unimposing two-story brick structure providing confidential outpatient treatment for previous in-patient residents and, very occasionally, outpatient appointments for immediate family members of the previously contained.

She made do with merely pulling up on the emergency brake, when what she'd really wanted was to yank it out. Relaxing for a moment—trying to relax—she checked herself in the rearview mirror and then checked on Troy, mostly silent in the passenger seat for the entire ride. Legs falling apart, body reclining, chin to chest, and forearms resting on his inner thighs. She would've mistaken his expression for boredom had it not been for the jangling legs, betraying the thoughts she was unsuccessful at wrestling from him despite many leading questions.

"Good to go!" Laura hoped her voice conveyed courage Troy could take into his appointment with Dr. Harvey. She'd already relayed her version of Troy's unusual behavior. Now Dr. Harvey would hear Troy's take on the events.

They'd barely sat down in the waiting room when Dr. Harvey appeared at the door leading to the inner offices. Laura closed the *Psychology Today* she wasn't reading and dropped it in the seat behind her.

Dr. Harvey raised his hand, both in greeting and to halt Laura from following along behind her son, like she'd done on the first day of nursery school. "I'll come get you *after*," he said, and the heavy door swung shut, swallowing the doctor along with her son.

Laura picked up a copy of *Vanity Fair*, and the glossy cover photo of an actress with a saccharine smile trembled in her hand. She tossed the magazine onto the side table. She sat down, she stood up. Breathed, held her breath. Paced.

A young couple checked in with the receptionist. The woman touched her husband's expressionless face, gave his name, and confided that they were there for his first in a series of ECT appointments. She whispered the acronym to make the idea of electroconvulsive therapy lest objectionable, for herself, not her husband. Her husband didn't appear as though he'd object to much of anything.

"Honey? We can sit down now." The woman was shaking worse than Laura, all the while keeping a hand on her husband's arm, no doubt afraid he'd die and leave her behind.

Laura had once thought avoiding expressing her worst fears, even to herself, could forestall them.

Hot and cold at the same time, Laura shrugged off her suit jacket. She balled the navy weave against her chest. She rocked on her heels, and the motion activated a wave of memory.

Jack's blood-stippled right hand had straddled the revolver's hard rubber grip. His fingers clenched the trigger. His left hand had rested in his lap, gold wedding band gleaming, palm open and beckoning.

Laura had sat beside him on the futon, facing forward, and stroked the smooth-skinned length of his forearm. She'd held his hand between hers, matching up three sets of fingertips. Finding the gesture ineffective, she'd pressed her lips to his still-warm palm and wrapped his fingers around her offering, hoping the kiss would remind him of their love for an eternity.

A tsunami of a heat flush rolled over her. She race-walked to the single stall ladies' room, locked the door behind her, and splashed her face with cold water, sprinkling her blouse in the process. She was not about to throw up. Not here, not now. No way. *Don't think, don't think, don't think.* She swallowed purposefully.

Three raps on the door.

"Someone's in here."

"It's Carol."

Laura wiped her hands with a coarse wad of brown-flecked paper towel, shot into her blazer, and buttoned to cover up the wet mess she'd made of herself. In her breast pocket, she found Aidan's folded note and rubbed his words between her thumb and forefinger. A deep breath, and she pushed through the heavy metal door and hung a sunny-side-up smile on her face for the benefit of Carol, the receptionist who'd vacated her post to chase her down. Nothing was going on here.

"Dr. Harvey can see you now."

Laura nodded like a bobblehead doll and walked alongside a woman she'd known slightly for years, a woman who'd known all the gritty nuances of her personal life.

"You look amazing," Laura said, noticing Carol's considerable weight loss, then wished she'd kept her mouth shut. What if the healthy appearance was due to grief or disease? One never knew.

"Weight Watchers." Carol touched her hair, drawing Laura's attention to the new addition of red highlights covering up the gray. "It's the only thing that works." Then, eyeing Laura, "You've always been such a tiny thing. What's *your* secret?"

"Oh, well." Stress, sleepless nights, widowhood, the possibility of a life-threatening disorder snaring her son. "Why, Carol, I don't *have* any secrets from you." Laura made sure she caught the woman's horrified gaze dead center. Once in a

while, Laura couldn't resist stepping into a character completely unlike herself and shocking the pants off people. She'd
never tried skydiving or bungee jumping, so this little thrill
would have to suffice. She found the necessity of allowing so
many professionals front-row seats for observing her family life
hugely unpleasant. As far as she was concerned, letting a
health-care professional measure her height and weight vio-
lated her privacy.

They rounded the corner, and soft crying trickled from the
waiting room. The young woman who'd checked in her husband was sitting alone, pressing the heels of her hands into her
eyes, as though she'd already witnessed enough horrors. Laura
wanted to tell her everything would be all right. Her husband
wasn't feeling a thing. He'd awake disoriented and headachy,
and he'd most likely behave more like his usual self after a
course of repeated treatments. But the facts that came next
prevented Laura from speaking. ECT never provided a long-
term solution or prevented the inevitable. If a man wanted to
commit an act of violence—either homicide or suicide—no
person or procedure could stop him.

Dr. Harvey poked his head into the waiting room and ushered her through the connecting doorway. "So nice to see
you." He pounded her back, like a guest at a cocktail party.
She'd forgotten about the back thumping.

In the hallway, Laura noted the dated decor—beige pat-
terned flooring to mask scuff marks, cheap art prints on the
walls depicting a single rose, a raindrop, a bouquet of fall leaves,
nothing too complex. Everything cheerful and mundane. No
wailing Edvard Munch expressionist paintings. No impression-
ist van Gogh clouds curling into themselves. No cubist Picas-
sos encouraging the alternative placement of body parts. No
hint of the close quarters creativity kept with madness.

The sight of her son in Dr. Harvey's office, sitting in the
leather wing chair she associated with Jack, paused her at the

threshold. She thought, for a nanosecond, she was watching a brutally clear home movie.

Jack had favored seltzer water with a twist of lime, and Dr. Harvey had made sure the ingredients were at the ready for every visit. A slice of the fluorescent green fruit wedged atop the rim of Troy's clear plastic cup. He pressed his thumb to the top of his red-striped straw and slurped up a bubbly gulp from the bottom. So her son was having a great, good time, and she was falling apart.

Troy scrambled from the comfort of the wing chair. "I'm gonna wait outside. Okay?" He flew off before Laura could answer.

"Sit, sit!" Dr. Harvey said.

In addition to the back thumping, Dr. Harvey had also retained the peculiar habit of saying everything twice when particularly excited, his phrases like a double dose of optimism.

She chose a seat beside him on the overstuffed microfiber. The doctor's soft belly pressed at the buttons of his starched white short-sleeved shirt, his light brown hair had turned silver at the temples. And he still wore those beige chinos with the overdone pleats, the type she didn't think they made anymore. The very facts of him had once settled her nerves. She smoothed her skirt, waited.

"You've got a great kid."

She smiled, waited more.

"It's not at all unusual for an anniversary of a particularly stressful event to precipitate an extreme grief reaction. Especially if that grieving has never been fully expressed."

When had she prevented Troy's grieving? She refused to nod, despite Dr. Harvey's contagious gesture. One little *reaction* could detour the course of her son's entire life.

She pictured an ECT bite block in Troy's mouth, preventing her son's clenching teeth from sinking into his lips and tongue. She was sitting perfectly still but found herself breathing hard just the same. She clutched her blazer by either lapel to keep the fabric from opening and revealing her heart, thudding as though electrodes were disrupting its normal pacing.

Her sinuses swelled. Her ears pounded. Her gaze ratcheted over the dark painted woodwork, the bamboo blinds, the framed degree from Harvard Medical School, the walls that caged her.

"Look at me," Dr. Harvey said, in the way of a person used to taking charge.

She jumped to standing, following an instinct she didn't understand. On the third pass around the room, she replayed the conversation with Dr. Harvey and allowed the possibility she'd misunderstood. Perhaps he wasn't heading her son toward a definitive diagnosis of bipolar. One negative thought had spiraled her heart rate, which had further spiraled her thinking, until mind and body had wound around her chest, coming at her from both sides.

She settled into the soft cushion beside Dr. Harvey, and he continued talking, as though her side trip had never happened. In her ears, the pounding slowed to mid-grade agitation. The cotton-wad-in-the-throat sensation softened to a tickle of hair, and the hot pressure behind her eyes retreated.

"Troy described the anniversary events very much like you detailed them for me," Dr. Harvey said.

Right, she and her son were so much alike she could imagine what he was thinking. Usually.

"We attempted to get at what he was feeling, what might've derailed him." The exact details she'd craved for weeks. Turned out, Darcy wasn't her only offspring good at stonewalling.

She tried catching Dr. Harvey off guard. "Which was?"

"You know I can't divulge. A deal's a deal."

She nodded. Troy had agreed to speak openly with Dr. Harvey only when she'd assured him their conversation would remain privileged. She might never know the details of her son's mind, but she had a right to the general impression. "So would you say he had a manic episode, or what? I realize he exhibited some of the classic manic symptoms, but he's never been depressed." *That I'm aware of* scrawled clear as skywriting across her mind, trailing a secondary scribble of blame. "And depression usually precedes a manic episode, so perhaps Troy's just been anxious?" For the entire car ride to Belmont, she'd hung her hopes on the diagnosis of *anxiety*, the mainstream malady of the worried well.

Dr. Harvey coughed. "Excuse me a moment." He nabbed a fizzing beverage from his desk blotter, took a few swallows, and then set his lime-decorated seltzer water on the side table.

"Can I get you something to drink?" Dr. Harvey asked.

"Uh, gin and tonic?" Dr. Harvey formed his lips into an O before she let him off the hook. "Just kidding!" And her kids accused *her* of having no sense of humor.

Dr. Harvey angled toward her and took an audible breath. *Stay with me, Laura,* Dr. Harvey's eyes seemed to say. She examined his tiny downward-arching lashes shadowing his cheeks.

"The details you mentioned on the phone—his agitation, self-deprecation, the crying, sharing stories about Jack—if not for Troy's family history, I wouldn't have bothered having you bring him in to see me. Nothing sounded extreme, and what Troy shared didn't prove otherwise."

Her lungs opened, and she sighed. "Thank God."

"You understand, this certainly doesn't rule out the possibility of bipolar for either Troy or Darcy further down the road. We'll just have to wait and see," he said.

"Wait and see?" Hearing the phrase she'd told herself only validated her worry. She hoped she sounded only faintly hysterical. She was clean out of patience. She'd used up her quota on Jack, waiting to see how long it took for him to cycle between mania and depression, waiting to see how long each

episode lasted, waiting for his suicide attempts to earn the des-
ignation of *successful*. Dangerously warm again, she walked
across the room and took off her blazer, not caring whether
her blouse was still so damp her bra showed. Screw the blazer.
Deal with it.

Dr. Harvey got up and came to where she was standing by
his desk, digging her nails into her palm. He gentled his voice.
"I'm sorry I can't give you a more definitive answer at this
time."

He was trying to make her feel better, but his apology had
the opposite effect.

Dr. Harvey slipped a hand into his desk's side drawer, and
then passed Laura a business card. "Grace Snyder is a very good
therapist, easy to talk to, and much more accessible distance-
wise."

Grace Snyder's private practice was located in Peterborough. Well, that would certainly save gas. "I don't mind making the drive for Troy."

"I think *you'd* feel more comfortable talking to her than to
me."

"I don't understand."

"Have you spoken to anyone this year, joined NAMI or
any other survivors' groups, sought out any grief counseling?"
I know you haven't hung unspoken between them.

She shook her head, couldn't think of a damn thing to say.
How had the conversation turned? Her blouse had mostly
dried, but she might as well have taken it off along with her
undergarments. *Don't look at me.*

"Considering Jack's illness and what you've been through,
it's understandable you'd be concerned about your children's
mental health. It's not unusual for extreme worry to snowball
into a full-blown anxiety issue," he said. "Like what just happened here."

No, no, no. Laura's gaze slid from Dr. Harvey's to the closed window behind his desk. What did the man have against fresh air?

"A good therapist can give you tools to help you deal more effectively with your anxiety and help you recognize when you needn't worry," he said. "I've been wondering how you've been doing. When I got the message you'd phoned, I was sure the query concerned your mental state, and not the children's."

"Why?" She tilted her chin upward. She was never ashamed of her husband, but she'd always prided herself for being the glowing picture of mental health. She'd never thought of her behavior as extreme, until now.

"Because," he said, "you were always so strong for Jack and the kids, unusually so, and I've a sinking suspicion, despite efforts to keep this information from the general public, that you're also human."

Laura translated Dr. Harvey's shrink talk. *Human* meant *the worried well.*

She imagined telling Dr. Harvey about her night terrors and about the details of Jack's death that plagued her, right in his waiting room. But the perfect opportunity couldn't coax the words. Once you'd spoken your thoughts, they revealed a truth you damn well better be prepared to deal with head-on. Her truth could wait.

"You know, doctor, I've always respected your professional opinion, but this time you're wrong. I'm Super Laura to the Rescue." She took a wide-legged superhero stance, threw her blazer around her shoulders like a cape, and raised her arms to ensure safe flying.

He burst out laughing. "I've forgotten how funny Jack could be sometimes."

She could never remember who'd started the nickname,

Troy or Darcy, but Jack had made it into a term of endear-ment, and then gave himself several comic strip personas. *Super Bipolar Man, man, man, man,* he used to say, echoing like an old-fashioned cartoon character. She preferred his Super Writer Guy impression the best, her hero with fingers flying across the keyboard faster than the speed of sound.

Edging her way toward the door, she slid back into her blazer and buttoned the Peterborough therapist's card into her breast pocket alongside Aidan's note. "So nice to see you, Dr. Harvey." She offered her hand, and he turned the businesslike shake into a hug, reminding her of Jack's funeral. Dr. Harvey had hunched in the second row of folding chairs at the ceme-tery, crying uncontrollably, not as a doctor who'd lost a patient, but a man who'd lost a dear friend.

"Call me anytime," Dr. Harvey said, releasing his bear hug before she was ready.

The glaring absence of Troy in the lobby drove home the obvious reason behind her son's reaction. She and Troy were so much alike.

For a year she'd mourned her husband, the sick Jack, the man who made her so angry she'd wanted to scream. After the funeral last year, she'd hidden away the photo albums. She'd re-fused to look at pictures of Jack fishing with the kids on Her-mit Island, teaching them how to ski at Crotched, or the sun-drenched shot Darcy had taken of Laura and Jack during the CROP Hunger Walk. Two weeks ago, Troy's anger at Jack had broken, and the good memories, the good Jack memories had nearly broken Troy.

The good memories were so much harder.

"Dude," Troy said in his husky thirteen-year-old voice, when she exploded out of the Admissions Building. He stretched out across a granite bench, partially concealed beneath the cover of an ancient maple.

"Dudette," she corrected, and pointed to her vehicle.

Not a worry in the world, Troy had assumed she'd find him. He'd assumed she'd always keep him safe from harm.

But how could she keep her son safe when she was so utterly lost?

Chapter 24

The threat of vegetable oil frying potatoes into cancer-causing snacks did little to dissuade her son.

She pressed her back into the seat, making herself as flush as possible, so Troy could lean across her, reading the red-lettered drive-through menu. "Are you sure you can't wait?" she asked him for the third time since fitting into the end of the rush-hour line.

"Mom! I'm so hungry I'm drooling." He wiped his mouth for effect. "I, uh, didn't eat lunch."

"Troy Edward," she said.

"I'm sorry! I just wasn't really hungry earlier, and now I'm starving to death." Troy plopped back. "I've decided. Value meal three."

She nodded, gave Troy's order to the disembodied monotone voice coming from the pitted circular speaker, pulled up a car length to exchange cash for what barely passed for food, and then angled into a parking space. Letting Troy eat on the way home was a better use of time than making him wait until eight o'clock tonight. Eating that late was plain bad for his digestion, and like he'd said, he needed a full stomach for homework.

Troy took five minutes to gobble down most of his meal, mowing through a double-decker burger, large fries, and massive root beer, as if fast eating were a universal test of manhood. He didn't bother swallowing before diving into conversation, a habit Laura had cautioned him against since his toddler years, to no avail. "Tell Aidan we can have dinner another time. You should invite him over again. I could do my smoothies for dessert."

"It's okay, honey, no big deal. I'm sure he'll understand."

Laura took her cell from the console and speed-dialed first Elle, and then Maggie, knowing Maggie was teaching a yoga class and Elle forgot to take her cell to the shop more often than not. She left the same message for both friends, who'd insisted she call after Troy's appointment but weren't expecting to hear from her till later. *I found that misplaced book,* she told their voice mails; the code they'd agreed upon to mean Troy had not lost his mind.

Next, Laura called Darcy. The phone rang once.

"What's up?" Her daughter's voice, but not an expression Laura was used to hearing from her offspring. Even the intonation rang foreign, coming out all ghetto and attitude.

"Did I tell you Aidan invited us to dinner?"

"No. When would you have told me? Maybe in your sleep this morning?"

"All right, that's enough. I'm telling you now, but you sound as though you're not in a very good mood."

"I'm in a great mood. I mean I was. No way I'm going to dinner with you. I don't want to talk to *him,*" Darcy said, referring to Aidan.

"I was really hoping you'd come with me," Laura said. She wished Aidan could connect with her daughter, the way he'd connected with Troy. A girl couldn't have too many positive influences.

"Is Troy going?" Darcy asked.

"No."

Troy folded the last of the disease-causing french fries into his mouth, and then wiped his grease-splotched lips on his shirt, ignoring the stack of napkins.

"Is it okay if I make something for myself?" Darcy asked.

"You can't avoid Aidan forever. You're going to have to face him eventually."

"Why should I? He's not my father," Darcy said, drawing Laura back to Monday night's circular argument.

Give her strength. "How does fast food sound?" Laura asked, offering an olive branch to her daughter.

"Awesome!" Darcy said. "Large fries, please!"

Laura rested at the threshold to Darcy's bedroom; amazed they'd made such good time returning from Belmont. The southbound lane had come to a stop, while she drove northbound at fifty-five. Troy was camped out in his bedroom, his boy cave, bent over schoolwork, having declined her offer to talk about his appointment.

Laura opened Darcy's door wide enough to fit her arm and waved the white flag of a value meal. She licked her lips and stepped into the bedroom, expecting to hear Darcy laugh. Instead, she found her daughter stone-faced, sitting on her bed and clutching a throw pillow over her stomach.

"What did Dr. Harvey say about Troy?" Darcy snuggled the pillow closer and fidgeted a chenille pom-pom.

Darcy's heartfelt question about her brother proved layers of sensitivity. Troy was Darcy's constant sparring partner, but she'd defend her brother to the death. Ironically, when it came to Darcy's relationship with Nick, this character trait worried her the most.

Laura closed the door and placed the fast food on Darcy's dresser. She sat down on the bed, not too close, the way animal tamers lured skittish critters. She couldn't help but sigh, even though it usually irritated her daughter. She couldn't help but love her daughter more than ever. She couldn't help but break into a grin and share the good news. "It seems, Darcy, that your mother is off her rocker."

Laura inched closer and told Darcy as much as she knew. She left out the part where Dr. Harvey gave her the name of a shrink. She had no intention of signing up for weekly pity parties.

"We ended up talking about Dad's Super Bipolar Man persona," Laura said.

Finally, Darcy cracked a smile. Tears glazed her eyes. She went to the dresser for a tissue and turned her back to Laura. Darcy's shoulders shook, either from relief or lingering worry.

"Angel, Troy's fine."

"For now," Darcy said through her tissue, and she blew her nose.

Laura had never harped on Darcy's and Troy's genetic predisposition to their father's bipolar disorder. But what had Laura expected? Between Google and books, her kids probably knew more about bipolar than she did.

Darcy's turn to heave a loud sigh.

"I don't think . . . I don't believe Troy's going to get sick," Laura said.

"But you don't know that."

Laura sucked in a breath and considered lying, if only to convince herself. "No, I don't know that. I wish I could make you a personal guarantee for the future. I wish—" Dr. Harvey's phrase "wait and see" scrolled through her head. How could she share with her daughter what she could barely brook?

"Troy's fine, angel, and so are you."

Laura went to Darcy and wrapped her in a hug. She pressed her lips against the part in her daughter's hair. The sweet scalp scent reminded Laura of a newborn, brimming with potential. Whether Darcy realized it or not, she had her whole life ahead of her. She didn't have to end up like her mother, sidelined by the possibility of future disaster. "Try not to worry."

Darcy straightened, scratching her head. "I'd like to be alone now."

"I can stay—"

"Please," Darcy said.

"You're upset. You shouldn't be alone. If you shared—"

"Please, Mom, I *really* want to be alone."

Laura nodded and backed silently out of the room, responding to her daughter's polite request before it dissolved into something infinitely less pleasant. Patience wasn't Laura's favorite virtue, but she could fake it, at least when it pertained to waiting for her kids to open up and come to her.

In the bathroom, Laura checked her watch, and noted just enough time to jump in the shower before heading downstairs for dinner. Short of lying, she'd said everything possible to assure Darcy. And Troy, well, once again he'd proven how very much alike they were. Tonight, he'd calm his residual nerves by sticking his head in his schoolbooks. Tonight, neither one of her children needed her. Tonight, Laura doubted any book could stem her tension.

Chapter 25

Getting ready for dinner with Aidan set off a notion that arose not from Laura's mind, but from her body, traveling upward until it formed one concrete sentence. *I deserve happiness.* She revised. *I deserve moments of happiness.* A scene featuring a couple skipping along hand in hand through fields of heather while saccharine music played and then faded in time with the golden sunset belonged to unrealistic G-rated movies.

Under the showerhead, the water pulsed at her scalp and clarified her thoughts. When it came to certain areas of her life not related to her children, patience had altogether lost its luster. She rinsed the clogged razor close to the nozzle, then shook the shaving gel and lathered her upper thighs.

Out of the shower, she wiped the fog from the mirror, squeaking it clean, and stood on the bathroom stool. She couldn't make out her entire body, but surveyed her form in sections, beginning with her breasts. Not too bad, if she stood perfectly straight, no slumping. For the first time in years, her stomach lay flat, a diminished appetite the only benefit of widowhood. And her legs appeared sculpted, detailing not one but two separate curves at the calf when she rose to tiptoe, like a ballerina on pointe. She made the conscious decision to avoid viewing her bottom, much to the chagrin of Elle's voice in her head. *You need to know what you look like from behind*, her free-loving friend often said. To which Laura always replied with statistics, supporting her claim that attraction happened mostly in the gray area between your ears.

She stepped down from the stool, patted herself dry, and reached for the super-emollient cream, taking great care to slather liberally on those areas prone to roughness—elbows, knees, and the inexplicably dry patches on her bottom. Turned out, she was more concerned with the sense of touch than with vision, at least where her bottom was concerned. She knew what she had to do, how far she needed to go to get exactly what she wanted. She'd done it before, so it shouldn't have come as a surprise to her, this deliberate planning, and yet it shocked her, making her heart drum in her ears. The last great real-life plotting had taken place years ago, before she'd become an adult in the truest sense, before circumstances had gradually sculpted her like water over rocks. Even then, she'd acted out of character, or so she'd thought.

She worked the remaining cream into her hands, massaging the palms, and then briefly caressed below her navel— more to ascertain certain near-forgotten regions were still fully functional than to obtain a cheap thrill. All systems go.

She finished washing up, brushing and flossing, even gargling with the painfully strong mouthwash. She covered her face with moisturizing face tint to even out her skin tone and make the spray of girlish freckles across the bridge of her nose a bit less prominent. Considered and forewent the blush. She was already flushing. She opted for deodorant, but the decision to skip perfume was a no-brainer. Natural pheromones served her purpose.

Did it really matter what motivated a person? In the end, you were your actions. No more, no less. You forced a smile, and your body interpreted the movement of facial muscles, splashing brain cells with opiates and creating the feigned emotion. She worked mousse lightly through the crown of her hair, and then hung from the waist, using the diffuser to garner maximum volume for what, tonight, she recognized as a glorious mane. She tried out a forced smile in the mirror to test her theory, and, sure enough, her whole body sang.

Sailing on natural opiates, she hurried across the hall and unceremoniously slid off her wedding band, tossed it inside her jewelry box, and closed the lid. She selected a brand-new white T-shirt, one of the few staples she replenished every year, and a well-worked-in pair of jeans. The stonewashed denim hugged in all the right places. For shoes, she decided upon her favorite sandals with the half-inch heels. She was going for the understated look, unaware, approaching innocence, as much as a thirty-five-year-old mother of two could fake naïveté.

Yet, she must have convinced herself, because by the time she went down to the kitchen, her hands were really shaking, and she paused at the counter to steady herself. She dragged over the step stool so she could reach the above-cabinet wine rack and chose the cabernet sauvignon, remembering how on that long-ago fateful day she'd given her virginity to Jack she'd downed a shot of peppermint schnapps.

She was raising her hand to knock on Aidan's partly open door when he called out from the far end of the apartment. "In the kitchen!" She pulled the door shut behind her, and it locked with a soft click. In the unlikely event her kids needed her tonight, she'd hear them knock.

Aidan stood at the sink, washing his hands. "I'm just about ready for you guys." He gazed past her.

"Um. Guess I should've let you know. Darcy and Troy aren't coming. Homework," she offered as a quick alternative to a long drawn-out explanation. "But I brought wine." She held out the bottle, wishing she'd thought to pick up a gift bag on the way home, something to make the offer less like a regifting.

He wiped his hands on a paper towel. "Great, thanks. Would you like me to open it now?"

"Sure, why not?" she said, and Aidan fished in a drawer for an opener.

She glanced away and hoped she appeared nonchalant, rather than a woman badly in need of a drink.

Aidan's butcher-block coffee table took up most of the back room; his four overstuffed beige floor cushions outlined its perimeter. A hot plate perched at the center of the table atop a metal trivet, holding a heavy-looking iron stockpot. Plates of raw food surrounded the pot of gently boiling bouillon. The largest plate displayed chunks of creamy tofu, sliced shittake mushrooms, Chinese cabbage, and semitransparent leeks. Thin strips of steak lay across the smaller plate, like sunbathers stretching across a dock. Wide udon noodles roped inside a mismatched khaki bowl.

Only one meal called for this specific selection of raw ingredients. "Shabu-shabu," she said, and accepted a nice and full glass of wine from Aidan.

"You make swish-swish?" he asked, translating from Japanese to English.

"I don't make it, but I love it. I haven't eaten Japanese in years." On the rare occasions when they all went out to eat, they'd venture as far as Nashua, where they'd watch Asian chefs with sharp knives chop at a maddening pace, magically turning performance art into the most wonderful meals.

"I thought shabu would be fun for your kids. Dinner entertainment," he said, laying to rest the question of whether he had had an ulterior motive. Unlike her, Aidan's motives were pure.

He set out two sets of chopsticks and filled small red-lacquered dishes with dipping selections—duck sauce, sweet and sour, and her absolute favorite, ponzu, a citrus-seasoned soy. "Is anything missing?" Then, just as she was about to settle on a cushion, "A toast, to my first dinner guest!" Aidan said. "Not counting takeout pizza with Finn."

Filling a home with the personal sights, sounds, and smells of food christened a home like nothing else. "To new beginnings," she said, embellishing his toast.

They tapped glasses, then sipped. Aidan's smile took over his face. The rich wine flowed downward and kissed Laura's throat.

She started with the meat—clamping a strip between her chopsticks and inhaling the savory beef broth as she swished the red meat back and forth.

Beside her, Aidan slipped his chopsticks into the pot and swished his tofu, mirroring her movements. The ropes of muscles in his arm flexed. Her face tingled, and she chased the first tender morsel of meat with a healthy mouthful of wine.

Aidan chewed his tofu, and his tongue licked at the excess sauce on his bottom lip. "I've forgotten how much I like this." He grinned like a boy, content with small treasures.

"Me too. Delicious." She nodded, flushed from the food, the wine, her racing thoughts. She wouldn't let her mind wander from small treasures to small pleasures—even after the unchaste translation, a dirty little rhyming game. Instead, she drank more wine, filled her plate with every vegetable, and churned them through the broth, a woman on a mission toward a new beginning Aidan hadn't intended.

He passed her the noodles, regarded her carefully. "You remind me of Suzanne."

She dabbed at her mouth with a napkin and dug into the noodles with her chopsticks, waiting for an elaboration.

"One of my many sisters," he said.

Maybe she should've eaten before dinner, gorged on

crackers straight out of the box so she'd appear lacking any discernible appetite, like the Southern belles in *Gone with the Wind*. She imagined his sister Suzanne, an immense girl with beautiful dark eyes.

He laughed. "I swear it's a compliment. Suze is this tiny thing, so she shocks guys when she eats them under the table. Used to drink guys under the table, too, but she doesn't do that anymore," he said, letting her know his sister Caroline of He-Who-Must-Not-Be-Named fame wasn't the only member of Aidan's family with past issues. He leaned forward. "So does Darcy really have homework or is she avoiding me?"

She swallowed her mouthful of noodles, pulled her legs out from under the table, and kneeled on the cushion. "Darcy's avoiding you, but she'll come around," she said, interjecting confidence into her voice.

"And Troy?" Aidan asked. "I thought my bike buddy would show up."

"Troy got started on homework late. He had a doctor's appointment in the Boston area this afternoon." She stood up with her empty wineglass and took his, even though it was still half full. "I'll get us more wine."

She poured the wine and noticed a gray Bose sound system lurking covertly on the narrow shelf above the sink. A neighboring shelf housed a stack of CDs.

"Boston? Is something wrong?" he asked.

She should've kept her mouth shut. Sharing every detail of her personal life wasn't part of the plan. But the facts certainly spoke for themselves, a personal ad only a fool would answer: widowed white female, devoted mother of two teenagers predisposed to a serious mental illness, seeks companionship with attractive normal man. Any reasonably sane man would run for the hills, camp out, and live as a hermit until the end of his days, rather than pursue a meaningful relationship with her.

This could work to her advantage. She really liked Aidan and what she sought was a win-win situation. A relationship with her, the type necessitating actually garnering approval from each other's family and friends, could turn disastrous. All in one night, she could show and tell him exactly how much, or how little, she had to offer.

"I brought Troy to speak with Jack's old doctor, a psychiatrist who specializes in bipolar disorder," she said.

"That's what Jack had—bipolar?" Aidan scrambled up from his cushion and started across the room, a split-second response to a slight quaver in her voice.

"Exactly." She passed Aidan his wine and took a double sip of hers. "After Troy's outburst at dinner a couple of weeks ago, he was up all night, extremely agitated, and fretting over Jack memories. And"—her gaze dashed to the dinner table, and then back to Aidan—"because of Jack, the kids are predisposed to bipolar, but I needn't have worried. Troy is fine."

"How's he doing otherwise?" Aidan asked, all at once too close.

She wasn't the type of woman to start sobbing in front of a new friend. Dissolving into tears wouldn't convey an accurate portrayal, so she measured her words for stability. "Troy is absolutely fantastic." *Thank God, he's not Jack.*

"And you," he said, not giving her any space. "How are you doing?"

An innocent enough question, if it came from anyone other than Aidan. But she couldn't dismiss his unwavering voice, his steady gaze, or the way his feet pointed toward her, as if nothing else existed in the universe other than his awaiting her answer. Most people threw out a question and mentally moved on to the next subject before you'd even formulated a response.

Aidan wasn't one of those people, so Laura gave him what

approximated the truth. "I'm managing," she said, grateful the right verb had come to her. She hadn't said whether she was managing well or not, so she hadn't lied. *You wouldn't know the truth if it bit you on the ass.* Where had that expression come from? Crass, but she liked it.

Aidan stood perfectly still, as though waiting for a more detailed response to his inquiry into her state of mind.

An abrupt subject change seemed in order.

"Can I put on some music?" She replaced what must've been a troubled look on her face with a small smile and shuffled through Aidan's stack of CDs. Midway through, she discovered a classic Van Morrison recording that broadened her smile. "Do you mind?"

"Go right ahead."

She read down the list of song titles, remembering the soulful rock, the folksy lyrics. Very many years ago, she'd owned a cassette of the recording, but the tape had gone missing, lost in transit when she and Jack had moved from their last apartment. Jack had never liked Van Morrison. He took her listening to the singer-songwriter as a form of emotional adultery, as if she'd cheated on him with another artist.

Sliding in the beloved music allowed a pause of blissful anticipation.

She leaned against the counter so the steady beat of "And It Stoned Me" pounded through her. She didn't remember all the words, but the gist of the tune flooded back—taking joy from a simple day, complete with rain and sun, friends and— oh, yeah—liquid spirits.

"You picked one of my all-time favorites," Aidan said. When the song came around to the chorus for the second time, he caught Laura's gaze and joined in with the vocals. His voice flowed effortlessly, at once masculine and tender. Aidan sang for his audience of one, but his expression told Laura he'd chosen her from millions.

He combed his fingers through his hair, chuckling at himself, and she laughed with him. "Couldn't resist," he said.

He race-walked to the table, turned off the hot plate, then jogged up to Laura and raised his wineglass to suggest another toast. "To singing," he said. "Which I kind of, sort of, accidentally on purpose gave up about five months ago." Well, that explained the performance. Kind of, sort of.

They clinked glasses for a second time, and Aidan stared off into space. Energy buzzed around him. She tried naming the expression on his face, identifying layers of emotions: glee at getting back his sultry voice and a hint of regret at whatever had taken it in the first place. Her knee-jerk reaction pointed at Kitty. The time frame fit.

Laura took the brief lull between songs as an imperative to drink up because she knew what song was coming next, and the perfect opportunity it provided.

Tap, tap, tap. "Moondance" began with gentle percussion notes, four sets of three beats, rake on drum. A softer secondary swish followed the first resolute note, as though her heartbeat were knocking through the speakers.

She ran her fingers down the back of Aidan's hand until her palm lay flush against his knuckles and her fingers curled over his fingertips. He could've construed her hand on his arm as overboard friendliness, neighborly even, and she didn't want to leave any doubt in his mind. "Dance?" she asked.

He squinted at her.

"The song," she said, wondering about her next move, if this one fell flat.

He nodded, as if she'd spoken a full sentence, and glanced at their entwined hands.

"Here." She lifted Aidan's hand, arranged his warm fingers at the crook of her waist, and swayed against his palm before she lost her nerve. Stepping closer, he rested his free hand on her shoulder, the way kids slow-danced in middle school after a lecture on maintaining personal space. In time with the music, she swayed nearer, until she'd danced him up against the kitchen counter.

Maintaining eye contact was the hardest part—the way he saw her, really saw her, looking past the charade of her body. She couldn't stand it for another second, and she ran her fingertip along his jawline. No way he could mistake this gesture, a bold foray into personal space.

Still, just in case he didn't want this, didn't want her, she moved slowly and waited until his gaze fell across her lips.

"Laura," he said, and her name on his breath softened her. "You continually surprise me." His fingers smoothed the surface of her shoulder and journeyed to her waist, mapping her body with his hand. "Is this like a date?" he asked.

"Like," she said.

"Then I'd better kiss the girl." The faintest touch of Aidan's smiling lips opened her mouth. In time with Van Morrison's end of song vocal trill, his candied tongue tumbled into her mouth, sharing wine and citrus, ginger and honey. For this performance, he pulled her closer, letting her know he was hers.

"Crazy Love" played, and she smiled at the coincidence because she couldn't deny how nuts this looked, if anyone were looking from the outside. From the inside of her body, everything felt just right—his mouth an all-encompassing caress that warmed her down to her jeans. Hands in his hair, she deepened the kiss, and he pressed himself against her.

By the time "Caravan" sang of turning up the volume, they were both pretty loud, breath coming out in fits and starts, his hot mouth on her neck, and her hand playing truth or dare at the hem of his T-shirt. *There.* Her fingers traveled the expanse of skin over his nicely delineated stomach muscles, even silkier than she'd imagined.

She wanted more.

Now. She pulled away slightly and took him by the hand for the second time that night, and for the second time, he gave her that look, all quizzical and concerned. "We should go up to the loft." She hoped, prayed, he wouldn't ask her to expand on the notion.

He leaned his forehead against hers, then spoke all hushed, "You don't have to. You don't."

Ah, a man with four sisters, conscious in the way a woman had the right to say *no* up until the last possible moment. "Yes, but you see, I want to." Then, risking more than when she'd dared touching his stomach, "Unless, of course, *you* don't want to."

He nuzzled into her hair. "Oh, yeah, I want," he said, and turned the dimmer switch, lowering the loft-side ceiling light before following her up the ladder.

She climbed the ten steps to the platform and discovered her hands were shaking again, her body throwing up a signal of caution she had no intention of answering. She skirted a week's worth of Aidan's discarded clothing—scrubs, jeans, cotton socks—and lay sideways on his unmade bed.

He came to her and held her hands until the erratic energy ceased. When she was ready to start over, he went across the room and slid the closet door open, revealing a dumbbell and a stack of weights. He dropped to his knees and foraged through a built-in drawer.

Should she take off her clothes? Not exactly romantic, but no more ridiculous than their awkward removal by an impatient partner.

Years ago, fearing a gradual shedding would highlight her inexperience, she'd disrobed for Jack all at once. She'd stepped out of her button-fly Levi's and onto the threadbare Oriental in his hardback-scented office, like a butterfly emerging from a chrysalis. In subsequent visits, she'd relaxed and found the slow removal of clothing more gratifying, even when shirts tangled and pants bunched. Then, in recent years, they'd both taken to coming to bed naked whenever Jack's mood swung upward. For her, to get it over with, and for Jack, to avoid burdensome preliminary activities, like kissing and touching. Like looking at each other.

Jack could never win when it came to their arguments over his meds, so he chose to wage a horizontal war, using her body as his battlefield of choice.

"Laura?"

Aidan, this beautiful man, the essence of pure goodness in action, was calling to her from no more than four feet away. *Get the hell out of my head, Jack. I deserve this.*

Aidan held up a box of Trojans, not purchased for her, of course, but at least it was unopened. "Do you, are you . . . ?" He rubbed at the back of his neck, suddenly shy.

She hadn't planned this far ahead. "No, nothing," she said. Then, unable to filter her thoughts, "I've never been with anyone but Jack."

He opened the glossy box, ripped off a single packet, and then laid it on the pillow next to her. "You're practically a virgin," he said, and sure enough, his approving gaze made her new again, a woman without a past. He took off his shirt before lying next to her on his side and waited patiently for her signal to move forward, a very deliberate reserve, judging by the urgency his body was evidencing. "Come Running" played, the music drifting up to surround them, and in the instinctual dance of man and woman, they moved together.

A Renaissance man, she decided, losing track of time but not her habit of naming, controlling her experiences the way Adam and Eve held dominion over the Garden of Eden. Skilled in the art of appreciation, Aidan savored with all his five senses—visually exploring, inhaling her skin, touching, tasting, listening for her responses. The room spun, and she held on, digging her nails into the tender flesh of his shoulder blades.

Kneeling, he tore open the gleaming red packet.

"I can do it," she said. When she took her sweet time unrolling the condom onto him, he closed his eyes. His lips pursed.

Lover. She tried out the term as he lowered himself onto her. Then, in a split-second decision, urged her up so they were both sitting. In an equal position, she opened up and let him inside her. *Oh, God.* She'd forgotten how good it felt, how it could feel. Should. How it should feel.

Ecstasy, a state beyond reason and self-control, a trancelike state, leading naturally to *bliss,* an expression of heaven. *Exuberance* too; they both showed a joyous lack of restraint.

Clinging, kissing, rocking, the energy flowed back and forth between them. "Glad Tidings" played through to the final note until their bodies provided the only night music. Close, so close.

"Laura," he said, as though, yes, he knew the effect of speaking her name at just the right moment. *Oh, God. Rapture. Aidan.*

Then, for the best of reasons, she lost the need for words.

The alarm clock glowed a red two a.m. warning, sitting kitty-corner on the loft floorboards, and it took Laura a few seconds to make sense of it all. Aidan curled behind her, claiming her with his arms wrapped securely, the warmth of his body heating her back, his breath shallow like a sleeping child's. Just a sheet draped over them, and the comforter lay rumpled on the floor. She could neither recall the original arrangement of bedding nor the drifting into sleep.

She untangled herself from his bear hug, came to sitting, and ran her hand down the length of her body, wondering who she'd become. Laura, but not Laura. Aidan clutched a handful of sheets and rolled onto his back.

She hunted down the trail of her clothing and discovered

her jeans wrapped like burrito filling in the roll of the comforter, her underwear laid modestly beneath a pillow, and the white T-shirt folded multiple times upon itself and peeking out from the bottom of the sheets, keeping company with Aidan's feet. She couldn't help but wonder what on earth her bra was doing with Aidan's jeans, squashed up against the door of the closet.

She slinked back into her rumpled clothing and knelt beside the mattress. A rectangle of moonlight streamed through the skylight and showcased the curve of Aidan's face, his dark eyelashes, the length of his naked body. Pressure built behind her eyes, and she fought the urge to kiss the gentle slope of his mouth. His beautiful, sensitive, loving mouth.

What had she done?

Days ago, she'd told Aidan they shouldn't date because if her children knew, they might get emotionally involved. Last night, she'd come clean with Aidan, mostly, and shared her family's problems with him, if only to scare him away from drawing him into unfair emotional involvement with *her*. Last night, she'd intended nothing more than mutual sexual satisfaction, what the kids called friends with benefits.

Who the hell was she kidding? Last night, they'd made love.

Aidan blinked his eyes open. "Where are you going and why are you wearing clothes?"

She laughed, and the chuckle released wetness onto her cheeks. She batted it away. "I have to get to bed, my bed. And if my children find me walking around naked, I'll scare them to death."

Aidan came up on one elbow, regarded her face, and his gaze narrowed. "Laura," he said, sweet and soft and drawn out to soothe. He sat up and pressed his lips to her cheek, a streak of tears she'd missed, and her chest clenched. She stroked the back of his neck.

She had no right to pursue happily ever after with Aidan. She understood her place in life. She alone was responsible for her children. In one hand, she held the knowledge she'd never seek to make her relationship with Aidan anything more than what she'd originally intended. Her other hand held all her selfish wants, and the torture of the impossible completely unbalanced her.

Chapter 26

Technically, she was still a virgin.

So when her mother had asked, pressed the point, wondered out loud at whether she, Darcy, had been with Nick in the biblical sense, had allowed the penetration of a specifically male part of his body into her specifically female region, she'd answered *no*. Truthfully, they'd done everything else.

When they were alone, her clothes fell away as quickly as her inhibitions. High on Nick, her body urged her to give away more, not less, and do anything he asked. Maybe this not so gradual change should've surprised her, but it didn't. What really shocked her senseless was the way Nick had invaded not her body, but her mind. They'd taken to finishing each other's sentences, as though they were a quaint old couple celebrating their forty-fifth wedding anniversary. Sometimes, she'd know what he was thinking when they weren't even talking. The look on his face would give him away. And she could always tell, ten times out of ten, when the phone rang and he was on the other end.

"Nick," she said, after she'd raced from the living room and had scooped up the kitchen phone on its second ring. "You're back!" After Nick had suffered several of his father's I-swear-I've-changed phone calls, he'd decided to visit the wife beater in person. For the first time ever, Darcy had wished the weekend away, anything to span the seemingly insurmountable forty-eight hours Nick was spending with his father in Nashua. She'd refused more than one party invitation, actually got her homework done Friday night, and then passed all of Saturday biting down her nails, convinced Nick was in a terrible, nameless trouble.

"Hey, pretty girl. I'm on my way home," Nick said, his voice strangely thick. She thought she heard a motorcycle revving behind Nick's voice, passing him in traffic. "There's something I need to show you. Can I pick you up in, say, half an hour?"

"Absolutely." Just enough time to get ready for a date—fix her hair and pick out clothes, anticipating the fun of their removal.

"Later, gator."

So freakin' cute! Whenever Nick used one of those goofy phrases, clashing with his usual street talk, it only made her like him more.

She headed to Aidan's apartment to give her mother the update. Mom, Troy, and Lover Boy were getting ready to go hiking. Mom had even asked her to tag along. *As if!* She couldn't imagine how to fake not seeing through her mother's transparent game for an entire day, couldn't imagine how she could choke down her mother's story that she and Aidan were *just friends* along with the bags of trail mix they'd prepared. One of these days, it was going to slip out and it would *so* not be her fault. At her mother's age, she should be more careful. Darcy shuddered thinking about it, imagining them going at it, locked in a gross movie contortion.

She knocked on Aidan's door, and Aidan appeared, grinning like an idiot, his default expression. "Change your mind?"

"No," she said, and walked right past him.

Troy wore an unfamiliar black day pack, and Aidan tightened the belt so the weight rested on Troy's hips. "Now we're talking. Feel okay?"

"Feels super," Troy said. "Load 'er up."

Darcy could ignore the open containers of peanuts, raisins, dried cranberries, and white and dark chocolate chips lining Aidan's kitchen counter. But the butterscotch morsels watered her mouth.

Mom scooped Gatorade Frost powder into one of three empty Nalgene bottles and ran the tap. Blue puffs sprayed the air, replacing butterscotch with the taste of snow: raspberry with mint at the edges. "Nick's on his way to pick me up," Darcy said.

Mom screwed the Nalgene lid and gave the bottle three sideways shakes. "Where are you going?"

"Not sure. Greenboro Lake?" Darcy said, and her mother nodded, assuming Darcy had meant the public access side, where horny teenagers couldn't mess around unnoticed.

Mom set the bottle aside, and she turned around to ensure eye contact. "And how can I reach you?"

"Nick's cell?" Darcy said, since Nick would shut off his phone when they got busy.

"I'd like you to join us," Aidan said, and his happy-camper face got serious, his eye contact harder to ignore than her mother's. "You could invite Nick."

Darcy glanced at her mother. "Why not?" Laura said, as if Aidan were the dad in charge.

If Daddy were alive, he wouldn't have helped Mom prepare the family for a hike. He would've waited like royalty, writing or researching or sorting papers in his office, while Mom reviewed the contents of their packs, mixed gorp, and ensured last year's emergency whistles sounded clear.

From Mom's day pack, Aidan removed a bread bag full of sandwiches, and he zipped the stack of PB&Js into his own pack. He held both packs by the straps, then lifted and lowered the two weights.

If Daddy were alive, he would've hung back till it was time to leave. He would've let Mom do it all, instead of sharing the load.

"Come with us," Aidan said, "and I'll even carry your gorp. You know, to take care of quality control." Aidan winked at Darcy, and she accidentally smiled. For a split second, she pictured it: Mom and Aidan, her and Troy, a happy little hiking family.

For a split second, she replaced her daddy.

Darcy sucked air, but she couldn't get a full breath. "Can't." Her reed-thin voice ushered the sensation of Daddy's afternoon shadow roughing her face, and she fingered her cheek.

"Hang on a sec." Aidan unzipped his pack, dug down deep, and came up with his bag of gorp. He handed it to Darcy, killing her with butterscotch kindness. "I was planning on stealing your mom, anyway," Aidan said.

With an ache, Darcy's stomach cartwheeled. "What did you say?"

"Planning to steal your mom's gorp," Aidan said, and this time, Darcy heard the possessive *s*.

"I need to go change," Darcy said. Then, before Mom and Aidan had a chance to exchange one of their not so secret looks, Darcy stepped between them. She kissed Mom on the cheek and made a break for the Klein part of the house.

"That was random," Troy said, and her brother's clueless as usual comment nipped at Darcy's heels.

Troy didn't know everything.

He didn't know that, weeks ago, for the first time in years, Darcy had woken up in the middle of the night, wanting her mother. Not as a result of nightmare bad guys chasing her down the street, but from a sick tension striking when she'd remembered about Troy's bipolar genes potentially lying in wait.

After she'd checked on Troy, feeling slightly bizarre, she'd gone to Mom's room and found her bed not only empty, but also untouched—the coverlet snug and pillows neatly arranged. Okay, not even her neurotic mother made the bed before going to the bathroom in the middle of the night. Darcy couldn't smell anything, but maybe Mom was downstairs, getting ready to bake. If Darcy hurried, she could help.

She ran down the stairs with visions of baking in her head—gingersnaps, Mexican wedding cookies, shortbread with jam centers, moist chocolate macaroons bursting with coconut. At the threshold to the mudroom, she'd stopped short, her head snapping back against the sight of her mother's flannel-lined bed slippers angling toward Aidan's door, as though Mom had stepped from them while running, and then kept on going.

Her mother, the always proper widow Klein, was a hypocrite.

Darcy wished she'd had the foresight to record her mother's perpetual lecture on the dangers of premarital sex. Mom didn't seem too worried about pregnancy, disease, or a broken heart. Really, Darcy was surprised at herself for not figuring it all out even before finding the slippers. She should've known from the way Mom and Aidan stood too close, the way Aidan stared at Mom, pathetically magnetized, and, the biggest evidence of all, the way if Aidan caught Mom's eye, she'd quickly look away and raise a hand to her cheek.

Darcy ran up the stairs and headed straight for the hair spray she kept on the shelf in the bathroom, a necessary evil for days like today, foreshadowing summer humidity. She spritzed her head with the rest of the hair spray to smooth down her wild waves, even though Nick always said he loved her hair. He'd bury his nose in her hair and breathe deeply, as though he might inhale her. *Mmm.*

She added hair spray to her mental list of special items needed for the prom, touching the top of her head, a trick for remembering. She tapped her shoulders for the iridescent lotion, her chest for the strapless bra, her—well, Nick had said he'd take care of the condoms, purchase a brand-spanking-new box with her name on it. She didn't think she was the jealous type, but the idea of him dipping into a box he'd used for other girls made her want to tear it up into red confetti, find the sluts, and shove it down their throats.

Never mind. Nick was all hers now.

In her bedroom, she threw on a pair of stone-colored cotton pants and a lavender eyelet camisole, a dressier outfit than her usual weekend clothing. She was declaring today a holiday. This morning she'd awoken with the fierceness of realizing the obvious: she was in love with Nick.

She was working her feet into blue suede wedge sandals and simultaneously glossing her lips with cinnamon balm when Nick's Monte Carlo growled into the driveway. He honked the horn, and she snapped up her beaded purse, her heart flying down the stairs ahead of her. Usually, Nick would honk to let her know he was there, and then knock on the front door to keep her mother happy, proving that even a boy with a rusty car could have good manners.

Today, the car sat idling at the edge of the circular drive, facing the street with Nick behind the wheel, waiting for her. She swung through the screen door, kicked the side door shut, and raced to Nick's wide-open passenger-side door.

Nick turned and smiled at her.

"Oh my God!" His left eye squinted from the depths of a swollen lid. Sun glinted off the slit of violet-blue iris, and a matching hue formed a half-moon pool beneath his pale lower lashes. "What happened?" Instinctively, she touched his face.

He stiffened, inhaled sharply, and peered around her in the direction of her house.

"Nobody's home. Let's go inside." The way his gaze flitted made her jumpy, too. Made her want to take him up to her room, lock the doors, and bar the windows.

He shook his head. "I've got a better idea." He put the car in drive and careened onto the street. She tried holding his hand, but his fingers clenched around the steering wheel, turning white at the knuckles. And whenever she touched him, rubbing his shoulder or resting a hand on his leg, he'd have trouble breathing and his left eye would squint even smaller.

She squeezed her hands together in her lap. "I'm so sorry," she said, apologizing, even though she'd no idea what had happened. For once, Nick didn't take his eyes off the road, as though her gaze hurt more than her touch.

Pine scent further thickened the moist air, and they turned into the familiar drive leading to the vacant cottage. They'd taken to calling the property their own, even though they only parked in the driveway on their way to the lake for skinny-dipping and pressing curious prints into the sand.

The Monte Carlo roared to a stop. Nick jogged around to the trunk and took out his cooler. "Let's go."

She kept her hand on the back of his sweat-dampened T-shirt while they walked past the spot where they'd cut down the cottage-side hammock weeks ago just because it bothered her. Nick stopped at the back door, knocked, and then cocked his head. "What d'you know. Nobody's home." He turned the knob easily, and the door swung silently inward.

"When?" she asked, knowing he'd fill in the sentence to mean, *When did you work the door?* Nick's black eye wasn't scheduled, but she could bet he'd thought about this particular presentation for a long time and made sure everything would unfold according to plan. She couldn't wait to see what surprise he was saving for her in the cooler. She hoped it was covered in chocolate.

"So easy," he said. "Took me, like, thirty seconds to jimmy the lock. The place was asking for it. I'm surprised nobody's done it before." Nick held the cooler in front of him so they could fit through the door side by side.

"Oh, Nick." He'd done a lot more than breaking and entering. He'd even thought to open the window behind the cracked porcelain sink, lessening the musty smell. From the looks of the kitchen, he'd stopped by a few times to mop the black-and-white checkered linoleum, wipe the laminate counters, and scrub down the one item that hunched her shoulder into a shiver. Beneath a red, yellow, and blue stained-glass window sat an original built-in 1950s dinette, metallic red seats and all, direct from the diner of her dreams. Thankfully, today, no ghost of her father waited for booth-side service.

Nick slid the cooler onto the bench and leaned against the table, opening his arms to her. She kissed him lightly; she was afraid his whole face might hurt. They hugged until tremors moved through him, and she pulled away. Nick's black-and-blue eye closed. His good eye squinted, his face a lopsided grimace. "What happened?" she asked him again, and touched his face again, hoping he'd feel comfortable telling her in their cottage. "Please." She had to know so she could fix it.

He shook his head. "I don't know where to start."

"How about the beginning?"

"Like, when I was born?"

"You probably don't have to go back that far. Tell me what happened this weekend. Tell me who gave you the black eye." She had her theories, the obvious suspect, but Nick needed to tell her.

He held her around the waist, tugged her closer. "I'm so stupid for giving him another chance. I told him no way I was gonna see him again. No fucking way!" *Ouch.* A little too loud in her ear.

Darcy whispered, so Nick would lower his voice, too. "Your dad?"

"Him! Garrett, if you need a name. I don't have a father. And that's what I told him when he started in on me. The worthless, lazy piece of—"

Too tight. She wriggled out of Nick's embrace. "That's when he hit you?" she asked, like one of those TV lawyers, redirecting a difficult witness.

"No! That's when he started going nuts! Talking about what he was going to do to all of us. How easy it'd be to kill me, my mother, and my grandmother."

Darcy leaned against the table, and Nick paced back and forth, waving his arms. "Said he'd whack the three of us, and there was nothing I could do to stop him. It was all my mom's fault. He'd never wanted the divorce. Poor him. All he wanted was his family back. Was that too much to ask?" Nick stopped, center stage in the kitchen. "So I told him the truth. I said, 'You don't deserve my mother. You never did.' " Finally, his voice lowered. "That's when he came at me, swinging."

"Nick." He couldn't cry tears, so Darcy was doing it for him.

"Oh, don't you worry. I got him good, too."

She shook her head, wanting to make Nick's story go away. "So are you going to the police?"

"Are you fucked?" he said, and her mouth fell open.

"I'm sorry. I didn't mean that." He came to her and held up his shaky hands. "Garrett's making me crazy. See, I forget there's stuff you can't possibly know. Like how a restraining order's a useless piece of paper. And, if a guy wants to hurt your family, the police can't do a thing until *after* the fact."

Nick's story painted a black-and-white front-page image of three corpses beneath white sheets, taking the shape of Nick, his mother, and his grandmother. Beneath her sandals, the floor shifted, slick as black mud, and Darcy slipped into the chrome-edged booth.

"So I got some bad news." Nick slid into the booth next to her and draped an arm around her shoulder. "I was saving this place as a surprise for you. Our *honeymoon suite* for after the prom," he said, using a term she'd never heard him utter.

Darcy followed Nick's gaze through the doorway into the cottage's bedroom. On the floor, a single mattress took up most of the room. A sales tag dangled from the top of a white comforter.

"Maybe we can still come here," Nick said. "But just in case, I wanted to bring you here now."

Darcy stared into Nick's mismatched eyes, and he wiped the tears off her face.

"No prom?" She was embarrassed to admit it, but she was really looking forward to every ridiculous cliché detail, even balloons and crepe paper. Especially balloons and crepe paper.

"Oh, yeah, we're going. We have to go. It's our alibi. There's just the matter of a little something I need to take care of in the middle of the prom. Say, after we've been there for half an hour or so and made sure more than one group of kids has seen us. One group would seem like they were in on it."

In on what?

"Sweet princess," Nick said, responding to a bewildered expression he claimed she wore whenever he'd shoot off some street term. "Pass me the cooler. Would ya?"

Darcy lifted the cooler onto the red-and-silver doodle-swirl table, wondering how Nick would link today's snack with Saturday's prom.

Nick inhaled through his nose and huffed out through his mouth as he lifted two bulky dish towel–wrapped packages

from the cooler and set to unwrapping the larger of the two
with great care, seeming like he was making too big of a deal
out of the presentation—

Unless he was presenting a gun.

Even in the dusty light, the long black barrel gleamed,
aching her eyes. The trigger dangled, a lone silver claw hooked
in a come-to-me dare. The grip appeared rubbery and fake,
like a child's toy. Her brain flashed with two domino thoughts,
the second toppling the first. *I'll never let my kids play with toy
guns.* Then, *I won't live that long.*

"Beauty, isn't she?" he said, misunderstanding the way she
was staring at the revolver. "Smith & Wesson, holds six rounds,
.38 Special."

The gun Daddy had stolen from Mr. Mathers was a .38
Special, but some other brand.

Nick opened the smaller package, unfolding the stained
dishcloth as if it were expensive wrapping paper, and revealed a
rectangular box claiming to hold fifty .38 Special silvertip revolver cartridges. A whole goddamn arsenal. Enough to start a
small war . . .

Or kill your father.

A spiked head of nausea hammered at her throat.

The bubbly stained-glass window above the dinette caught
her eye, offering visions of ribbon candies stacked in a smooth
white candy dish. She narrowed her eyes so she could taste them.
Pucker-tart lemon for the burst of yellow light, maraschino
cherry for the pink-toned red, and raspberry for the cobalt blue
kept her from puking. But she wanted to break the glass, hear the
satisfying crackle and crunch, see the rainbow shards twinkle,
bust out into the sunlight, and never stop running.

With the prom as his alibi, their alibi, Nick was planning a
murder and asking for her *moral* support. How ironic.

Oh, Daddy, I get it now, the whole notion of irony!

Nick stroked her hair, and she turned back around for the

touch she couldn't get enough of. "You can't do this. I won't let you," she said. The words were her mother's, but her voice didn't come close to mimicking Mom's talk-sense-into-Daddy tone. *No, Jack, I won't let you go off your meds. Run away to Positano. Jump off the roof and fly to the moon.* How could Mom stand it, over and over again, without losing *her* mind? Had Daddy said those things because he knew Mom would stop him?

"What you gonna do? Have a little talk with Garrett? Ask him to play nice? Behave like a man?" Nick said, and Darcy thought of Aidan's Nick lecture. Pride, respect, and following house rules had nothing to do with murder.

Nick shook his head, and his jaw clenched. "Garrett's not a man, Darce. He's a psycho. You know, like Hitler gassing babies in ovens. Like Osama bin Laden wanting all Americans dead. What would you do if you had a chance to go back in time and kill a monster like that before he killed innocent people?"

Now she knew the gist of the English assignment he'd passed in without her editing, his answer to the philosophical question.

"What would you do?" he repeated. "You tell me."

"No, Nick." The idea of time travel overwhelmed her when she wanted time to stop.

"I'm really glad I spent the weekend with Garrett. It was like I saw the future, so I could decide what to do about it." Nick picked up the gun, aimed it across the room, and put on an expression she'd never seen him wear: heartless. "*Bang!* You're dead!"

Darcy's nails bit through the cotton of her pants leg, then her thigh.

Nick turned back to her, the gun aimed at the table. "Want to hold it?"

She swallowed, imagining the butt of a different gun. *The Colt,* she finally remembered. "Please, put it away."

Nick repacked his supplies, and his fingers worked the

towels into hospital corners. "It's not like this is all of a sudden. I was just hoping I wouldn't have to go through with it."

Of course not. These thing never were. Just turn on the news after a school shooting. The police always found evidence of a well thought out plan, a motive, and a boy—it was usually a boy—hell-bent on revenge. And family violence followed the same rules.

Nick clicked the cooler shut. "Yeah, I got most of it figured out, but something doesn't sit right. I was thinking after our visit to Nashua, we disappear for the rest of the night. Come back here or get a room somewhere, act like nothing happened."

She shook her head and accidentally blurted out the obvious answer. "We go back to the prom."

"Why do we go back to the prom?" he asked. "By going beforehand, we already got an alibi."

Telling him didn't mean anything. She wasn't agreeing. Besides, he'd figure it out without her. "You're right," she said. "Kids would remember the beginning because of pictures, deciding where you're going to sit, that sort of thing. The middle doesn't matter so much. Everyone's on the dance floor during dinner. But the end's when they do all the superlatives. King and queen and their court. That's when the teachers walk around, right? Kids are checking out the other couples, too, thinking they look the best. So they'd remember who was there and who wasn't. They'd *notice* if a couple went missing."

"God, you're perfect." He leaned in for a kiss, and she left her eyes open partway. Nick felt the same, but what his father had done to his face had vastly transformed him.

She grasped for something to unravel the plan, a thread left dangling. "What about fingerprints?"

"Another bonus from my visit to Nashua this weekend. Explains my fingerprints all over the apartment. It's a done deal."

No! Her father was a done deal. He'd decided to steal the gun from Mr. Mathers, get Mom out of the house, load the revolver, shove the barrel in his mouth, and pull the trigger. Every step of the way had offered him a chance to turn back. "Does anyone else know about this plan?"

"Dude I bought the gun from. He'll make sure Garrett's in the apartment alone at the right time."

The loose thread. She smiled without letting the expression reach her face. "Ever watch the news?" she asked him. "Not just the six o'clock, but one of those prime-time hour-long programs, when they talk to the criminal from jail? How do you think they catch the criminal, Nick? The criminal always tells one guy too many, either before or after the perfect crime." *Oops.* She didn't mean to sound so happy about it, so pleased with herself for discovering what she was absolutely sure would undo this sick idea stuck in Nick's head.

Nick touched her face, and the sensation moistened her eyes, reconfirming how much she loved him. "I'm not going to jail, princess." He widened his eyes, trying to make a point, but she didn't get it, couldn't fathom why the hair was sticking up at the back of her neck.

"How? What is it?" she asked, a shade short of hysterical.

I'm sorry, he mouthed. Nick leaned his head to hers so his words tingled her lips. "Worst case scenario, I got a bullet with my name on it."

For the second time in her life, her heart exploded in her chest.

Chapter 27

Even though they'd decided upon the White Dot Trail, the most direct ascent up Mount Monadnock, Laura had still turned into a straggler. Staying up late every night for the past month with Aidan, and sneaking back to her own bed at five a.m. had exhausted her. Her heart pounded in her ears, drowning out a thrush's flutelike phrasing. Her breath burned the back of her throat. She yanked off her day pack, tied her sweatshirt around her waist, and guzzled Gatorade. Only half of the blue liquid ended up in her mouth. The other half dribbled down the front of her wicking shirt.

"Drinking problem," she mumbled, even though Troy and Aidan couldn't possibly hear the joke.

Light filtered through the branches of striped maple, beech, and yellow birch, cascading down the rock path like water down a falls, and the sun's direct rays spotlighted her beautiful guys as they trotted effortlessly up the boulders en route to the summit. She wiped her mouth with her hand. Damn infuriating slip. She'd meant her beautiful son and her dear *friend*, whom she was planning to break it off with as soon as she could find the right words.

Their relationship was not going as planned. She'd managed to keep the extent of their friendship a secret from her children and friends. She'd even convinced Aidan that with her all-too-public history, going out for a real date within a twenty-mile radius of Greenboro would invite unkind gossip. But feeling a tug she couldn't answer and Aidan's constant push for her to accompany him to his friend Finn's house for dinner was getting the point across. She'd better end it before both of them got hurt.

The trouble was, whenever she'd try telling herself tonight was the night, she'd find herself in Aidan's bed, ablaze with equal parts lust and happiness.

She took another sip, getting the Gatorade entirely in her mouth this time, and slipped her arms back through the day pack straps. Where did those easy on the eyes guys go?

She made a microadjustment to the waist strap for comfort, took a generous inhalation of mountain air, and continued forward as the path opened up into a view of a knob she knew from experience would prove a false summit. Looking left and right, she couldn't see any blazes on the hardwoods indicating a route Aidan and Troy might've taken in error. Well, fine. She'd continue without them and catch up with them at the top.

With Troy at his side, Aidan burst from the woods and onto the trail. "And we're back!"

God help her, but the sight of her favorite man with her favorite boy sent her heart to her throat, like a girl with a wrenching crush. Or a grown woman with an irresponsible affair. "Where'd you go?"

"Bushwhacking." Troy grinned clean across his face, and Laura made the translation to *bathroom break.*

"Really now?" She looked from Troy to Aidan and judged the two males equally pleased with themselves. "Am I missing out?"

"Yes," they answered her together.

Aidan hastened to her side. "You okay? Are we going too fast for you, *old lady*?"

"Fine and dandy," she said, using a too-old-for-her expression to highlight their age difference.

Walking ahead of them, Troy laughed, surely thinking Aidan's teasing nonspecific, instead of an allusion that, out in the open, heated Laura's cheeks. Just last night, in response to her claims of getting old—an assertion she'd meant as the opening line for her Dear John speech—Aidan had embarked on a detailed exploration of her anatomy for the sole purpose of declaring her body both beautiful and youthful. According to his medical training.

Aidan curled an arm around her shoulder and leaned his head to hers. "Let's tell Troy we're going steady."

"Aidan." She ducked out from under his arm and picked up her pace. They'd settled on the phrase "going steady" to describe their relationship, the anachronism ringing a sweet old-fashioned sound reminiscent of poodle skirts, sock hops, and innocence, and not at all indicative of their covert operation.

He caught up in half a step. "C'mon. I'm crazy about him. Poor kid has the same sense of humor as I do." True enough. They both found soaking her *accidentally* while washing her station wagon highly amusing slapstick comedy.

"Let's tell everyone, *Laura*." Aidan tapped her bottom in time with the slow pronunciation of her name, and she immediately regretted having admitted the effects of his dulcet voice speaking her name with such deliberate kindness.

"Don't," she said, taking on a clipped tone. Letting Troy catch Aidan groping her would cause more damage than a public announcement.

Aidan stopped at a stretch of bare rock face. She'd seen him without a stitch of clothing, but never more vulnerable than now, paused with his palms open to her. "I'm beginning to think you don't trust me," he said.

"Aidan—"

"Who cares what other people think? This is about *us*."

He was asking her to see their present-day relationship as separate from her past, separate from her children's future, when the whole continuum of her life strung like glass beads along frayed yarn.

She tried to dislodge the whirligig sensation in her stomach making her want to embrace Aidan and never let go, despite the consequences. Clearly, Troy had taken a shine to Aidan. As for Darcy, the fact her daughter refused to come hiking with them today said it all. The friction between Darcy and Aidan was palpable. Laura needed to keep a close eye on Darcy and her too-serious-for-a-fifteen-year-old relationship with Nick, and not give her daughter an excuse to push away from her.

"This is about my children," she said. Even though she realized her initial attraction had as much to do with his sensitivity as physique, she'd truly hoped that deep down he was stereotypically male, exuberantly grateful for a no-strings arrangement.

"I like your children," he said, wavering in neither his stance nor his expression.

"Really? You like Darcy?"

"Despite my better judgment, yeah. I find her highly amusing."

Laura could imagine how highly amusing Darcy would become if she discovered her mother was sleeping with Aidan, despite all of her lectures on premarital sex. The word *hypocrite* resounded in her head, spoken in her daughter's best accusatory voice.

"Highly amusing wears on a person." Laura walked past Aidan-of-the-earnest-stare and up the stretch of boulders.

One step at a time, she angled for a secure toehold, when there was none. Lug-sole traction against smooth rock, arms out for balance, she climbed sideways, making use of the valley between boulders in lieu of an actual support. Above the tree line, inviting-looking tarns peeked out from behind layers of sap-green springtime hills. She gazed out as far as possible, willing her eyes to see the faintest ghost-shadow curve.

With Troy only slightly ahead of her, she glanced down the path she'd ascended, amazed at the steepness and how far she'd already come. Amazed Aidan had retained the precise distance from her she'd initiated, while keeping her and Troy within his line of sight.

She waited for Aidan, and together they caught up with Troy at a monstrous rock cairn. They climbed into a hair-whipping wind, and Laura spotted the geological survey benchmark imbedded in granite.

They'd hit the summit.

"You're supposed to kiss the marker," she told Aidan.

"Love to." He shrugged off his pack, dropped down into a push-up position, forced his lips into an exaggerated smooch, and lowered to the patina-green disc five times, clapping in between.

Troy followed Aidan's example, performing ten clapping push-ups to best Aidan's show. "Your turn, Mom."

She dropped her pack onto the rocks along with theirs and blew the marker a kiss.

"Do it!" Troy said.

She supposed she deserved this. She forced one push-up with pursed lips, and then flipped over, arms and legs splayed like a starfish. The playacting quickly turned into real exhaustion when she realized budging was entirely out of the question.

Aidan stared down at her. "What should we do with her?"

"I have absolutely no idea." Troy pushed on her lightly with the toe of his boot, and she gazed past him.

Aidan knelt beside her, pressed two fingers to her wrist. "She'll live." He stood up and puffed out his chest. "We strong men are going exploring," he said, letting her know he was teasing. He'd told her countless times how much she impressed him with her physical abilities, a strength she'd gained through necessity.

Laura raised her head. "Aren't you thirsty?" she asked Troy.

"Real men don't need water!" Troy said, and bounded off after Aidan.

Only her thirst pried her off the hard bed of rock. She scrambled to her pack and unzipped it carefully, making sure the plastic trash bags didn't go sailing across six states. She took out her half-full Nalgene and downed the rest of the Gatorade, grateful there were no witnesses to her unladylike gulping. She found a smooth spot on a boulder and arranged her pack behind her head.

Thumb Mountain appeared like an unimpressive hillock, near enough to touch. She could see Mount Kearsarge and Mount Osceola, their peaks easily discernible without binoculars. But believing in the fourth mountain, over one hundred miles away, required a profound faith she thought she'd lost until she heard her voice. "Mount Washington."

Gazing up into the cloudless sky, her eyes lost focus, and her eyelids fluttered shut. Three more times she tried keeping them open, and then the effort turned futile. Her lightweight jacket crackled in the breeze.

Wind-garbled, Aidan's voice touched her ears.

Troy's footfall thumped beside her. "There's this wicked cute girl," Troy said. "If I ever get up the nerve to talk to her—"

"What's her name?" Aidan asked. No way would Troy

give a name. The last time Laura had heard directly from Troy, her son still thought girls had cooties.

"Charlotte."

"So you haven't talked to Charlotte yet?" Aidan said. "What's the deal? If you like this girl, then don't let the chance blow by or you'll seriously regret it. There was this girl I liked in junior high, and I never got up the guts to talk to her. Found out years later she had this huge crush on me. I just never knew it."

Was that true? Laura couldn't imagine Aidan lying, but any girl catching a glimpse of him would find her tongue twisting in her mouth like a salted pretzel.

"Uh, I don't know," Troy said.

"Does she take off whenever she sees you, kind of avoiding you?"

"Yeah! And she's really friendly. She talks to all the other guys during track."

"Man, Troy, that's classic," Aidan said. "She's not shy. So why wouldn't she talk to you, unless she's all freaked about talking to you for the same reason you're worried about talking to her?"

Troy's voice squeaked. "Ya think?"

"Yeah, I do."

"Thanks, dude!" Troy said, and Laura couldn't help but grin like an idiot. Or a mom realizing her baby boy was growing into a fine young man.

"Look who's awake," Aidan said.

She scrambled to sitting.

"Guess we can't leave her here, Troy. Good idea though."

"I'm not at all concerned," Laura said. Aidan had left the outside pocket of his pack unzipped. She snapped up the spilling contents and jumped to standing. "I've got your keys!" she said, and dangled them in front of Aidan's face.

Tactical error. Aidan closed his hand over hers and smiled

into her face. When their eyes met, she fought the urge to raise a hand to his face and kiss him full on the mouth. The resistance dusted her fingers with perspiration.

In her peripheral vision, Troy studied their playfulness, as if he were collecting data. Her son could certainly benefit from a man like Aidan. Unless she did something stupid like dating Aidan openly and their relationship crashed, making Troy the unintended victim.

All the more reason to break it off tonight.

Eight forty-five p.m., and Laura's favorite means of distraction wasn't working.

After having phone-visited with Elle for thirty minutes and having spoken with Maggie for about ten, Laura promised herself she'd make it to the next book club meeting. For the first time in weeks, she'd be able to spend time with friends without worrying about Aidan-related fibs of omission. No more fear Maggie would read her madly in love aura or that Elle would take one look at her face and declare her lit with afterglow.

Laura sat on her bed with her back against two well-plumped pillows, her knees bent, and the hardcover book club selection beside her. Each time she'd tried beginning the novel, her eyes would leave the page, and her thoughts would follow. Tonight, she was planning on stating her case to Aidan, and then bolting. What at first stung mightily would result in a smaller net pain.

She hoped.

She kept glancing at the window, willing the obnoxious rumble of Nick's vehicle to roar through the screen, so she could begin the second half of her evening, the part she was dreading. Nick's old wreck had become synonymous with the before-curfew return of her daughter, and Laura had grown fond of the rusty Monte Carlo and its driver. Almost.

For now, she was keeping an open mind and an open door.

Nick's car rumbled into the driveway, and Laura peeked out her window. Leaving the engine running, Nick came around to the passenger side, and Darcy emerged from the car, only to disappear behind Nick's body.

Laura stepped away from the window. A few nights ago, Laura had once again asked Darcy whether they were having intercourse, and the way Darcy had held her gaze led Laura to actually believe her daughter's denial. Given their intensity of courting, however, Laura wondered how much longer that statement would hold true.

Laura recognized the tell-tale signs of a girl falling in love: the way Darcy had all of a sudden stopped making plans with her best friends, the way she hummed unconsciously under her breath, and the way she stared off in the middle of dinner, a piece of half-chewed food forgotten between her teeth until Troy gave her a prod. Even if Laura hadn't discovered the unique method Darcy and Nick had devised to keep their literal connection open by staying on the phone through the night, she would've known by the unusual luminescence in her daughter's face, a sheen she'd recently noticed in her own reflection.

Soon that would end.

Nick's car door slammed, and his car roared from her driveway. The screen door smacked shut. Instead of remaining downstairs and eating straight from a carton of ice cream, Darcy's usual post-date activity, her daughter trampled up the stairs to her bedroom. Laura took her daughter's action tonight as synergy, a sign that ending her relationship with Aidan was meant to happen, even though the thought upended her stomach.

Laura checked herself in the mirror. No hair fluffing tonight or formfitting clothing, but she didn't want to leave Aidan with the image of her as a total hag. She wrangled her hair into a covered ponytail holder befitting the tied-back seriousness of the occasion. Laura had given Aidan a preview by stating they needed to talk, and before he'd thought to erect the classic male unreadable mask, she'd glimpsed a look to rival any horror movie actor.

She stretched her calves, as though preparing for a sprint to a finish line she couldn't imagine any joy in crossing. When she'd started the affair, she'd experienced first-time jitters. Nothing to compare with the task before her.

She could envision breaking up with him, but she couldn't imagine her life after their conversation. Somewhere in the course of her relationship with Aidan, folding into the mix along with the role of lover, he'd become one of her best friends.

Partway through her kitchen, she glimpsed the door to Aidan's apartment, wide open and waiting. She trudged into the studio and closed the door behind her.

Aidan sat in the leather recliner, clutching his guitar in much the same way as her daughter hugged a throw pillow. He set the guitar aside and sent her a smile she'd come to believe was special order, for her eyes only. Then, seeming to remember her conversation preview, his mouth turned down. "Would you like something to drink?"

She shook her head, unable to speak as she committed his eyes to memory.

"Sit with me then," he said, and patted his thigh.

Instead, she perched on the chair arm. Her hand twitched with the memory of stroking his hair, touching his face, and forgetting about reality. She gripped the leather. "We can't do this anymore."

"Why not?" he asked, an invitation for her to state her case concisely, instead of the crumbs she'd been dropping for days.

Mustering all her debate skills, she gathered her thoughts, setting them in a black-and-white domino row she thought would click-clack to their inevitable breakup. "I'm in no position to date." She answered his quizzical stare, the slight shaking of his head. "I'm the mother of two teenagers. They're fine now, thank God they're fine, but I can't guarantee they won't develop their father's disorder. I'm flattered you appreciate them, but pulling you into my life as anything but a friend was utterly selfish on my part. You're a wonderful man, and you deserve more than what I can offer."

"Laura." He touched her face, and she swallowed the tears clogging her throat. "So your family's not perfect, but you're perfect for me. You're beautiful and talented and funny as hell, when you're not worrying about every worst-case scenario. Why can't you see yourself the way I see you? You have so much to offer."

"Parenting two teens isn't the same as being a friend. You think you know what you're getting yourself into, but you don't."

"Let me decide."

"No. It's not just you I'm concerned with. When you figure out what my life is really like, the long-term commitments, you could run like hell, and I can't say I'd blame you. Thing is, by that time, it would be too late for me to save my kids from more loss."

"I don't scare that easily. That's what family's about, but you already know that," he said, and she couldn't avoid the gaze that looked past all of her faults. "That's why I love you."

Laura's body flashed hot and cold, thrill and dread. A pin-sharp ringing pierced her ears. Every cell in her body wished she could do the wrong thing: grab her second chance at happiness while ruining Aidan's first.

She'd do the right thing because she loved him, too.

"You're so young," she said. "You're going to want children of your own one day, and I've no idea if I'd want any more."

"We'd decide together."

"There's more." She held her hand over her heart, and her pulse beat through her fingers, up her arm, and out through her lips. "There are things I haven't told you."

"What sort of things?" he said, and beneath his question Laura heard, *I've got it*, his take charge, take over, take care phrase.

She didn't need to make him think she'd totally lost her grip. She didn't need him to look at her that way, either, as though she were beautiful, no matter what. So she set out a chronicle of her near-miss panic attacks, night terrors, and wide-awake finding-Jack memories that plagued her, describing each scene as though she were recounting a secondhand experience.

None of these symptoms of anxiety had surfaced since she and Aidan had started sleeping together. That fact wouldn't serve her argument.

Aidan nodded almost imperceptibly. He spoke in the pragmatic tone of a medical diagnosis. "Post-traumatic stress disorder."

"Delayed onset," he added, when Laura opened her mouth to protest.

"I wasn't a soldier on a battle field," she said. Her denial sprang up visions of chaos, human suffering, and bloody death. "Okay, maybe you're right. But naming what I have doesn't cure the condition."

She stood up, and the air temperature dropped, Aidan's warmth slipping away from her. A chill hunched her shoulders, and she hugged her arms across her chest.

"I'm releasing you from any obligation. You're free," she said, and her voice tripped on her jump-rope heartbeat.

Aidan's brows hunched, and his head tilted to one side, as though he were trying to decipher a crazy woman. "You don't get to decide this one alone. We're great together, and you know it. You just haven't admitted it yet."

"You can't stop me from breaking it off with you," she said.

"Listen to Laura is Laura's house rule number two, right?" Aidan said.

"Sure?"

"The problem is you're not making any sense," he said, a cherry-picked insult.

For the first time, she knew what Nick must've felt on the receiving end of Aidan's lecture. For the first time, she knew what it felt like on the receiving end of Aidan's disappointment.

"Laura," he said. His voice smoothed around the curved letters of her name, and the rest of the world fell away. He stood and rubbed the cold from her arms. In the blink of his eyes, she saw herself as he saw her, just a woman in love with a man.

"Aidan's house rule number one. I always win," he said, and the image cut to black.

Chapter 28

Nine fifteen p.m., Mom sneaked downstairs to get busy with Lover Boy. Nine twenty, Darcy sneaked out her bedroom window and climbed down the fire escape. Her legs warbled beneath her. Her pulse pinched between her ribs. She started down the street, and then glanced back at Aidan's apartment. The studio light glowed warm and bright, and she let herself imagine going to Mom with her Nick problem. She imagined Mom's face, all alarm and concern. She imagined Mom wrapping her in her embrace. She imagined crying into the curve of her mother's neck.

Then she imagined everything going terribly no-second-chances wrong.

If she told Mom about Nick's crazy-sick plan to kill his father, Mom would call the police. If the police went after Nick, no way he was going to jail.

I got a bullet with my name on it.

Darcy shivered in the cool dampness and willed her legs to move. Under the cover of a moonless night, her eyes adjusted so she could see the soft edges of lawns and houses, the irregular shapes of cars lining driveways. She dashed across the town's street-lamp bright center, through the candy-on-her-tongue fragrance of blooming lilacs, the dark woodsy aroma of fresh mulch. She pumped her arms to power past the gleaming dark storefronts.

Darcy darted down side streets and race-walked until she came to the familiar cape. Home to sleepovers and pillow fights. Home to Cam.

Her breath rasped out before her, and she rang the bell. A dog barked in the distance. The Mathers' minivan wasn't parked in the driveway, but a television sounded from inside the house. Darcy peered through the glass top of the door in time to see Cam's gangly legs trampling down the stairs from the second floor.

He opened the door and blinked at her. "Darcy," he said.

"That's me!" she sang out, wanting to make Cam grin. Instead, she started to cry.

Cam glanced over his shoulder. He stepped onto the front stoop and went in for a hug. All it took for her to really lose it.

Darcy slobbered with relief into the cotton of Cam's black T-shirt and inhaled the slightly musty boy smell of her best friend forever. He'd gotten her out of trouble countless times. Last Halloween, Mom had suspected Darcy's involvement in a town-wide egging, and he'd sworn she'd helped him take his two-year-old sister, Emily, trick-or-treating. When Darcy had gone skinny-dipping in the Carsons' pool—the time she wasn't caught—he'd claimed a dip at Stevie's and a borrowed suit. And once, he'd let her copy off his algebra test because if she'd flunked, her mother would've killed her.

"What's the matter?" he said when she'd finally caught her breath.

She wiped her cheeks with her hands and blinked at Cam through blurry eyes. "It's Nick." Her voice came out in a whimper.

Cam considered her for a moment, gave her arms a pat, and took a step back. His mouth worked, as though he tasted

Nick's name and found it lacking. He shook his head, three slow side to side movements. "Sorry, Darce, but you're better off without him. The kid's serious messed-up bad news. Heard about him busting Jared's windshield."

Nick had slammed his palms against Jared's windshield right in front of her, but she hadn't noticed the glass cracking. Had Nick?

She stared at her usually gossip-hating friend. Two things became clear. Cam thought she and Nick had broken up, and he was glad.

That would make it a lot more difficult to get Cam to help her figure a plan to save both Nick and his father.

"I really need you," Darcy said, and Cam turned to the sound of feet bounding down the stairs.

Long thin legs, cutoff denim shorts. Smooth blond hair, purple barrette at one side. Heather came to the screen door, carrying Cam's little sister against her hip. Curly-headed Emily rubbed her eyes. Her chubby hand opened and closed at Darcy.

Darcy smiled and returned Emily's toddler wave, missing the days when Cam had needed both her and Heather to help babysit. Through the screen door, Darcy caught Heather's gaze. For a second, Heather's eyes seemed to register Darcy's tear-streaked face. Then, in the time it took for Darcy to think, *Love you*, Heather hardened her eyes and turned to Cam. "Em wants you to read *Goodnight Moon*."

"I'm in trouble," Darcy blurted out. Details about Nick, the boy Heather hated, swelled in Darcy's throat. The details proved Heather's warning. Darcy didn't really know Nick.

But that didn't stop her from loving him.

"Breakup," Cam supplied, when Darcy didn't say anything.

Darcy bit the inside of her cheek and gulped back tears.

With a toss of her head, Heather flicked her hair from her

eyes, a snooty move she'd perfected last summer. "Told you so," Heather said to Cam. "Told you you'd hear from her when they broke up."

Darcy would've called Cam, would've stopped over sooner, but Heather had gotten to him first. She couldn't compete with Cam's crush on Heather. Besides, Heather had needed Cam more. Until now.

"Bummer about Nick," Cam said. He gave Darcy a half-hearted hug, a quarter-hearted smile, and slipped back into his house. Heather passed Emily to Cam, and the toddler waved bye-bye to Darcy. This time, her chubby palm faced inward.

Darcy mimicked the toddler's wave. *Bye, cutie-pie Em. Bye, Cam and Heather.*

Heather started to close the door, but Darcy couldn't let her. "You were right about what you told me," Darcy said, and Heather froze in the doorway. "*It* is a big deal." Darcy used a pronoun for "being gay" in case Heather hadn't yet come out to Cam.

Heather glanced over her shoulder at Cam. "Duh, he knows," she said, and shut the door.

Weeks ago, Heather had walked half a mile in the dark to tell Darcy she was gay and to ask for support. Instead, they'd ended up arguing.

Now, she supposed, they were even. Now she was all alone.

At the town center, Darcy dropped to her knees and puked in front of the lilacs. Then she brushed herself off and ran back to her house because she'd already lost valuable time. Lights were off in Aidan's studio. Ditto Troy's room, but Mom's light blazed.

Back in Darcy's bedroom, she kicked off her sneakers so she could pace back and forth between her bedroom and the bathroom without alerting the house. Three hours later, she was still walking in circles, round and round Nick's plan that put her in the driver's seat of his getaway car. Nick was planning on giving her driving lessons and teaching her the laws of the road, so she could break all the others.

No matter how hard she tried, she couldn't imagine a successful getaway. The police would run them off the road, and they'd plunge into the Merrimack River. The cold current would press the oxygen from their lungs, suffocating them.

Another scenario had her driving at seventy miles an hour into a Jersey barrier, and Nick's ramshackle Monte Carlo crushing like a can of beer against a football player's head. The car would explode, killing them instantly.

If they weren't so lucky, the flames would start slowly, trickling from the burned-up engine and crawling up the hood. Trapped in steel jaws, the flames would lick their bodies, their flesh melting like wax figures in a museum inferno.

Another movie in her mind played like a little kid's riddle: black and white and red all over. Nick would bound up the staircase to his father's apartment, and his father would fling the door wide and shoot him point-blank in the face. Nick's bright-red blood would mist the air and stipple the railing.

Or father and son would shoot each other.

No way out, no way out, no way out.

Pressure wrapped her temples in a vice, and her stomach growled with a queasy ache. Darcy threw open the medicine cabinet. She filled a Dixie cup, tossed down two ibuprofens, and then sputtered on the water. Her gaze glued to her mother's stash of meds.

She knew what she needed to do.

Chapter 29

For Laura, one night without Aidan had proven to be torture.

Wearing her favorite comfort socks, Laura dangled her legs over the edge of the bed and stretched them out before her. She examined the socks' turquoise and amethyst stripes, and the robin's-egg blue raised flowers. Finding beauty in simple objects helped her forget the battlefield of her mind. How nothing made sense anymore. How her logic didn't even seem, well, logical.

Damn it!

She was doing it again, questioning all the good solid reasons she'd given Aidan for ending their relationship. Even after replaying their conversation, she sensed something vital was missing that would hold the reasons together and solidify her argument.

Laura plodded down the stairs and into the kitchen. A white envelope stuck out from beneath the ceramic canister of flour. Aidan had written Laura's name in caps, so she couldn't miss it. She tore the glued-down flap, unfolded the crisp letter, and recognized the words of Rainer Maria Rilke.

Only once, she'd told Aidan about the poem she'd tacked onto the wall of her undergraduate study carrel for writing inspiration. She'd told him that every time she'd read it, the first line assaulted her. She'd told him that she could've stayed right there, blissfully lost, pondering the layers of meaning.

I believe in all that has never yet been spoken.

She batted at a tear, read the rest of the paragraph:

I want to free what waits within me so that what no one has dared to wish for may for once spring clear without my contriving.

Below the poem, she found Aidan's prose, his tidy handwriting as precious to her as the angles of his face.

You're stubborn, and I love you, he wrote, an observation and a reminder.

She flew out of the kitchen, paced the mudroom, tried focusing on the dust motes playing in a shaft of light flooding through the window, and her mind shifted to the pores of Aidan's face, the gentle slope of his hips, the crevices of his lips. He loved her, but his love didn't alter the facts of her life.

He'd called her *stubborn*, a close cousin to the term "control freak" she'd overheard Darcy use in reference to what her daughter considered unfair rules Laura set for her children's well-being. As if somewhere along the line Laura's boundaries had become errant, misguided, and completely inappropriate. As if over the years, the limits she'd created said more about her marginalized fears than realistic threats to her children.

As if Laura's defenses had driven away the best man she'd ever known.

Darcy was gnawing at the soft flesh of her forefinger because she'd already bitten down the nail. She caught her reflection in the smudged rectangular mirror inside her locker door, and her sore finger fell from her mouth. The school day hadn't even started, and already the darkness beneath her eyes made her look old, like maybe nineteen or twenty. Lockers opened and closed around her, voices thrummed past, and a girl's for-show squeal sounded down the hall.

Funny, Darcy had always had trouble imagining herself past

her teens, but today, she could see clear in either direction. She envisioned herself married, with a baby even, pushing a stroller to the park, a paperback under her arm and a bottle of spring water in the undercarriage netting. She peeked into the carriage and folded down the pastel-blue knit blanket away from her infant son's face, and he squinted against the sunlight.

"It's okay, Jack," she said.

In a daydream, you could name your firstborn after your father without anyone looking down at you. In a daydream, you could love whomever you chose without shame.

Darcy-the-Mom settled onto a wooden park bench beneath a maple tree and slid out her book. Not fiction, but a book on gardening. She wanted to start her own business. Combining her passions, she'd grow a garden entirely made up of edible flowers, and then create cake recipes using their petals.

Apple blossoms on casual yellow cakes reminded her of grandmothers in picnic-ready wide-rimmed straw hats with starched yellow ribbons tied at the back. Roses and violets were best for formal celebration cakes. And little-kid-birthday-party pansies enchanted her. Their cheerful purple-and-yellow faces would smile up at her from a whiskey barrel beside her doorstep.

Half a dozen lockers down, Heather unhinged her lock and flung the door wide. The chipped blue metal door clanged against her neighbor's. She peered around five students, waited the prerequisite three seconds, and then showed Darcy the back of her head, earning a high score for lively hair tossing.

So immature! Darcy simply could not tolerate passive-aggressive girly crap. God, she missed Heather!

The very first time Mom had let Darcy and Heather plant a whiskey barrel of pansies, they'd been preschoolers. On the way home from Humpty Dumpty, Mom stopped at Lakeside Acres, and she let them choose four varieties of pansies: burgundy, yellow, deep drenched purple, and white with blue inkblot centers. At home, Darcy and Heather ended up with as much soil in their hair as in the planter. Gray sweat streaked their faces. Dirt smudged their shoes.

But Mom had let them learn by doing.

Another loud metallic clang warned Darcy that Vanessa was across the hall at her locker, arriving when all the other students were leaving for first period. Unlike Heather, Vanessa wasn't *trying* to attract Darcy's attention; the girl was just naturally loud. At high school graduation, they should give Vanessa a fiery red tassel to turn alongside the school's standard blue-coiled mortarboard rope for the superlative Most Obnoxious.

"Darce!" Vanessa slammed her locker and came bouncing over, as if on a pogo stick. "Where were you Saturday? You missed everything!"

Darcy shrugged. "What did I miss? Did Boomer win another beer bong contest?" At last year's unchaperoned spring fling, the two-hundred-pound football player had funneled one beer bong too many, and then, smiling, stepped out onto Vanessa's parents' porch and blew chunks across the horrified crowd of kids. Five minutes later, he'd gone back for more.

"Better." Vanessa's cheap rose perfume wafted into Darcy's personal space. Vanessa's cheeks flushed, and energy poured off her. She glanced around Darcy toward Heather and lowered her eyelids, grinning at the floor. "I was with Stevie."

"Uh-huh." Poor innocent boy. She'd send her condolences. Darcy shut her locker.

"That's not it." Vanessa widened her eyes and spoke through bubble gum breath. "Stevie and me were scouting out a place to, you know, get busy, and you won't believe what we found."

"Try me."

Vanessa smiled without parting her lips, savoring the moment. "I think I know why you and Heather aren't talking."

"I doubt it." Each day, she'd walk by Heather's locker, trying to transmit an extra sensory apology that never hit its
mark. Last night's transmission hadn't worked, either. "Look, I
need to go."

"Okay, okay." Vanessa leaned closer. "I saw her, Heather.
She was making out with some girl. They were, like, totally all
over each other, their hands under each other's shirts—"

"Does she know you saw her?" Darcy's mind raced to the
PA system, wondering how she might dismantle it before
Vanessa thought to transmit an impromptu morning announce-
ment.

"Yeah! She was flipping out, fixing her clothes."

"What did you say?"

"You know, the usual when you walk in on a couple. *Sorry,
carry on, as you were*, that sort of thing."

"Was Stevie there? I mean, did he see?" Stevie was even
quieter than Heather. Most likely, he wouldn't tell a soul.

"He has eyes! Anyway, I wanted to tell you first. I'm dying
to know if that's why you guys don't hang out anymore. Did
she try to nail you or something?"

Darcy wanted to say "Are you a fucking idiot?" but she already knew the answer.

Looking into Vanessa's dark almond-shaped eyes made
Darcy long for Heather's sea-glass blue. "Nothing like that. It
was something personal." Like all the time she'd wasted hanging out with losers like Vanessa and going out with boys who
spread lies about nailing *her*. Somewhere along the line, Darcy
had strayed from her original course. She should've stayed
closer to home and focused on the people she loved: Heather
and Cam, Troy and Mom.

Weird, but Darcy couldn't imagine her mother without
picturing Mom's just-a-friend Aidan.

"So you knew, right? Was she checking you out all the
time? Did she ever ask you to do anything?"

Vanessa was trying to trap her and get her to say something, anything, to enhance the gossip about Heather. She'd seen Heather kiss a girl, information that might mean nothing at all if Darcy could convince Vanessa to forget it. Keep your friends close and keep your enemies closer. Darcy had figured out back in middle school Vanessa spun the rumor mill, and she'd purposely made friends with the miller.

Darcy glanced over at Heather. Her blond head bent into her locker, no doubt trying to pick up the thread of their conversation. She even thought Heather's narrow shoulders trembled slightly from the effort of remaining so still. Heather had nothing to be ashamed of, but by the time Vanessa got through with her, she wouldn't be able to show her face.

"The triplets," Darcy said, and she made sure her expression betrayed no trace of sympathy.

Vanessa blanched. "What does that have to do with anything?"

"Everything." Luckily, even Vanessa had done something she was ashamed of.

Moisture clouded Vanessa's eyes. "You promised you'd never tell."

Darcy smiled and inhaled success. "I lied."

"I'd say I was drunk."

"That's not how you told it. You only had a couple of beers. You figured they were triplets, so it was almost like doing the same boy three times. Pulling identical cabooses, right? Vanessa Murray pulls a train. Worse than strapping a mattress to your back."

Vanessa chin snapped sideways. She shook her head, small rapid-fire movements, as though trying to dislodge the memory.

"Oh, c'mon. You must know that's what everyone already says about you. You practically say it about yourself. So, really, calling you a whore wouldn't be much of a stretch."

Vanessa bit at her quivering lip, and then her gaze darted to the right. She worked her gum. Each chew notched her eyes rounder until they opened into a wide smile. "The nightmare!"

Darcy's stomach clenched around Daddy's secret, as though it were hers.

The last time Vanessa had slept over, they'd camped out on the living room floor, and Vanessa had awoken with a start, Darcy's father standing over her. Vanessa's scream had sent Daddy scrambling to his studio, a finger pressed to his lips. He'd shut the door seconds before Mom had come tramping down the stairs, an excuse lighting on Darcy's lips: Vanessa had had a nightmare.

Mom hadn't needed to know Daddy's OCD was flaring, compelling him to count the kids sleeping under his roof repeatedly. Or so Darcy had thought.

She shouldn't have covered for Daddy's nuttiness.

Darcy's stomach relaxed, and she could breathe again. "Go right ahead. Tell everyone."

"Wha–at?"

"You heard me. I couldn't care less."

Vanessa's jaw flapped open, and she mouthed, *No.*

"So I'll go ahead and tell about those triplets. If you don't mind."

"Don't do it."

"Triple the fun."

"Please, Darce, don't!"

The begging almost got to her. "Here's the deal. Keep your stupid mouth shut about Heather. You didn't see a damn thing. Ask Stevie real sweet to keep quiet about it, too."

Vanessa scraped her fingers through her scalp and distributed the oil down to the ends, exactly the way she'd behaved when she'd originally trusted Darcy with her story of sleazy regret.

"Then I won't spread your little three-part story. Okay, my friend? I'm going to tell one person about your story, so there will always be two people watching to make sure you keep your end of the deal." Really, she wouldn't tell a soul, but she needed Vanessa to believe someone else held the means to ruin her already mangy reputation. Just in case.

"So what was it you saw in the woods?" Darcy asked.

Vanessa's lips curled. Her nostrils flared, and her breath hissed through her teeth with another type of sleazy regret.

"Give it."

"Nothing," Vanessa whispered.

Darcy glanced over her shoulder and found Heather exactly as she'd left her, an ace at playing statue. "Could you speak up?"

"I didn't see a thing."

Darcy pushed air upward with her palms, raising Vanessa's volume. They both looked at Heather, and she turned completely around.

"I didn't see a thing!"

Darcy nodded. "You can go now." She didn't bother watching Vanessa leave; she'd already given that girl too much of her attention. Instead, she went to Heather.

Her best friend scrambled inside her locker, tossing books and notebooks into her backpack. Her polished blond hair swished, scenting the air.

Darcy inhaled mangos, pineapples, and coconuts. "I've missed you. LU," *Love you.*

Heather swung the loaded backpack onto her narrow shoulder and clicked the locker door shut. She turned to Darcy, revealing her heart-shaped face, her eyes the color of frosted sea glass. "Thanks."

Darcy crossed her hands at the wrists, one half of their best friends forever handshake. Back when they were in preschool, they couldn't walk from the Play-Doh to the sand table with-

out holding hands. Once, they'd even braided their hair together, interlocking wispy white-blond and coarse auburn
strands.

Heather did another imitation of a statue, staring at Darcy's
hands, as though she'd offered her ABC gum: already been
chewed.

The first-period bell shrieked through Darcy's eardrums,
pain coming from both sides.

"I'm sorry," Darcy said, when the bell finally stopped ringing.
She tried projecting everything into her apology. She understood
how much she'd already hurt Heather, and she hoped forgiveness
would extend into the future, if her plan went no-second-
chances wrong.

Heather's gaze flitted around the empty hallway. "We're already late."

"Better late than never?" She shifted toward Heather, angled her face until she caught Heather's gaze. *Please.*

Darcy's chin quivered, igniting a mirror expression in
Heather, like when they were in elementary school and one
scraped knee set off two identical wails.

"Not now," Heather said, as if she had all the time in the
world to decide, as if tomorrow were a sure thing. Heather's
pink-and-green hibiscus print backpack jounced down the
hall and disappeared around the corner.

Darcy took a turn at statue. Her hands remained crossed at
the wrists, and she waited for an answer that wasn't coming.

"Not now" might mean "never."

Chapter 30

Five days before the prom was probably the only chance Darcy would get to wear the to-die-for prom sandals. She walked behind Nick on tiptoe toward the cottage, clutching the two bottles of soda she'd just purchased from Yogi's, careful not let the heels of her glittery silver sandals dig into the soil and aerate the overgrown path. She smiled, giggly with nerves, at the senseless practice. Clearly, she was worried about the wrong things, like a prisoner on death row fussing over the menu for her last meal.

Nick opened the cottage's door, set down the cooler, and then came back for Darcy. He swept her into his arms like a fantasy prince would, and she latched her fingers behind his neck, not wanting to let him go.

He set her down in their retro kitchen, snapped on his business face, and continued with yesterday's crazy-sick plan. "We do pre-prom at Stevie's," Nick said. "Go to the prom for exactly an hour and a half. We do the couples photos, chat with the teachers, and make the rounds to all the tables. Then we drive to Nashua, make it there by nine the latest, and you wait two blocks away on Vine."

Darcy's pulse accelerated, a whirring in her ears, as she reviewed her counterplan. She might not know Nick as well as she'd thought. But if she screwed up, she was counting on her belief Nick would never hurt her.

Unless that was another lie she told herself.

"Then we go back to the prom, easy-peasy lemon squeezie," Nick said. "Did I miss anything?" Nick tried a grin, and Darcy pictured the scared six-year-old boy, a towhead in fire-engine-red footed pajamas, hiding behind his bedroom door, watching helplessly as his father beat his mother. Nick seemed to imagine the past could've happened differently, as if he could've helped his mother ten years ago by killing his father on Saturday.

Darcy couldn't let him.

"Nick? Don't forget my little red present."

"For after?" Nick asked, stumbling over his words.

Remarkably, they still talked about returning here to the cottage after the prom and the murder, and spending the night, as though the two events—murder and deflowering—would take place in universes light-years apart.

Darcy took Nick's hand, wondered whether years from now she'd remember the square shape of his fingernails, and how the back of his hand felt cool while the palm radiated heat. She wondered whether "years from now" would even happen. She glanced at the cooler and met Nick's eyes. "Right, we're waiting till after the prom. But I was thinking, maybe we could rehearse now with the usual."

He bit at his lip, and his for-real smile deepened her breath. "Twist my arm," he said.

She snatched up their sodas and led him into the bedroom. Late-afternoon light shone on their clean, white, untouched bedding.

Sometimes, you had to do the opposite of what was expected. Sometimes, nothing was as it appeared.

Sometimes, you had to betray the boy you loved.

Nick kicked off his sneakers and tossed his black hoodie onto the wood floor, the sleeves splayed in surrender.

Darcy uncapped the sodas and handed Nick his bottle. "I'm sorry" lighted on her tongue, and she sipped her Sprite, swallowing her apology. Nick gulped down half his caffeine-free Coke, and she waited for him to taste her betrayal, bracing for an accusation she couldn't deny.

Instead, Nick set his Coke on the floor and pulled back the bedding. He shrugged out of his T-shirt, unzipped, and stepped from his jeans.

Darcy took a deep breath to slow her racing heart. She lowered herself to the mattress and stared into the shadowed corners of the room. She worked the straps of the sandals over her heels. Kneeling, she tugged her T-shirt over her head and unhooked her bra. From behind, Nick's hands cupped her breasts. His mouth heated her neck, and he pressed into the small of her back.

She turned to face him. Guilt strung her spine, from the ache of her tailbone to the chill at the nape of her neck.

Fingers interlaced, hands behind his head, Nick lay on his back, and Darcy set not to lovemaking, but an act of love.

When Nick was finished and sated, he rolled from his back to his side, his eyes already half-moons. "Don't let me sleep for more than half an hour. Okay, princess?"

"Don't worry. I'll take care of everything."

And she had. After she'd bought their sodas at Yogi's, she'd laced Nick's Coke with the Valerian drops she'd swiped from the medicine cabinet. She knew from experience the herbal sleep aid wouldn't harm him.

She pulled the comforter up to Nick's shoulders, the final piece of her three-part plan to sedate him: herbal sleep aid, sexual release, physical warmth. But she wasn't sure until Nick's breathing had turned shallow whether her plan even had a chance. She wasn't sure how much time her plan had bought to save him.

Darcy gathered her clothes and crept into the kitchen.

After she'd slipped her clothes back on, she gave her attention to the cooler and its contents, the gun and ammo beneath threadbare pear- and peach-covered dishrags.

Before they'd met, Nick might have carried out his plan on his own. The fight with his father would've followed the same path—the same angry words spoken, and the blows would've still landed on their mark, leaving purple bruises beneath Nick's pale lashes.

The past, Darcy couldn't change, but the future lay before her, acre upon acre of flat open landscape, waiting for her design. She tiptoed to the bedroom doorway, peeked at Nick for one last time, and saw all of him. The scared little boy, helpless against the strength of his father, twitching with every blow that met his mom. The angry teenager, plotting violence against violence. Now a third version of Nick peeked over the horizon: Nick the man.

She snatched the cooler from the dinette table and slipped Nick's car keys in her pocket to give herself a head start. She clamped the sandals under her arm, eased open the back door, and shut it soundlessly behind her. Pine needles pricked the soles of her feet. She ran past Nick's wake-up-call loud car and headed for the main road, hoping she could hitch a ride home before Nick came to and realized the girl he'd thought he could trust had betrayed him.

For all she knew, Nick's father's temper would never move beyond the length of his arms, the curl of his fists. Not every father carried his threats through to the most extreme conclusion.

When Darcy had argued with Mom about Aidan lecturing Nick on respect, Darcy had said, *He's not my father.* She should've added, *Thank God.*

Thank God, every man wasn't her father.

Darcy was willing to take the chance because she couldn't

accept the alternative. Bottom line, she couldn't help Nick kill his father, and she wouldn't help him destroy himself, either.

The way Mom had taken care of Daddy had taught Darcy you never give up trying to help the people you love. She would bring the gun to Mom and tell her about the murder plot.

This time, no one would die.

Chapter 31

Laura was throwing a pity party, mourning the relationship she'd killed.

She'd fashioned her bedroom into a nurturing nest, complete with long-stemmed white calla lilies arranged in a cut-crystal vase on her night table. She'd taken a tray upstairs outfitted with green tea in a rooster-decorated porcelain teapot and matching china cups and saucers she rarely used. While the tea had steeped, she'd invited Maggie and Elle. Steaming cups in hands, Laura had confessed the whole Aidan story.

Neither of her friends had been surprised. Laura had been successful in hiding neither her madly in love aura nor her afterglow.

All three women agreed Laura had screwed up massively when she'd broken it off with Aidan.

Maggie drank down the rest of her tea and set her cup on the bureau. She regarded Laura for so long, Laura thought Maggie must've been reading her aura against the light walls. "It's easier than you think," Maggie finally said, using the title from a book on Buddhism Maggie read at least once a year.

"Meaning, I should meditate my way to enlightenment?"

Maggie laughed. "Meaning, you should tell Aidan you made a mistake and you want him back."

Exactly what Laura had been thinking all day, ever since she'd debunked last night's misguided logic. But whenever she imagined the scenario, a cottony sensation lined her mouth, and her heart misfired. What was stopping her?

Maggie came across the room and kissed Laura on the forehead. "And now, dear heart, I must be going. I've a class to teach."

Elle stood and smoothed her skirt.

"You too?" Laura asked.

Elle bent down to hug Laura and whispered in her ear, "You deserve someone wonderful like Aidan." Then when Laura's eyes threatened to tear up: "About time you ended your sex drought."

Maggie took her and Elle's teacups and placed them on the tray. "That's right. It's good for you. Balances the chakras."

Laura was still smiling when Maggie's and Elle's vehicles fired up and left her driveway. The hot tea lit her skin, and she rolled the coverlet off her jeans and pushed back the sleeves of her T-shirt.

The rumble of an unfamiliar car's engine turned into the driveway. A car door slammed, and the rumble trailed down the street. Moments later, the broken screen door banged the frame and echoed through the bedroom window. Troy was spending the night at Michael's. And Darcy wasn't supposed to return home until later.

Unless her daughter had forgotten something she couldn't live without.

Laura's stomach tensed, and she ran down the four steps to the landing, chewing at her cheek. "Darcy?"

"Mom?" A whittled-down version of her daughter's voice spoke, and then Darcy materialized at the bottom of the stairs, barefoot and carrying a battered cooler. Darcy's hair, brushed and hair sprayed when she'd left for school this morning, now frizzed around her face, fringing her daughter's pallor.

"Angel?"

Darcy left the cooler on the bottom steps and came flying up the staircase, arms spiraling, as though Laura's voice had unhinged the rest of her. At the landing, she caught Laura about the neck.

"I can't—we have to—" Darcy wrestled with her breath, and Laura breathed for both of them.

She guided Darcy into her bedroom and slid over the tea tray so they could both sit down. She culled through Darcy's jumbled speech and determined her daughter had stolen Nick's car keys so he couldn't come after her and hitchhiked home, an activity Darcy wouldn't have admitted to unless the reason were unimaginably worse.

"Darcy?" Laura waited for her daughter's breathing to slow, waited until Darcy looked her in the eye. Laura waited till she could push the question through her throat. "Did Nick hurt you?"

Darcy shook her head, suddenly quiet.

"Okay. Bare bones," Laura said.

Darcy sucked in a breath, her eyes bulging in her head. "Nick's father used to beat his mom. He beat up Nick and threatened to kill him, his mom, and his grandmother, so Nick got a gun to kill him first." She gulped the air. "And if the police come after Nick, he'll kill himself, and I snuck off with the gun."

Tides roared in Laura's ears.

Beat, kill, gun.

Laura's mind short-circuited, unable to process this horror story, coming from Darcy's lips.

"I wouldn't help him go through with it. I don't want to hurt anybody."

"Of course not. You're a good girl, Darcy," Laura said, and the statements sent her daughter into a crying jag.

She tried jolting her daughter into rational thought. "Darcy! Where's Nick?"

"At the cottage. I left him sleeping at the cottage," Darcy said, as though Laura should have a clue about some cottage.

"And the gun. Where's the gun?"

"I took the gun. I . . ." Darcy glanced at the tea tray set at the foot of Laura's bed, the night table.

"Where is it now?"

"I don't know!"

"You took the gun, and then . . ."

Darcy's gaze flitted around the room.

"And then?"

"Nick, his car keys, the cottage—"

The screen door smacked against its frame. Footsteps pounded through the mudroom, the kitchen, the living room floor.

"It's in the cooler!" Darcy jumped up, but Laura sprinted ahead of her and slammed the bedroom door in her face.

Laura raced down the stairs, made it to the landing—

Too late.

Nick stood at the foot of the stairs beside the open cooler. Red-faced and panting, he jabbed bullets into a revolver, and a bitter tang coated Laura's tongue.

Nick snapped shut the gun's cylinder and aimed the revolver at Laura's head. "Where's Darcy?"

"She's not here," Laura's said, and her hand flapped against the banister.

She'd give Nick her baby girl over her dead body.

A dark bruise blackened Nick's left eye socket, evidence of his father's beating. Not much different than what Darcy had emotionally endured from Jack.

Laura looked Nick in the eye and saw a scared boy, shaking

in his untied sneakers. "Put the gun down, Nick. You don't want to do this."

Laura's bedroom door sprang open, and Darcy tore down the stairs to the landing.

Nick pointed the gun at Darcy. "Get down here!"

"It's okay, Mom. I'll go with him."

Laura jutted out her arm and stepped in front of her daughter, like when she'd halt a six-year-old Darcy from crossing against traffic. "Darcy told me about your father."

"I don't have a father!"

There was a reason for the fire escape, beyond an easy means for her daughter to sneak out. If only her daughter would understand her message. "Darcy, go to your room!"

"I'm not leaving you."

Was the gun a double-action revolver, like the weapon Jack had pilfered, requiring nothing more than a moment of impulsive action?

One pull on the hook trigger could end Laura's life.

A cacophony of garbled voices. A collage of still frames. The same story replayed in slightly altered versions. Laura as a child, aching for the father who'd abandoned her before she was born. Laura from a year ago, mourning the husband who'd killed himself after a long illness.

She focused on Nick's eyes and took a step, her hand stiff as ice against the railing. "You're a good son, Nick, trying to protect your mom."

"Don't talk about her! You don't even know her! You don't even know what he did to her!"

"You're right. I don't know what it was like for your mom. But I know how impossible it is to handle a man who's out of control. All I ever wanted was to keep Darcy and Troy safe from their dad. All I ever wanted was to keep their dad from hurting himself. I never even thought about myself. I bet your mom never thought about herself, either."

Laura hesitated, breathing into her stomach. "I'm sure her only thought was to protect you. How would she feel if you got hurt now, Nick? How would she feel if she lost you?"

Her gaze strayed to the gun, the gleaming black barrel, and her mind trundled back to the day she'd found Jack's body.

Blood had bearded her husband's clean-shaven face.

Her legs failed beneath her. She slipped against the railing, and Darcy squealed.

Laura propped herself upright. Chest jackhammering, she walked down the rest of the stairs, and Darcy, damn it all, followed.

Nick's hands trembled the gun. Sweat beaded along his forehead. He met Laura's gaze. "Don't make me shoot you!"

Darcy stepped from behind her mother. "Let me talk to him."

Laura started to pull Darcy back, and then she stopped herself. Laura had been the one person who could reach Jack, and Darcy would know how to reach Nick. Her daughter knew Nick better than anyone.

Nick probably knew her daughter better than she did. The plain truth stung Laura's eyes.

"Guns are for cowards, and I know you're not a coward." Darcy shook her head. "Not like my dad."

Laura had thought keeping her opinions about Jack to herself had safeguarded Darcy. Unlike Laura, Darcy wasn't afraid to speak the truth. "And your dad's just the same. He's a coward, Nick. Only a coward would whale on his son. Only a coward would beat his wife."

A groan rumbled from Nick, and when Laura started forward, Darcy gestured for *her* to stay put. "He's a coward, Nick, but you're not. It took guts for you to tell your dad how you felt about him and your mom.

"It wasn't your fault when your dad beat your mom. But if

you kill your dad, you'll hurt her worse. You're better than that, Nick. You're better than your father."

Her daughter knew exactly who she was. Brown pixels flash-blurred Laura's vision.

Darcy's steadfastness could kill her.

"Darcy?" Nick said, looking around like a little boy lost.

Darcy reached her hand out to Nick, the identical gesture Laura had used to pull Jack back to safety when he was dangling over a precipice.

Nick's jawline flickered, setting off a tremor across Darcy's shoulders. "Give me the gun."

Nick's lips trembled.

"Please, Nick."

A lifetime of hurt blazed behind Nick's eyes. "Why did you take off on me?"

"Because I love you, Nick," Darcy said, and her daughter's voice choked on *love*. "And I couldn't let you hurt yourself."

Nick's face went white. Tears trickled down his cheeks, and he handed Darcy the gun. She passed it to Laura, and Laura placed it in the cooler.

When Darcy touched Nick's cheek, he gave in to sobbing and collapsed in her arms, their embrace a homecoming and a farewell.

At the bottom of the stairs, Laura sat with her daughter, as if the treads were transfixing them. The air hummed white noise. Paisley filaments drew spiral paths in the early evening sun flooding through the front door's sidelights.

Outside, three car doors slammed in rapid succession: the backup cruiser, and the arresting officer, shutting Nick in the backseat of his patrol car and then slamming his driver's side door. An arrest Laura had initiated. Despite Nick's family history, he needed to take responsibility for his actions.

She hugged Darcy against her shoulder. Darcy opened her

eyes and looked up. Her gold-speckled irises shone, her pupils constricting, adjusting to the light. "I'm sorry, Mom."

"Whatever for?"

"I messed up. You were right to worry about me and Nick."

Darcy let Laura wipe the tears from her face with her fingertips. For once, she didn't pull away. "I'm so proud of how you handled the situation. Thank you for trusting me."

"I should've told you when Nick first started scaring me. I thought I could handle him myself."

When Aidan had spoken to Nick about Darcy's curfew, Laura had knee-jerk reacted as if Aidan had taken over her responsibility. In truth, he'd only helped her carry the burden. "Even adults don't always make the right choice first. Being a grown-up just means making the right choice before it's too late. You're the brave one. You saved yourself, and you saved Nick."

"I miss Nick already."

"I know, honey. I know. It's really hard."

"D'you still miss Daddy?"

Laura sighed. "All the time."

"Me too! I love him, even though he messed up a lot."

"Sweetheart, his choices weren't your fault."

"I know that, Mom. I'm not Daddy. I can only control what I do," Darcy said, repeating a statement of Laura's. For the first time, Darcy infused it with true understanding. "But it still hurts!"

Fresh tears slid down Darcy's cheeks, and she rested her head on Laura's shoulder. Vibrations traveled from the center of Darcy's chest. Sobs convulsed her body, radiating heat. The wetness pooled against Laura's neck, a safe haven for her daughter's pain, but not a cure.

The heat of Darcy's body melted Laura's numbness, and her mind cleared. The roles of Laura-the-caregiver-wife and

Laura-the-widow had overshadowed her relationship with Aidan.

Darcy was right. Laura was a control freak. She'd taken the offensive and had insisted on orchestrating every aspect of her relationship with Aidan. Seducing him, keeping the relationship a secret, and then trying to scare him away before he could leave her. All the supposed logical reasons Laura had given Aidan for breaking up had been a conditioned response born of her fear.

Aidan was right. They were great together. The problem was she wasn't brave like her daughter.

Laura rubbed Darcy's back, and her breathing slowed, mirroring Laura's cadence. "I'm sorry, Darcy. I should've been more honest with you about how your dad exhausted me emotionally, instead of lecturing you on self-respect."

No wonder Darcy had become involved with a troubled boy, narrowly escaping disaster.

When Darcy took a sharp breath, Laura did, too, and they inhaled together. "I should've been more honest with myself," Laura said. She'd given her mind, body, and spirit away to Jack as if she didn't even matter. "No wonder you think I'm a hypocrite."

Darcy straightened, smiling weakly through her tear-magnified eyes. "Does this mean you're going to stop sneaking around and come clean about your *friend* Aidan?"

Heat flushed Laura's cheeks. Darcy had known all along. Laura had fooled no one but herself.

"Want another shocker?" Darcy asked.

"There's more?"

"I wanted to hate the guy, but I like him, and I think you two make a nice couple."

"Oh, Darcy, I don't know. I don't think I should—"

What if Laura could actually show her daughter a healthy relationship where the partners supported each other? Aidan had already proven to her time and again he could do that, if only she'd let him. If only she could summon the courage.

"I'm scared," Laura said, admitting to her daughter what she'd never before admitted to herself. "After your father—"

"He's not Daddy."

"Well, I know that."

"So why suffer?"

Laura stared at Darcy. When had they switched places, and her daughter become the voice of reason?

Aidan's truck screeched into the driveway, and he burst through the front door, all traces of calm stripped from his face. His rich voice thinned. "Finn's police scanner—heard the call—drove across town—" he said, but he looked as though he'd run across town. His wide-eyed gaze took in Laura and Darcy, and then zipped around the corners. "Where's Troy?"

"It's okay. He's at a friend's." Laura's throat swelled with the knowledge Aidan loved her son. He loved her family.

"Go for it, Mom," Darcy whispered, and she kissed Laura's cheek.

Maybe it really was that simple.

Laura took a deep breath. "Aidan's rule number one. You always win," she said, and his waiting-for-Laura-to-make-sense expression clouded his face.

It was high time Laura made sense.

Right in front of her daughter, she went to Aidan and kissed the bafflement off his handsome face.

Aidan laughed, the sound more beautiful because she'd inspired it. His happiness reverberated through her chest. His arms wrapped around her waist.

His strength only made her stronger.

She stroked his lopsided dimple, the curve of his smile, and met his gaze. "You win. You're right. We're great together," Laura said. "Welcome home."

Chapter 32

By mid-August, the honeymoon was over.

Aidan stretched across their bed, so that his feet touched her, the way she liked it. His lips curved into a soft smile, content, even in his sleep. His scattered belongings—bike sneakers, half-balled socks, cast-aside scrub bottoms—reassured her that everything had changed.

Today marked the second week of Aidan's rotation into pediatrics. No more cake fifty-hour weeks. As Aidan had warned her, on required rotations from the emergency room, residents worked up to eighty grueling hours. Sleep was a luxury.

Laura kissed Aidan on the warm pulse of his temple. With a grin, his eyes flashed open. He took her around the waist, pulled her on top of him, and tickled her neck with his mouth till she shrieked with laughter. "I brought you coffee," she said when he released her and came to sitting. "You have twenty minutes before I kick you to the curb."

"You can't get rid of me that easily." He winked and took his steaming mug of coffee from Laura's hand.

"Nope, you're like a bad penny," she said. A joke, since she told anyone who'd listen Aidan was her *lucky* penny.

She and Aidan had decided telling their friends and families they were going steady fell short of the truth. Instead, they'd shown how they felt by sending out wedding invitations and throwing a July Fourth party in the backyard for one hundred and fifty guests, with Elle and Maggie as bridesmaids, Darcy as the maid of honor, Aidan's friend Finn as an usher, and Troy as the best man. Aidan's mother, sisters, aunts, and uncles inflated Laura's extended family from zero to seventy-five. Fine by her.

Although she'd known Aidan for less than six months, she had absolute faith in his integrity. She admired the way he spent his days—from his occupation saving lives to making sure they included Darcy and Troy in family decisions. Miracle of miracles, Darcy was coming around to accepting Aidan, which didn't prevent her daughter and husband from butting heads. And Troy and Aidan continued to bond over sports and outdoor activities. Aidan promised to take Troy camping whenever he could finesse a couple of days off. Troy knew Aidan wouldn't disappoint him. Laura measured her relationship with Aidan not by the month on the calendar, but by the strength of their love and mutual respect. Their marriage would endure whatever life offered.

Twenty minutes later, they were standing in front of the house on the cement step. Laura rose on tiptoe, prepared to give her freshly showered scrub-ready husband a get-to-work-on-time pristine peck on the lips. Instead, he pulled her into a deep kiss that threatened to make them both late for work. "Don't hold dinner for me," he said, and jogged to his truck. The engine roared to life. The truck made it to the edge of the driveway before it backed up to where Laura was standing.

"What's wrong?" Laura said.

Aidan leaned out of his window. "Uh, forgot to tell you I love you," he said, and then sped from the driveway and onto the street, leaving Laura with a hand pressed to her heart. "Love you too."

Outside on the deck, she awaited the sunrise. The first rays winked and twinkled, squinting between the peaks of the distant mountain range, and then pouring across the green fields. Sunlight blazed, and she shielded her eyes, taking in the goodness in tiny sips.

She was learning not to gulp up all the beauty at once, learning to trust in steadfast abundance.

Darcy's sunflowers skirted the deck, and a warm breeze combed through the enormous heart-shaped leaves as the blossoms tilted their yellow ruffle-trimmed faces toward the mountains. Darcy had taken up gardening in the middle of June, and along with the sunflowers, she'd planted vivid purple violets and sherbet-orange daylilies, highlighting their white farmhouse with splashes of color.

Each day, Laura would discover a new plant making a home in their yard, and Darcy kneeling, up to her elbows in soil. Sometimes, Darcy would even coerce Heather and Cam into joining her. Without fail, on the days when Darcy worked alone, a crease would form between her brows, and Laura could almost see her daughter's mind shifting to Nick, wondering where he, his mother, and his grandmother had moved to after the courts had placed Nick on probation.

No sounds of waking teenagers trickled down the staircase. For the moment, they were securely tucked into their beds. For the moment, they were healthy and well. Her mind was peaceful when she stayed in the moment.

She left her supporting roles of wife and mother in the kitchen and sailed through the unlocked door of her writing studio: Jack's old studio she'd feminized with lavender paint. She settled into her ergonomic chair, waited for the screen to hum on, checked her notes, and rocked gently, picking up the thread of her story. Her fingers hovered above the keyboard.

For inspiration, she spoke her favorite Rilke poem in her head but couldn't contain the last line, reverently connecting creativity with God: " 'I will sing you as no one ever has, streaming through widening channels into the open sea.' "

Just a few chapters into the novel, and the story was already taking a circular path—a hero's journey where the hero left the everyday world to learn old and new lessons, and then returned home, wiser for the voyage.

EQUILIBRIUM

Lorrie Thomson

ABOUT THIS GUIDE

The following discussion questions are included to
enhance your group's reading of *Equilibrium*. For a
little something extra, serve the delicious gingersnaps
Laura bakes using the recipe that follows.

DISCUSSION QUESTIONS

1. How does Darcy see her mother at the beginning of the novel? Discuss the ways in which that perspective changes by the end. Talk about how Laura and Darcy switch roles over the course of the story.

2. Jack used to tell Laura that the most obvious reasons for a character's actions were usually wrong, excuses masquerading as explanation. How does this apply to Laura's relationship with Aidan? Laura says that Aidan is the polar opposite of her late husband. Do you think this makes him a good match for Laura? Why?

3. How are Laura's and Darcy's relationships to Jack similar? How do they differ? And how does that affect the way they cope with his death? How does Aidan help Laura see her relationship with Jack differently? How does Nick help Darcy see her relationship with her father differently?

4. Compare Darcy's and Troy's memories of their father. How did his actions toward each of them influence their grieving?

5. How does Troy deal with his grief over Jack's death? Laura believes she and her son are very much alike. Do you agree?

6. How do Laura and Darcy view Nick differently at the beginning of the story? Does this change by the story's end?

7. What are the similarities between Darcy's and Nick's relationships to their fathers? In what ways do Darcy and Nick express the same emotions differently?

8. When Darcy first meets Nick, she thinks of herself as Daddy's girl. Even though she's embarrassed by how her father ended his life, she's always looked up to him. Has her relationship with her father changed by the end of the story? How?

9. Laura mentions her mother, a woman who kept to herself and might've died from never having reached out to others. Do you think Laura sees herself in her mother? Are there similarities? By the story's end, how has she learned to take her mother's life as a lesson in reverse?

10. How had Laura tamped down her emotions in response to Jack's? Is that coping mechanism now working in her favor or against her?

11. At the beginning of the story, Darcy's best friend Heather is struggling with a secret that she later reveals to Darcy. The reveal forces a temporary wedge between them. How do keeping secrets, and the resulting fallout, factor into other aspects of the story?

12. Discuss how Darcy and Troy react differently to Aidan.

13. As an adult, how does Laura now view the way her relationship with Jack began? How does that factor into her romance with Aidan? How does Laura's early relationship with Jack lead to Laura's concerns about Darcy and Nick?

14. In what ways do Elle and Maggie support Laura? Why is Laura reluctant to tell them about her relationship with Aidan?

15. Laura stuck by Jack through his struggles with bipolar disorder. Do you have any personal experience with it? If so, how has that influenced the way you read *Equilibrium*? Do you think she could have—or should have—done anything different with Jack?

Gingersnaps

2 cups unsalted butter, softened
2½ cups dark brown sugar, packed
3 eggs, room temperature
¾ cup molasses
4½ cups unbleached all-purpose flour
¼ cup ground ginger
1½ teaspoons ground cinnamon
1½ teaspoons baking soda
½ teaspoon salt

1. Preheat oven to 325 degrees. Line the baking sheets with parchment paper. In a large bowl, cream butter and brown sugar. Beat in eggs and molasses. In another bowl, sift flour, ginger, cinnamon, baking soda, and salt. Use a wooden spoon to stir dry ingredients into wet. Cover with plastic wrap and refrigerate for thirty minutes.

2. Either use a pastry bag to pipe one-inch rounds or drop batter by the teaspoonful onto the parchment-covered baking sheets. Leave two inches between drops to allow for spreading.

3. Fill a small bowl with warm water and wet your finger. Press finger into drops to flatten. Bake ten to thirteen minutes until brown.

4. Lift parchment off cookie sheet and set on cooling rack. Remove cookies from parchment when firm.

5. Enjoy about six dozen cookies!